MW01631558

Read all of the Cats 'ı

The Cajun Queen: Fortune Hunters descend on the tiny northern town of Four Oaks seeking a century-old ancestral fortune. After an explosion rocks the hotel, killing two, a break-in at a local emporium is soon to follow, and Anya detects an unseen presence lurking upstairs at the art gallery. The unprecedented series of disasters takes an even darker turn when a body is discovered in the trunk of the art curator's car. Anya is led to wonder if there are hidden messages behind the rune tiles and tarot cards a mysterious cat known as Ching leaves lying around. Adding to the drama, Ethan Notah has returned with a desire to pick up where they left off. Anya is surprised to learn that not everyone is happy to see them reunite.

Rise of the King: Anya is a newly minted billionairess, and Cats 'n' Cocktails is a huge success, but Ching is suddenly missing. All's well that ends well when he turns up at the lake house minutes before a blizzard is set to strike. Still, it's a mystery to Anya how he found his way through the woods. Anya receives an invitation to visit old friends of Martine's in New Orleans, and The Christmas Train sounds like an exciting mode of travel. With Ethan unable to accompany her—she, Tate, Ching, and Don Pedro ride the rails alone. Tate confesses his true feelings to Anya, but all decisions must be put on hold while Anya searches for a connection between Ching's mysterious aversion to potatoes, two suicides, and murder.

Black Maria: What do jewel thieves, an escaped prisoner found guilty of murdering his wife, and the card game known as Black Maria have in common? Only Ching knows for sure.

Splittin' Aces: Having sorted out her romantic feelings for Ethan and Tate, Anya has married the man of her dreams and started on a blissful new journey. The honeymoon is cut short, however, when the sheriff's niece is murdered. Tate is asked to assist federal agents in the investigation. The stakes are high as Tate goes undercover to infiltrate a dangerous cartel and gain the trust of a crime boss who's been operating a clever horse race-fixing scheme. Luckily, Ching is the favorite to win.

Aces and Eights:
Part One: It's ten years later, and Anya's life is about to change in a big way. The past resurfaces, and there is a reason for hope, but Ching has his own agenda. He's hot on the trail of drug traffickers, and this time, Anya is well in tune with his otherworldly premonstrations.

Part Two: The rightful heir to The Notah Ranch at Big Timber, formerly The Hart Ranch, has stepped forward to file a claim, and Ethan fears he will lose the ranch. Anya calls in the big guns to assist: her friend and lawyer, Beau Nithercott, and of course, Ching. Following another disastrous turn of events, Anya discovers that Nigel has been keeping secrets.

Judgment: Just when Anya thinks she's embarking on a whole new chapter in her life, someone makes a dramatic return. Anya's world is shattered, and once again, it's time to reconsider the future. Meanwhile, Mason Stevens's sister-in-law has been found murdered, and his own wife has disappeared. Ching points to clues hidden deep within the belly of the ark.

The Cajun Queen

Faith Waitstill

Bad Ax Press

Cajun Queen
Copyright: 2021 by Faith Waitstill
Cover image and design: ebookpbook.com

ISBN: 978-1-7371953-0-6 (paperback)

This is a work of fiction. Names, characters, places, and incidents either are the product of the author's imagination or are used fictitiously, and any resemblance to actual persons, living or dead, business establishments, events or locales is entirely coincidental. The author does not have any control over and does not assume any responsibility for second or third-party websites or their content.

All rights reserved. No part of this book may be reproduced, scanned, or distributed in any printed, audio, or electronic form without permission. Please don't engage in or participate in piracy of copyrighted materials. This violates the author's rights. Purchase only authorized versions.

It is with the utmost gratitude that I humbly dedicate these works to The Creator of all things seen and unseen …

“In the ascent of the ‘staircase of refuge,’ to the left-hand side, three cubits up from the floor are 40 talents of silver.”

—Author unknown. This text was discovered engraved on an oxidized copper scroll in Israel by archeologists. Broken in half like a treasure map, the scroll is said to describe sixty-four locations where gold and silver are hidden all over Israel.

ONE

When Anya McClean stepped from her vehicle, the first pair of eyes to meet her own were Ching's. She was instantly transfixed by his hypnotic yellow-green gaze, serenely eyeing her from the glass catwalk.

The catwalk joined together two buildings at the east end of Main Street, both of which, through unfortunate circumstances, now belonged to her.

Anya thought she perceived the slightest flick of Ching's tail before, one by one, he was joined by four more pairs of curious eyes. They were all staring down at her, ears alert and whiskers twitching. Two other cats, who were not immediately present, were also permanent residents here.

They had all moved back to town that morning for the grand opening and the fall festival kickoff. Upon arrival, she'd realized that in all the commotion that went along with rounding up seven cats, loading them into multiple carriers, and cramming them into her truck—she'd left her cell phone behind. This had required a return trip to the lake house with less than three gallons in the tank and no fueling stations along her route. If all the world was a stage—this morning's opening scene hinted that a farce was afoot.

Anya's attention was diverted toward the left-facing building as the fresh new neon hummed and sprang to life.

Her friend and manager, Desda March, must already be inside, making last-minute preparations. She noticed that Tate's old blue pickup was parked out front too.

Her peripheral vision then drew her attention to the right facing building where a couple stood eyeing her at a distance. Anya slid her sunglasses to the top of her head to glean a clearer perspective. First impressions told her that while they were definitely from outstate, they weren't tourists.

They were an interesting pair, very chic, early thirties. Of the two, the man stood out the most to Anya, made conspicuous by virtue of his exemplary height alone. He towered well above his diminutive counterpart, who probably couldn't cast a shadow at sunrise greater than his in the shade. Otherwise, whether consciously or unconsciously, they mirrored one another. Both had dark hair, both were clothed entirely in black, and both continued to return her stare from behind dark sunglasses.

Suddenly the woman flashed a smile and danced across the street to Anya—hand outstretched. Her male companion was quick to follow, his long legs closing the divide in fewer strides.

"Anya McClean by any chance?" she asked, venturing a guess.

Anya nodded, extending her hand to grasp the woman's own.

"What a lovely coincidence!" she exclaimed. "Perfect timing!"

Her gentleman companion agreed, shaking Anya's hand as well.

"I'm Nyx Bellemore, short for Nyxon, an old family name. This is my husband, Aedan. We drove out here from Philadelphia in answer to your ad."

Registering the look of confusion on Anya's face, the woman pointed to the building behind her.

"The emporium you listed for sale? We would love to see it when you have time. We have a shop of our own in Philly, and we love the vibe there, but we're looking to relocate to a place where we can set down roots—raise a family. We've been keeping an eye out for opportunities in smaller communities that are safe, but with a pulse, you know? This little town is absolutely darling! Precisely what we've been searching for," Nyx explained.

"Oh!" Anya laughed nervously. "The emporium! Yes! I would be happy to show it to you. I also own the building connected to it, and today is our grand opening. I'm afraid I'm going to be tied up all day until close. I can spare a few minutes right now if you want to take a quick peek. If you like what you see, we can schedule a time for a lengthier visit tomorrow."

The Bellemores removed their glasses in concert to study the signage, the pink neon silhouette of a cat in profile, eighteen feet tall, its six-foot tail curving around the green deco lettering of the establishment's logo.

"Cats 'n' Cocktails? What kind of an outfit is it?" Aedan asked.

"It's a rescue bar and grill," Anya replied. Noting their blank expressions, she added, "Maybe you've heard of cat cafes?" Anya had discovered early on that the concept of cat cafes was an expedient way of describing her new venue.

"Oh, yes! Of course!" Nyx exclaimed, giving Anya's forearm a friendly squeeze. "So, instead of a cafe, you've opened a rescue bistro! How fabulous! I love it!" Nyx clapped her hands in approval.

"The first of its kind in the nation—possibly the world," Anya replied.

"And are those some of your rescues up there? They've been keeping a watchful eye on us." Aeden said, pointing to the crew surveilling them from the catwalk.

"Oh, no … they actually live here. They belonged to the woman who used to own the emporium. She passed away a couple of months ago." The words stuck in the back of Anya's throat.

Nyx paused to reflect on this new information. "I'm so sorry. She must have been a very dear friend of yours. More like family?"

Anya pressed her lips together and gave a nod of confirmation.

Nyx paused to contemplate the sign above the emporium. "Martine's Mystical Treasures...," After another moment's consideration, she asked, "Is that the original sign?"

Anya's jaw dropped. It was a little known fact that Martine had changed the signage decades ago. What had led Nyx to suspect such an odd piece of local trivia? How could she have known?

Both Bellemores turned to look at her expectantly.

"Actually, there *was* another sign, many years ago." Anya felt a pressing need to create some space between herself and the Bellemores. This exchange was causing too many memories of Martine to surface all at once. She slid her glasses back into place to dull the overall intensity of the experience.

"I knew it. I could feel it," Nyx said. "The original is beneath this one, is it not?" she called out, sprinting across the street again to stand beneath the sign. Aedan was right behind her, leaving Anya hastening to bring up the rear.

"This place … ," Nyx said, throwing her arms open wide, "it was much more than a new age shop, a place to sell trinkets, talismans, incense, and the like, wasn't it?" It was more of a statement than a question. "Forgive me, but, was Martine practiced in the arts of spiritual divination, tarot readings, cartomancy?"

The question brought on a flashback, a hazy snapshot from the past in which Anya saw herself seated across the table from Martine, watching her configure what she'd called the Celtic Cross.

"Yes, they say she had a real gift," Anya replied. "Her name was Martine Decoudreau, but around here, she was affectionately known as the Cajun Queen. She was a wonderfully strange woman, beautiful, and kind, and I miss her terribly."

A respectful silence passed between them before Anya recovered her voice and proceeded to delve a bit deeper into the history behind Mystic Treasures. "In the 1800s, this place was a bank. There's an old vault in the basement where Martine used to do her readings. She ran this shop and lived in the rooms above it. She also took in stray and orphaned cats, seven to be exact. She believed that stray cats instinctively choose their future owners. She never turned away a seeker."

"In some parts of the U.S., there were laws against so-called fortune-telling," Aedan said.

"Still are in some states," Nyx chimed in.

"True. Changing the sign could have been an attempt to avoid prosecution," Aedan speculated.

"Well, I was too young to remember it, but I've been told that the original sign is an illuminated image of the tarot card known as *The High Priestess.* No name, just the words: *Your questions answered within.* I don't know when or why it was covered up, but given her … close ties to our sheriff, I never understood the necessity. The prosperity and vitality of Four Oaks is reliant upon the strength of its tourism. It may have been purely a business decision on her part. She may not have wanted to draw the wrong kind of attention," Anya explained.

Another glance at the now deserted catwalk brought on a surge of loneliness. Anya felt despair rising in her chest. She'd been fighting to keep her emotions in check all morning. Today was not only the grand opening of Cats 'n' Cocktails, but also the start of a whole new chapter in her life. She had timed the opening to coincide with the town's annual fall festival, a new season for a new beginning, but Martine would not be there to share it with her. It was heart-rending.

The other shop owners were busy setting up their street-side vending carts and beverage stands, while closely monitoring her interaction with the two attractive strangers. At the far end of the quarter-mile strip, some men were hard at work setting up the bandstand,

and beyond that, a few carnival rides were being tested. Along with the opening of Cats 'n' Cocktails, they were this year's newest attraction.

"We'd love to take a quick look inside. We promise not to take up too much of your time. I have a good feeling about this place already," Nyx Bellemore affirmed.

"Sure, I have the key right here," Anya replied.

The deadbolt turned stiffly from disuse, its tumblers thudding hollowly within. Anya gave the door a shove. It swung open freely, and they all stepped inside. After flipping on the lights, Anya felt immediately compelled to glance at the newel post at the foot of the stairs. Sadly, she felt certain that Ching would never sit sentry there again.

Her eyes swept across the empty room with its soaring ceiling and dusty shelves. Nyx and Aedan moved thoughtfully throughout the wide-open space, pausing to stare out of the front and side windows, no doubt envisioning their own plans for the shop. Could they feel the residual energy of the Cajun Queen? It was truly palpable to Anya—like the air itself was electrically charged.

Nyx paused beside the staircase, resting one hand on Ching's now abandoned newel post, and gazed upward to where the door to Martine's residence stood ajar. Anya had decided to leave it open for the cats. They were accustomed to having access, but she doubted they would spend much time here anymore.

"The stairs lead up to Martine's old apartment. I was hoping to retain that space for the cats. The catwalk adjoins our two buildings. It's exactly as she left it, and they're used to traversing back and forth between the two upstairs residences. It's been a long-running routine for them. They've always been allowed ingress to the emporium and the pub as well."

The Bellemores looked at her with eyebrows raised.

"Small town," Anya said with a shrug.

Nyx clicked her short black nails against the wooden staircase post, while indulging in a moment of quiet introspection.

"I can feel their energy in this place," she said. "Cats are extremely prescient, you know? Like them, I can … sense things."

Anya couldn't remember how many times she had heard Martine say the same thing about her cats.

Martine had believed, that Ching, in particular, had left her many signs over the years using tarot cards, playing cards, rune tiles—even dice. She had also claimed to receive clairvoyant messages through a process of observing the cat's movements, a practice known as ailuromancy. Recent events and concomitant twists of fate had served to open Anya's mind to the possibilities.

"I would like to meet Martine's cats. If we seem to have a connection, maybe you'd consider selling the entire building to us so we can live upstairs. Will you think it over?"

Anya had never imagined any future owner bringing such an offer before. She had never pictured Martine's cats residing with anyone other than herself and Martine, and yet—there was something about this engaging couple that tempted Anya to reimagine the possibilities. Could there be a new beginning in this place still so awash with Martine's indomitable spirit?

Anya was surprised to hear herself say, "I'll give it some thought." Her tone indicated how unlikely she was to accept, but—there it was.

"Good then. I really think it could work. I have a feeling. Many feelings … as a matter of fact," Nyx murmured, her focus shifting to the locked door beside the stairs. Tentatively she tried its knob. She looked questioningly at Anya.

"That's the door that leads to the old vault I told you about." Anya fiddled with the keys. "Give me a second. I'll unlock it for you."

Nyx placed her hand on Anya's arm and shook her head. "Let's leave that for another day. Shall we? Today is *your* big day, and we promised not to take up so much of your time. I think I can speak for us both when I say that we've seen enough. It's perfect for us, and we would like to take it—with or without the upstairs apartment, but please … be open to the possibilities. I think the cats will take to us brilliantly," Nyx predicted.

Aedan nodded and smiled warmly in agreement.

"Are you staying at the new hotel?" Anya asked.

"Yes! Very modern. Excellent accommodations," Aedan replied.

"And the Williamses—John, Keisha, and Derrick—are delightful people. So friendly," Nyx added.

The fact that Nyx had made a note of all three of their names wasn't lost on Anya. It was an affable quality.

"What's going on here today?" Aedan asked, with a sweeping arm gesture toward the bustling street-wide preparations. "Looks like some sort of celebration is in the offing. Judging from the cornstalks and hay bales, my guess would be fall festival?"

"Yes, we hold annual week-long festivals here at the start of every season. You should plan to attend. Meet some of the townspeople," Anya replied.

"Definitely! We will! Good luck with your opening! You may see us wander in later," Nyx said. "Call us at the hotel tomorrow, so we can talk more about our plans. Hopefully, we can reach an agreement before we have to return to Philly?"

Anya furnished the pair with a contemplative smile and promised to do just that. She watched as they strolled away, arm and arm up the street, trying to envisage what sort of neighbors they might make. Admittedly, there was something inexplicably familial about the beneficent Bellemores.

TWO

The old black walnut door still marked the entrance to the pub, its brass pull handle dulled and scarred by age. Anya rested her hand on it and drew a deep breath. She'd been in such a hurry to return to the lake and retrieve her cell phone that she'd dropped off the cats without so much as a glance around at the new place. Apart from that, she hadn't been inside for more than two months.

Squinting her pale green eyes, she transitioned from the bright sunlight into the soft glow of the interior. Beyond the wooden door was a second set of doors. They'd been added as a safety measure to deter any willful defectors from escaping when customers entered or exited the premises.

"Are you frowning? Is something wrong? Who were those people I saw you talking to? They weren't inspectors, were they? Are we still going to open today?" The panic-stricken stream of inquiries was spilling from her manager, Desda March.

Desda was another permanent fixture, so to speak.

She'd been the manager of this operation from its inception back when it was a little pub known as McClean's.

"No, no! It's so bright outside that my eyes needed a minute to adjust," Anya replied, surveying the finished results of what had been a painstaking renovation.

Desda leaned against the wine cooler, folding her arms across her chest. "So, then who were those people? I've never seen them before. Didn't look like tourists."

"They're from Philly," Anya explained. "They're interested in buying the emporium. In fact, they want to take the whole place, including the upstairs apartment. Nice people, but before I make my decision, I'd love for you to meet them too. I consider your instincts infallible."

Desda merely raised her eyebrows in question, numerous questions, Anya imagined.

Anya shifted her attention to Tate, who appeared to be stifling a grin. He'd been sitting at the bar, keeping company with Desda all morning, waiting patiently for her arrival. She went to hug him and found herself overcome with emotion. It was a bittersweet moment. So many transformative events had preceded this day, some of which had been painful.

Tate Blackledge, Anya's best friend and a skilled craftsman by trade, had been tasked with transforming McClean's Pub into Cats 'n' Cocktails. It had been an arduous process, undertaken solely at his direction. He'd incorporated his own designs into her original concept and created a revolutionary backdrop—an industry first—that was truly one of a kind. He'd begun the work in the months following Martine Decoudreau's death, with very little input from Anya. She had spent that time in seclusion at the lake house, coping with the major life changes that had resulted from the loss of her dear friend. Tate had come by almost daily to keep her updated and share pictures of the project's progress. His unflagging enthusiasm had helped her through one of the worst times in her life.

Anya tossed her glasses on the bar and raked her fingers through her long dark hair, feeling a sense of awe. For the next few minutes, there was nothing but suspense-filled silence as she took a look around the room, attending to each and every aspect of the newly designed space.

Only two elements remained of the original pub. The first was the second-story office above the bar. From its windows, she could monitor everything that went on down below.

The second was the one-hundred-year-old bar and back, constructed from one massive piece of mahogany, masterfully carved by a local artisan of his day.

Considering its age, the hulking expanse was a historical treasure, and it could seat twenty with room to spare.

Two cat-friendly features had been a large part of the renovation project. One was a climbing wall, the other a system of interconnected beams, at ceiling level. Tate had designed them both based on the well-known fact that cats enjoy escaping to high places. Each was an impressive feat of engineering.

The climbing wall consisted of sisal wrapped climbing poles, of varying lengths, that adjoined carpeted footpaths. The footpaths led to other built-in features such as rope bridges, hammocks, perches, and hidey-holes for smaller cats, treats, or toys.

The system of interlocking wood beams he'd constructed was anchored ten feet above the main floor. They were accessible to the cats by way of several ramps. The ramps had been strategically located in remote corners so as not to obstruct the flow of customers or waitstaff. Tate had created a forerunner, or prototype, of this feature years ago at Martine's lake house where she and the cats had spent their summers. She'd commissioned him to design and install it for her own cats to enjoy. Next to squirrel watching, it was the most popular feature of the home.

The updates to the pub had also included new furnishings, light fixtures, and a brand new color scheme in black, white, and gray. It gave the place a contemporary feel and reflected the sophisticated taste of the project's decorators—Elizabeth and Jules Colburn, owners of the Colburn Design Studio.

Gone were the old barstools, their black leather seats cracked and torn with age. The heavy oak booths, dusty ceiling fans, and the old tables and chairs—scratched, scuffed, and worn—were gone as well. In their place were newly reupholstered booths, cushioned barstools with backrests, and a variety of new table groupings, both large and small.

The most ambitious phase of the renovation had involved the inclusion of a white stone fireplace. At Jules's insistence, and to Tate's consternation, a couple of stonemasons had been brought in from Thief River Falls to erect the facade, after which he and his brother, Rob, had run the gas line and vent. An informal grouping of studio couches and chairs now hugged its rocky hearth.

The new glassware behind the bar was gleaming. Festive string lights had been strung about the room. Several large flatscreen TVs had been added. An enormous aquarium, teeming with brightly colored tropical fish, had been set into one wall. Below it a carpeted bench provided an ideal viewing platform for cats and customers alike.

"What do you think? Is it what you expected?" Tate asked.

Anya laughed. "It defies expectations. Only you could conceive of something like this. The pictures on your phone don't begin to do it justice," she replied, walking over to take a closer look at the aquarium.

Out of the corner of her eye, she caught a flash of cream-colored fur. A well-rounded tabby, known as Zia, was sashaying down the length of the bar—moving like a slow-rolling stream. When she reached her favorite spot at the far end, she stopped short and registered a look of surprise. Desda's husband, Paul, was absent from his usual seat. Zia was very attached to Paul March and the undivided attention she received from him. The cloying little female circled around three times and settled herself into a compact bundle, content to await his inevitable appearance.

"I hope you don't mind. I let Zia come down after you dropped them off this morning," Desda explained. "I didn't think you'd want them all racing around here today, but Paul will be here soon to keep her company."

"Where did that come from?" Anya asked, pointing to a new mirror mounted on the wall behind the bar. It was enormous, framed in silver, with the *Cats 'n' Cocktails* logo emblazoned across it. She went behind the bar to examine it more closely, tracing her fingers over the frosty white lettering.

Desda smiled. "That's from Ethan."

"Wow ... it's fantastic!" Anya exclaimed.

"He had to return The Pero Cat. It was one of the pieces reported stolen from that gallery in New Jersey. He was asked to turn it over to the authorities," Desda murmured, anxiously combing her fingers through her platinum blond curls.

The Pero Cat, to which Desda had referred, was a beautiful piece of mosaic artwork that Ethan Notah had bought for Anya at The York Gallery. The now-shuttered gallery had been at the center of four homicides, only months ago. It was an unwelcome reminder of the recent misfortune that had befallen the town. Anya chose to dismiss it without comment.

Still clutching her cell phone, she glanced at the time and then tossed it beside the cash register. In less than three hours, they would open the doors on her new venture. *Friends for Life*, the rescue organization Anya had arranged to partner with, would be bringing six cats available for adoption today. Knowing firsthand how notoriously averse to change cats can be, she had proposed that the adoptees arrive a few days earlier to give them a chance to warm up in advance of crowd-sized introductions. The director, an unflappable optimist named Nancy Dunn, had assured her that wouldn't be necessary. The candidates were remarkably adaptable, easygoing, and people-oriented. "Couple of hours, tops," she'd said, "that's all they need."

Anya remained skeptical.

Desda had placed two shot glasses and a bottle of single malt scotch—the good stuff—on the bar beside Tate.

"Shall we have a toast?" Tate asked.

"Definitely. Grab the scotch and come upstairs with me. I need to do a headcount, make sure the cats are all set for the afternoon," Anya said.

Once upstairs, they found Hester and Possum, a female calico and a gray female tiger-striped cat, asleep on Anya's couch—legs and tails entwined. This was pretty status quo, as the two were practically inseparable. Benny, an orange male tabby, was asleep in a puddle of sunlight near the door to the terrace. A quick check of her bedroom, dining room, and kitchen indicated that the other three must be next door at Martine's. Anya motioned to Tate to follow her across the catwalk to search for them.

When they reached the kitchen, they encountered Don Pedro. He was sitting on the counter, perfectly camouflaged between two glossy black ginger jars. He was presently engrossed in laundering his shoulder but paused long enough to appraise her with his one cloudy green eye. The other eye had likely been lost in a catfight. He'd been living on the streets a long time before arriving on Martine's fire escape one cold winter's night.

The veterinarian, Doc Lafferty, had not been able to determine any physical anomaly behind the eerie color of the cat's one good eye. There was no cataract, and it afforded him with seemingly perfect vision. Martine had said, of Don Pedro's eye, that having one eye open to the spirit world would cause it to be partially obscured to ours. She'd been prone to say things like that, shivery things that gave you the chills.

Don Pedro regarded Anya in the disinterested manner that cats so often do when their needs have all been met. He gave his shoulder another swipe or two, glided smoothly to the floor, and disappeared into the living room—his sleek black tail hugging the corner as he slid by.

Anya had yet to discover Ching's whereabouts at either residence. Trailing Don Pedro with intuition as her guide, she finally came upon the lithe, buff and cream-colored tabby, the feudal overlord of the four-legged freeloaders. He'd arranged himself in an exalted position on the fireplace mantel, affecting the air of an august statesman. Anya noticed that the eagle-eyed ruler's focus was trained on something across the room. Tracing his line of sight, she spotted Luther, an enormous white Turkish Van—huddled in the corner. The twitching whiskers and shifty-eyed gaze suggested that he was guarding a "treasure".

Anya crept forward for a closer look. Don Pedro

shimmied past her to perform his own inspection. It was one of Martine's dice, one of the many tools she had used for spiritual guidance in her readings. The One was showing. Over the years, and through her close acquaintance with Martine, Anya had managed to acquire a rudimentary understanding of the symbolism attached to the tarot cards. She knew nothing, however, of the omens said to be indicated by the dice. Whatever its meaning might be, it had certainly generated concern among the cats—particularly Ching.

Don Pedro imbued the dice with a cagey glare. Lifting his nose to the air, he gave a series of mighty sniffs, attempting to gain more information on this specter. When his senses failed to provide additional intel, he shrank from its presence, emitting a sinister sounding "kak-kak-kak" from the back of his throat.

Instinctively, Anya reached forward to retrieve the die.

Suddenly, an unholy shriek pierced the air and shattered the peace—bringing Tate running from the kitchen! It had come from the direction of the fireplace.

Anya turned to see that Ching was in crouching position on the mantel. His haunches were raised, and his shoulders were gathered high like gargoyle wings.

Luther whirled around and scrabbled madly from the room, narrowly avoiding a collision with Tate.

Ching shrieked and yowled again, bushed his tail,

and dove to the floor. He leaped over Luther in his haste to exit the room. Anya could hear him thundering down the stairs that led to the sanctity of his emporium.

Don Pedro gave his right ear a furious scratch and made a leisurely exit—strolling off at a measured pace in perennial pursuit of Ching.

Anya scooped up the die and slipped it into her pocket. "Never a dull moment when Ching's around," she said to Tate with a heavy sigh. "Come on. Let's have that toast."

They stood together in the kitchen, calming their collective nerves, while Tate poured them each a celebratory shot.

"Where's Rob this morning? Is he going to stop by?" Anya asked. Rob was Tate's younger brother and his partner in the construction business they operated.

"Rob is on a job site in Dixon, but he'll probably come by later. I have to leave soon to meet him over there. That's why I'm dressed like this," he said, tugging on the brim of the old, blue trucker-style hat he always wore. From beneath his cap, the long layers of his sun-drenched hair fell nearly to his shoulders.

As he handed her a glass, he flashed that charming, well-cultivated smile of his—the one that had the power to compel and captivate. Tate Blackledge had been blessed with the innate ability to attract anyone or anything he set his sights on. He was purely magnetic. On the surface was this breezy kind of confidence—but something in those dark blue eyes hinted at a more serious nature, just below the surface—one that was slightly cool and calculating.

He gently clinked his glass against hers and raised it slightly in the air.

Anya raised hers too. "To you, Tate," she said, breathing a sigh of relief at having reached the end of the journey. "I'll never be able to thank you enough for making all of this possible. I'll never be able to tell you how much your friendship has meant to me all of these years, either. I love you."

Tate gave a thoughtful nod. "I have no words. I love you too, and you're welcome," he replied. "To us," he added.

With the toast complete, Anya excused herself while she made a trip down to the emporium to search for Ching.

She pinpointed his eminence sitting calmly near the front door—staring blankly out at the street. Less than five minutes had passed since his portentous outburst, but for Ching, it was little more than a distant memory, now stricken from the cat's mind. He allowed Anya to pick him up but insisted on performing his limp, wet rag routine in her arms. It was a catly means of protest.

"This is against my better judgment, young man, but I think you'll be better off with me and Mrs. March today. Cut us a break, though, will you? Try to keep out of trouble," Anya instructed him on the way up the stairs.

Tate laughed and shook his head when she rounded the corner, grappling with the incorrigible feline. His majesty's tail dragged the floor as his rear section drooped further past her knees.

Together they traveled back across the catwalk and down the stairs to Cats 'n' Cocktails.

When they reached the bottom step, Anya was stunned to find herself immediately surrounded by her friends and fellow Main Streeters. "Surprise!" they cheered, raising their glasses.

Desda had gathered everyone, nearest and dearest, to mark the occasion with a little pre-party in advance of the official inaugural.

Anya was speechless. Ethan came over and handed her a toasting flute. He was smiling, but his eyes visibly darkened when he saw Tate right behind her with scotch and glasses from their toast in hand.

She and Ethan had resumed their relationship last spring, upon his return from Minneapolis. He'd spent the last six years there, attending a veterinary college. Since then, she'd been battling his misimpressions that there was something more on Tate's mind than friendship.

Desda took Ching from her so she could make the rounds. Anya hugged and thanked everyone for such an amazing tribute. It was a pinnacle moment, the capstone of her life's work to date.

Anya had all but forgotten Ching's mid-morning episode until he leaped up onto one of the new barstools between Sharon Bailer and herself. The Bailers owned a little hot dog shop across the street known as Let's Be Frank. Ching drew back his lips, giving the appearance of a sneer. Anya tried to ignore him and focus on what Sharon was saying.

"Jules certainly pulled out all the stops on this endeavor, and Tate's an architectural genius! You have a real hit here, Anya. Your mother would be so proud of you. Martine, too," Sharon said.

Ching made a low grumbling sound, and Anya stroked his neck fur to quiet him.

"Honey, I've got a job over in Chenoah Falls," Sharon's husband said, coming alongside her. "It's gonna take up most of the day. I wouldn't look for me until sometime close to dinner." Roger often did plumbing work to supplement their income. "This place is incredible, Anya," he added. "Best of luck. Sorry I have to run." He planted a kiss on Sharon's cheek, gave a wave to the room, filled with friends and neighbors, and dashed out the door. Anya noticed that Sharon recoiled from his parting kiss, and her smile had been transformed into something more akin to a grimace.

The Bailers had been high school sweethearts, married twenty-five years. Sharon was tall and slender with scraggly brown hair she wore straight and to the shoulder. In her day, she'd been head of the prom committee, student council secretary, and played point guard on the girls' varsity basketball team. Roger, in contrast, was both of average height and weight with graying hair and warm brown eyes. He hadn't done anything special in high school other than escort Sharon around. Raising a family and operating a business together for a number of years had taken their toll. Their marital meltdowns were legendary on Main Street and, more often than not, conducted in public.

"Something wrong?" Anya was prompted to ask.

"Wrong? No, nothing's wrong. Nothing at all," Sharon said, feigning a smile, but the veil had been lifted. She was clearly irritated with Roger. Sharon looked away for a second to recover herself more fully. Unfortunately, that's when Ching decided to make his move.

For whatever reason, he began yikking and yowling at a prodigious pitch, until his repeated mewling had caught the attention of everyone in the room. When the howling ceased, he took to marching in circles—left, right, left, right—lifting his paws in a macabre, ritualistic fashion. The disturbing display continued for what felt like an interminable length of time until the cat finally showed signs of winding down. He blinked his eyes to clear the fog, gave himself a stiff shake, and took a swipe at Sharon's glass like he was swinging for the fences! Having doused her in champagne, he turned tail and charged down the length of the bar, toppling several other unattended glasses in his wake. In need of an escape route, Ching tried to shoulder his way into the kitchen, but the door had been cat-proofed—by order of the inspectors—so he turned and pounded up the stairs instead.

These episodes of his always meant something, something dark. This was Ching's death march. To Anya, it had come to signify the prediction of an untimely death, often one of an innocent victim—though the latter had not always been the case.

In years past, she would have turned to Martine to make sense of his behavior, but that was before…

THREE

Before …

Anya McClean, mid-to-late twenties, and sole proprietor of McClean's Irish Pub, emerged from an establishment known as Bagels Baked Goods & Beyond with coffee and breakfast in hand.

Bagels Baked Goods & Beyond was an excellent example of what had become a local practice of using stylistic devices in the naming of one's shop. In the town of Four Oaks, flowers and gifts were purchased at The Twisted Tulip, Pie in the Sky served the best homemade pies—eat-in or carry-out, and at Let's Be Frank, you could order hotdogs fifteen different ways. An amazing selection of books could be found at Bell Book & Candle, though contrary to what the name implied, there were no bells and no candles. Bearing that logic, it might come as no surprise that the local candy store, Candy's Canes, sold over fifty kinds of candies—but not one candy cane, not even at Christmastime. Idiosyncrasies of this nature were deemed inconsequential. Particularly on Main Street, shops and restaurants were designed with the tourist in mind. It was the theater of it all that mattered here, logical or not.

Four Oaks was one of seven small outliers, or bedroom communities, of a larger city called Chenoah Falls. The combined population was somewhere in the neighborhood of twenty-five or thirty thousand, with the people in the city alone accounting for nearly half of that.

The city and its surrounding towns had been built on the lumber and fur trades. When the fur trading industry went south, and much of the forests had been laid bare, the region turned to tourism to sustain its growth and well-being.

On the surface, Four Oaks was a friendly, welcoming community—safe, yet well connected, but like most small towns, it was also a place where everyone knew everyone else, and newcomers were always suspect. The population of the city was forever in flux, but here—the residents came from families that went back as many as four or five generations. The outside world might be a turmoil of change, but in this small northern territory, nothing much ever changed, and everyone liked it that way.

The date on the calendar read May 6—seven weeks since the official start of spring—but here in the north country, it had yet to take hold. If you could concentrate on the sun's return and abide the morning chill, you might be able to convince yourself that winter had finally blown itself out. Anya, however, was more winter-weary than usual and longed for much warmer weather. Being confronted by another windy morning was discouraging—to say the least.

She crossed Main Street to Martine's Mystic Treasures, an emporium next door to her pub. Martine Decoudreau, known affectionately to locals as the Cajun Queen, was the proprietor there, and she was a most interesting woman.

The sign in the window still read closed, but the door was open. Anya scanned the interior for signs of Martine, but she was nowhere in sight. Her presence, however, was otherwise indicated by muffled noises arising from the old basement vault. The centuries old emporium had its origins in banking. Martine used the vault to do tarot readings for clients.

"What's got in to you? Why can't you behave? Drop it!" Martine shouted.

A frantic scuffling sound was heard as a scrimmage for the stairs ensued. Anya turned to see Martine's cat, Ching, come bounding up the basement steps. He skidded to a halt at Anya's feet where he froze—legs splayed, belly flattened to the floor. He had something in his mouth which he immediately surrendered. The cat shot her a look meant to impugn her and slithered away under a nearby rack of candles and incense.

Anya set her coffee and bagels down to retrieve Ching's prize. It was one of Martine's tarot cards. There were tiny teeth marks on one corner.

Martine was an expert when it came to the tools of her trade. She could divine the answers to your questions from the tarot, dice, regular playing cards, rune tiles, and even tea leaves. Anya had once seen Martine intuit messages by holding personal possessions or trinkets belonging to a querent's loved one.

Anya's mother, Kate, had been Martine's best friend, but she'd never given much credence to Martine's craft or what Martine called Ching's warnings. She had, however, admitted to witnessing some eerie coincidences on more than one occasion.

The card Ching had dropped was an odd-looking card known as the Moon. The images depicted on the card were disturbing: A full moon, its face in partial profile, was shining down upon a winding road drawing unseen travelers toward twin towers on the horizon. In the foreground, a dog and a wolf opposed one another across a dark pool of water from which a crayfish emerged.

"Martine!" Anya called out, announcing her presence on the way down the stairs.

The frustration emanating from the inner sanctum was tangible. Martine was seated at her table with her head in her hands. It looked like a cyclone had hit the place, a cyclone named Ching.

"What happened here?!" Anya exclaimed.

The bracelets around Martine's wrists rang as she threw up her hands in disgust. "I was doin a readin for Mrs. Bailer dis mornin, when Ching flew into one of heez cat fits. I was about to read da Celtic Cross when he jus began screechin and howlin! I don why he so crazy." Martine paused to take the card from Anya's outstretched hand. "Suddenly he grab dis card and raced away—kickin all da cards to da floor as he go. Mrs. Bailer left in a hurry, she did. He been racin up and down da stairs in a torrent ever since."

"Spooky card," Anya said, as she helped Martine right the room.

"Depends on da position in da overall spread, but wid Ching I have to take da card at face value. He know I got a letta from my sista down New Orleans yestaday."

"Sister? I didn't know you had a sister," Anya replied.

Martine nodded. "She comin for a visit. Since he see dat letta, he got sometin stuck in heez craw. He tryin to warn me—and he exactly right." Martine produced an envelope from a pocket hidden somewhere within the folds of her aqua sea-green gown.

Anya read the letter, written on pale blue stationery, emblazoned with a gold pelican in the lower right-hand corner. The contents had been frantically scribed. In short, it was an urgent request for Martine's help in a matter that was tantamount to blackmail—accompanied by a death threat. It seemed that her sister, Tame, had been receiving letters from an unnamed source demanding an enormous sum of money—or else!

"Ten million dollars?" Anya frowned, looking up at Martine. "Is there any reason for this person to believe she has access to that kind of money?"

Martine shrugged. "We both inherited well, but dat was years ago, and certainly not in keeping wid such a vast amount. Whatever she had, she's likely squandered most—if not all—of it by now."

"She doesn't expect you to come up with it, does she?"

Martine rolled her eyes in response.

"Does the sheriff know about this? I want you to fill him in right away."

"Perhaps I will share it wid him, but he has no jurisdiction in New Orleans. What can he do? Tame say she already notify da proper authorities down dere."

Anya thrust the letter at Martine. "I don't care. I want you to tell him. Something isn't right. Something is very wrong here. Your sister is in danger. You could be too if you get involved. Why don't I know about this sister?"

"I don talk to her in years. Always so much trouble wid dat one."

Bells jangled from above, announcing the presence of a customer, and they made their way back upstairs.

Anya noticed that Ching had emerged from his hiding place and was now sitting stiffly posed on the newel post beside the steps. His eyes were forward-focused, trained on some invisible point in the distance. He looked more like a sergeant at arms than the unopposed leader of Martine's feline housemates.

Martine motioned to the customer to indicate that she would be right with her. "Ethan's party is tonight, Sha, yeah? It's been a long time since you see him. I have to work late, but you bring me back a piece of cake. Tell me all about it. I gave Desda my gift for heem. Oh, and it's gonna rain, so you be sure and take da truck," she said.

"Rain? The forecast called for clear skies through Wednesday," Anya replied.

Martine shook her head. "No, dat's wrong. Possum been starin out da window all mornin—mutterin to herself, and washin her ears. Storms comin," Martine insisted, gesturing to the little gray female tabby sitting near the door. Hearing her name, Possum turned to provide them with a worried look.

Anya had learned of many superstitions associated with cats from Martine over the years. It was bad luck to see a white cat at night, but good luck to see one on the road in the daytime. The sudden appearance of a stray tortoiseshell cat could be the harbinger of accidental death—but to dream of such a cat might foretell luck in love. Everyone knew that it was unlucky for a black cat to cross your path, especially while traveling by car after midnight. But few knew that to reverse this, one needed only to turn their hat around backward and mark the windshield with an "x". These and more were the words of wisdom from the Cajun Queen.

"OK, I see you later den," Martine said, squeezing Anya's wrist before rushing off to her customer.

"Wait, Martine, there was a pelican on the stationary. Why?"

"State bird of Louisiana," she replied.

On her way out the door, Anya retrieved her coffee and breakfast—now cold. Having lost her appetite as well, she deposited them both directly into a sidewalk receptacle outside of McClean's.

Desda March was behind the bar, emptying one of the small dishwashers they used for barware.

Smoky Mabrey, whose real name was Bob, was sipping Irish coffee and keeping Desda company. Smoky and his wife, Helen, were the owners of Smoky's BBQ.

"Hey there, Smoky," Anya greeted their early morning customer.

"Top o' the mornin to ya. What's the news? I heard an ugly rumor somewhere's that you're gettin ready to shut this place down for a while. No more Irish pub? Where do you expect us regulars to go to blow off some steam?" he asked, only half-jokingly.

"Well, I don't know how to break it to you, Smoky, but those ugly rumors are true. Won't be until August, though, and only for a couple of months. And you can get back to blowing off steam right here when it's over."

Anya had decided to expand upon the concept of cat cafes by converting McClean's into a cat rescue bar and grill. There would be a full renovation done on the place, and she was already lining up rescue organizations to partner with when they reopened.

She smiled to herself as she pictured Smoky and his fishing buddies playing darts and doing shots on Friday nights surrounded by cats. It was comical, really. Dogs maybe, but cats … never. Still, she knew somehow they would adjust. Nothing could chase away her regulars.

"Well, gotta run. Helen and me are smokin racks of ribs for Ethan's party. Actually, I'm doin the smokin. Helen's concocting side dishes. See you two ladies up at the ranch later?" he asked, ambling toward the door.

"You betcha," Anya replied with a wave.

"See ya later," Desda echoed in kind.

The party that currently had everyone's attention was for Ethan Notah. He'd recently returned, credentials in hand, after having spent the last six years away earning his veterinary degree. A celebration had been planned for later that evening at his father's ranch to honor his achievement and to welcome him home.

The Notahs' ranch was officially called The Mustang Ranch and was situated on the banks of a 430-acre man-made lake known as Lake Increase. It had been formed in the 1800s by the damming of the Chenoah Falls River. Some of the wealthy families in the area also had lake houses there. Martine had a sprawling home in the community, directly across the lake from the Notahs.

Only a few horses remained at the ranch that had once been home to about a hundred head, but none were American Mustangs. The name referred to another popular pony—the Ford Mustang, and the Notahs had about four hundred acres of them in varying conditions, housed in massive stables that had been converted into garages. They were in the business of selling reconditioned classics and parts to collectors. It was apparently a very lucrative operation. They'd even sold a few cars to a big Hollywood producer once for a movie he was making—the name of which no one could ever seem to remember.

Typical of their small-town upbringing, Anya and Ethan had known each other all of their lives. Their families were well-acquainted, they moved in the same social circles, and they'd graduated the same year from the same high school.

Post graduation, Anya had chosen to pursue a business degree at a local college. Ethan had landed a full scholarship at an outstate university in Minneapolis where he planned to obtain a veterinary degree. When it came to covering his living expenses, he'd refused his father's offer of money and taken a job working in Doc Lafferty's veterinary clinic instead to save up. In the years before he went away, Anya and Ethan had begun a more personal relationship, one that Ethan had been reluctant to put on pause when it was time for him to leave for Minneapolis. Anya had insisted on ending their relationship, pointing out the fact that most long-distance relationships were doomed from the outset. It was a point of view with which Ethan had staunchly disagreed. He'd launched a vigorous campaign of resistance, promising to come home on weekends or fly her up to visit him, but Anya had held firm to her beliefs. In the end, he'd had no choice but to concede to her wishes.

Soon after, Anya had been forced to withdraw from her own classes for a semester when her mother passed away quite unexpectedly. In the months that followed, she'd decided to scrap her college plans altogether and take over proprietorship of McClean's.

Six years had passed, during which Anya had endeavored to build her own life, but Ethan had always been somewhere in the back of her mind. She had to admit that she was both nervous and excited about the party tonight.

"So, these are the gifts we all bought for Ethan," Desda said, placing three boxes on the bar between them. Each was elaborately wrapped and tied up in satin ribbons and bows. "This big one is from Paul and I. The flat, square one is from Martine, and this long skinny box is from you. I had them all wrapped at The Twisted Tulip."

Anya smiled. "Thank you, Desda." Desda was always on top of every detail.

Anya had purchased a silver St. Francis of Assisi medal for Ethan. The patron saint of animals seemed like an obvious choice. Desda had ordered a set of whiskey glasses and chilling stones. The glasses had black pawprints on them.

"What did Martine get him?" Anya asked.

"A clock for his future office. It has the staff of Asclepius on it."

Some in the medical community claim the staff of Caduceus, a rod with two snakes wrapped around it, is the official symbol for medical doctors or veterinarians. In actuality, it is the staff of Asclepius that was the original symbol, a rod with a single snake wrapped around it. It wasn't surprising that Martine would make this distinction. Her father had been a doctor.

"Ananda and Craig are coming in at five to relieve us," Anya said. Ananda Reese and Craig Capinetti were longtime and much relied upon employees.

"Oh, good! That will give me time to go home and change before the party," Desda said.

Out of nowhere, as is often the case with cats, Martine's calico, Hester, materialized. She slyly slipped a paw into Desda's cup of water and licked it. She liked to drink from her own water bowl the same way—with a dip of her paw. Desda gently shooed her away.

"Paul and I are planning to get there a little early to help set up. Want me to bring the gifts with me?"

"OK, sure. That would be great," Anya agreed, happy to relinquish this task. It would spare her the necessity of having to track Ethan down in order to bestow her gift. She preferred to leave it up to him to seek her out if he felt so inclined.

The workday dragged on endlessly. To make matters worse, Anya happened to catch Desda yawning, resulting in a phenomenon in which they traded yawns—back and forth for hours—while stealing glances at the clock.

When Ananda and Craig finally arrived to relieve them, and Desda had shuffled out the door to her car, Anya decided to head upstairs for a quick nap to recharge. She wanted to be in top form for this long-awaited reunion of sorts. She jogged up the stairs, collapsed on the couch, and fell fast asleep.

No more than an hour had passed when Anya was awakened by a vague sense of heaviness on her chest, as if something was exerting downward pressure. It was accompanied by an odd prickling sensation on her cheek. Upon opening her eyes, she found herself face-to-face with Ching. He was lying on top of her, mere inches from her nose. He'd grown impatient waiting for her to awake and had begun stroking her cheek with his whiskers.

Ching let out a stentorian yowl and knifed his tail from side to side.

Two other warm bodies were coiled near her feet, those of Hester and Don Pedro.

Anya squinted at the clock—ten minutes past six. Had Martine forgotten to feed them? She had mentioned that she would be too busy working to go to the party. Perhaps work, or the situation regarding Tame had caused the cats' dinnertime to slip her mind.

Anya crawled off of the couch and stumbled over to Martine's apartment—via the glass catwalk. Instantly, there were seven cats at her heels, yikking in protest at the lateness of their dinner hour.

Martine's cats were given kibble only as a side dish. The main dish was always something like salmon, chicken, turkey, or duck. She liked to prepare homemade delicacies for them, simmered in broth and served on blue and white china.

Anya located several cans of red salmon in the pantry and took great pains to arrange it attractively on the customary plates. She filled a separate bowl with kibble, refreshed their water, and policed their commodes in the laundry room. The sounds of tiny fangs, clicking loudly on plates, meant that she was free to attend to her own needs.

She popped down to McClean's to check on Ananda and Craig. The pub's regulars were already in evidence—seated at the bar. The rest of the Saturday night crowd wouldn't arrive until much later, around nine or ten o'clock. Everything was under control, so Anya grabbed a sandwich from the kitchen and devoured it on her way upstairs to shower.

After she had blown out her long dark hair—flat-ironing it until it was stick-straight—she dressed in jeans and a jade green and white tee that complimented her cool green eyes. She briefly considered wearing a new pair of platform wedges, but Possum's and Martine's warnings of impending rain prompted her to reach for her field boots instead. A little eyeliner, a sweep of mascara, and a pair of silver hoop earrings completed her preparations.

Anya grabbed her jacket and was on her way out the door with a commercial-sized tray of McClean's "famous" hot wings in hand when she noticed little Possum sitting in McClean's front window. The little tabby was still fussing and muttering to herself. Anya again decided to heed the warning and chose to take the Land Rover instead of her small convertible. In the case of a heavy storm, there could be flash-flooding, and the roads up near the lake sometimes washed-out. The truck was the safer choice.

It was about a twenty-minute drive to Lake Increase, along narrow winding roads. Long stretches beneath the dark canopy of two-hundred-foot white pines alternated with equally vast expanses of farmland or cultivated pastures that had sprung up in response to the Timber Culture Act. By the late 1800s, the area had undergone such heavy clearing by the lumber industry that the government had started offering free acreage to anyone willing to farm it—provided they were also willing to plant several acres of trees.

Driving through the picturesque countryside, Anya's thoughts turned to Ethan Notah. Roughly three hundred or so Native Americans still lived in the area, mostly Lakota and Ojibwe. The Notahs were Lakota. Sam Notah and his sons, Ethan and Nigel, were all well over six feet tall, with shoulder-length black hair and impenetrable dark eyes. The fiercely defined cheekbones and sharply angled jawlines were also attractive features that all three shared—adding to the powerful, if not intimidating, presence each man possessed. They had many friends in the area who spoke well of their charitable nature, clever wit, and strength of character.

Ethan and Nigel had been raised solely by their

father, Sam, and there was never any mention of their mother. Anya had once been told that she had run away with a hired man when the two boys were very young. Anya's father had left too when she was little, and her mother had never spoken of him either.

When she saw the old Notah Ranch sign, weather-beaten, gray, and seasoned by age, she slowed her vehicle. Rain would transform the lawn parking into a muddy maze of potholes and tire ruts, so she decided to park on a patch of gravel near the road instead. After a quick peek in the mirror, she pocketed her keys, grabbed the tray of wings, and trekked up the hill toward the house.

FOUR

The party was in full swing, as evidenced by the sound of music and an abundance of laughter coming from the house on the hill. The oaky smell of bonfires burning intermingled with the scents of wet leaves, cold lake water, and fresh night air, creating a heady mix.

Noni Landale was waving to her from one of many food-laden banquet tables. Anya saw her chance to unburden herself of the cumbersome tray of wings she was carrying.

"I saved you a couple of compartments in this buffet warmer. Here, let me help you," Noni said, taking the tray from Anya and transferring the wings to covered warming bins. She paused to sweep away a few stray strands of her auburn hair and adjust the pins in her bun before adding, "You can leave your tray with me if you like. I'll drop it off tomorrow." The Landale's Log Cabin restaurant was right next door to McClean's and Mystic Treasures, which made Noni's offer one that Anya could accept in good conscience.

She continued to loiter about near the tables for a minute or two, surveying her surroundings with nervous incertitude until she heard the sounds of familiar voices calling to her. Anya turned to see Ethan's brother, Nigel, his girlfriend Cecilia Bennedetto, and Tate Blackledge crossing the lawn to join her.

"We saw you coming from the kitchen window," Tate said, handing her a beer.

As best friends, she and Tate had always spent a lot of time together, but even more so in recent weeks. Tate owned his own construction company, and they'd been collaborating on her plans to transform McClean's into a rescue bar and grill. Tate was going to oversee the entire project for her.

Anya gratefully accepted the beer and greeted all three of her friends with a hug.

"I'm so glad to see you. I wasn't sure if you'd come," Cecilia said.

Anya knew that wasn't true. Cecilia knew full well the history between her and Ethan. She knew Anya would make an appearance there that evening.

Anya threw Cecilia a sideways glance that conveyed her skepticism and replied, "I was promised free beer."

Cecilia rolled her eyes and laughed. "Don't be glib," she meekly enjoined.

While Tate was Anya's best friend, she'd known Cecilia the longest. Her parents owned a business on

Main Street too, a restaurant known as Bennedetto's Surf and Turf. Cecilia's parents had been friends of her mother, so they were confidantes of long-standing acquaintance.

"Ethan's been looking for you," Nigel said. "Last time I saw him he was on the porch, talking to Pops and Sheriff Wakefield."

Nigel Notah was Ethan's younger brother, by little more than a year. Personality-wise, they were very different people, but the physical resemblance between the two was astounding.

"I'm sure we'll run into one another at some point," Anya replied noncommittally. She resisted the temptation to look toward the porch and suggested that they all grab a table instead.

Cecilia shook her head. "It's too chilly out here for me. There's a small group hanging out in the kitchen if you care to join in. Besides, I think I see Lila Stevens over there, and if one more person checks my hand for an engagement ring tonight, I'm going to scream."

The whole town had been waiting for her and Nigel to finally make an engagement announcement. If there was anything the people of Four Oaks loved more than a festival, it was a wedding—and this one was sure to be the event of the century. More than once it had been said what a beautiful bride Cecilia would be, and what a striking couple they made—Nigel Notah, tall, dark, and handsome, and Cecilia Bennedetto, the dark-eyed, raven-haired, Italian princess. She was also the only child and beloved daughter of Cossima and Alessandro Bennedetto—the wealthiest family in town.

"If you haven't eaten, there's enough food out there to feed us all for a month! Try the raspberry ribbon cake. I made it myself," Cecilia called out as she and Nigel headed back toward the house.

"She wasn't kidding, was she?" Anya remarked to Tate, looking out over the nearby tables of food. In a community such as theirs where most everyone was involved in food and beverage services of some sort, it was probably not so surprising.

There were trays of deli sandwiches from Drexsler's Deli, hamburgers and ribs from Smoky's BBQ, hotdogs from Let's Be Frank, Crab cakes from The Pirate's Cove, the wings from McClean's, and buckets of fried chicken from Landale's Log Cabin. There were two whole tables given over entirely to side dishes. Coleslaw, two kinds of potato salads, chips and dips, mac 'n' cheese, macaroni salad, pickles, olives, grapes, and melons rounded out the spread. The dessert table was equally overflowing with lemon bars, a coconut cake, a chocolate cake, pans of brownies, Cecilia's ribbon cake, and an assortment of pies from Pie in the Sky.

She and Tate grabbed a couple of sandwiches and some chips. Anya also got a slice of Cecilia's raspberry ribbon cake for Martine. Juggling two plates and a beer, she followed Tate over to the nearest available table.

Anya had always considered Ethan to be the best-looking man in town, but sitting across from Tate now, she realized that many would argue that the title belonged to him. He was tall, lean, and well-built with a casual manner and an inviting smile. The long, tousled layers of his ash-blond hair fell in hapless disarray, inches below his collar. He was insightful, intelligent, and dangerously charming. Often times she'd wondered if he'd purposely affected this boy next door allure as a way of disguising another side—one that was covertly clever, impassioned, and designing. Without a doubt—there was something subtly seductive in those dark blue eyes he kept shyly shaded beneath the bill of his hat.

"You've done a lot of work for Martine, spent a lot of time with her. Did she ever mention that she has a sister?" Anya asked him.

"Yeah, as a matter of fact, I seem to remember her mentioning something about a sister. She's an antiques dealer in New Orleans where Martine's family is from. They're not very close. She's kind of the black sheep in the family, I think. Why?"

"She's coming for a visit. Martine isn't exactly happy about it. Sounds like she wants money."

"Hmmm … when is she coming?"

"I think she arrives tomorrow."

Tate responded with a satirical grin. "That should be interesting, especially if she's anything like Martine. I'll look forward to hearing more about that after you meet her."

Anya's train of thought was interrupted, seeing that Jimmy Shaw had pulled up a chair at the end of their table.

"Tate and Anya, I've been looking for you two!"

Jimmy was a close mutual friend of theirs. He lived in the city and ran an organization known as Chenoah Falls Stray Rescue. It was a shelter for stray and abandoned dogs. In addition to running the shelter, Jimmy made the local news regularly in connection with his efforts to break up illegal dogfighting rings. He was a big man with a tough exterior, but beneath that long hair, scruffy beard, and armfuls of tattoos, he was a gentle person with a huge heart.

"Jimmy! I'm glad you're here," Anya said. "I've been meaning to call you. I want to hold at least one more fundraiser for CF Stray Rescue before I close down McClean's for renovation."

"Oh yeah, that would be great!" Jimmy replied. "We're trying to add a new wing, and our cash flow is getting pretty tight. Let's get together on that soon, if you're up for it."

McClean's often collaborated with CF Stray Rescue on fundraisers. They were a big hit with the locals, who were always generous with their donations. Even so, with the number of dogs he endeavored to care for at the shelter, Jimmy was always in need of support. He was also continually looking to expand his operations which required funding as well.

"Speaking of renovations, did you get your permits approved yet?" Tate asked her.

"Not yet, but I see Nick Larkin over there. Maybe he knows something," Anya replied, waving at Nick until she'd caught his attention. Nick returned the wave and made his way to their table.

"Hey, guys!" he greeted them, shaking hands with Tate and Jimmy and giving Anya a friendly hug. He shoved his wavy brown hair up under the bill of his cap and said, "I bet you two are wondering about those permits." Nick and Lisa Larkin were the owners of a restaurant called The Pirate's Cove on Main Street. Nick was also on the town council.

"Tate and I were hoping you might have an update," Anya said.

"They're on this week's agenda, so you'll be hearing something soon. You won't have any problems, though. Don't worry about a thing."

"Great! With any luck, you'll be approved by the end of the week, and I can start ordering materials," Tate said.

"Yep, it's in the bag. No worries," Nick replied with confidence. "Get those supply orders ready to go."

Just then Helen Mabrey sidled up to the table and handed Jimmy a large paper sack. "Here you go, honey," she said, smiling down at Jimmy with caring blue eyes.

"Doggy bag for my four-legged friends," Jimmy explained. "Thanks, Helen!" he called out after her as she shuffled off.

Nick rubbed his chin and looked around. "Has anybody seen Ethan?" he asked. "Lisa and I are leaving soon, and I haven't had a chance yet to say hello."

"As a matter of fact, looks like he's on his way over here right now," Jimmy replied, looking past Anya's shoulder.

As Ethan moved in to join their group, Anya was quick to avert her eyes. She was stunned to see that he looked exactly the way she remembered him, the long black hair—sweeping below the shoulders of his leather jacket—the darkest eyes she'd ever seen. The irreverent smile that lingered at the corners of his lips confirmed that the waggish, slightly arrogant manner he'd possessed was also still in effect, adding to his disarming appeal.

"Ethan, welcome back," Nick said. "It's great to see you!"

"Good to see you too," Ethan replied, shaking hands all around.

"Listen, Lisa and I have to go pick up the kids, but

I wanted to invite you to drop by The Pirate's Cove sometime soon. It'll be on the house," Nick said.

"Thanks, I'll be sure to do that," Ethan assured.

Once Nick had gone off in search of his wife, Ethan sat down next to Anya, straddling the bench.

"Anya, I was hoping you'd come," he said.

Anya suppressed a shiver. The smooth warm tone of his voice brought on a flood of emotions.

She threw him a fleeting glance and a guarded smile. "Ethan, welcome back."

Ethan gave her a playful shoulder bump. "Thank you, it's good to be back. Been a long time."

Anya could feel his eyes on her, attempting to assess her reaction to this unofficial reunion, even as she remained rigid beside him, loathe to reveal any insight.

"When did your flight get in?" Jimmy asked.

"This afternoon actually. Haven't even had time to unpack," Ethan replied without so much as a glance in Jimmy's direction.

Anya shifted uncomfortably and sighed. She happened to meet Tate's gaze across the table and registered what she interpreted as a disapproving look.

"What do we have here?" Ethan asked, draping his arm around her neck while reaching for his inside pocket. He produced a long, slender gift-wrapped box. It was the present she'd bought for him. Desda must have given it to him earlier. Without further comment, he tore away the paper and opened the box. Ethan held up the medal, admiring it reverently. The polished silver gleamed in the moonlight.

"Hey! The patron saint of animals. I've got one too," Jimmy said, revealing a similar medallion that he wore around his own neck.

Ethan winked at her, beaming that magnificent smile of his as he worked to secure it around his neck. "Best gift of all. I'll wear it always. Thank you, Anya," he said sincerely.

Anya nodded and relinquished a genuine smile.

"Anyone need another beer?" Tate asked, abruptly ending the moment. Everyone accepted his offer, and he departed to fill the order.

"Be sure to thank Martine for me too," Ethan said. "I'm not sure when I'll get by there to see her, sometime soon, but please tell her the clock is fantastic."

"I definitely will," Anya affirmed.

"How is our Cajun Queen, by the way?"

"Martine never changes. You'll find everything around here is pretty much the way you left it," Anya replied. She noticed that Ethan was staring at her again. She knew he was deciding whether or not to read anything into her response.

Jimmy cleared his throat. "So, Doc Lafferty told me to tell you to give him a shout now that you're home for good. Maybe he's gonna offer you a position or something," Jimmy interjected.

"That's what I'm hoping, Jimmy. I'm going to stop by the clinic on Monday or Tuesday, as soon as I get settled in," Ethan confirmed.

"Man, that'll be great. We'll get to work together all the time," Jimmy said.

Doc Lafferty had a booming veterinary practice in Chenoah Falls, practically next door to Jimmy's shelter. It had always been Doc's plan to bring Ethan into the practice once he graduated. The Doc was a real animal lover, and he took care of all of Jimmy's dogs free of charge. Anya knew that Ethan hoped to be able to buy out Doc someday and take over the practice.

"Ethan!" Old Sam's voice was suddenly heard, calling to him from the front porch.

Ethan turned to look over his shoulder. "Oh-oh, looks like Pops wants me for something," he said, getting to his feet. "Jimmy, see you soon, probably right after I drop in on Doc."

"Do that. We'll grab lunch and a beer at Sawyer's to celebrate," Jimmy replied.

Anya was surprised when Ethan leaned down to hug her. He buried his face in her hair and whispered, "Don't … go … anywhere." He lingered with his arms around her for several seconds more before heading off in the direction of the house.

"Where'd Ethan disappear to?" Tate asked, arriving with their beverages.

"Old Sam called him away," Jimmy said, gesturing toward the front porch.

Tate glanced up at the house where Nigel, Sam, and another man were waiting on Ethan. "Oh, that customer of Nigel's must be here. Nigel said he was coming up tonight from somewhere down south."

Another hour or so of friendly conversation commenced, during which Ethan did not return. Eventually, Jimmy left to go see to his dogs, and Tate's brother, Rob, came to collect him.

"We need to get an early start in the morning. Got a roofing job over in Five Pines. Let me know when you hear about the permits," Tate said in parting. Anya said she would.

She stuck around for another hour or so, hoping Ethan would make it back to her, but he never did. It was understandable. As the guest of honor, he was in high demand.

She'd just finished bringing home the win with Paul March in a game of washers against Noni and Larry Landale when she heard the first rumble of thunder somewhere off in the distance. Anya counted to twenty before she saw the accompanying blink of lightning softly illuminate the clouds that were gathering overhead.

With the rain threatening to bring the festivities to a close, Helen, Smoky, Desda, Cecilia, and several others came running from the house. Anya joined them in gathering up the many trays of food which they whisked away to the safety of the Notahs' kitchen.

On the way to her vehicle, she took one last look around for Ethan and spotted his towering frame adjacent to the porch. His father and Sheriff Wakefield must have gone inside, but Ethan was still talking with Nigel and the other man—the customer of Nigel's Tate had spoken of. They seemed to be deep in conversation. Anya watched as the stranger ground out a cigarette beneath the heel of his boot. Whoever he was, she was certain that he wasn't from the area.

The winds rose up sharply, and she could feel the electrical charge in the air. There was another rumble of thunder followed more closely this time by a brilliant flash of lightning.

Anya grabbed the cake she'd saved for Martine and a small bag of treats for the cats and ran for the truck. Another violent crack of thunder shook the ground as she dove behind the wheel. There was an audible sizzle as a jagged bolt of light knifed across the sky.

Wind-driven rain and quarter-sized hail made for slow travel on the way back to town. It was a pretty violent storm, but it moved through quickly. By the time she pulled up in front of McClean's and Martine's Mystic Treasures, it had all but subsided. The aftermath left her surroundings looking more like winter than spring in Four Oaks. The streets and sidewalks were white, blanketed by hail. It crunched beneath her feet as she climbed out of the truck.

Anya ran upstairs to check on the cats and to parcel out the crabmeat she'd brought them from the party. The smell of seafood brought all seven racing to the kitchen, where they devoured it rapturously the second the plates hit the floor.

Martine's shop was empty, so Anya descended the stairs to the vault, cake and fork in hand, and found the Cajun Queen seated at her table.

"Thank you, Sha," Martine said, smiling a bit smugly.

"Raspberry ribbon cake, courtesy of Miss Bennedetto. It looks terrific," Anya said, handing the plate and fork to Martine.

"I tol you it would rain." Martine chuckled. "Dat ole Possum try to tell you too, eh?" The chuckle became a knowing laugh.

Anya gave a conciliatory nod. "That you did. Ethan was sorry you couldn't make it. He said to tell you, and I quote, that the clock was fantastic. He'll be around to tell you himself after he gets settled in."

"Ah! Good! How is Ethan?"

"Well, I'm tempted to say that he hasn't changed a bit, but I didn't get to spend much time with him. There were so many people there. He's hoping Doc Lafferty might hire him at the clinic."

"Wouldn't dat be nice? I love for him to work wid Doc Lafferty. Heez a good man," Martine said, smiling warmly at the mention of her cats' veterinarian.

Anya shifted uncomfortably in her seat as Martine reached for a deck of ordinary playing cards, instead of the fork, and began to shuffle them vigorously.

"I don believe my sista's claims of blackmail. Dat one never tells da truth. I wan to ask da cards to show me da true intentions behind her visit. I can't do it alone. Sit wid me a minute?" she asked.

As hard as Anya tried to avoid being anywhere near Martine when she channeled otherworldly entities, the woman somehow managed to drag or trick her into it every now and again.

Almost immediately, a card flew out. It was the four of clubs. Martine positioned it on the table in front of her and silently laid out three more cards, face down below it.

"Da central issue is da four of clubs. Da devil's bed-post," Martine announced without so much as a trace of concern.

Anya felt a shiver ripple up her spine and down both her arms.

Martine flipped over the other three cards, pausing to study them with her amber-colored eyes.

"Past, present, and future," she said, gently tapping each card. "OK… so, da overall message comes from da four of clubs. It wanted to come out right away. It cautions not to blindly accept what others tell you. It is a card dat warns of deceit. No surprises dere."

Martine then turned her attention to the other three cards in the spread. The card in the past position was the five of hearts.

"Dis card talks of jealousy and ill will, but it is in da past. No surprises dere either. In da present position is da king of spades. Dis one draws my attention da most. It is a warning about a self-servin, dark-haired man coming toward the querent." Martine paused to consider this card at length before continuing. "Da third card is da card of da future, circumstances yet to unfold. Nine of spades—bad luck, perhaps leading to an unforeseen accident."

"An accident?!" Anya exclaimed. "Have you told the sheriff any of this yet?"

Martine shook her head. "No, did you see he was at da ranch tonight?" Her bracelets jingled while she swept up the cards.

At that moment, Ching came into the room. He ascended effortlessly to the table's surface beside a box that held a vintage Kabala game. He positioned himself directly above a picture of the eye of Zohar that was printed on the lid and sneezed. Having finished his late-night snack, the cat commenced with his post-dining ablutions.

"Ching want me to ask da Kabala," Martine said.

Everything that cat did was a sign to Martine. Ching paused to trill his tongue, making an odd breathy sort of sound.

As if in answer to Ching's utterance, Don Pedro slipped out from between two books on a nearby shelf.

Martine gently slid the box out from under Ching, who unflinchingly carried on with his bath. Anya watched her assemble the contents with grave reservation.

The Kabala, in theory, was intended to be marketed as a game, much like the Ouija Board, but the way Martine used it, it was far from a game.

She set up the circular board with the tiny tarot cards encircling the perimeter and the eerie glowing eye of Zohar at the center. Ching paused to watch in fascination, as each new element emerged.

Anya became aware of a presence behind her and turned to see Zia entering the room. In one fluid motion, she leaped onto Anya's lap to observe.

The rest of the cats were right behind her. First came Luther, wagging his great plumed tail, followed by Hester, Possum, and Benny bringing up the rear. They appeared transfixed by the flurry of Martine's movements, each seeking out a vantage point from which to witness whatever magic was about to be made manifest.

Martine placed the marble on the teetering track that encircled the board. The board tilted zanily—careening from side to side—while the marble whirled madly round and round.

Anya realized she'd been holding her breath and shook her shoulders, forcing herself to relax.

All seven cats were intensely focused, tracking the marble as it spun around the track. Several of them began making guttural sounds deep in their throats, and Hester let out a spine-tingling, "Arooooo-oooo!" Don Pedro bushed his tail, crouching and hissing at the glowing eye of Zohar as the marble came to rest in front of one of the cards. Ching placed his paw firmly on the marble, and Martine drew the corresponding card.

"Da Tower," she whispered. It was a frightening card depicting death and destruction. A dark ominous tower was engulfed in flames, the result of a terrifying lightning strike. A crown drifted aloft above the scene, blown high into the air by the explosion. Two people, wearing expressions of horror, tumbled from the windows toward the ground below.

Anya was astonished by Martine's unwavering calm in the face of such a grim omen. Unperturbed, she merely tapped the card to her lips and said, "Destruction, trauma, chaos. Unstable foundations will be torn down to make way for a stronger, new beginning. A cycle is ending, perhaps in a way dat is shocking." Martine replaced the card in its original position and smiled. "Unless dere jus tryin to tell me da roof was damaged in da storm," she added with a wink.

That's when Ching let out a shriek and donkey-kicked the board hard with his back legs, sending everything clattering to the floor. He paused to squint his yellow-green eyes at Anya, gave his shoulder a few congratulatory licks, and strolled casually out the door.

Zia sauntered after him, landing on the disembodied eye of Zohar. It spun away under the table and was knocked into a corner of the room.

The others filed out, one by one, as quietly as they had entered.

Martine twisted a few lengths of her long braided hair. The distant look in her eyes signaled to Anya that she had retreated into her own private thoughts.

"Well," Anya sighed, struggling to regain her composure, "that was all very disturbing. I don't know why I let you involve me in these things. You *will* call the sheriff in the morning, correct?" It was more of an order than a question.

Martine reached for the fork and smiled.

FIVE

Sunday was warm and bright. Voluminous white clouds, some tinged with gray, floated above, buoyed along by a light spring breeze. Despite the previous night's storm and visit to Martine's, Anya was in high spirits and ravenous for breakfast when she entered Landale's Log Cabin. Glancing around, she was relieved to see that she was ahead of the usual Sunday morning rush. There were still plenty of tables available.

"Anya!" a voice called to her. Anya was happy to see Lila and Mason Stevens motioning to her to join them.

The Stevenses were the owners of an enormous ark-shaped restaurant. Its perimeter was guarded by life-size replicas of giraffes, bears, elephants, and lions, and all were naturally arranged in pairs. One would logically expect the restaurant to be named Noah's Ark; however, the six-foot tall red letters on the roof read: Two By Two.

Mason was originally from Missouri, where there had once been a restaurant called Noah's Ark. Though now defunct, it had been a thriving landmark. He had replicated nearly every detail in his own restaurant, including the homestyle fried chicken dinner special, but out of respect, he had chosen an original name. It was wildly popular with the tourists, whether visiting locally or just passing through.

They all exchanged cheerful hellos and good mornings, as Anya slid into the booth across from them. Lila handed her a menu.

"Have you ordered?" Anya asked.

"No, but here comes Holly now," Lila replied. Holly was the Landales' daughter. She worked waitstaff on weekends and on her breaks from college. She was dressed like a pioneer, the uniform that all of the Log Cabin employees were required to wear.

"Good morning, folks! What can I bring you?" Holly asked.

Anya was still weighing her choices. She was torn between two pictures, one that featured the three-egg breakfast with bacon, and hash browns, and one that had a stack of pancakes, golden brown and dripping with maple syrup.

"Good morning, Holly. I'll have a plain bagel and a glass of orange juice," Lila said confidently before hastily reconsidering. "On second thought, better bring me a smidge of cream cheese on the side."

"And you can bring me the Belgian waffle—strawberries and powdered sugar on the side—three strips of bacon, country-style potatoes, and coffee," Mason said.

Holly turned to Anya then, tapping her pen on her pad expectantly. Anya caved to the pressure and ordered the pancakes *and* the three-egg breakfast with coffee.

Holly thanked them politely, swept up their menus, and dashed off to put their orders in.

"So," Lila began, leaning forward in a conspiratorial manner, "have you heard about the new art gallery that's going in the old furniture store next to Bell Book & Candle?"

"No, I have not," Anya replied, duly intrigued. In a small town such as theirs, gossip ranked as a cottage industry, though no one admitted to trading in it. People preferred the term "news" when it came to exchanging enticing bits of information that were not widely known.

"The new owner or artist in residence, as I believe she refers to herself, is a Miss Sidra York and the gallery itself will be called The York Gallery," Lila continued.

"She came into the restaurant last night for dinner. Lila and I were on our way out, and we kind of bumped into one another at the hostess station," Mason explained.

"What's she like?" Anya asked, as Holly arrived with their food.

"She's kind of reserved," Lila said, snootily tossing her long brown hair for effect.

"Kind of a snob, if you ask me," Mason added, digging into his waffle.

Lila gave his shoulder a shove. "That's not very polite."

"No, but it's true," Mason mumbled.

"Wow, that's some news. I wonder how the Colburns will react. They do a fair amount of business in that area, paintings, photography, wall hangings, sculpture, and other decorative stuff," Anya pointed out.

The Colburn Design Center was a full service decorating studio operated by two sisters—Elizabeth and Jules Colburn. Their services were retained by all of the wealthiest families in Four Oaks. The bulk of their clients, however, were online or located in big cities. One of them was always out of town on business, it seemed, with the other remaining behind to run the shop.

"Won't Elizabeth be livid?" Lila snickered behind her napkin.

Jules Colburn was congenial and approachable, but her sister, Elizabeth, had a saturnine manner that was haltingly abrupt and often downright offensive.

"Now that's not polite," Mason said, pointing out his wife's double standard.

"Well, I doubt that Jules will be threatened by a little competition. She may even see it as an opportunity to collaborate on future projects, but Elizabeth is a different story," Anya agreed.

"I saw Sidra talking to her neighbor, Elijah, this morning outside of his bookstore. Wouldn't that be nice for him—if they were to hit it off, I mean?" Lila speculated.

Anya raised an eyebrow. "I always got the impression that he and his cat were confirmed bachelors."

"Speaking of cats, how are the plans for Cats 'n' Cocktails going?" Mason asked.

"We're still waiting on permits, but Nick Larkin is confident they'll be approved. Meanwhile, Tate's working on the plans. He has some unique ideas."

At the conclusion of breakfast—Lila signaled to Holly to bring the check. "Our treat," she told Anya. "No arguments."

People were starting to pour into Landale's, right on schedule. Three new arrivals caught Anya's attention, two of whom she knew all too well.

Anya thanked the Stevenses as they departed, and stayed behind to greet the three men who had spotted her as well. Ethan pointed to Anya's booth when Noni met them at the door. He and Nigel were in the company of the stranger she had seen them talking to when she was leaving the ranch the night before. The three tactically circumvented the waiting crowd and made their way over to join her.

"Anya, thanks for saving us a table this morning," Ethan said, grinning slyly while sliding into the booth across from her.

"No waiting in booth four," Anya replied, returning the smile.

Nigel slid in beside her, looking like death warmed over from too much celebrating.

The stranger sat next to Ethan, oblivious to the stir he'd created among his fellow diners. Every head in the room had swiveled in his direction, taking notice of his appearance and in whose company he had arrived.

The newcomer was average in height and build, with wavy brown hair and hazel eyes. Overall, he was rather scraggly and unkempt. He had a scruffy beard, the result of more than three days' growth, and his clothes had the rumpled look of someone who'd been sleeping in their car.

"Anya, this is Daniel Freeman. Daniel, this is our friend, Anya McClean. She owns a locally sanctioned pub, two doors down from here, known as—you guessed it—McClean's," Ethan said, making the introductions. "Daniel is a collector from Lafayette. He came to buy a set of white leather buckets for his '69 Mustang from us. We made him such a great deal he's decided to stick around and do a little fishing with us before he heads back."

"Lafayette, Louisiana?" Anya asked.

"Very good, Miss. Nice weatha ya havin here. Already hot and humid as hell where I'm from," Daniel replied—employing the time-honored custom of mentioning the weather.

Anya couldn't quite agree. A little hot and humid sounded like an improvement over brisk and windy.

"Great party last night," Anya said to Ethan.

"Yeah, until the storm came up. I assume you made it home OK? I looked around for you, but you had already gone," Ethan replied.

"First crack of thunder, and I was on the road," Anya said. "Wasn't soon enough, though. I had to drive through the thick of it, hail and all. Took me about forty minutes. At least the roads didn't wash out."

Ethan rolled his eyes. "You didn't drive your little car, I hope."

"No," Anya replied. She was tempted to tell him that Possum had warned her to take the truck but thought better of it.

"We dropped in on Martine a few minutes ago. I wanted to thank her for the clock. She hasn't changed a bit. It was good to see her. Ching seemed really happy to see me. I wasn't sure he'd remember me."

"Smart cat," Anya replied. "So, are you missing the city yet?"

"City? No," he said—laughing and shaking his head. "There's nothing about the city that I'll be missing.

I had to quit coming home here for visits because it made me so homesick. There were a few times that I wasn't sure if I was gonna make it, you know? No, I'm very happy to be back. By the way, Jimmy Shaw filled me in on your plans for Cats 'n' Cocktails. I'm really excited for you. Sounds like you have a big renovation planned. Who's doing the work?"

"Tate Blackledge," she replied after a moment's hesitation.

Anya noticed Ethan shift uncomfortably in his seat. "Tate, of course. The guy does good work."

Anya drained her cup of coffee and nudged Nigel to let her out of the booth, just as Holly came to take the three men's orders.

"What? Running off so soon?" Ethan protested.

"I'm afraid so. I received some exciting news this morning that I'm eager to confirm," she replied.

"Oh, really? And what might that be?" Ethan asked.

"Oh, I probably shouldn't say. I wouldn't want it to be construed as gossip," Anya said with a wink.

"Then you're not from around here," Nigel mumbled, collapsing into the booth again.

"Well, you won't hear it from me, but Candy Corbin is headed this way, and I'm gonna bet she will be only too happy to fill you in."

"Pay for your breakfast, Miss McClean?" Ethan offered.

"Too late, the Stevenses beat you to it," Anya said. "Mr. Freeman, it was nice to meet you. I hope you enjoy your visit. I'm sure the Notahs will show you a good time—though Nigel here may need a day to recover first."

Anya was still standing beside their table when Nigel ordered coffee—no food.

"Hey, eat something. I'm not getting in a boat with you until you look a little less green," Ethan warned. "I don't suppose you'd want to come fishing with us?" he ventured, redirecting his focus toward her.

She and Ethan had gone fishing a few times together, but Anya hadn't been so much a fan of fishing as she was of spending time with him.

Anya wrinkled her nose. "I don't think so," she said with a shrug. "Maybe next time."

"How about a card game then?" Ethan persisted. "Want me to set something up?"

They had spent many nights playing cards with Nigel and Cecilia in the past. They'd shared a lot of good times with them. Ethan was getting warmer, but it still wasn't quite what Anya had in mind. She decided to accept the invitation anyway. Perhaps it was at least a place to start.

"Sounds good! Let's do that," she agreed.

Nigel was groaning and holding his head, digging the heels of his hands into his eye sockets. Anya patted his shoulder, pityingly, waved goodbye to Ethan and Daniel, and made her way toward the exit.

She passed by Candy Corbin on her way out. Candy was the owner of a candy store named Candy's Canes where no candy canes were sold.

"Anya! Are you leaving?"

"Yes, I … "

"Have you heard about the new art gallery?" Candy asked, interrupting Anya in mid-sentence.

"As a matter of fact, I have, but do you see the Notahs over there? I don't think they've heard the news," Anya replied, pointing Candy in their direction.

Anya waved to Ethan to catch his attention. He noticeably frowned in return. He wasn't a big fan of Candy. He always said she talked so much it made him dizzy.

Anya was smiling to herself, as she walked up Main Street, amused by the predicament she'd left Ethan in.

SIX

Anya's interest had been piqued by the prospect of a new art gallery in Four Oaks. She felt compelled to see this much-rumored addition to Main Street for herself. She decided to take her time, though, as she made her way up Main Street, navigating the cobblestones and taking in the familiar sights.

The gaslight lamp posts were already flying the flags of the season, miniature blue and white banners that announced: "Spring is Here!" The sidewalk tables were all uniformly shaded by turquoise blue umbrellas. Enormous flower pots were interspersed among them, each one overflowing with a riotous mix of colorful blooms. Such were the hallmarks of spring in Four Oaks.

In summer, the lamp posts would be trimmed out in sailing flags to welcome the boaters who arrived in droves to enjoy the area's lakes and rivers. The turquoise umbrellas would be retired, and the coconut grass umbrellas raised in the summer months would make their debut.

The fall theme was predictably Halloween, and the flags flown from the lamp posts wished everybody a happy one. The flower pots were replanted with mums and joined by bales of straw, scarecrows, and piles of pumpkins. Red, gold, and green umbrellas twirled above the sidewalk tables during the autumn months.

Winter ushered in the Winter Festival, which was mainly for the locals. Frequent heavy snowfall and glacial temperatures kept all but the skiers away. There were Christmas trees in every window, except the deli where the owners celebrated Hanukkah. Sparkling holiday lights were strung about the street, accompanied by festive pine garlands and banners that read: Happy Holidays. Snowshoeing races and snowman building contests were also traditional highlights of an otherwise desolate time of year. Anya thought the best part of the winter season was the sweet smell of hickory kept burning in the fire barrels on both sides of the street.

As she drew nearer to her destination, she saw that Elijah Whip, the owner of Bell Book & Candle, was polishing the doorknobs on the door of his shop. It was his compulsion to do so many times throughout the day. He was a fastidious man, if not a little neurotic. He was also a bachelor, fortyish, and exceedingly shy. For many years, the women of Four Oaks had been relentless in their matchmaking endeavors where Elijah was concerned, but their efforts had yet to produce a lasting union.

His enormous white cat, named Ichabod, not Pyewacket as logic might have dictated, was watching her from the display window. He was perched atop a tall stack of coffee table books.

"Good morning, Anya," Elijah greeted her cheerfully.

"Good morning, Elijah, Ichabod," Anya replied.

The prodigious cat eyed her with feline indifference.

"Gonna be a busy summer. Farmer's Almanac predicts a fair amount of rain this year. Rain's good for business—the bookstore business anyway," Elijah remarked.

Anya nodded, acknowledging the well-founded reasoning behind the bookseller's conclusion. "Have you met your new neighbor?"

"Oh, yes! Sidra York! She's very nice. She came in yesterday to introduce herself to Ichabod and me. Bought more than a hundred dollars' worth of art books. Ichabod likes her very much," he replied.

From his effusive response, it seemed to Anya that Elijah liked her very much as well. But what need would an experienced art dealer have for mass-market coffee table books geared toward the average consumer?

"It's going to be a beautiful gallery. Tate and Rob Blackledge did an outstanding job," Elijah said, using the same cloth he'd been using on the doorknobs to polish the lenses of his glasses.

Anya was surprised to hear that Tate had been involved in the project. He hadn't mentioned the gallery or Sidra York at the party the night before."

"It's not open yet, and I'm afraid she's gone for the day, but I recommend you take a peek through the window—if you don't think it's too intrusive. It's really going to be something! She mentioned wanting to buy me out, you know? Said I should take the bull by the horns and fulfill my dream of moving the shop up to Patawomek Street near Lake Increase, but I told her no. Ichabod's not ready to go. Not just yet." Elijah slid the cloth back into his pocket and reapplied his glasses. He smoothed his head of thinning blond hair and squinted in the direction of the gallery. The recollection of Sidra's suggestion that he should relocate appeared to have caused him a moment's anxiety.

"I suggested she contact you to make arrangements for her grand opening. I hope you don't mind," Elijah went on to say. "I told her you knew all of the best people to work with if she needed any help with the catering. I think she liked the idea. She's planning a fancy reception, I guess." His smile returned then, and he drummed his fingers playfully on the window, to gain the attention of his cat. "Even Ichabod has been invited to attend," he added.

Anya was suddenly at a loss for words. She had never seen the man smile so much.

"Well, thank you for the referral, Elijah. I'm looking forward to meeting her, and I believe I will take that peek. Have a good day," Anya said and, with a parting smile, continued on her mission.

"OK, but don't smudge the glass!" Elijah warned.

The windows were sparkling clean across the front of what had once been an old furniture store. Anya ventured a quick look over her shoulder before peering inside. It was dark, but she was astonished by what she could observe. Soaring coffered ceilings, dark wood plank floors, and three enormous crystal chandeliers set the scene. Not one, but two, ornate iron spiral staircases rose three stories above the showroom floor from opposite sides of the interior. New recessed lighting had also been installed, strategically placed to reflect downward on numerous framed and unframed oils, watercolors, and acrylics—mostly abstract in design. Across the main floor, sofas and chairs had been arranged to create several intimate groupings that might be utilized for private consultations. Anya wondered if the concept was entirely Sidra York's. It looked very much like Jules Colburn's taste. Perhaps the designing sisters had already made contact.

On her way into McClean's, Anya saw that there was now a silver BMW with Louisiana plates parked in front of Mystic Treasures. The sound of voices raised in anger drew her eyes upward where she saw that the windows were open. Were they arguing? A wave of apprehension engulfed her.

"Martine's sister is here?" she asked Desda, who was presently expelling nervous energy by scrubbing down the bar. It was easy to deduce from the look on her face and all of this strenuous activity that Desda had heard the commotion too.

Desda nodded grimly. "Martine mentioned she was coming this morning when I opened up the pub. I didn't know she had a sister. I think they're arguing up there. I heard shouting."

"Did you meet her?" Anya asked.

Desda shook her head no. Deciding to give the counter a break, she turned to the nearest cooler and gave it equal time—scouring away at the stainless steel. Anya thought it was a good time to change the subject—lighten the mood with the latest town gossip.

"Did you know we're getting a new art gallery?"

"Yes—The York Gallery! I haven't met the owner yet. I hear she's a bit of a snob. I suppose it comes with the territory. Artists of all types tend to carry the diva gene."

Anya made a face at her for articulating such a false stereotype.

A few minutes of protracted silence passed while Anya procrastinated over going upstairs to meet Tame Decoudreau.

"Aren't you going up?" Desda finally asked.

Anya sighed, "I guess I have to, don't I?"

"What's she doing here?"

"I'm not sure," Anya lied, thinking it best to keep the details between herself and Martine for the time being. "I get the feeling Martine doesn't trust her, though. She's never even mentioned her until she got a letter from her saying that she was coming for a visit." Anya sighed, steeling herself for whatever might lie ahead and started up the stairs.

She took the catwalk over to Martine's, hoping she wasn't about to interrupt some kind of family feud. That would be awkward. As she passed the stairwell that led to the emporium, she saw the outline of Ching seated perfectly erect on the newel post below. Entering the kitchen, she thought she detected the peppery sweet aroma of cardamom and clover. Another one of Martine's skills was blending her own scented oils, some of which she sold in her shop. It was in the living room that she found the two women, seated opposite one another on the two white chesterfield sofas that flanked the fireplace.

"Martine?" Anya inquired within—announcing herself with a degree of hesitation before poking her head into the room.

"Ah! Good!" Martine said as both women rose to face her. "Anya, I wan you to meet my sista, Tame."

Anya was astounded by the woman who turned to meet her gaze. Like Martine, she was very petite and possessed the same exotic facial features, most notably an alien glow in her amber-colored eyes, but that's where the similarities ceased. Martine, with her beautiful long braids, flowing gowns, and wrists full of musical bracelets, stood in high contrast to her sister, who embodied the style of today's urban chic. Tame's makeup was expertly applied, her nails were perfectly manicured, and the soft brown layers of her shoulder-length hair were tipped in platinum. She wore a white strapless dress with an asymmetrical hemline and silver-toned sandals on her feet.

"So, you are Kate's daughter. It's a pleasure to meet you," Tame said, extending her hand toward Anya. Anya couldn't help but notice that she also didn't speak with a Cajun accent or an accent of any kind.

"Nice to meet you," Anya replied, shaking her hand. Right out of the gate, there was something about her that made Anya uncomfortable, a strange vibe, something dark. Maybe it was only what Martine had shared with her that was creating this sinking feeling inside. Anya released her hand and instinctively stepped back.

"Technically, we have already made one another's acquaintance, but you were very small and wouldn't remember," Tame said, resuming her position on the couch.

Anya remained standing, intent on keeping the introductions short.

"I was sorry to learn of your mother's passing. You look like her," she added. It wasn't true but was more the kind of thing people said when they didn't know what to say.

"Thank you. Will you be staying with Martine while you're in town?" Anya asked.

Tame laughed. "Oh, no! I think not. I'm staying at the hotel. I'll only be in town a few days, but my sister is a busy woman. I don't want to be underfoot," she replied.

At that instant, Ching, who had left his newel post, decided to make one of his heart-stopping entrances. He raced across the room to a carpeted climbing pole in the corner. All jaws and claws, he scaled it to the ceiling in a leap and a bound. Without hesitation, he flew from the top of the pole to the fireplace mantel, where he paused to hiss venomously at Tame.

"Ching!" Martine scolded, reaching out to contain him, but Ching was airborne again—exceeding her grasp. He landed with a thud and galloped out of the room.

Tame laughed nervously but was clearly shaken by Ching's aggressive rebuke. "I don't think Ching is so happy to see me."

"Don pay any attention to heem, crazy cat," Martine huffed.

The distinct absence of regional dialect in Tame's manner of speaking continued to arouse Anya's curiosity. What had prompted this gentrification? Had she taken pains to dump the accent out of some business-related necessity, or had she left it behind in Paris where she and Martine had attended a private university?

Anya's thoughts were interrupted by the hollow-sounding footfall of gun boots coming up the back stairs. An authoritative male voice called out to Martine, and they all turned to see Sheriff Kieffer Wakefield enter the room.

At six-foot-three, in full uniform and wide-brimmed Stetson, the sheriff had a fiercely commanding presence. He was somewhere in his mid-fifties, with dark hair, turning silver, but physically, he was in fighting trim. His deep-set analytical eyes held the power to discern your motives, assess your true nature, and see right through to the depths of your soul. He was a strikingly handsome man—never married but hotly pursued—who seemed on the surface to prefer the company of his dog. Those who were closest to the sheriff and Martine, however, knew that their public friendship was privately much more. Anya realized that Martine must have taken her advice and told him about Tame's troubles.

"Ladies," he addressed them in a professional tone while removing his hat. "I think Desda's looking for you," he said, glancing at Anya. *Translation: Please leave, so I can get to the bottom of this.*

"Thank you, Sheriff. I will go directly to see to that," Anya replied—grateful for an excuse to cut her visit short. "Tame, very nice to meet you. I hope your visit is a pleasant one. See you later, Martine."

That's when she noticed that Ching had returned to launch a sneak attack. He was army crawling toward Tame on his belly, wholly undetected by his target. Anya intercepted him without skipping a beat and carted him off across the catwalk to her own apartment.

"Take a break from chaos. I recommend a nap," she told the cat as she deposited him on her couch.

About an hour had passed when Anya happened to glance up from the bar in time to see the sheriff pulling off in his Blazer. Moments later, loud voices could be heard coming from next door. She and Desda exchanged worried looks at the sound of angry footsteps, pounding down Martine's stairs. From where they stood, they saw the door to the emporium swing open violently, and Tame exited the building. She marched to her car, made an abrupt U-turn, and sped off toward the hotel.

"What's this all about?" Desda asked once more. Her usually cheerful blue eyes held a look of concern.

Anya shrugged. "I'm not altogether sure," she

replied—still not ready to fill Desda in. In truth, she didn't have too many details herself.

"I've got a four o'clock appointment with Lisa Larkin," Anya said, deftly changing the subject. "I'm thinking of having The Pirate's Cove cater our next CF Stray Rescue function. We haven't set a date yet, but I saw Jimmy at the Notahs' last night, and we're going to set up something soon. I want to give Lisa a heads-up, so she can start on the preliminaries."

McClean's had its own kitchen, but the stray rescue events were overwhelmingly attended by locals. Inviting a new restaurant to cater each affair was an opportunity to change things up. It was also good publicity for the restaurants and an opportunity for community service.

"Mmmm ... crab cakes, fish tacos. I've been waiting for you to work them into the rotation. Tell Lisa I said hello," Desda replied.

"Oh, and Ching was bothering Martine's sister, so I shut him up in my place. Now that she's gone, will you run up at some point and reopen the catwalk for him—in case he wants to go home?"

"Sure thing," Desda affirmed.

On her way out, Anya had to step over Don Pedro, who was batting around a smooth white tile near the stairs. It was imprinted with a symbol similar to the mathematical sign for greater than/less than. It was one of Martine's rune stones. Anya left him to his fun.

It was a long walk to The Pirate's Cove, which was located near the far end of the strip. Anya waved to Freya Hale, who was watering the flowers outside of Pie in the Sky.

"Nice day!" Freya remarked, shielding her eyes to peer at the sun.

Alessandro Bennedetto was sweeping the sidewalk outside of Bennedetto's Surf and Turf. Cecilia was lounging nearby at one of the umbrella tables, engrossed in her phone, probably texting Nigel.

Elijah Whip was cleaning the glass on the front door of his shop. Ichabod was watching from the other side.

Anya had just passed The Colburn Design Studio when a thunderous BOOM knocked her straight to the ground! Instantly, everything bowed and swayed, contracting in the wake of a powerful drag flow. This was closely followed by violent quaking as the energy reversed and expanded outward. The air shimmered—rippling with sonic, wave-like reverberations. Anya looked up in time to see a second detonation rock The Four Oaks Hotel. Doors and glass windows, three stories high, blew out, projecting deadly, jagged shards high into the air. Glass, bricks, and rebar rained down upon the street and sidewalks. Anya covered her head.

The desk manager, Lance, staggered out and collapsed in the street, followed by one of the maids, the hotel chef, and a waiter.

The haunting images of the tower card flashed through Anya's mind. Clouds of dust and debris hung suspended in mid-air as the whole world ground to a halt.

SEVEN

The hotel had, in part, collapsed. The charred remnants, smoldering bricks, and twisted rebar had transformed it into a kind of ghastly, post-apocalyptic vision. Clouds of dust and thick black smoke belched out into the street as it heaved its dying breath.

The twin blasts had been powerful enough to shatter many of the other storefront windows on Main Street. Directly opposite the hotel, at Two By Two, one of the giraffes now lay dismally on its side. A deafening silence permeated the atmosphere as debris rained down, and everything came to a stop. Then … chaos …

People began amassing in the street. There were many frantic shouts to call for the sheriff and 911.

Anya staggered to her feet just as Desda and Martine came rushing to her side. That's when it first occurred to Anya that Tame had returned to the hotel—only moments before. She had most likely been inside at the time of the blast.

Jules and Elizabeth came running out of the design studio, to stand in stunned silence beside them all.

Theories were already circulating rapidly, uttered in hushed tones by voices in the crowd.

"How could this happen?"

"Had a boiler blown, or perhaps a vat of grease had exploded in the hotel's kitchen?"

"Had it been an accident or sabotage?"

The sheriff's Blazer skidded onto the scene, accompanied by his orders to clear the street. The distant shriek of sirens approaching from the direction of the Chenoah Falls Bridge pierced the air. The townspeople withdrew to the sidewalks.

Anya put an arm around Martine's drooping shoulders while the incredible scene continued to unfold. Things like this didn't happen in Four Oaks.

When the first responders started arriving, everyone was ordered back inside. The western half of Main Street was jammed with police cars, fire engines, ambulances, and news crews, forcing everyone to retreat to the east end of town. McClean's was the logical place to gather, and it was standing room only within minutes.

By the time the first news report aired on local station KCFV, Sheriff Wakefield had already regretfully informed Martine that her sister had been one of the casualties resulting from the explosion. A hush fell upon the crowd at McClean's while they listened to the official report:

> *"Two people lost their lives late this afternoon in an explosion at The Four Oaks Hotel. Their names are being withheld pending notification of family. The hotel was completely destroyed by two separate detonations. Initial investigations point to the possibility that backpacks, containing homemade pipe bombs, may have been left in the hotel lobby, concealed by a grouping of potted palms. The hotel's owners have been notified but were not immediately available for comment. Police do not have anyone in custody, and there are no persons of interest, nor possible motive known at this time."*

Though the victims' names had not been released to the media, everyone in town knew that a traveling salesman named Ronald Gillespie and Tame Decoudreau were the two who had perished that day. The Four Oaks grapevine went into high gear with people speculating about potential motives and suspects. There was some conjecture as to whether or not Tame had been the intended victim, but for the most part, suspicions centered on poor Ronald Gillespie. Why was he in Four Oaks? What was his destination? What was the nature of his business?

Martine and the sheriff had chosen a dark corner booth in the room, where they were presently conversing in private.

Desda was holding down the far end of the bar. Her husband, Paul, was there too, comforting Zia.

Anya took the middle ground, with Tate occupying a barstool near her. She suddenly realized that, in all of the turmoil, no one had remembered to feed the cats. She motioned to Craig, who once charged with the task, promptly dashed upstairs to see to their dinner. Anya watched as Zia bounded down the length of the bar and leaped up the stairs on Craig's heels. If Martine's cats really did possess a sixth sense, Zia was obviously tuned into hers.

"Anya," a voice called to her from behind. She knew it was Ethan even before she turned to see him there. He was wearing a rain jacket, shiny and wet. His long black hair was dripping as well, tied back by a few of its own sleek strands. Was it raining? She'd been too busy or too numb to notice. Wholly drawn in by him, as she always was, she failed to notice Nigel beside him until he voiced his regrets and inquired about Martine's whereabouts.

"She's over there," Anya replied, motioning to where the two were huddled, "talking to the sheriff." Anya opened two beers and passed them over to Ethan and Nigel.

"I didn't know she had a sister. Where is she from? Why was she here?" Ethan asked.

"New Orleans, same as Martine. Tate's the only one who remembers her mentioning that she had a sister."

Tate and Ethan exchanged a look.

"You have business in town today?" Ethan asked.

Tate nodded. "Rob and I had some finish work to do on The York Gallery."

"Martine never mentioned her to me until she received a letter from her saying that she was coming for a visit," Anya continued. "They hadn't spoken in years. Don't repeat any of this, please, but she was in some kind of trouble. She came to ask Martine for help. It didn't go well. Desda and I heard them fighting."

"What kind of trouble?" Nigel asked.

"Blackmail, death threats. Martine brought the sheriff into it. It sounded pretty serious," Anya whispered.

"You don't think this trouble she was in is connected to what happened here today, do you?" Ethan asked.

Anya shrugged. "Why don't you ask Old Sam? The sheriff seems to share everything with him. If they're withholding any details from the public—he would know," she suggested.

Ethan and Nigel's father, Sam, otherwise known as Old Sam or Pops, often served as deputy and was the sheriff's closest confidante.

"Hey, Anya," Craig said, returning from his mission. "I found this on the steps. I think one of the cats must've been playing with it. I figured it might belong to Martine." He handed her the rectangular rune tile she'd seen Don Pedro playing with earlier. She thanked Craig and slipped it into her pocket for the time being.

"Jimmy called earlier," Ethan said. "He saw the news reports. He wanted me to convey his sympathies to you and to Martine. He said to tell you not to worry about calling him this week to schedule that fundraiser. He suggested waiting a few weeks until things settle down."

"Oh, no," Anya said, shaking her head. "I don't want to put it off that long. It will be a positive distraction from all of this. I think we're going to need something upbeat to help everyone shift focus and get back to normal around here."

Ethan glanced around the room. "You might be right about that."

"So, where's your buddy from Lafayette? I thought he was going to stick around for a while," Anya asked.

Nigel shook his head. "You know… it's the damnedest thing. You won't believe this, but he was on his way to check-in at The Four Oaks Hotel right before it blew up. Poor guy was pretty shaken up. We had a tough time convincing him not to hightail it home."

"He's staying over at the Ambassador Hotel in Chenoah Falls. We're going fishing in the morning," Ethan added.

Anya noticed that the sheriff was rising from the booth now. He placed a comforting hand on Martine's shoulder, said a few more words, to which she nodded, then he put his hat on his head and strode determinedly through the crowd to the door. Martine went directly upstairs after he'd gone.

They were predictably busy at McClean's all night. Anya had chanced to see Tate on his way out and had waved goodbye, but she'd somehow missed that moment when Ethan and Nigel had made their exit.

By closing time, the area around the hotel had been cordoned off, the streets were empty again, and the crowd at McClean's was thinning. Desda, Ananda, and Craig had closing operations under control, so Anya decided to look in on Martine.

She found her in the living room, surrounded by her support group. Hester, Possum, and Don Pedro were curled up on the sofa across from her—legs and tails entwined. Luther and Benny occupied a nearby chair, and Zia was asleep in her lap. Ching was conspicuously absent.

"I hope I'm not disturbing you," Anya said. "I was just on my way to bed, and I wanted to see if you needed anything first."

"No, Sha," Martine replied, staring into the fireplace at the last glowing embers of the dying flames. "I'll be leaving in da morning. I have to go to New Orleans to make arrangements for da burial. I'll have to close up Tame's house and also her antique shop. If dere was no will, an auction will be held, sometime after da probate court finishes wid it. I may be gone a week, but you will take care of da cats, yes?" she asked.

"Yes, of course. Don't worry about a thing. I'll take very good care of them while you're away," Anya assured her.

A sizzling sound emanated from the fireplace as the last flame flickered out.

"Does the sheriff have any leads?" Anya asked.

Martine shook her head, "No leads, but dere is one troubling new detail. He tol me dat he checked wid da police in New Orleans, and dey have *not* been in touch wid Tame and were *never* made aware of da attempts to blackmail her."

Anya frowned. "I thought she told you that she had reported it?"

Martine stared wordlessly into the darkening firebox.

What did this new information mean? Why hadn't Tame informed the authorities in New Orleans? Had she invented the blackmail story?

"Wake me if you need anything," Anya said as she turned to go.

After brushing her teeth and changing for bed, Anya discovered that Ching was already nesting in her covers. He'd evidently been digging around in the vault again, too, and had pilfered a playing card. The Ace of Diamonds was lying on her pillow. That's when she remembered the rune tile Craig had recovered.

She went to the hamper to retrieve it from the

pocket of her jeans. She knew she couldn't disturb Martine. Instead, she performed a computer search of their meanings, one that unleashed her deepest fears. A chill ran through her as she read aloud the interpretation for the rune tile: "Kenaz … torch."

"Mau!" came the clarion comment from Ching.

Don Pedro had been playing with this tile, minutes before the hotel had been decimated by pipe bombs. Next, Anya looked up the Ace of Diamonds. There were several interpretations listed, including unexpected wealth, monetary gains, or possibly an inheritance. An inheritance? Martine and Tame's parents had passed away long ago. Martine had remarked that Tame had probably already gone through her half. It didn't seem to fit.

Following this, Anya lay awake reviewing the Kabala's portent of the tower card, and its quite literal depiction of an explosion and two people who were falling to their deaths. Prior to that had been the messages Martine had received from the playing cards. There was the warning of the self-serving, dark-haired man, deceit, ill will, and the potential for accidents, not to mention the ominous four of clubs known as the Devil's Bedpost.

Anya tossed and turned for most of the night, trying to make sense of it all. The events of the last two days spiraled around and around in her head. One thing persistently plagued her mind. Maybe it was her small-town mindset, a predisposition toward suspicion when it came to strangers, but there had been several new arrivals in town on the day of an unprecedented tragedy. The last conscious awareness she had as she drifted off to sleep was not a thought, but a sound—the muffled thud of the sheriff's boots going up Martine's backsteps.

EIGHT

When Anya awoke, Ching was gone and so was Martine. Anya discovered the note she'd left for her when she shuffled to the kitchen for coffee. It was propped against the coffee pot.

Dear Anya,
I know you will take good care of the cats while I'm gone, and I thank you for that in advance. They are all behaving quite strangely—especially Ching. Last night he dug a hole in one of my kitchen chairs and tore out the fur lining of my slippers. I think they somehow sense what has happened. Do you think they were watching from the catwalk when the hotel blew up? The sheriff will bring me home from the airport when I get back.
Love,
Martine

Ching was notably absent when Anya went over to feed the cats and police their commodes, but she didn't have to look far to find him. He was sitting atop the newel post in the emporium, guarding the Cajun Queen's shop in her absence.

He had indeed done a number on one of the kitchen chairs. Anya couldn't help but think it was no great loss. The vintage 1960s dinette, with its orange leather bucket chairs, had always looked out of place in what were otherwise elegant surroundings.

She was about to leave when a book on the kitchen table caught her eye. The title of the book was: *Trappers and Traders—North American Legends.* A page had been bookmarked. Anya flipped to the page. To her amazement, she found herself looking at an archived photograph of an antique desk—one she immediately recognized. It was the same one that currently occupied a space in Martine's study at the lake house. The caption confirmed it. The desk had belonged to James Beckwith, a distant relative of Martine's. The lake house had also belonged to him when it was nothing more than a four-room cabin. It had undergone several additions since being handed down to Martine.

Anya had heard the stories about James Beckwith and his partner, Charles Firth, many times over the years. The two men had been instrumental in putting Four Oaks on the map. They had made their fortunes in the fur trade in the 1800s. They were what the locals referred to as "coureurs des bois", or runners of the woods. According to Martine, it was a term given to unlicensed independent traders, sort of like bootleggers.

James Beckwith had also opened the bank in town, which was now Martine's emporium. McClean's had been Beckwith's trading post. His primary residence had been above it, where Anya presently lived. Many of the original businesses in Four Oaks had been raised on loans from Beckwith's bank.

Paging through the book, she saw that the photo of the desk was one of several illustrations in a chapter detailing the lives of both men. She was stunned to see a picture of Martine's emporium and McClean's when they were the bank and the trading post. The sign above the trading post read simply: Beckwith's, and the bank was called The Bank at Four Oaks. The streets were unpaved, and the sidewalks were wood planks. There were hitching posts outside of all of the buildings. It was somewhat surreal to see. There was a photo of the lake house when it was just a cabin and another in which the two men were shown standing in front of the bank. A small Native American woman stood slightly behind Charles Firth. The caption identified her as Firth's wife and a member of a local Hidatsa tribe.

Martine had once told her that Firth's estate had been passed to James Beckwith, not his wife, after his death. Women couldn't own property in those days, and that would have been even truer in the case of Native American women.

Legend had it that, in an attempt to evade the tax collectors—Beckwith had stashed away millions of dollars, either in or around his cabin, inside the trading post, or in the bank on Main Street. He'd died without ever telling a soul where he'd hidden his assets. The chapter detailed this intriguing mystery, as well.

Skimming the chapter's text, Anya thought she detected an unfavorable opinion of the two men, on behalf of the author, and perhaps rightfully so. He seemed to imply that their dealings with the local tribes were less than honest and far from mutually beneficial.

Anya put the book back on the table. Where had the book come from? Had Tame brought it? What was so significant about the desk that it warranted a bookmark? These and other questions that were beginning to arise would have to wait until Martine's return.

Anya showered and dressed in a hurry before heading over to Landale's Log Cabin for breakfast. She didn't have much of an appetite, but she hoped to overhear some new details about the bombing—if in fact there were any.

She sat at the counter where the farmers in their feed caps and the Silver Sneakers Club women sat, drinking coffee and sharing the latest "news".

"Damn tourists! I was rollin down the road yesterday

on the tractor, pullin a trailer with my cultivator parked on top, when this character with outstate plates comes flyin up over the hill. He was half in my lane, and I had to swerve to avoid him! Tipped my trailer and lost my cultivator."

"Ought to be a law against it. Let 'em do some time in county."

"Lot of black raspberries and acorns around already. Hope it don't mean a hard winter's comin."

"Nah, more likely means a hard summer."

"I hate those damn berry thickets around my pastures. Almost lost one of my lambs when it got caught up in it. Took me twenty minutes to free it."

"Don't curse the berries around my wife. It's the wild saskatoons and thimbleberries she's after for her jams and jellies. Ever had thimbleberry syrup on hotcakes?"

Apparently, the farm co-op wasn't discussing the hotel bombing this morning, and the news coming from the Silver Sneakers brigade was no more enlightening.

"Fran had the baby last night at eleven thirty-eight. It's a boy. They're going to name him Jack."

"How do you like that visiting minister? I think his sermons are very uplifting. I heard he's been offered a job in Dubuque, though."

"My son-in-law finally got a promotion. Maybe now they can move out of that broken-down rental home they've been living in."

Larry Landale brought Anya some coffee and a doughnut, but he hadn't heard anything new either. The mission was a bust, and left her feeling edgy and distracted. Later it would occur to her that the strict avoidance of any "news" linked to Tame, Martine, or the bombing at the counter that morning might have been due to a conscious awareness of her presence there.

On her way back to McClean's, she was surprised to see Desda, motioning excitedly to her from the front door.

"Anya, where did you go? I was about to come looking for you. You'll never guess who's upstairs."

Anya frowned and shook her head.

"Sidra York! She's waiting in your office. She wants to talk to you about catering arrangements for the gallery opening," Desda replied.

Anya thought the meeting was a bit ill-timed. Grand openings weren't foremost on anyone's mind today. On the other hand, Sidra York was new in town and didn't know anyone involved in yesterday's catastrophe.

Anya glanced up at the office, located on the second story above the bar. Its bank of windows allowed her to keep an eye on McClean's while she worked. Through the windows she could see that Sidra York was there, seated, waiting patiently, but she was not alone. Hester and Don Pedro were there too.

"Oh, boy. I see trouble. Better get up there," Anya said, racing up the steps.

When she burst into the office, she was out of breath and greeted Sidra York with an unsteady hand.

"Miss York? I'm Anya McClean. Allow me to welcome you to Four Oaks," Anya said in a practiced, professional manner.

Sidra shook her hand without bothering to rise.

The gallery curator was a fairly young woman, late thirties or early forties, very slender, with shoulder-length blond hair and brown eyes. Anya was momentarily distracted by the heavy eyeliner she wore. She looked to be wearing false eyelashes as well.

"Thank you very much," Miss York replied, stiffly. "I know you must be busy, so I'll get right to the point. I'm here upon the recommendation of Mr. Whip, the proprietor of Bell Book & Candle. I want to host a reception at the gallery for the grand opening, and Mr. Whip suggested that you might be in a position to assist with the arrangements."

Wow, straight to it, Anya thought to herself. She had hoped to exchange a few pleasantries before getting down to business—things like: *Where are you from? What brought you to our little town? Have you started to feel at home yet? Elijah is a nice man, isn't he? How do you feel about cats? Where were you when the hotel blew up?*

She could see that wasn't going to be part of the program. "Yes, of course. We'd be happy to assist," Anya affirmed. "We can provide the beverage service, and there are several restaurants I can think of that would be in a position to cater the hors d'oeuvres. Do you have a preference, or would you like me to select one? And what is the date of the opening?"

"By all means, select one. I'd prefer to leave all of the details to you, if you don't mind. Just let me know when you need the check. We're planning to open Saturday. I realize it's extremely short notice, especially in light of ... recent events. If it can't be done, I completely understand. Simply advise me as to the earliest possible date, and we will adjust accordingly."

The choice of the word "we" had not escaped Anya's notice, nor had the untimely appearance of Ching, who was slinking around the side of Sidra's chair. His lips were drawn back in an odd sort of sneer.

"Opportunist," Anya muttered.

"Excuse me, what's that?" Sidra asked.

"Oh, nothing. Just making a mental note," Anya covered. She pretended to rifle through some papers on her desk while she pondered the possibilities behind Sidra's allusion to a partner, the other half of "we", so to speak. She'd been under the impression that Sidra was the sole owner of the gallery. Did she have an associate, or was she in the habit of referring to herself in the third person?

Anya was forced to drop this line of thinking as, unbeknownst to Miss Sidra York, there were now three cats in the room, intent on sizing her up. Hester moved in for a quick sniff of her ankles.

"Oh!" Sidra jumped, feeling the wet nose on her leg.

Hester jumped too and hopped sideways out of the room.

Ching, still wearing a look of contempt, leaped onto the arm of Sidra's chair, sniffed her hair, and rolled back his lips—fully exposing his fangs. To Anya's horror, he slowly raised his paw as if he meant to take a swipe at her.

"Ching!" Anya admonished him. She stamped her foot, startling Sidra *and* Ching. He sprang from the room as Sidra leaped from her chair. Anya shooed Don Pedro out too and quickly closed the door.

"I'm so sorry about that," Anya said to Sidra, who was understandably shaken and anxious to leave.

"That's all right. Simply let me know if the date will work, and if so, perhaps you could supply me with a menu when you call for the check," Sidra requested.

Anya had already decided to use The Pirate's Cove for the York Gallery opening. Though she'd initially contacted the owner, Lisa Larkin, about Jimmy's function, she and Jimmy had yet to set a date. She was sure that Lisa would relish the opportunity to cater Sidra's gala, and there were a number of other restaurateurs she could approach for Jimmy's benefit. Anya thought Sarah Katz over at Drexsler's Deli might like to collaborate on that.

"I'll confirm the date with you tomorrow after I've had time to connect with my sources. Can I assume that there was no damage done to the gallery? You were very close to the point of … impact."

Sidra smiled coolly. "No, none. We were very fortunate. I believe the woman next door to you lost her sister? We haven't officially met, but I was terribly sorry to learn of her loss." The words were intended to convey sympathy, but the tone was lost in translation. Anya found her to be very flat and unreadable in both word and action.

"Yes, it was a tragedy. Things like that don't happen around here. It was quite a shock," Anya acknowledged.

"Well, with any luck, the police will apprehend a suspect soon. It was lovely to meet you, Anya, and thank you so much for taking over the catering details for the opening. Whew!" Sidra said, drawing a finger across her brow for effect. "I'm glad to check this off of my to-do list." She shook Anya's hand once more and turned to go. Anya hid a grin. The back of Miss Prim and Proper's skirt was covered in fine white cat hairs.

NINE

Anya needed to place a few orders with her beer distributers, so she put her call to Lisa Larkin over at The Pirate's Cove on hands-free.

As it so happened, it was Lisa who answered. "Ahoy! Pirate's Cove, this is Lisa. How may I help you?"

Anya was surprised when Ching instantly materialized, apparently recognizing the voice he associated with his favorite seafood restaurant.

"Hi, Lisa. It's Anya. How are you?"

"Anya, how are you? How's Martine?" she asked.

Anya's initial response was inaudible, muffled by Ching's muzzle snuffling into the speaker phone.

"What's that? Sounds like you have a cold," Lisa said.

Anya gave the cat a shove. "No, that was Ching. I have you on speaker because I'm also on the computer right now."

Lisa laughed. "Oh … I see. Hello, Ching," she replied sweetly.

Hearing his name, Ching stiffened his tail and gave himself a vigorous shake.

"Going back to your question, Lisa, I'm fine. Martine's pretty shook up. She's on her way to New Orleans to make final arrangements for Tame and to settle the estate."

"Ugh … horrible. Were she and her sister very close? I never knew she had a sister."

"Neither did I. They hadn't spoken in years."

"Wow, did she give Martine any advance notice of her impending arrival, or did she show up out of the blue?" Lisa gently probed. Anya knew the whole town was still trying to establish whether there was any connection between Tame and the bombing of the hotel. Who could blame them?

"No, Martine knew she was coming. It was sudden, but expected," she replied. Out of respect for Martine, Anya chose not to elaborate. Thankfully, Lisa seemed satisfied that there was nothing more to know.

"So, shall we reschedule our meeting for CF Stray Rescue?"

"Actually, there's been a change," Anya said.

"Oh?"

"Yes, I still don't have a date for Jimmy's thing, but the owner of the new art gallery, Sidra York, has asked me to set something up for her grand opening. Have you met her yet? I thought you might want to cater the food, and we'll run beverage service," Anya explained.

"No, I haven't met her yet, but she's made a definite impression on those who have had the pleasure."

Anya smiled at Lisa's less than subtle overtone.

"Still—I would love to do her grand opening with you! Thanks for thinking of us. I have so many ideas running through my mind already. I assume it will be an elegant affair?" Lisa asked.

"Definitely elegant," Anya affirmed, "and definitely short notice. She wants to open Saturday. What do you think? Can you swing it?"

"Whoa, that is short notice, but you know what? We can handle it. Can you come over here tomorrow, around eleven or so? I'll draw up the menu today, and tomorrow we'll drink some wine, have a little tasting of the hors d'oeuvres I've selected, and catch up!"

"Can't wait!" Anya said, jotting down the time on a nearby scrap of paper.

Her next call was to Jimmy Shaw to set a date to host his event, but he was "out on rounds".

Out on rounds could mean many things, but for the most part, Jimmy started and ended his days the same way. He and his volunteers would divide up and scour city streets and surrounding communities for abandoned dogs and stray packs. They would offer them food, most notably hotdogs, and water for days, weeks, sometimes months on end. It was painstaking work, designed to earn their trust. Then and only then could he and his volunteers get close enough to slip leads around their necks and transport them to the shelter and salvation. At this moment, Jimmy was probably crawling around under an abandoned house, searching a vacant building, or combing through some other treacherous locale.

There was another side to Jimmy's world, a darker, more insidious side that involved locating, raiding, and rescuing dogs from illegal dogfighting rings. These raids always took place under cover of darkness and always in the worst part of blighted urban or depressed rural areas.

Typically, as many as five to ten dogs were recovered on these missions. This required the use of several vehicles and willing volunteers. Anya's Land Rover had substantial cargo capacity, so she had been enlisted a few times to help. Back at the shelter, the dogs received the medical care they needed and underwent months, or even years in some cases, of rehabilitation ahead of making the adoption list.

The jailbreaks, as Jimmy liked to call them, were perilous, to say the least. Dogfighting was big business—and if there was a lot of money on the line, the ring runners could be dangerously confrontational.

In nearly every case, the criminals were apprehended, and Jimmy made it a point to testify at their trials. The maximum sentence for animal abuse and operating an illegal gambling ring carried fines upwards of fifty thousand dollars and up to five years in prison. His dedication to the cause, the severity of the penalties, and the widespread news coverage of his efforts had all but eliminated these abuses in the region—though not entirely.

Anya had just finished placing her orders when Ethan suddenly appeared in the doorway. He was not alone.

"Excuse me, Miss. We don't have an appointment, but might we have a minute of your time?" he asked, affecting a humorously formal tone.

"It's highly irregular, but if you must," she replied, playing along.

Ethan and one of the other new faces in Four Oaks, Daniel Freeman, stepped into her office, wearing hip waders and clutching handfuls of fish.

"Caught a lot of fish today up near the beaver's dam," Ethan announced with a gratified grin.

"As well I see. I'm glad I didn't wear *my* big rubber pants today. That would have been downright embarrassing," Anya said, rolling her eyes at the sight of them. "Did you even consider sending a text, maybe a picture or two, spare me this assault on my senses?" she added, wrinkling her nose.

Ethan laughed. "Yeah, for a second I didn't think Desda was gonna let us in."

The odiferous combination of lake water and fresh fish was as powerful as it was pungent.

"Whew! Wow! You two have quite an odious presence!" Anya exclaimed, rising from her chair. "Let's go out of here, please. Come on," she said, leading them out of her office and into her kitchen.

"I thought you might want a couple of these beauties for Martine's cats, but...," Ethan said, pretending to be offended.

"No, no. We thank you very much for thinking of us, and your timing couldn't be better," Anya replied, gesturing toward the faces of Possum and Hester, who, having followed their noses, had now located a source of interest. Anya had once read that a cat's sense of smell is fourteen times stronger than a human's.

She invited them to store the rest of their catch in the refrigerator for the duration of their visit. Daniel sat at the table while Ethan cleaned and filleted a couple of bass. Anya got out a pan, butter, an egg, and some cornmeal to prepare them.

"Sure is a lot of cats. I'm a dog man myself," Daniel remarked as the rest of the troop drifted in.

Anya wondered if he knew just how unappreciated his comment was in this household.

Seven sets of twitching whiskers remained at a distance, glancing warily at the dog man while their lunch was prepared. Anya doubted that they would concede to eating in the same room with the unknown visitor, so she served them in the dining room.

"So, how are you enjoying your visit, Daniel?" she asked.

"I've enjoyed it greatly, yep, sure have. Da Notahs have been very hospitable indeed, but I'll be headin on back to old Lafayette tonight. Gotta get home to my wife and to work on Friday," Daniel said.

"Well, I hope you're not letting the sheriff run you off prematurely," Ethan said.

Daniel shook his head. "No, no. Not at all."

Ethan turned to Anya and said, "Sheriff Wakefield came around this morning under the guise of grabbing a coffee with Pops, but he sure had a lot of questions for Dan." To Daniel, he added, "I hope he didn't make you feel too uncomfortable."

Daniel waved his hand and shook his head again.

"The sheriff? Really?" Anya found this most curious.

"Yeah, it was kind of weird. He tried to be casual about it, but it felt a lot like an interrogation," Ethan explained.

"Da sheriff was jus doin his job is all. Folks is waitin on him to arrest somebody for dat hotel bombin. Me bein a stranger in town, it's only natural he'd want to question me some. Small towns are like dat when it comes to outsiders. It be da same down Lafayette, so I don take no offense," Daniel assured him.

Anya's mind was racing. Had the sheriff really questioned him because he was a stranger in town, or was there something more to it? Tame and Daniel had arrived within a day of one another. Both were from Louisiana, albeit different cities, that is, if Daniel was really from Lafayette. Did the sheriff suspect that he was somehow involved? Had he really come to buy car parts from the Notahs, or had he been the one blackmailing Tame? Had he tracked her here? When she failed to come up with the money, had he killed her by blowing up the hotel? Admittedly, there was some question as to whether Tame had been the victim of blackmail in the first place. She had lied about reporting it to the New Orleans Police. Perhaps it was all a coincidence, and she was letting her imagination run wild.

"Have you heard from Martine?" Ethan asked.

"No, and she left so early that I didn't get to say goodbye. She did leave me a note. She's worried about Ching. He's been acting strange," Anya replied.

Ethan laughed. "Stranger than usual?"

Anya laughed too. "Yes, stranger than usual—believe it or not."

She noticed that Daniel was staring at the tabletop, toying with a stray paperclip he'd discovered. He had mentioned a wife, but he wasn't wearing a wedding ring. Still, that wasn't proof positive that he was being deceptive.

"Maybe you heard about my friend, Martine?" she asked, abruptly shifting her focus to Daniel. "Her sister, Tame Decoudreau, was killed in the hotel bombing."

"Yes, da sheriff mentioned dat," Daniel replied, without looking up.

Dissatisfied with the brevity of his answer, Anya decided to double down. "Tame was from Louisiana too—New Orleans. Ever get down there? It's not too far from you."

Daniel flipped the paperclip over and over in his fingers. "Nope. Ain' never been dere. I'm afraid dat ain' my kinda town," he replied.

It was an odd claim and one that was hard to believe. For Anya, it was a red flag.

She noticed Ethan was frowning at her, ill at ease with this line of questioning. She decided to turn down the pressure by steering the rest of the conversation toward him instead of Daniel.

"Do you remember me telling you that I heard Martine and Tame arguing just before the explosion?" she asked Ethan.

Ethan nodded, still seemingly perplexed.

"Turns out, Tame had alleged that she was being blackmailed. She wanted Martine to give her some money. When she refused, Tame was furious. She stormed out and minutes later … well, you know the rest."

Anya cautiously glanced at Daniel. He had looked up at the mention of blackmail, but he was staring blankly at her now too. In Anya's opinion, his response lacked the discomposure of someone who had been directly involved. In the absence of any observable stress reaction, she decided that he was either a gifted actor or simply not responsible.

"Are you saying that you think Tame was the target in the bombing?" Ethan asked.

Daniel went back to fidgeting with the paperclip.

"Not for certain, but it's a possibility."

"I hope Sheriff Wakefield gets to the bottom of all of this soon. The whole thing has got everybody on edge," Ethan said, before deftly changing the subject. "So, have you met the owner of the art gallery yet?"

"Yeah, she came by today, actually. We're the open bar for her grand opening Saturday. The Pirate's Cove will be doing the catering. You should come," Anya replied.

"I might do that. It will depend on how my meeting goes tomorrow. I may have to work on Saturday," Ethan said. He stood up then to retrieve their catch of fish from the refrigerator.

"Oh? Are you meeting with Doc Lafferty?" she asked.

Ethan smirked. "Why don't you ask Candy Corbin?" he suggested, referencing the little joke she'd played on him at breakfast the previous morning.

Anya made a face.

"Well, we better take off. Gonna have a little farewell cookout for Daniel with Pops and Nigel," Ethan said with a smile.

"You're really not going to tell me?" Anya asked.

In response, Ethan winked and left without further comment.

"It was very nice to meet you, Daniel. Have a safe trip home," Anya said, feigning a smile.

"Thank you, Miss. Pleasure to meet you too," Daniel said, shaking her hand and hurrying after Ethan, who could already be heard descending the stairs.

Anya went into the dining room to collect the plates from the cats' lunch. She frowned, seeing that the fish was untouched. Not a bite had been taken. She had never known them to turn down freshly prepared fish of any kind. Cornmeal, she thought. That must be it. They'd probably never been offered anything breaded and fried. Martine was prone to poaching or simmering things in broths. Cats could be irritatingly finicky if you dared to divert from the usual presentation—no matter how slight. When it came to cats, variety was not the spice of life. It was a transgression. Anya scraped the fish from the plates into the trash can and took the bag directly to the dumpster out back.

It was after 4 a.m. when Anya, asleep on the couch, was jolted awake by several loud thuds, hissing, growling, and a chilling howl she knew had come from Ching even before her eyes had registered his position in the room.

The cat was in full attack mode, crouching in the

hallway, facing the catwalk. His tail looked like a spin duster, and the fur along his spine was bristling.

Don Pedro landed on the table behind her and began clicking his teeth.

Fur flew as Zia, Possum, Hester, and Benny went scrabbling from the room. Luther was nowhere in sight.

Anya was frozen, debating on whether to investigate or not. Suddenly she heard an indecipherable noise coming from the direction of Martine's apartment. Ching shrieked, and Anya rushed to lock the door on her side of the catwalk. She immediately called the sheriff and ran downstairs to McClean's to wait.

TEN

McClean's had been closed for hours, and the place was shrouded in darkness. Anya hurriedly flipped on all of the lights and watched from the window for the sheriff to arrive. She didn't have long to wait. Within minutes, he was pulling to the curb, closely followed by the Chenoah Falls Crime Scene Unit. The shimmer of broken glass covering the sidewalk in front of Martine's reflected brightly in their headlights. Anya rushed out to meet Sheriff Wakefield, standing by as he inspected the emporium's shattered front door.

"What the … hell is going on around here?" he cursed, shifting his hat toward the back of his head. He paused to survey the street in both directions as if he half expected to see some sign of the perpetrator lurking nearby. He motioned to her impatiently, indicating that she should wait in his Blazer while he and the detectives went in to have a look around.

The sheriff was exactly right, Anya thought, climbing into the front seat of his truck. What was happening in their quiet little town? First, the hotel and now this? Until yesterday, the greatest offense visited upon Four Oaks had been the occasional shoplifting or dine and dash.

She turned her head as the lights abruptly came on inside Martine's shop. She could see the sheriff and the detectives moving throughout the space, making a careful inspection of the scene. Anya was on tenterhooks, waiting for the sheriff to return with his assessment. She tried to calm herself by using a deep breathing exercise Martine had taught her, practiced by Tibetan monks, but the results were less than satisfactory. Eventually, he re-emerged and slid into the driver's seat beside her.

"Nobody's inside or upstairs. Door's still locked to your side. Want me to take a look anyway?" he asked.

"No, I'm sure it's all right," Anya said.

The sheriff sighed wearily. "Doesn't look like anything's missing. Only Martine will know for sure. I don't know what they were after, but they went through the place pretty good. Once the detectives have finished dusting for prints and collecting evidence—should there be any—I'll get Tate out here to replace the door. It would be nice if you and Desda could straighten up a bit in there for Martine before she gets back."

Anya noticed that the sun was beginning to rise. The sky was streaked with red, pink, and gold.

"If you hear from Martine, don't mention any of

this. Let's keep it to ourselves for now. I'll tell her when I pick her up at the airport," he added.

"Have you heard from her?" Anya asked. "Do you know when she's coming home?"

The sheriff shook his head no as he fished through the crumpled butts of stale cigars that filled his ashtray. Finding one that looked like it had a little life left in it, he produced a lighter from his pocket and set to stoking it. "Cats over at your place?" he asked, rolling down the window to release the dense cloud of smoke that filled the cab.

Anya stifled a cough and nodded silently.

"Maybe you should go on up to Martine's house at the lake. Take the cats with you. Stay there for a while. I'm going to suggest she move up there herself until we sort this out along with the hotel bombing and whatever it was that was going on with her sister."

"OK," Anya murmured in agreement. She climbed out of the cruiser, feeling numb from the neck down as she watched him drive away. She gazed up at the sky again, randomly recalling the old adage: Red sky at night, sailor's delight. Red sky at morning, sailor's warning.

Anya crept toward the nearest window, glass grinding under her feet. There were a few items strewn about the store, but the cash register was closed. She noticed that the door leading to the vault was open.

What was this about? Somehow, it didn't have the look and feel of a burglary.

On her way into McClean's, she noticed the lamp post out front had been struck. Had the intruder fled in a vehicle? Had he crashed into it in his haste to flee the scene?

Several of the cats were watching her through the door of McClean's. They took flight, charging back up the stairs to safety when she entered. Anya locked the door behind her, something she wouldn't normally do now that the sun was up. The sheriff's suggestion that she and the cats move up to the lake was a good one. They would all feel safe there. It would be a peaceful respite from all of this recent turmoil.

She went upstairs to open cans of boned chicken for her furry companions, mixing in a little warm broth. Then she went to pack a couple of bags for the trip up to the lake.

Anya took the quickest shower she'd ever taken in her life, feeling vulnerable and a little fearful. After dressing and grabbing toast and coffee, she sat stiffly on the couch to wait for nine o'clock when Desda would come in to open.

At seven o'clock, she heard someone pounding on the door downstairs. It was Tate. He was there to replace Martine's door.

"Anya, are you OK?" he asked when she let him

in. He grabbed her and hugged her a little frantically. "What the heck is going on around here?"

Anya smiled, remembering the sheriff had said the same thing just a couple of hours ago.

"I haven't been inside yet, but I had a peek. Was anything taken? Cash register is still there," he noted.

"Sheriff Wakefield couldn't tell if anything had been taken. He mentioned that it looked like someone was looking for something specific."

"Well, it's a mystery to me what anyone could be looking for in there. Are the cats at your place?"

"Yeah. They heard the break-in. Someone was upstairs in Martine's apartment. Ching started howling, and the rest of them scattered. I think he scared the prowler away. I locked the door to my side and called the sheriff."

Tate frowned and rubbed his eyes the way he always did when he was feeling anxious. "I don't like the sound of that," he said, shaking his head. "You shouldn't be here alone with everything that's been going on. Especially not after this."

"The sheriff suggested I take the cats and move up to the lake. I'm going to do that later today. I'll stay up there until Martine gets back. I'm actually looking forward to it. It'll be safe. I can relax and take it easy."

"Good idea," Tate agreed. "Why don't you let me help you out with that? What time do you want to go?"

Anya thought about canceling her meeting with Lisa and leaving straight away, but Sidra's opening was in four days. Lisa would need time to place orders and prepare. All things considered, she resolved to keep the appointment. She and the cats would still be settled in their new surroundings by dinnertime.

"I have to meet with Lisa today about catering The York Gallery opening, but I'll be ready to go after that, say about three o'clock? Tell you what, if you can help me out—I'll make you dinner," Anya offered.

Tate grinned. "That's a deal. I'll look forward to that. See you later," he replied, giving her another reassuring hug on his way out. His genuine concern had helped to steady her and lift her spirits.

By the time nine o'clock rolled around, and Desda finally showed up, the new door had been installed, and the sidewalk had been swept clean. There was nothing to indicate to Desda that anything out of the ordinary had happened. She listened in utter disbelief while Anya relayed the disturbing details.

"I don't believe it! We've never had a break-in around here! What could they have been looking for? Could they have known that Martine was out of town?" Desda speculated.

Anya shrugged. "I don't know. The sheriff seemed mystified. He suggested I take the cats and move up to the lake house. I'm thinking about getting an alarm system."

Desda scrunched her eyes shut. It was a distasteful thought that perhaps they weren't as immune to crime in Four Oaks as they'd previously believed.

Anya suddenly felt a lack of energy. The toast she'd eaten hours ago wasn't going to get her through the day, so she decided to head over to Bagels Baked Goods & Beyond.

She was surprised to bump into Sidra York, who was on her way out of the Cruz sisters' shop. Anya noticed that she was carrying a small bag and two large coffees.

"Oh! Good morning, Anya. How are the arrangements for our grand unveiling going? Have you managed to procure a caterer for us?" Sidra asked.

Anya was quick to note the strange dual person reference Sidra had again employed, not to mention the two coffees she was holding.

"As a matter of fact, I have," Anya replied. "The Pirate's Cove will be handling the affair. We'll do it on Saturday, just as you'd hoped. I'm meeting with Lisa Larkin this afternoon to discuss the details and sample the menu items she's selected. Do we have a start time for Saturday?"

"Yes, one o'clock," Sidra confirmed. "Thank you so much! Be sure to let me know when you'll need the check. I couldn't be more thrilled," she gushed as she tottered away on three-inch heels.

Cobblestones, heels, and two boiling cups of hot

joe—a recipe for a disaster, Anya thought. She watched in amusement, curious to see whether she would stop at Bell Book & Candle. One of the coffees might be for her new friend, Elijah. When she continued on past the bookstore, Anya went inside the bakery.

"Ladies," Anya greeted Kathleen and Donna Cruz with a smile.

The Cruz sisters were a pair of good-natured, clubby types in their early forties. They were both single, though it was rumored that Donna had been married once. There had been a lot of speculation and salacious gossip surrounding Donna's past, but no one really knew if any of the stories were true. Both women were small in stature but otherwise appeared to sample their wares a bit too much.

"Hear about the break-in at Martine's yet?" Anya asked, knowing full well they probably had.

"Oh, my gosh, yes," Kathleen gasped.

Word travels fast, Anya thought.

"Is it true that they made off with her cash register and smashed everything in the store?" Donna asked. Her eyes grew wide in horror at the images her own words had conjured in her mind.

Anya shook her head and chuckled at how twisted the "news" always became as it was passed along.

"No, nothing was broken, and the register was undisturbed. Doesn't look like the motive was robbery, but we won't know for sure if anything was taken until Martine returns."

"Not robbery? Then what?" Donna questioned.

Anya sighed. "Exactly. We don't know."

"Well, thank God you're all right, and Martine was away. Are the cats OK?" Kathleen asked.

"Yes, they're all fine. We're moving up to the lake later on today."

"Good idea. What a harrowing experience," Kathleen said, fanning herself with a napkin.

"So, I see you've both met the new artist in residence, Sidra York. I ran into her on my way in. First impressions?" Anya asked.

"She comes in every morning," Kathleen replied, rolling her eyes.

"Two large coffees and two French toast bagels," Donna added with similar effect.

"You two don't seem to like her much. How come?"

"She's a phony and a scam artist, that's how come," Kathleen blurted out. "She's been cozying up to Elijah Whip ever since she came to town. She's been trying to talk him into moving his shop up to Patawomek Street, near the lake. She doesn't care about his dreams and future plans. She's gunning for his square footage is all. She wants to expand her own space, and she's not even open yet."

"Yeah, she's really got her hooks in him—pegged

him for an easy mark right away. She's gonna charm him right out of his little bookstore," Donna asserted.

"Well, I did hear something about that, but you know I have heard him mention on several occasions that he might move his shop up to the lake someday," Anya pointed out.

"Idle chit-chat. He doesn't really want to leave all of us. We're family here on Main Street. She's trying to take advantage of him," Donna insisted.

"Yeah, and the break-in at Martine's might be just the ammunition she needs to convince him to pull up stakes," Kathleen huffed.

"You said she always orders two coffees and two bagels. I thought she was the sole proprietor of the gallery. Does she have a partner over there I don't know about?" Anya probed.

Donna and Kathleen raised their eyebrows in tandem and exchanged a wary look.

"We assumed she was buying breakfast for herself and Elijah," Donna said.

"I thought so too when I saw her leaving with two coffees, but I watched her walk right on by the bookstore," Anya replied.

A heavy silence prevailed while the sisters filled her order. Anya felt a little guilty and a tad mischievous for having stirred the pot. She had clearly heightened the sisters' suspicions with regard to Sidra York, but perhaps with good reason. Sidra's recent references to "we" and "us" along with her routine order of breakfast for two were all indications, in Anya's opinion, that Sidra had a secret partner of some sort. She made a mental note to ask Tate about this. Maybe he would have more information.

The walk to The Pirate's Cove that afternoon was an eerie one. Mr. Safety Glass repair trucks were in evidence at several locations, replacing store windows that hadn't survived the blast. Crime scene tape still surrounded the crumbled remains of the hotel, and a giant crane was hard at work, righting the toppled giraffe in front of Two By Two.

The Pirate's Cove was another tourist favorite on Main Street, especially among families with small children. The exterior was that of a clipper ship's hull—jutting out over the sidewalk. Authentically constructed from wood, it was weathered, worn, and gray. Inside, the place was more Captain Hook than Captain Bly. Being a family restaurant, historical references to pillaging, plank-walking, and rum swilling had been rejected in favor of more socially acceptable images, such as dolphins, swordfish, and mermaids. The wooden booths were carved cut-aways of lifeboats. Faux taxidermy whales and marlins spy-hopped around the room. The whole place was draped in fisherman's nets where decorative starfish, shells, and seahorses made a pretense of having become ensnared. A sign above a large treasure chest near the front door was an invitation for children to take a souvenir on the way out. It was filled with interesting little trinkets and toys.

"Anya!" Lisa called and waved to her. They exchanged heartfelt hugs and greetings, after which she ushered Anya over to a nearby booth presided over by a chainsaw carving of a bluefin tuna.

Lisa Larkin had a bright and breezy quality about her. She was so energetic and youthful that you would never guess she was the mother of four children. In her striped tee and canvas boaters, her long blond hair spilling out from under a bucket hat, she looked the part of a ship's first mate.

"I had the chef prepare all of the appetizers I'm proposing for Sidra's opening so we can have a tasting," Lisa announced—her blue eyes sparkling. "I know McClean's is providing the beverage service, but I thought we'd try out a few wine selections as well, see what pairs best with the food. I'm sure you carry some of the same bottles we do," she said with a grin.

Anya was most agreeable and settled back to enjoy the delightful atmosphere, while Lisa disappeared into the kitchen in search of the chef.

Lulled by a soundtrack that featured the intonations of surging surf and gentle waves—punctuated by the occasional foghorn—Anya felt the tension of the past few days start to slip away.

A waitress in a mermaid server's uniform shuffled over with a carafe of wine and two glasses. Anya smiled sympathetically as she shuffled away again. She always felt a little sorry for The Pirate's Cove waitstaff. The chef was the only employee not required to dress on theme. When Lisa returned, she had the chef in tow, wheeling a cart full of hors d'oeuvres. He presented the offering with a flourish of pride: baked stuffed shrimp with clams, crab cakes with a drizzle of ginger-citrus vinaigrette, mini-grilled Cajun shrimp kabobs, bacon-wrapped buffalo shrimp, smoked salmon squares, and toasted brioche rounds with crème fraîche and caviar.

Anya and Lisa passed the next couple of hours nibbling, sipping, and catching up on "news".

"Well, thank God for Ching, or you might have come face-to-face with that prowler," Lisa acknowledged with a shiver.

Anya nodded. "My hero. It was all I could do to force myself to take a shower after that. I was pretty spooked. I was never so glad to see Tate in my whole life as when he showed up to replace the door. Before that, I'd been perched on the edge of the couch, watching the clock, waiting for Desda to arrive. She doesn't like the idea of an alarm system, but I'm leaning toward having one installed. What do you think?"

"I have to admit, I hate to see our dear little town succumb to a few bad apples, but Nick has raised the idea as well," Lisa replied. "Does Martine know about the break-in?"

"No, Sheriff Wakefield wants to wait to tell her when he picks her up at the airport. She has a lot on her mind right now, so I guess that's best," Anya said.

"You said she and her sister weren't very close?"

"No, but it was a shocking loss, considering the circumstances. Tame had a house and an antique shop in New Orleans—but no will—so Martine will have to deal with all of that too. It will have to go through probate court, of course."

"It's all so eerie. You know they've eliminated any connection to that poor salesman. Seems he really was just a squirrel guard rep on an overnight stay, heading home from his last sales trip. There's nothing questionable about his activities, known contacts, or his life in general."

Last sales trip in the truest sense of the word, Anya thought, grimly.

Lisa raised an eyebrow and nodded, as if reading her mind.

Anya frowned then. "Squirrel guard?"

Lisa chuckled. "I don't know all of the specifics, but have you ever seen squirrels run across power lines? Squirrel guard keeps them from getting electrocuted."

"Huh, ... interesting," Anya replied. Realizing that this new information strongly indicated that Tame was the intended victim in the bombing, Anya decided to change the subject to the woman who had prompted this little get-together in the first place.

"Have you had the opportunity to meet Sidra York since we last spoke?"

"Still no, but I hear she's trying to swindle Elijah out of his shop. I sure hope he doesn't give in to her overtures. Sounds like a con artist to me, but I'm happy to make the commission," Lisa said with a wink.

Anya laughed and raised a glass in solidarity. Lisa's response, while amusing, was also proof of the lightning speeds with which news traveled in this town.

Halfway through the second bottle of Albarino Rioja, Anya happened to glance at her phone. "Oh-oh, three o'clock. I've got to run. I'm taking the cats and moving up to the lake today. Tate volunteered to help me. I'm supposed to be meeting him now at McClean's. I don't want to keep him waiting," Anya said, hopping out of the booth. "Thank you for everything. I really needed this. Give my best to the chef, Nick, and the kids!"

"You bet! Glad you enjoyed it," Lisa said. "Here's a copy of the menu for Sidra and our bill for the catering service, of course. See you on Saturday."

They exchanged a quick hug, and Anya was off and running again.

ELEVEN

Anya jogged the distance between The Pirate's Cove and McClean's. She could see that Tate's truck was already parked at the curb. When she blew in the door, flushed and breathless, she saw that Desda was keeping him company at the bar.

"Sorry, I'm late. Lisa and I were so busy catching up that I guess I lost track of the time. Forgive me?" she asked, pressing a small cellophane packet into Tate's palm.

He smiled and removed the tiny green plastic paratrooper, complete with a paper parachute, from its wrapper. He held it up for inspection.

"A little treasure from the treasure chest at The Pirate's Cove? There was a time when this would have meant we were going steady," he said. He was laughing, but she noticed that he slipped the tiny trooper into his pocket.

Anya beamed a smile at him. "Yeah, I knew you'd like that." To Desda, she said, "Would you ask Ananda or Craig to run this over to Sidra York? It's a menu and the bill for catering."

Desda confirmed that she would.

Tate accompanied Anya upstairs to help her round up the cats. Their unsuspecting quarries were presently lounging about in her living room. All she had to do before they started loading carriers was to close a few doors to their well-known escape routes.

Anya had little to no trouble coaxing Zia, Hester, and Possum into the first two coaches. They were the most cooperative of the bunch.

Tate managed to catch Don Pedro off guard and sweep him in beside Possum. This sly bit of gamesmanship prompted loud howling from the offended party—a warning to the others to evade at all costs.

Benny began to race around and around the room—flying over tables and chairs. He sailed to the top of the fireplace mantel and then down to the floor again—darting his eyes madly about the room. He honed in on the couch, planning to seek refuge underneath, but unfortunately for Benny—Anya was able to grab him before his disappearing act was complete. She dragged the struggling ball of orange fur gently out into the open and into an empty carrier. Though this maneuver impinged greatly on his dignity—Benny gave up the fight.

Luther tried to make his getaway by scrambling through the glass catwalk toward Martine's until he saw that Tate was already there to thwart his escape. He made a quick check of the access doors to the emporium and to McClean's, but finding both were closed, he was forced to surrender. Dejectedly, he allowed Tate to corral him with Benny. They hauled the first three cat coaches out to Tate's truck before returning for Ching.

Ching, who had been watching the mad fray from the top of the bookcase, struck a sanguine pose and waited for his cue. Anya knew that he preferred to travel alone and to enter his transport of his own accord. Once she'd opened the door to his carrier, Ching slid gracefully to the floor and strutted over to his waiting chariot. He entered without objection, and Tate whisked him out to her truck.

Anya raided McClean's walk-in freezer and the refrigerator, packing up everything she would need to make dinner. She also grabbed a few bottles of Verite 2013 La Joie from the cellar—the perfect red for the steaks she was planning to grill.

While Tate loaded these additional items into the rear cargo space of her truck, Anya went upstairs to retrieve her luggage. As an afterthought, she dashed over to Martine's to grab *Trappers and Traders—North American Legends.* Instinctively she knew that there was something significant about the desk, something linked to the real reason behind Tame's visit. There was a reason the photo had been bookmarked. This move up to the lake was her chance to make a closer inspection of the real thing.

Climbing behind the wheel, Anya felt happy to put the embattled little town in her rearview mirror for a while. She was looking forward to a relaxing week at the lake.

"Mau!" came the shrill vote of confidence from Ching. It was as if the cat could read her thoughts.

She and Ching made the rest of the trip in silence—racing along beneath the treeline. The sun's rays darted in and out of the canopy above them, glinting off the leaves and flashing off the chrome inside the truck's cab. With every mile she logged, Anya felt a greater peace. When they finally pulled up in front of Martine's, the transformation completed itself. Anya was swept away by the serene beauty that surrounded her. She'd been there many times over the years, of course, but it never failed to impress.

The house itself was a sprawling lakeside rambler, encircled by two-hundred-foot tall aspens, pines, and Douglas firs. There were three fireplaces, as evidenced by the three stone chimneys that rose above the cedar shake roof. A wall of windows across the back of the house overlooked the lake. The home had undergone several additions over the years to increase its square footage, but the original cabin with its chinked logs and wavy glass windows had been preserved as the centerpiece. Tate had been the contractor each time Martine had wanted to expand.

The cats, having gotten their first whiff of lake water, knew they were home and commenced to yikking and yowling, demanding their release.

Their human counterparts were happy to comply, quickly gaining entrance to the house and dashing inside. Joyfully liberated, the cats raced to the windows at the rear of the house, eager to pinpoint every squirrel and bird on the lawn. She and Tate watched them for a minute or two, their collective heads down, rear quarters raised, tails knifing. It was an amusing scene.

Anya turned her attention next to the soaring ceilings, open to the rafters. A cross-connecting system of rough-hewn beams traversed above the main rooms, two stories overhead. Their grand and glorious heights were accessible to the cats from two ramps located in the corners of the living and dining rooms. This was the forerunner of the feature Tate was planning to create for Cats 'n' Cocktails.

"This place is truly a wonder," Anya said, contemplating the elegance and warmth that the lakeside retreat evoked. It was a testament to Tate's talent when it came to design and craftsmanship.

Tate smiled and nodded, accepting the compliment with a well-deserved degree of pride. His professional skills and subsequent success had not come easily. He and his brother, Rob, had been raised by their grandparents, following their parents' divorce. Both had gone to trade school, but most of what they knew they'd learned while working after school and on the weekends with their grandfather. He had also been a skilled craftsman by trade.

Tate helped Anya unload the rest of her supplies, several bags of groceries, and a couple pieces of luggage which she tossed into the guest room.

Upon her return, she noticed that Ching had slipped into Martine's study, where he was now seated on top of the desk. Something had obviously caught his attention, and Anya found herself intrigued.

She went into the cozy space—nestled into the section of the house that was the original log cabin. She sank into the chair behind the desk, watching with interest while Ching clawed at the center drawer, trying to get a paw inside.

Anya assisted his efforts by sliding it open for him. To her surprise, Ching climbed into it and lay down, settling himself on the pile of papers inside. Common sense led her to consider that the cat might merely be looking for a place to nap. However, her intuition told her that there was something more going on here than a cat's instinct to nest. Ching stared at her through eyes resembling huge black orbs in the dim light. Anya wished she could read the cat's mind.

Aware that Tate was watching with interest from the other room, Anya decided to postpone the investigation and prepare dinner instead.

Tate followed her into the kitchen, where he opened the wine, and she set about washing greens and tomatoes for the salad she was planning to make.

"Martine probably has some scotch around here if you'd rather have that," Anya said.

"No, the wine is fine. Want me to marinate the steaks?" he asked.

Anya realized that Tate had probably spent more time at Martine's than she had over the years. He certainly seemed to know his way around her kitchen.

She watched with interest while he rounded up a variety of ingredients: Worcestershire sauce, soy sauce, salt, pepper, garlic powder, hot sauce, and olive oil.

"Why are you looking at me like that?" he asked, glancing up with a grin on his face. "You probably use the packaged stuff, don't you?"

Anya laughed. "No, but I assumed you did."

"I can do more than swing a hammer, you know," he replied, raising his eyebrows. He mixed everything together in measured amounts and poured it over the steaks.

With their preparations complete, they made their way out on to the deck, taking the food and the wine with them.

"Lisa didn't mention anything about the permits today?" he asked, firing up the grill.

Anya slapped her palm to her forehead. How had she forgotten to ask Lisa about that? She guessed it was because, ever since she'd learned that Tate had done the work on The York Gallery, she'd been devising a line of questioning aimed at getting him to divulge any insider's secrets he might have about Sidra York.

"No, and I didn't think to ask. We were so absorbed in the planning for The York Gallery opening," she lied. "I heard that you and Rob did the work on the gallery. What do you think of Sidra York and her partner?" Anya asked, employing a little strategy in her quest for information.

"Partner? I never met any partner," Tate said, shaking his head, "and I don't really *think* about the clients, Anya—only the projects." He looked over at her and smiled.

It wasn't the response she was looking for. Maybe she was way off base. Evidently, Sidra hadn't left much of an impression on Tate in general.

"She's very friendly, don't you think?" Anya asked, hoping to provoke him into elaborating on his previous comment by making an absurd statement of her own.

Tate started laughing at this, refusing to take the bait. "Friendly, hmmm … you don't believe that for a minute. I don't know what you're up to, but I'm detecting a thinly veiled attempt to grill me for information. Shame on you. What has she done to arouse such suspicion, if I might ask?"

"I think it's kind of a mismatch, a woman like that settling in a place like Four Oaks. Did she happen to mention what drew her to the area?" Anya asked.

"No," he said simply.

"And to your knowledge, she doesn't have a partner of any kind, at least not that you've seen?"

Tate put the steaks on and refilled both of their glasses. "No. Now what is all this about?" he asked again.

"Well, first off, she has a running routine of picking up breakfast for two every morning at the Cruz sisters' bakery. Also, when I met with her to discuss plans for her grand opening, she said: *we're planning to open on Saturday,* and *we'll adjust accordingly if that's too soon.* Either she's in the habit of referring to herself in the third person, or she has a partner lurking in the background. Why hasn't anyone met this partner? It also might interest you to know that she's trying to get her hands on Elijah's shop. She's been encouraging him to move the bookstore up to Patawomek Street. The word on the street is that she's more interested in acquiring his square footage than his friendship," Anya explained. "Furthermore, in case you haven't noticed, some pretty strange things have been going on around here lately. It's not every day a hotel gets bombed, and we've never had a break-in on Main Street, until now."

Tate calmly turned the steaks, closed the lid, and took a seat across from her. For a moment, she wondered if he'd heard a word she'd said.

After another minute's consideration, he replied, "Well, I agree that some strange things are going on around here lately, and some of what you've said is admittedly curious. Still, I'm not sure what any of it has to do with the hotel bombing and a local burglary."

"And that's another thing," Anya interjected. "The sheriff doesn't think the break-in at Mystic Treasures was a burglary."

"Even so, aren't you conflating people and events that may or may not be related? Have you allowed for the possibility that it could all be coincidental? I don't know if Sidra's hiding dark intentions, but then again, it's not my habit to pry into people's activities or motivations, except for maybe yours," he replied.

Anya was baffled by his response. She suddenly got the feeling that Tate meant to change the subject.

"Seen much of Ethan since he's been back? Other than at the ranch the other night?" he asked.

"As a matter of fact, he dropped by McClean's with that buyer of Nigel's, Daniel Freeman," Anya replied—slightly jarred by Tate's abrupt segue. "They'd been fishing, and he gave me a few for the cats."

There was an intractable silence as Tate appeared to weigh his options, deciding whether or not he wanted to pursue this new line of inquiry.

"So, I guess that's starting up again, huh?" he asked.

"What? You guess what's starting up again?"

Tate studied her expression. His blue eyes were dark and serious. He took off his cap, swept his hair from his eyes, and folded his arms across his chest.

"Come on, Anya. You know exactly what I'm talking about. You and Ethan. Gonna get back together now that he's home?"

Anya was astonished that Tate would be the least bit interested in the state of her love life.

"I don't know. We haven't discussed it, if that's what you mean," she replied.

Tate laughed. "It's not really the kind of thing you discuss, is it? It's just something you do. What's to discuss?"

Anya frowned in confusion. This was evolving into a stranger conversation than the one she'd initially wanted to have.

"Somehow I get the feeling you don't think it's such a good idea. Care to explain? I thought you and Ethan were friends."

"We are, but I'm talking about you. A lot of time has passed since you two were together, Anya. We're not kids anymore. Things change. People change.

I don't think you should rush into anything. Take it slow. Think it over," he said.

Anya wasn't sure how to respond. Since when did Tate care who she got involved with romantically?

She was relieved when, over dinner, Tate decided to steer the conversation toward their plans for Cats 'n' Cocktails. He'd been working on a budget for the project, so she could apply for the construction loan as soon as the permits were approved.

They had barely finished eating when they heard a knock at the front door. It was Ethan. Anya waved him inside from the deck.

"Hey, are you all right?" he asked, stepping outside to join them. He leaned down to give her a hug, but his eyes were locked on Tate's. "I had a couple of early appointments in the city. I didn't hear about the break-in until I went by McClean's to see you. Desda told me you were up here."

"Yes, I'm all right. It was scary, but I'm OK now. You're too late for dinner, but can I offer you a glass of wine? I don't know if Martine has any beer up here. I can look. If you're hungry, I'm sure I can come up with something in the kitchen," Anya offered.

"No, I'm fine, really," Ethan replied.

She gestured to him to take the seat beside her. Ignoring his decline of wine, she retrieved a flute from the kitchen and poured him a full glass.

Ethan was still staring at Tate. Both men seemed circumspect with regard to the other's presence.

"You helped Anya cart her friends up here today?" Ethan asked.

Tate cleared his throat, shoved his plate aside, and leaned forward—resting his arms on the table. "Yeah, the sheriff called me to replace Martine's door. Glass everywhere. He'd suggested that Anya stay up here at the lake for a while, so I volunteered to help her make the trip."

Ethan met his response with a somber glare while Tate remained impervious.

"Well, I have some information for Anya about her permits that you'll probably want to hear too," Ethan said. "Pops ran into Larry Landale yesterday. He's on the town council, you know. He said to tell you that your permits are all approved."

"Oh, fantastic!" Anya replied, looking to Tate. She was startled to see that he'd risen from the table. Apparently, he intended to leave.

"Well, that's exciting," Tate said in a stilted tone that oddly lacked any genuine enthusiasm. "That's what we've been waiting to hear. I'll finish up the supply list. We can go over it together when it's done." He bent down to hug her goodbye. "Looks like you'll be seeing a whole lot more of me in the months to come," he added with a wry smile and a glance in Ethan's direction.

Ethan shifted in his chair and cupped a hand over his eyes.

Before Anya could get to her feet, Tate raised a hand, indicating that he could show himself out.

"Thanks for dinner. Let me know if there's anything else you need," he said.

"You're welcome," Anya replied, "and thanks again for helping me out today. You know I really appreciate it."

Anya watched him walk to the door where something outside caught his eye. "Is that Jubal Carson's dog, Mr. Bones, out there in your truck?" he called out to Ethan.

"Oh, damn," Ethan replied, sighing and rubbing his eyes. "Yeah, that's Bones. Doc Lafferty brought him in for his annual checkup today. I'm supposed to take him home. I completely forgot."

Everyone knew Jubal Carson and his dog, Mr. Bones, by virtue of the fact that they'd both been around so long. Jubal was approaching ninety years old and didn't drive anymore, so whenever it was time for the dog's checkup, Doc Lafferty picked him up. Ethan must have offered his chauffeuring services as well.

"Jubal's practically my neighbor. Want me to drop him off for you? Save you a trip?" Tate offered.

"Really?" Ethan sounded surprised. "That would be terrific. I'd be very grateful."

"Sure, no problem. Bones and me go way back. You guys have a good night," Tate said with a parting wave.

"Oh man, I can't believe I forgot about Mr. Bones," Ethan said once he'd gone. "I was so worried about you I guess it slipped my mind. The reason I came by McClean's today was to tell you that one of the appointments I had this morning was with Doc Lafferty. I told him I had a little money to invest, and he offered me a partnership! Naturally, I accepted. I was so excited that I went straight to the pub to tell you. That's when Desda told me about the break-in, and well, in all the excitement, I somehow lost sight of my passenger."

"Oh, Ethan, that's fantastic! I'm so happy for you! I know a partnership was what you were hoping for, and now it's happened. Congratulations," Anya exclaimed, leaning over to hug him.

"Thanks, Anya. I'm pretty excited. I'm sorry about the scare you had, and that I wasn't there to help you."

"No, don't be. You couldn't have known."

They decided to finish the wine on the deck. It was a beautiful, crystal clear evening with not so much as a single cloud to obscure the blanket of stars that were emerging.

Ethan reached over and picked up a flashlight that had been left sitting on the railing beside him.

"Do you realize that Pop's ranch is somewhere right through those trees? I can almost see this place from there in the winter—when most of the trees are bare.

How's your morse code?" he asked, grinning playfully while making the flashlight blink on and off. "When Nigel and I were kids, we had separate bedrooms with windows that faced the same tree. We saved up our allowance to buy a couple of flashlights. At night, when we were supposed to be sleeping, we would aim them out our windows at that tree and talk to each other for hours in morse code."

Anya smiled at the memory. She could picture the two of them doing that.

There was a pair of binoculars on the table that Martine kept handy for bird watching and such. Anya reached for them. In the residual light that lingered, they took turns scanning the lake for ducks, snakes, and turtles. That's when she noticed something peculiar, something at a distance from them.

"Hey, take a look down by the beaver's dam. Tell me what you see," Anya said, passing him the binoculars.

"Wild turkey. A whole rafter of them … and smoke … " Ethan's voice trailed off as he continued to study the scene. "Got some campers, maybe?" he murmured.

"Why are they camping out there? It's too early in the season for the campgrounds to be full," Anya pointed out.

"Yeah, not to mention it's illegal to start a fire down there. I'll let the sheriff know about it. It's not safe," Ethan replied.

"You were over that way fishing the other day. Did you see anyone else?"

Ethan shook his head. "Not a soul."

They polished off the wine just as the mosquitoes arrived, and the night was at an end.

Anya couldn't help but feel a little disappointed when he'd gone. Perhaps they weren't about to resume their relationship after all, she thought.

She hadn't seen hide nor hair of the cats since they'd disembarked from their transports. The offer of a late-night snack was the fastest way to perform a head-count, so she searched the pantry for something that would suffice. She would make a run to Hop's Market tomorrow when they opened to stock up on their favorites. Finding a couple of cans of white chunk chicken breast, Anya quickly arranged it on plates while all seven of her housemates chorused their appreciation.

With everyone well and accounted for, she decided to focus her attention again on the mystery of Martine's desk. When she reached the study, she was met by a scene of chaos. The room was in utter disarray. The papers that had been in the drawer were now strewn about the place. Of course, Ching was responsible, but why? Had he been looking for something? A cat toy? A forgotten treat from his last visit? Anya gathered the papers—some bearing the tiny teeth marks of the perpetrator along their edges—and deposited them on a corner of the desk. She sank into Martine's well-worn desk chair and felt around inside the empty space, left to right, back to front. Nothing. She shoved the chair back a ways and inspected the underside. Zero, zilch, nada. Anya had no idea what she was looking for, but instinct prompted her to persist in her efforts.

At that moment, Ching sauntered in on long slender legs and glided effortlessly to the desktop. He bypassed her efforts to contain him and instead made a beeline for the drawer. Once inside, he marched about the interior like a master sergeant in charge. Around and around he went, lifting each paw in turn in the most peculiar fashion. It drew to mind the expression: *Cat on a Hot Tin Roof.* When this failed to trigger a response from Anya, he started digging furiously in the bottom recesses. She knew the cat was frustrated that she wasn't getting his message, but sadly, Anya really didn't have a clue.

Afraid the cat might actually injure himself, Anya scooped him up and cradled him, attempting to calm him.

Ching would have none of it and began to struggle and protest fortissimo!

Anya clapped her hands over her ears and used her elbow to nudge the drawer closed. She was beginning to feel a little frustrated herself. There wasn't anything special about the desk, at least not that she could see. It was just a desk—solid oak, four legs, three or four drawers. What was she missing? She was still mulling the possibilities, when she was struck by a sudden impulse. Rummaging through the side compartments, she quickly obtained what she was looking for, Martine's pearl-handled letter opener. As if anticipating her next move, Ching circled again, a sign that he favored this newly conceived approach.

Anya's heart was pounding with anticipation. She opened the drawer and slid the letter opener in and around the edges and corners. The base shifted slightly and then tilted upward, allowing her to remove it altogether.

"A false bottom!" Anya exclaimed.

"Mau!" Ching declared triumphantly.

It was an intriguing discovery, though a hollow victory. The secret chamber was empty.

Ching, however, seemed curiously vindicated. He left the room with a flick of his tail and not so much as a backward glance.

TWELVE

On the morning of The York Gallery's grand opening, Anya awoke wrapped in the resplendent comforts of Martine's luxe guest room. Martine had called to confirm that she would be unable to return home until the following week, so Anya, as the cats' official steward, had magnanimously agreed to stay on. Truth be told, she reveled in the opportunity to extend her retreat in such sublime surroundings.

She crawled out of bed at 5 a.m., navigating around several cats, still in the throes of a deep sleep. She'd fiddled with the timer on the coffee maker the night before and was relieved to see that the brew was hot and ready when she stumbled into the kitchen. She decided to grab an empty cup and take the whole carafe out with her on to the deck.

The air coming in off the lake was fresh and invigorating. Its waters shimmered with the waning beams of moonlight that reflected off its gently rippling surface. Anya was captivated as she watched the darkness recede, little by little, in nearly imperceptible increments, replaced by the steady rise of the sun. The chirping refrains of crickets and the rustling retreats of raccoons slowly faded, overtaken by the joyful singing of the birds and the scolding chatter of squirrels.

She was grateful that her role today would be minimal, limited to overseeing the beverage service. The Larkins would be charged with the larger task of coordinating their regular restaurant service with that of catering the food for Sidra's gala. To top it all off, it was also the start of the Four Oaks Spring Festival, and that meant a steep influx of tourists.

By 7:30, Anya was showered and dressed in an aqua tunic dress and a pair of matching sandals with a four-inch wedge. She was digging in the couch cushions for one of her earrings that had mysteriously disappeared from an end table when something caught her eye.

It was an old black and white photograph, an original taken of the Beckwith cabin. It was hanging on the wall above an antique sideboard, but it was tilted at a wild angle. Ching was sitting to one side of it, meticulously washing the base of his tail.

Anya scowled and moved to right it. She didn't want to be confronted with the immediate task of sweeping up a pile of glass when she got home.

"You behave yourself while I'm gone today, mister, or next time I leave Don Pedro in charge," she said, gently stroking his head.

Four Oaks was in full festival mode when she pulled to the curb outside of McClean's. Though spring had officially sprung weeks ago, the scheduled celebration was always held later in the season when the temperatures had moderated, and the threat of a late snow had passed.

As early as it was, she seemed to be the last one on the scene. Every shop and restaurant was open, and the musicians were setting up on the bandstand at the far end of Main Street. Martine's Mystical Treasures was the only shop that was dark.

Anya met Craig at the door. He was on his way out with the first of several commercial-sized coolers of wine and beer destined for the gallery.

"Hey, how many of these are we bringing?" he paused to ask.

"I'd planned on three," Anya replied, "but make sure there are enough outlets. We might have to go with two and restock as the day goes on. Text Nick Larkin and ask him how many outlets they're going to need. That's going to be the determiner."

Craig gave a thumbs-up and rolled on up the street.

That's when she noticed that he'd already laid out the ramps and planks needed to get the coolers across the cobblestone street. Craig was always thinking ahead. That's why she imagined that, someday, he would probably be the one to inherit her place.

Desda and Ananda had apparently arrived ahead of her as well, and, having finished morning prep, were enjoying Bloody Marys at the bar. It had always been their custom to toast the start of each new tourist season with a pitcher of Bloody Marys, blue oceans, or brandy slushes, except for the Winter Festival, when Anya blended up a punch bowl of her famous ice-cream eggnog.

Desda had Anya's at the ready, handing it to her as she took the seat next to Ananda.

"Why did I think I was early?" Anya asked.

"You are early," Desda said—adding, "early for you, anyway!" She and Ananda snickered at Anya over their celery sticks.

"How are the cats? How is Ethan doing?" Desda asked.

Anya knew it was the latter she was most interested in. Everyone in town was always trying to affect their union. She hadn't spoken to Ethan since Tuesday when he'd come by to tell her about the offer from Doc Lafferty, and it was a subject that slightly irked her.

"Cats are content. Haven't seen Ethan since Tuesday," she replied curtly.

Desda took the hint.

After Bloody Marys, Anya and Desda joined Craig in completing the last of the deliveries to be made to the gallery. Desda's husband, Paul, was already there setting up the beverage station, which was comprised of two banquet tables placed end to end and draped in crisp white table linens. Behind them were two large coolers with glass fronts, one for beer and one for wine. Between the two coolers was a temporary shelving unit on which the new glassware they'd ordered made for a glittering display. They were ready to go well ahead of schedule.

Next came the Larkins, Chef Ripert, and their entourage of servers, dressed in black and white formal attire- no pirates or mermaids today. Had Lisa borrowed the waitstaff uniforms from Bennedetto's? Right behind the servers was the kitchen staff, transporting the hors d'oeuvres in a Main Street parade of dining carts. There were also several coolers, a dish and flatware cart, and at least one cooking cart.

At five minutes to one, Sidra York emerged from her office on the second floor balcony and prepared to make her descent. She was dressed in a classic black sheath dress and black stilettos with titanium heels. Her long blond hair was elegantly braided and pinned up with tiny pearl clips.

Anya watched with interest as the curator turned and exchanged a few words with someone presently occupying her office. The encounter was so brief, if Anya had blinked, she might have missed it altogether. Still, she was certain of what she'd witnessed. There had been a conversation, but with whom?

Sidra closed the door and glided down the nearest staircase, the well-rehearsed smile plastered smugly on her face. Having located Anya in the crowd, she floated directly over to her.

"Everything looks amazing, don't you think? I couldn't be more pleased with the results," Sidra effervesced.

"Absolutely," Anya agreed. "The opening is sure to be a success. Please let us know if there is anything else you need," Anya entreated.

Sidra grasped both of her hands and thanked her again before making her way over to Nick and Lisa Larkin to bestow in kind platitudes of gratitude.

Thirty minutes later, the gallery was teeming with patrons. Sidra was clearly in her element. Anya continued to observe her as she made the rounds, introducing herself, answering questions, and expertly steering potential customers toward works of art— presumably in accordance with their taste. The servers had been instructed to shadow her with trays of aperitifs and hors d'oeuvres, providing Sidra with a mode of introduction among the attendees. The woman knew how to work a room.

Anya was admiring Sidra's polished business acumen when she spotted Jules Colburn. She was leaning over the railing of the gallery's left-facing staircase, deeply engrossed in an oil painting. It had been hung at a height best viewed from a point that was at about mid-flight.

"Hi, Jules," Anya said, climbing up to stand beside the town's chief decorator. Their last meeting had been under less convivial circumstances.

"Oh, hi, Anya," she replied, continuing to study the portrait of a woman with a grossly elongated face, nose, and neck. The eyebrows and eyes were also glaringly exaggerated.

"Are you a fan of … Modigliani?" Anya asked, squinting to read the artist's signature.

"That's just it," Jules whispered discreetly. "I'm a collector, not an expert, mind you, but I think this Modigliani is a forgery."

"What makes you think so?" Anya asked, discreetly lowering her voice.

"The pigments used here don't look authentic, and do you see the crackle pattern? Modigliani was an Italian painter who lived in France in the seventeenth and eighteenth centuries. French canvases from that time period have spiderweb-like crackle patterns. Italian canvases have a pattern like untidy brickwork. This pattern is too perfectly aligned. Elizabeth is the expert, but she's somewhere over the North Atlantic at this hour, on her way to Sweden," Jules replied while checking the time on her phone. "If she were here, she could say for sure. Cossima Bennedetto wants to purchase it today, but I'm going to advise her not to."

Elizabeth was Jules's sister and partner at the

Colburn Design Studio. In addition to her undergraduate degree in interior design, and her jointly held master's degrees in business and art history—Elizabeth had spent a year abroad focused on museum studies.

Anya was stunned... Her eyes swept over the walls of the gallery, where a great many oils and acrylics had been displayed. Granted, most reflected the mainstream commercial works of modern artists of lesser pedigree, but Jules's observations called into question the provenance of a sizeable collection, representing tens of thousands of dollars. It suddenly occurred to Anya that it might be best if Sidra didn't see them conferring in front of the alleged forgery. She grabbed Jules by the wrist and guided her down the stairs toward the main floor, where they continued their talk.

"When will Elizabeth be back?"

"A week to ten days."

"I think you should have her take a look at it. If it is a forgery, it will have to be reported, and Sidra's entire collection will have to be re-authenticated. Maybe she was duped by a disreputable dealer. Even Sotheby's has fallen victim to forgeries," Anya pointed out.

"No," Jules said, shaking her head. "A dealer of Sidra's supposed caliber would instantly spot the same defects I did."

"I think you should keep all of this under your hat until Elizabeth has a chance to render her opinion.

After all, you wouldn't want to risk your reputation by falsely accusing Sidra. If she is a fraud, charges will need to be brought. It would be best not to alert her to your findings."

Jules agreed. She would advise Mrs. Bennedetto to only put a deposit down on the Modigliani for now.

"Your sister must have had to amass quite a collection of art books in order to do her research," Anya remarked casually, hoping to disguise a purposeful comment as one more offhanded in nature.

Jules frowned and shook her head. "Art books? No, not really. I mean, she has a few in her own personal collection. Elizabeth authenticates the provenance that accompanies everything we buy and sell using online auction catalogs, historical records, and observational notes from industry experts."

Anya thought it was an interesting piece of insight.

When Anya left to check on Craig and Ananda, Main Street was thronged by tourists. Every umbrella table between the gallery and McClean's was occupied. Lines were in evidence at the sidewalk vendor carts and soft-serve ice cream dispensers. The band had dozens dancing in the street. Smoky had fired up his smokers curbside, accompanied by a banner which read: *Smokin on the Main.* Anya noticed the sheriff was standing in front of Bennedetto's, buying cannoli from their streetside cooler.

Anya spent the next hour or so assisting Craig and Ananda behind the bar at her own pub before sending Craig to relieve Desda at the gallery. He needed to be on hand when it came time to help Paul pack up. By about quarter to four, the lull between the late lunch crowd and the early dinner crowd was in effect. Anya had just enough time to pick up a check from Sidra, make a quick trip home to feed the cats, and get back to McClean's to work until close.

The patrons had also thinned considerably at the gallery. A few of the local faces had found time and opportunity to slip away from their own businesses to attend. While many were there to show their support for the town's newest transplant, Anya felt sure that some were simply there to indulge their own curiosity.

Two friendly faces she saw, lingering nearby, were those of Elijah Whip and his cat, Ichabod. Elijah was cradling the complacent heap of fluff, engaged in what appeared to be a pleasant chat with Sidra. They were laughing and smiling. Anya watched with interest as Sidra affectionately locked arms with Elijah and stroked Ichabod's head with her acrylic crimson claws.

"Isn't that interesting?" said a voice beside her. The curious display had not been lost on Desda, who had swooped in for a closer look.

"Mm-hmm, very. I think he's rather smitten," Anya agreed with a sense of uneasiness.

Desda shook her head in awe. "Smiling … laughing. I think Elijah's falling head over heels."

Anya feigned confusion. "Elijah? I was talking about Ichabod!"

Desda gave her a shove. "Good for him. I've been on the lookout for a good match for that man for years," she acknowledged.

"You and the rest of the town's yentas," Anya murmured. She noticed then that Desda was tapping what looked like a check on her chin. "Hey, is that our check?"

"Yes, I took the liberty of collecting it for you. They make a handsome pair, don't you think?" Desda gushed, continuing to eye the exchange taking place between Elijah and Sidra.

"I heard she tried to talk Elijah into handing over his bookstore, so she could expand her gallery," Anya replied. She enjoyed goading Desda.

"What?! Where'd you hear that?" Desda exclaimed a bit too loudly.

"From Elijah. He said Ichabod wasn't ready to move yet, so he declined her invitation to buy him out."

"Well, you better know she won't go breaking Elijah's heart if she knows what's good for her," Desda grumbled. "She'll be run out of town on a rail!"

"To be sure, though I can't remember the last time I heard that euphemism," Anya said with a wink while prying Sidra's check from Desda's grip. "I'm going to run out to the house and check on the cats, but I'll be back to close. You can go home, get some rest," Anya said.

Desda nodded absently, glaring at Sidra over her shoulder. "Before you go, there's a beautiful mosaic over there you might want for Cats 'n' Cocktails. It's on the left, near the stairs, but now I kind of hate to see you spend a nickel in this place," Desda muttered.

Anya strolled over to the area Desda had indicated and found the piece she had described. It was an enormous work, entitled: *The Pero Cat.* It was a silhouette of a cat created entirely of sea glass, shells, gems, and colorful art glass tiles. It was truly breathtaking and probably priced out of reach, but Anya made a mental note to inquire about it later.

Upon entering Martine's house, it was readily apparent that Ching had indulged in one of his cat fits during her absence. The damages were limited to a toppled floor lamp and one of Martine's books. There were shredded pages scattered all over the main room. He'd even gnawed the corners of the volume bare. The book was or had been a book of nature photographs of flowers, trees, vines, and animal wildlife native to the area. There was a label on the inside cover that read Bell Book & Candle. Martine had probably purchased the book from Elijah for landscaping purposes.

"Bad, Ching!" Anya scolded him, spotting the princely potentate watching from a beam up above. An air of pride emanated from his upturned whiskers.

"That's it! From now on, Don Pedro is in charge!" she bellowed as she dashed around, gathering up the mess. Hearing his name, Don Pedro lifted his head to look at her questioningly. He and several other cats were napping in the puddles of late afternoon sunlight that were streaming through the windows.

After disposing of the soggy remnants left behind in the wake of Ching's mayhem, Anya quickly changed into jeans and a McClean's T-shirt, policed the cats' commodes, filled their water, and arranged a few plates of canned salmon for their dinner. She was grateful for the abundance of canned salmon in Martine's pantry. There hadn't been time to run to the market.

There also hadn't been much time to play with the cats in recent days. She couldn't help but feel a pang of guilt that she wouldn't be around to entertain them this evening either. Their favorite game was a simple one, involving a long pole to which a longer string was tied. Anya swished it around the room while the cats all took turns leaping, pouncing, and trying to outdo one another's acrobatic feats.

Having little opportunity to expend his energy through play might account, at least in part, for Ching's misbehavior, she thought. Anya vowed to set aside plenty of time in the morning for playtime and brushing.

Satisfied that order had been restored, Anya took one final glance around and registered one notable exception. Ching had skipped dinner and was instead curled up asleep on the old sideboard beneath the photo of the cabin. The photo was tipped to one side again. What was that cat trying to communicate? Only Martine would know. She saw signs in what others dismissed as catly mischief.

Back behind the bar at McClean's, Anya was met by startling news. Another minor disaster had occurred right after she'd left the gallery. She couldn't believe her ears as she stared across the bar at Tate, listening to him describe the details of Elijah Whip's near brush with death.

"Yeah, it was unbelievable. They were all really lucky, I guess," Tate said. "The place had pretty much emptied out. Sidra, Elijah, and Ichabod were standing under one of those massive chandeliers hanging in the gallery. They were drinking wine, having a fine time when suddenly Ichabod leaped out of Elijah's arms and made a dash for the door! In a mad panic—Elijah rushed after him just as the thing came crashing down, right where they'd been standing! Glass and crystal everywhere! The damn thing just cut loose. I guess that cat of his pretty much saved his life."

Anya, aware that her jaw had dropped, closed her mouth and blinked her eyes in disbelief. She was unable to speak. Only minutes ago, Ching's attack on the book from Elijah's store had seemed like an isolated act of mischief, perpetrated by a bored cat. Had Ching somehow sensed that Elijah was in danger? Did the cat really have visions as Martine had often claimed? It was impossible, irrational, but somehow it felt like more than a coincidence.

Anya raked her hands through her hair. "I can't believe it. It's like a curse or something. We're having a real run of bad luck around here," she said, shaking her head. "Where are Elijah and Ichabod now?"

"Well, they were both pretty shook up, but no injuries. I think they went on home to recover from the shock. Knowing Elijah, I'd say they're probably curled up in bed, sipping warm milk," Tate replied, chuckling as he pictured it.

"Is the sheriff investigating? Was an inspection or anything done to discover how such a thing could happen?" she asked.

Tate frowned. "Why would the sheriff want to investigate something like that? It was an accident."

"What if it wasn't an accident?" Anya said, lowering her voice. She leaned in closer to Tate and whispered, "Remember when I told you that she's been trying to buy Elijah out so she could expand the gallery?

Wouldn't it be convenient if he were somehow … out of the way?"

Tate dropped his head in defeat. "Oh, no. Not this again. Sabotage? Oh, Anya, you're killing me," he said, starting to laugh. "I gotta tell ya, me and my crew hung those chandeliers ourselves. They're awkward and extremely heavy. It took three of us on extension ladders to hold them, while a fourth guy bolted them in. Not to sound like a chauvinist or anything, but I don't see how a woman her size could pull that off. I think the old plaster in that place gave way. Hey, you know, I bet the blast waves from the hotel bombing shook it loose. It was an accident, that's all. Don't let your imagination play tricks on you. I think you're a bit overwrought with everything that's been going on around here lately," Tate said, attempting to reassure her.

Anya recomposed herself for appearances' sake, but her thoughts had returned to the mystery surrounding Sidra's standing order of breakfast for two and the feeling she'd had earlier that someone had been upstairs in Sidra's office. Maybe she hadn't done it alone. Maybe she'd had help.

THIRTEEN

Anya crawled out of bed early on Sunday in time to catch another spectacular sunrise. She stumbled through the living room toward the nearest lamp and clicked it on to light the way. On the second leg of the journey to the kitchen, she noticed Ching was in the study, sitting in the drawer of Martine's desk. Sometime in the night, he'd managed to open it enough to scrunch his mutable form inside.

She paused to peer in the doorway, unintentionally startling him with her presence. Ching jerked his head in her direction and crouched. He squinted his yellow-green eyes at her like a cat burglar caught in the act.

Anya chose to ignore him for the moment and continued on with her own mission. Balancing a cup, the sugar bowl, and the entire carafe of coffee, she made her way out on to the deck in time for the opening act. Sitting quietly in the darkness, listening to the sounds of creatures scurrying through the forest that surrounded her, she felt peaceful and more clearheaded than she had the previous night.

Tate was right. She had simply allowed her imagination to run wild. She was exhausted, and her nerves were a little frayed, perfectly natural considering recent events. A hotel bombing, a mysterious break-in at Martine's shop, and now Elijah's close call, it was a wonder the whole town wasn't suffering from PTSD.

Sidra hadn't tried to whack Elijah by sabotaging a chandelier, and Ching hadn't had a premonition. He was just a headstrong cat, prone to mischief, who frequently indulged in capricious behaviors like shredding books, sleeping in drawers, and tilting pictures on the walls.

As the sun peeked over the horizon, and the first bird trilled its cheerful morning song, the first of the cats' loud demands for breakfast ensued. When the last plate had been licked clean, Anya kept her vow and engaged them in a rousing round of "string", after which everyone got a thorough brushing.

Another busy day lay ahead of her, so Anya skipped her own breakfast and headed straight for the shower. She dressed casually in jeans and a sheer red blouse with a matching camisole beneath, but she spent a little more time than usual on her hair. She gathered the sides into a messy half-bun in the back and flat-ironed the lengths that fell past her shoulders until they were straight and shiny as ribbons. She also took the time to frame her tired green eyes with a touch of black eyeliner and a sweep of mascara.

The busy day ahead would begin with a visit from Nick and Lisa Larkin. They were coming by soon to have lunch and to drop off her permits. Anya unlocked the front door in preparation for their arrival.

Tate was coming later to pick up the permits and to go over the list of supplies he would need to order for the Cats 'n' Cocktails project. They were also going to set a launch date for the renovation. McClean's would have to be closed for a couple of months to undergo the work.

Anya also planned to reach out to Jimmy Shaw again, and last, but not least, Ethan, Nigel, and Cecilia had invited themselves over for dinner, drinks, and cards. Ethan had hinted that Nigel and Cecilia had exciting news to share. Anya was pretty sure she knew what it was.

It was this final entry on the day's agenda that had prompted her to spend so much time primping. She was still waiting for a sign from Ethan that he might want to resume their relationship.

At eleven o'clock, on the dot, Anya heard meowing coming from the front of the house. Luther was spinning in circles near the front door, pinwheeling from side to side. He was using his enormous tail to bar the rest of his housemates from being the first to greet the Larkins.

Martine's cats adored Nick and Lisa. There were a few possibilities that could explain why such an honor had been bestowed upon them. Perhaps they knew that the Larkins were cat owners themselves, a feline duo known as Calico Jack and Jolly Roger. Another theory was that certain aromas, originating from The Pirate's Cove, could be detected by the cats, appealing to their gustatory sensibilities. Personally, Anya had surmised that it was because Lisa always came bearing treats for the scallywags, and today was no exception.

"Hel-lo, Anya! Hel-lo, kitties! I've brought treats for you!" Lisa called out, bending to pet each one's head as they encircled her.

"I know you've been waiting for these!" Nick exclaimed, waving an envelope containing the permits for Cats 'n' Cocktails.

"Oh, thank you. Come in, come in," Anya replied.

Lisa made her way to the kitchen to serve the cats' lunch. They darted around her, expressing their gratitude with earsplitting shrieks of delight.

Nick and Lisa had also brought along a light lunch of bread and Caprese salad to share with Anya.

"I guess you heard about Elijah and Ichabod's close call with the chandelier yesterday?" Lisa called out above the din emanating from the kitchen.

"I did," Anya replied. "Have you seen Elijah today? Do you know how he's doing?" she asked while they gathered around the dining room table to eat their own lunch.

Both Larkins shook their head no.

"I don't want to raise undue suspicion, but I don't trust that York woman. I've been hearing things about her that I find … well, disturbing," Lisa said.

"Like?" Anya ventured, encouraging Lisa to continue.

"Well, of course, it was you who told me she'd offered to buy Elijah's shop, so that she could expand the gallery. Isn't it all just too convenient that, after declining her offer, he was almost killed yesterday, in her gallery, nonetheless? I heard another interesting tidbit as well. My sources say she picks up breakfast at Bagels Baked Goods & Beyond every morning. Every day it's always the same. She gets two French toast bagels and two large coffees."

Anya tried to hide her amusement, covering a smile with her free hand. Obviously, Lisa had been talking to the Cruz sisters.

"And it gets better," Lisa continued. "The first couple of times Sidra came in, she ordered two regular coffees. Now, she always orders one regular and one decaf," Lisa said, pausing for dramatic effect. "What do you make of that?" she added.

Anya felt a tingling sensation at the back of her neck. "She's trying to cut down on caffeine?" she heard herself say, even though she knew what Lisa was implying, and she herself had been operating under the same supposition for weeks. She remembered vividly the impression she'd had that Sidra had been speaking to someone upstairs in her office yesterday at the grand opening. If someone had been there, what possible reason could she have for keeping this associate under wraps?

Anya made the quick decision not to share these details with the Larkins, but a devious plan was beginning to form in her mind. She was determined to confirm or dispel these conspiracy theories once and for all. It was time to make an impromptu visit to The York Gallery.

"Possibly, but I'm not the only one who's wary of her. I overheard Sharon Bailer asking Desda March if Sidra was a closet smoker."

Anya frowned. She was surprised that Desda hadn't mentioned this conversation to her, but that was probably because Sharon Bailer was the source.

"Yep. Desda said that she had no idea. Sharon told her then that she'd seen Sidra make quite a few trips upstairs to her office that day—no small undertaking considering the heels she was wearing. Following one such trip, Sharon claimed that she'd detected the faintest hint of cigarette smoke—underscoring the zephyr of perfume the woman wears. Sharon doesn't think

Sidra, with her gleaming white teeth and flawless skin, fits the stereotype of a smoker. She thinks Sidra has a mystery guest upstairs."

Anya had her own reservations regarding Sidra York; still she couldn't help but be a little astonished by the widespread incertitude Sidra was drawing from the locals. Whether or not she was deserving of their mistrust, Anya couldn't be sure, but she couldn't remember a time when anyone new to town had generated such prodigious cynicism. She was about to share Jules's assertions that at least one of the paintings at the gallery might be a forgery but thought better of it. Widespread misgivings were already in circulation. It would only serve to fuel the Four Oaks rumor mill.

"Hmmm … ," Anya murmured, focusing on her salad, "I must admit it's peculiar, but without any proof, it's really nothing more than baseless conjecture. There's no crime in offering to buy Elijah out. He's talked about moving his shop up to Patawomek Street many times over the years. And what's most likely to be behind the fall of that chandelier, sabotage or an unfortunate accident? Tate and his crew installed them, and he's of the opinion that the old plaster couldn't support the weight, or that the explosion at the hotel shook it loose. And maybe Sidra is a closet smoker. There's no crime in that either. Sharon thinks she knows everything—a self-appointed expert—but of course, she doesn't have any evidence to support it," Anya pointed out.

Lisa looked a little deflated, and Anya felt a little guilty for shooting her down, especially since she was secretly harboring suspicions of her own.

"Hey, here's something strange you might not have heard," Nick interjected, changing the subject. "We ran into the sheriff at Landale's Log Cabin earlier—on his way in for coffee. He says they still don't have any leads on the hotel bombing or the break-in at Martine's, but he has been trying to track down some folks that have been camping out by the beaver's dam. A concerned citizen reported seeing a campfire burning down there the other night. You know that's a no campfire/no cookout zone. Signs are posted all around the area to that effect. Evidently, he went out to investigate it. The sheriff located their campsite, but the campers were long gone. He said he's been asking all of the local fishermen to keep an eye out in case they come back."

Anya's ears perked up instantly. She was sure Nick was talking about the small fire she and Ethan had observed through the binoculars. Ethan had said he was going to call it in.

"The most intriguing detail is this: The sheriff found traces of blood in a pile of leaves and on a few of the rocks this person used to encircle their fire. Nothing big, mind you, but some sort of minor injury was suffered by whoever had been camping there. Interesting, huh?" Nick asked.

Alarm bells were going off in Anya's head now. Her mind flashed back on the spray of broken glass covering the sidewalk outside of Martine's store the night of the break-in, less than twenty-four hours before the unauthorized campfire was spotted.

"Mrroww!" Ching howled, abruptly inserting himself into the conversation. He leaped up to the table beside Lisa.

"Aww … isn't he sweet? He wants to thank us for that tuna we brought him," Lisa said, stroking Ching's silky coat.

Anya wasn't so sure that was Ching's intention.

At the conclusion of a most enjoyable lunch, Anya thanked the Larkins profusely on behalf of herself and the cats, and bid them farewell.

It was twelve-thirty. She had just enough time to run into town and pick up a few essentials for this evening's dinner and card party before Tate would arrive.

The community that encompassed Lake Increase had its own Main Street known as Patawomek Street. Patawomek was a Native American word that roughly translated to "they bring it". It was a reference to the origins of the town itself. The town's founders had operated trading posts and dry goods stores. They had traded their wares for fur pelts, beadwork, leather goods, and such—*brought to them* by the Native Americans, trappers, and settlers who had once lived in the area. It was only about a half-mile down the road, and Anya made the decision to walk there.

As the bustling enclave of picturesque shops and family-owned eateries came into view, she realized, with regret, that she had failed to enjoy the majestic surroundings along the way. She had been too engrossed in formulating the details of her plan. She intended to unmask Sidra's secret stranger or else put these rumors to rest. Whatever the outcome—by morning—the truth would be known.

The market on Patawomek Street was called Hop's Market. Next to Hop's was a popular party planning service called Eventful. As Anya approached the market, the door to Eventful swung open, and three familiar faces came piling out. They were all clearly excited, laughing and talking at once. The faces belonged to Sharon Bailer, Lila Stevens, and Cecilia's mother, Cossima Bennedetto. Anya was surprised to see them, especially Sharon Bailer. She'd played a featured role in one of the more controversial topics she and the Larkins had discussed over lunch.

"Anya!" came the chorus of female voices that greeted her there on the sidewalk.

"Did you hear the news? Nigel has proposed to Cecilia!" Cossima exclaimed.

It was news the town had long been awaiting. Anya had suspected it was the news they were planning to share with her that very evening.

"Oh, how wonderful! How exciting!" Anya extolled with a hug for her dear friend's elated mother. "I'm actually here to shop for a dinner party I'm having for them tonight, so if you see either of them, don't tell them that you ran into me. I don't want to ruin the reveal," Anya said.

"Yes, of course! I won't mention it," Cossima agreed, holding a finger to her lips. "But, you let me supply the food, eh? Alessandro has been cooking since four o'clock this morning. He's making his mother, Luna's, famous spaghetti and meatballs in Bolognese sauce and lobster ravioli. I assume Ethan will be coming tonight? I'll call him and have him stop by to pick it all up on his way over."

"Wow … Grandma Luna's spaghetti and meatballs and lobster ravioli," Anya murmured. "Definitely in the top three of my all-time favorites. I haven't had either in years."

Cossima nodded knowingly. "Yes, so you accept. I'll pack it all up along with some nice antipasti and something for dessert. I'll see what looks good."

Anya smiled and gave her arm a grateful squeeze. "Am I to assume you've enlisted the services of Eventful in planning some sort of engagement party?" she asked.

"Exactly right," Cossima affirmed. "Alessandro and I are throwing a big celebration for them this Friday night at our house! Eventful has agreed to arrange for a five-course meal to be served and a string quartet for the after-dinner cocktail party on the terrace," she replied.

The other two women bobbed their heads effusively, unable to slip a comment in otherwise. Cossima had barely taken a breath since they'd chanced to meet.

"You'll be receiving a formal invitation, of course," she continued, "hand-delivered due to the short notice- and no gifts! Cecilia will have a shower later on. I hope you can attend?"

Anya watched Cossima finally take that breath before replying, "I wouldn't miss it for the world!"

"Ohhh ... , I know you wouldn't, darling." Cossima beamed and embraced Anya warmly once more. Then the three party planners dashed off to continue their agenda.

With dinner now being provided by the Bennedettos, the remaining items on Anya's handwritten shopping list were: crackers, cheeseballs, raspberry sangria. The details were all in her head. She procured a couple of mangoes, two containers of raspberries, raspberry liqueur, bottles of French Rose, and lemon-lime soda, cheddar cheese, cream cheese, pecans, and crackers.

She also grabbed cans of deboned chicken and turkey for the cats.

Exiting the market, she instantly realized her error in deciding to walk to the market. She'd forgotten to estimate the number of heavy bags she'd be carrying on the return trip. Struggling along with her cumbersome load, she kept hoping Tate would pass by on his way to Martine's to meet her. Of course, he did not. The cats were monitoring her exertions from the front windows as she labored to the door with her parcels.

"Freeloaders," she muttered, unburdening herself in the foyer.

FOURTEEN

Friends routinely phoned Anya on her landline or any line they thought they could reach her on. That was because she was notorious for leaving her cell phone behind. She'd left it behind that morning when she'd set out for Hop's. Anya knew she must have received a call in her absence because Ching was presently sitting on the answering machine. He often alerted her to missed calls in this way. It was a habit she'd made an informal study of since she and the cats had moved up to the lake.

When Ching sat on the answering machine, it meant she'd missed an important call, though not necessarily one that was important to her. The cat had his own idea of which calls to the house should take priority. Calls from Desda, Tate, or the Larkins, for instance, were always dutifully reported. He adopted a fickle approach when it came to reporting calls from Ethan and Cecilia, directing her attention to those messages only about fifty percent of the time. On the other hand, there were some callers he ignored altogether. She'd been hoping for a call from the sheriff all week to further test her theories regarding Ching's VIP list, but, so far—no call from him had come.

She made two separate trips from the foyer to the kitchen, depositing her groceries on the island before playing the message. It was Jimmy Shaw returning the call he'd missed from her a couple of days ago. Anya called him back as she unpacked her shopping bags.

The first half of their conversation was business as usual. They decided to hold the fundraiser a week from Friday, which would allow them plenty of time to promote it on local radio and social media. Jimmy also agreed to help tend bar that day. Being a complete amateur, and a hopeless one at that, his misadventures in mixology were half the fun.

With these details out of the way, Jimmy next revealed that he'd had a secondary purpose in mind when he'd phoned her that day—one that Anya had not been prepared to hear.

"I've spent the last couple of months investigating another dogfighting ring that's popped up in the area," he said. "One of our volunteers came upon some intel on social media, and we've been looking into it ever since. I've made a few trips out there myself, under the radar, of course. I can't get a definite head count, but I think there may be as many as eight dogs on site. The police have been out twice to search the property, but somehow, they keep getting tipped off in time to move the dogs and cover their tracks. My contacts tell me that the chatter on the web points to a possible fight this Friday night, so we're going to hit the place *Thursday*, before any harm comes to the animals. I sure could use you and your Land Rover if you can summon the courage. I know you hate this sort of thing, but I'm going to need a few vehicles for that many dogs. Ethan has volunteered to ride with Tate, and Nigel will go with one of my volunteers, a girl named Kelly. She has a truck and has offered her help. How 'bout it? We can roll together," Jimmy said.

Anya paused, seeing that Tate was now walking up the driveway. She waved him inside.

"OK, Jimmy," she said, trying to disguise her reluctance. "Happy to help," she was amazed to hear herself say. She'd gone on these search and rescue missions before, and they were scary to say to the least. Jimmy was a tough guy to turn down, though, and Anya knew he needed her help.

"Great! We'll meet up at the Notahs' ranch around one a.m. This place we're going to is actually on your side of the river—on the outskirts of Dixon," Jimmy replied.

Dixon was a rough town. Thankfully, they didn't get too many customers from Dixon at McClean's since it was about forty minutes away, but, whenever they did, it nearly always ended with the police being called.

"Sheriff Wakefield and Sam Notah will be waiting at the Chenoah Falls Bridge on our return trip. If anybody tries to pursue us, they'll have a big surprise waiting for them there," Jimmy said, roaring with laughter.

The very suggestion that there might be a chase was numbing to Anya. She hung up the phone and stared blankly across the room at Tate. He was down on the floor, surrounded by all seven cats, doling out treats from his pockets.

Ching was especially fond of Tate. Did he know or somehow sense that Tate was the creator of his beloved second-story playground? Had he been present when Tate had installed the overhead beams he adored?

Looking past Tate into the guest room, Anya could see a tattered book lying on the floor. It appeared to have been the subject of some recent criminal mischief—another misdemeanor act of vandalism that had taken place in her absence. She knew it was *Trappers and Traders—North American Legends* even before she excused herself to retrieve it. It lay open to the bookmark, but the page that featured James Beckwith's desk, along with several other pages, had been ripped from the binding and strewn about the room. She shoved them back inside, closed the book, and returned it to the bedside table.

"Let me guess," Tate wagered as Anya rejoined him in the living room. "That was Jimmy on the phone."

Anya nodded. "I don't like these jailbreak missions. They make me nervous. I've gotta sell that Land Rover—buy a compact model."

Tate laughed as he scooped up Ching, who allowed himself to be draped around Tate's neck and shoulders like a fur collar. Ching nuzzled his cheek affectionately, oblivious to Anya's present state of unrest.

"You'd never survive the Four Oaks winters without a truck; besides there's no need to worry. There are at least six of us going. You can stay in your vehicle. All you'll really have to do is drive."

Nonetheless, Anya was dubious. Dogfighting was big business, even for a small operation. The money they raked in was in the tens of thousands, sometimes hundreds of thousands for the larger, more organized rings. These people always had guns and were always ready to protect their investment. She was glad there were people like Jimmy Shaw in the world to stop them, but she preferred to read about it in the newspaper afterward rather than experience it firsthand as a member of Jimmy's hit-squad.

Anya suddenly felt like sangria. Tate got out the supply list he wanted to review with her, while Anya concocted the first batch of the day in one of Martine's crystal punch bowls.

"So, did you manage to get some sleep last night? You were pretty upset about Elijah's near miss with the chandelier. Still suspicious of Sidra, or did everything look less ominous in the light of day?" Tate asked.

"To be honest, I initially felt like I had been overreacting, and then I had lunch with the Larkins. They delivered the permits," Anya replied, handing the envelope to him. "Let's say the chandelier was an accident. Fine—but I'm not the only one harboring suspicions about Sidra. Tongues are wagging. Other people in town think she has a secret partner, too—one she hasn't introduced to anyone. There is some evidence underpinning the speculation that someone's been hiding out upstairs in Sidra's office." Anya watched closely for a reaction from Tate, but it was clear from the look on his face that he hadn't heard the rumors that were circulating.

"The other day you mentioned something about breakfast for two and references Sidra had made to 'we' and 'us'. Now people think she's hiding somebody upstairs in her office? Why?" Tate looked predictably skeptical.

"Sharon Bailer—," Anya began.

"Oh, no! Sharon Bailer?" Tate flung himself back in his chair at the mention of the town's most notorious gossip.

"Just wait," Anya said, intent on continuing with her explanation. "Do you happen to know if Sidra smokes?"

Tate shook his head. "I met with her once for about

thirty minutes and again for about ten seconds to pick up a check. Why?"

"Sharon noticed that Sidra went upstairs to her office quite a few times during the grand opening. Following one such trip, she passed by the Bailers, and Sharon claimed she smelled like smoke. Granted, she could be a closet smoker, but the general consensus is that someone else was present that day. Someone who, for whatever reason, never made an appearance."

"That's it?" Tate asked, resting his chin in his hand.

"No, that's not it. That same day, I saw her on the balcony. I could swear I saw her exchange a word or two with someone in her office. She tried to be discreet about it, but I know what I saw. After that she closed the door and came downstairs."

Tate leaned forward with increased interest. "OK, I don't care so much about what Sharon Bailer's opinion is, but I confess to being somewhat intrigued by what you saw. How sure are you that she actually spoke to someone in her office?"

"Ninety-percent. I know that's not enough, but considering the rest of the evidence, I'm fairly convinced."

"Still, what does it mean? Suppose she has a secret partner. There's no law against that."

"No, but there are laws against art forgery," Anya blurted out. She hadn't intended to share that information with Tate, but his persistent pessimism had provoked her.

Tate raised his eyebrows. "Art forgery? Tell me more about that."

Anya related the details of the conversation she'd had with Jules Colburn. Tate listened intently. Jules was someone he respected. They were close friends and longtime associates. Whenever Jules had a project that required a construction expert, she always went to Tate.

After relating the inconsistencies Jules had noted while inspecting the Modigliani, Anya went on to apply another one of her own theories. "If Sidra had done her homework, she would have realized that there was a lot of old money in this town, a lot of potential clients. That alone would make Four Oaks a prime target for an art forgery scheme. She might have mistakenly underestimated the level of sophistication among our residents, leading her to wrongly assume that a small town like this would also be a soft target. I think it could explain why and how she wound up in Four Oaks," she said.

Tate listened attentively, but Anya could see by the look on his face that she'd failed to overcome his cynicism.

"So, let's review," Tate replied in a calm, discriminating tone that Anya found irritating. "After the explosion at the hotel and the break-in at Martine's, your suspicions turned to Sidra York. When you first mentioned all of this to me, you said you thought it was odd that someone like her would want to open an art gallery here. You were also concerned about her interest in acquiring Elijah's square footage, and you now suspect that she has a secret partner of some kind—someone behind the scenes who apparently doesn't want to be discovered. Added to this, we have a possible motive for her coming here, which involves fraud and an art forgery racket of some kind. So, what are we saying? That she handpicked this town to open an art gallery as a front so she could blow up a hotel, burglarize an emporium, and scam people out of money by selling forgeries?"

Hearing Tate describe it in those terms made Anya feel a little foolish. He was right. On the whole, it didn't make any sense. While the jury was still out on whether any kind of art forgery had been committed, there wasn't any evidence or even a possible motive connecting Sidra York to the bombing or the break-in.

Anya sighed. "I see your point, and you're right, but I can't help it. My instincts tell me something more is going on here."

They spent the rest of the afternoon drinking sangria, going over facts and figures, and a few new ideas Tate had for Cats 'n' Cocktails. Zia spent the afternoon napping on Tate's lap.

"Here are the three most important numbers to focus on," Tate said, circling three sums at the bottom of three long tabulated lists. "This first number is what I estimate the project will actually cost. The second number reflects potential overages, which will be adjusted after I have some inspections done on your place. We need to open up the walls in some areas, have a look at the electrical, the plumbing, etc. The third number is the amount you should ask the bank to loan you."

Anya felt extremely apprehensive. She'd never applied for a loan of any kind, and she was looking at a very big number.

Tate reached out and covered her hand with his own. "Hey, there's nothing to worry about. Think of it like a mortgage, but instead of thirty years, I predict you'll have it paid off in five with the kind of business your place does."

"I know. I've done the math a million times. I've just never had to go to a bank for anything. It's a little daunting, but I'll make an appointment with Ben Jacobs in the morning," she said. Ben Jacobs was the chief loan officer at The Bank of Chenoah Falls.

"Why don't you let me go with you? Do you have any idea how many construction loans I've gotten over the years? Between my house and my business, I've needed plenty. They know me over there. Lean on me. Let me handle it. You won't have any problem getting that loan—I promise," he assured her.

"Really? You'd do that? You'd go with me?"

"Of course. I probably should anyway because they might have a few questions about the timeline and the size of the crews that you won't be able to answer."

Anya frowned, feeling uneasy again about the whole process.

Tate laughed and gathered his paperwork. "Give them a call. Let me know when they want to meet. Everything will be fine, you'll see," he said on his way to the door.

"Do you have to go?" she asked. "Why don't you stay? Ethan, Nigel, and Cecilia will be here soon. They have a big announcement. We're going to have a little party here tonight," Anya said.

"Oh, really? I assume that means they're finally going to do it? Tie the knot? That's terrific!" Tate exclaimed.

"I have it on good authority that it's finally official," Anya replied.

"Well, I'd like to stick around, but I have a lot of new videos to edit, render, and upload tonight. The process takes hours."

In addition to his construction business, Tate had two social media channels that were very popular and highly subscribed and donated to. One was a DIY type of renovation/remodeling channel. The other was a lesser-known endeavor that he only discussed openly with his closest friends. It involved Tate's other passion, a fascination with all things paranormal.

As he explained it, it worked something like this: An ongoing list of well-known and reputedly haunted locations were generated by his subscribers. The sites that received the most money in donations became the focus of future investigations. He and Rob would travel to these locales and either film or livestream the entire experience. The end result included interviews and research, as well as any mysterious or inexplicable occurrences.

Anya had always wanted to tag along on one of his adventures. She felt silly admitting it, but she found it all rather compelling. For the most part, his investigations turned up hoaxes, but there had been a few positively chilling experiences.

"OK, but you're going to miss Grandma Luna's spaghetti and meatballs in Bolognese sauce and lobster ravioli," Anya said, trying her best to tempt him.

"Oh . . . really? I *love* Grandma Luna's Bolognese sauce *and* her lobster ravioli. You're making this pretty hard on me, you know?" With one hand on the doorknob, he looked back at her and said, "I'll tell you what—freeze any leftovers, and when we get the loan we'll celebrate. Just you, me, a bottle of scotch—the good stuff—and Grandma Luna's pasta and lobster ravioli. Martine will be home by then, so we'll do it at my place."

Anya hesitated for no more than a second or two before he added, “Say yes, Anya.”

“Yes,” she said, smiling. “Thanks for offering to go with me to the bank. I feel better about it already.”

“Trust me. It’s no big deal. We’ll be approved the same day and walk out of there with a big check. Well, I’ll walk out of there with a big check. You’ll walk out of there with a big bill!” he said, laughing.

Anya shoved him out the door.

Less than a minute later, Ethan showed up. Anya looked over to see him standing in the doorway, his arms full of to-go bags from Bennedetto’s.

“Hey, was that Tate I saw leaving?” he asked without so much as a hello.

“Yeah, now that we have the permits, it’s time to get the loan, order supplies, and move forward,” she replied. “Tate’s going to go to the bank with me. He’s obtained quite a few loans from them over the years. He says it will be no big deal, but I can’t help feeling a little anxious.”

“Huh, well, I’m sure he knows what he’s talking about. The guy tore down his own house, built a new one, and started a construction business. It takes a lot of money to do that. I’m sure he’s familiar with the process. You won’t have any problems. It’s all going to work out. Don’t worry,” Ethan said.

He pushed the front door closed with the heel of his boot and strode toward the kitchen.

"I guess you already know what all of this is about tonight? Cossima mentioned that she ran into you outside of Hop's," Ethan said, changing the subject.

"Yes, but I'm still planning to act surprised, so don't blow my cover," Anya replied, adding, "I'm so happy for Nigel and Cecilia. I think everyone's been looking forward to that wedding."

Shortly after that, the door opened, and Nigel, Cecilia, and Cecilia's diamond ring arrived. The two-carat sparkler made for a dazzling display on her outstretched hand when she crossed the threshold. Anya came from the kitchen to greet them.

"Wow! That's quite a chunk of ice!" Anya exclaimed. "Let's all go into the kitchen. Ethan's in there. I can't wait to hear all about it!"

When they reached the kitchen, they saw that Ethan was not alone. Ching was sitting beside him on the counter, watching him unpack the spaghetti and meatballs Bolognese, lobster ravioli, bread, antipasti, and frozen cups of affogato for dessert.

"So, when's the big day?" Anya asked the happy couple as she served them all glasses of sangria and rolled her cheeseballs in pecans.

"We haven't set the date yet," Cecilia said. "It'll be sometime in the spring. Martine cautioned us to wait six months after August's solar eclipse. By the way, I was hoping you would be my maid of honor."

"I would love to! Wait … did you say you talked to Martine?" Anya was a little bewildered. She'd only heard from Martine once since she'd left.

"Yeah, she phoned the Notahs last night, looking for the sheriff. Nigel broke the news."

"She didn't happen to say what day she'd be coming home, did she?" Anya asked, veering a little off-topic. She and Desda had yet to clean up over at the emporium.

"No, but the sheriff probably knows," Nigel replied.

The eclipse Cecilia was referring to was the total solar eclipse coming up on August twenty-first. It was to be the first total eclipse visible in the United States in ninety-nine years.

McClean's would be closed for renovation, but the town council was expecting record crowds. Behind closed doors, the councilmen and women were said to be planning something special to mark the occasion. Desda had mentioned it a couple of weeks ago. A reliable source had divulged to her that the celebration was to be dubbed: The Super Solarbration.

Anya was about to ask Cecilia why Martine had urged them to wait for six months after the eclipse to marry, when Cecilia volunteered the answer.

"Martine said eclipses have very powerful energy and bring large scale beginnings and endings for up to as long as six months after their occurrence. This one is particularly significant, being the first of its kind in ninety-nine years. She said we should let the energy subside. I don't know. Anyway, we decided to take her advice. She's promised to do our charts and recommend an auspicious date," Cecilia explained.

Knowing Martine as she had all of these years, Anya wasn't nearly as astonished by Cecilia's explanation as she was by Ethan's self-restraint. On the surface, he appeared to be savoring a taste of the sauce, but Anya knew better. He was fighting an impulse to issue a wisecrack regarding what he referred to as Martine's voodoo superstitions.

Anya made a new batch of sangria, and they all went out onto the deck, so Anya could hear the story of Nigel's proposal. It was an amusing account as related by Cecilia:

"Nigel had invited me over for a romantic dinner which he had promised to prepare himself. He said Old Sam and Ethan would be out for the evening, so we'd have the place all to ourselves. Naturally, I was skeptical, but he insisted he had it all under control."

Anya noticed that Ethan and Nigel were grinning.

"Well, imagine my surprise when I arrived and saw Old Sam sitting on the porch with the dogs with seemingly no plans to go anywhere anytime soon. Furthermore, when I went into the kitchen, I found a pot of meatballs simmering in sauce on the stove, but

Nigel was nowhere in sight. I asked Sam where Nigel was, and he told me Nigel had gone into town to pick up a shipment of car parts he'd bought in an online auction. Then, get this—he tells me I should probably go ahead and make the spaghetti, finish up the salad, and if I didn't mind, Butternut could use some fresh water, oats, and straw."

Butternut was Cecilia's favorite horse at the ranch—but that was clearly beside the point.

"I'm thinking, *Does Pops not see that I'm standing here in a dress and heels?* I was supposed to be *served* a romantic dinner, not *cook* one for him and Nigel. I was furious, thinking how typical this was. Getting angrier by the minute, I put a pot of water on the stove to boil and went back out to the porch to pull on a pair of Nigel's muddy old boots he'd left lying there. Pops didn't move a muscle. Didn't say a word! Nothing. So, I stomped off toward the stables to tend to little Butternut. I fed and watered her and pitched some fresh straw into her stall. After that, I was a mess! My hair was halfway falling down and sticking to my face. My dress was covered in oat and straw dust. I was about to charge back up to the house to give them both a piece of my mind when I saw Nigel standing at the stable door with the dogs. Cross galloped over to me with a little scroll attached to his collar that read: Will you marry me? Nigel got down on one knee and held up the ring. The whole thing was a setup! Of course, I accepted. When we walked in the house, there were flowers and candles and champagne! Dinner was already prepared, and Ethan and Sam congratulated us before they left for the evening!"

Ethan handed Anya his phone, so she could see the pictures he'd taken of them: Nigel, dressed in his suit, and Cecilia, looking dusty and disheveled—showing off her ring for the camera.

"Risky joke!" Anya laughed. Daring to incite the wrath of a Bennedetto was like poking a sleeping badger with a stick.

After dinner, they played hearts until almost midnight. Ching and Don Pedro watched the game with great interest. More than once, Ching ventured a paw in the direction of the discard pile, only to be denied each time by a gentle wave of Anya's hand.

Ethan remained behind to help her clean up after Nigel and Cecilia left. Anya hoped he had another purpose in mind, but twenty minutes later, he was on his way out the door. Just when it seemed she was to be disappointed again, Ethan reversed course.

He turned around to face her, hands on hips, and asked, "Where are we at here, Anya—you and me?" His dark eyes searched hers, gaging her reaction. He folded his arms across his chest, a sign that hinted at closely guarded emotions. "Or maybe I should start with you and Tate," he continued. "Is there something going on there that I should know about?" Ethan stepped back onto the porch. His towering frame hovered far above her. "I know it might sound crazy, but I was kind of hoping you might wait for me," he said.

Anya stared up at him and swallowed hard. "Nothing is going on between Tate and me. We're friends, that's all."

Ethan put his arms around her and buried his face in her hair. "Let's pick it up then, Anya," he whispered. "Let's pick up where we left off. I know I had to go away for a long time, but that's over now. There's no reason for us to ever be apart again."

Anya reached up to comb her fingers through his long dark hair and smiled. "I love you, Ethan, and I did wait. I waited for you."

Something in his smile told her he was immensely relieved to hear her speak those words.

"I love you too, so much. I never stopped," he said. "So, you'll go with me to Nigel and Cecilia's engagement party on Saturday?"

"I can't wait," she replied.

They shared a long, lingering kiss goodnight—the first in six years. She watched him go, feeling overjoyed. She hadn't been wrong to wait for him after all.

When he'd gone, her thoughts returned to Sidra York and the rumor mill's assertions of a secret partner. Though Tate had managed to point out the failure in her logic to some degree, he hadn't been able to quell her curiosity with regard to that aspect of the situation. Tomorrow she would get up early and pay a little visit to the gallery. If she timed it right, she would discover for herself whether or not this phantom associate existed.

On the way to bed, she glanced out at the lake, lucent in the soft glow of the moon. For an instant, she could have sworn she'd seen a flickering light, beaming through the trees from across the lake. Its glow was intermittent—a series of long and short blinking lights as if someone were trying to signal in morse code. Anya smiled.

FIFTEEN

In the morning, Anya was surprised to find that Ching was the only cat in her bed. With his head on the pillow and his legs tucked under his chin he closely resembled a cocktail shrimp. This behavior was entirely out of character for Ching. She could only imagine that he must be missing Martine.

There would be no time for coffee on the deck today. Anya showered, dressed, and attended to the cats' needs before she hit the road with coffee to go. The success of her plan was predicated on precise timing. She had to be ready to move as soon as Sidra left the gallery for Bagels Baked Goods & Beyond.

Anya parked a few doors up from The York Gallery—in front of Smoky's BBQ. Less than a minute had passed when Sidra appeared. She exited the gallery and made her way down Main Street in her daily pursuit of two coffees: one regular, one decaf, and two French toast bagels. As Anya had hoped, she hadn't bothered to lock the door behind her. In a flash, Anya was out of her truck and moving stealthily toward the entrance. Her heart was pounding as she kept her eyes trained on Sidra, who, for the moment, remained utterly unaware of Anya's progress toward the gallery.

"Anya! Oh, Anya!" came the voice of Lila Stevens, hailing her from across the street. She came skipping over from Two By Two to meet her.

Anya cringed. Sidra had just entered the Cruz sisters' establishment. Time was of the essence. There wasn't a second to lose.

"Hello, Lila," Anya sighed, irritated by this ill-timed interruption.

"So? Did you get to see Cecilia's ring last night? Isn't it gorgeous?" Lila effused.

"Indeed I did," Anya replied, struggling to keep her tone free of the exasperation she was experiencing.

"I'm so excited for them. I can't remember the last time we had a wedding in Four Oaks! It's so … well exciting!"

As yet, Anya had not taken her eyes off the bakery's door. She was nodding and praying for a miracle when another voice came to the rescue.

"Lila! Telephone! Your mother!" The voice belonged to Lila's husband, Mason, who was motioning to her from the entrance to the ark.

"Oh, gotta go. Have a great day!" Lila called out, rushing off as quickly as she'd come.

Anya breathed a sigh of relief and slipped inside

the gallery, where she surveyed the main floor for signs that anyone else might be present. The showroom was empty. Another lucky break for me, Anya thought.

She turned her gaze upward toward the office on the balcony above her. The light was on, but there was nothing unusual about that. Sidra was probably already on her way back, but Anya had to risk taking a closer look.

Consciously aware that she was holding her breath, she started slowly up the stairs. Suddenly, a thin curl of smoke, so faint that it was almost imperceptible, wafted out into the air above her head. Anya immediately halted her ascent and froze in place as the curl was dissipated by a denser cloud. Someone was there!

While she was weighing her options, deciding whether to advance or retreat, she heard the door open below. Anya's heart sank. Sidra had returned, and she was caught in the act. She knew she had to compose herself and move smoothly into Plan B mode. Anya had taken care to devise a ready-made excuse to justify her visit—should some unforeseen twist of fate require it.

"Excuse me? Can I help you?" Sidra called out. "Anya? What can I do for you?" she asked, shielding her eyes as if she was having trouble identifying Anya's unsanctioned presence on the stairs.

"Good morning, Sidra!" Anya greeted her cheerfully, hurrying back down the steps to the main floor. "I thought you might be upstairs in your office,"

Anya said, careful to keep the inflection in her voice congenial.

"I was out. Getting coffee. Was there something you needed?" Sidra asked succinctly.

The smell of tobacco was unmistakable and drew several involuntary upward glances from Sidra. Anya pretended not to notice.

"I came to see about a mosaic piece you had on display at the opening. It was a silhouette of a cat," Anya replied, in a tone that she hoped conveyed innocence.

"Yes, I believe the piece you're referring to is *The Pero Cat*, but I'm afraid it's been sold," Sidra replied.

Initially, Anya's interest in acquiring the mosaic had been genuine. Since then, many factors had served to cool that interest.

There was an awkward silence during which Anya thought she heard the muffled creak and soft thud of a door being closed on the second floor.

Sidra had set her purchases down on the nearest table and was now staring at her with her arms folded defensively. "I would offer to make an inquiry for you, but I happen to know it's the only one of its kind," she said.

"Maybe the buyer would consider selling it to me," Anya submitted. "I'm sure you have a record of the sale upstairs in your office." Anya knew she was pushing it, but she was on a bit of a high, feeling fully vindicated by the confirmation of her suspicions. Instead of fear—newfound courage had arisen in her.

"No need. I remember very well who purchased it. It was Ethan Notah. I believe you know him? He said it was a gift for someone special."

It was Anya's turn now to be sidelined by the unexpected. Ethan had been working at the clinic on Saturday and couldn't attend the opening. How did he know about *The Pero Cat*? Had Desda steered him toward it? Had he purchased it for her—for Cats 'n' Cocktails?

Sidra's hand flew to her throat as a snide burst of laughter escaped her. "Oh, dear! Perhaps *you* are that special someone? I hope I haven't put my foot in it." The disingenuous apology was laced with something more akin to contempt.

"I'm not sure, though it's possible. I won't tell if you won't," Anya countered. It was a bold response that was loaded with innuendo.

Sidra was careful not to signal that she had grasped Anya's meaning.

Another awkward silence ensued as both women dug in their heels, determined to stand their ground.

That's when Anya noticed that the curator's hands and smock were dotted with paint smudges. "Been doing a little painting?" she asked, not bothering to disguise the accusatory edge that had crept into her tone.

Sidra brushed her hands together and smoothed a few invisible wrinkles in her top. "Yes, I've been endeavoring to give several of the upstairs rooms a fresh coat of paint—as time permits, of course."

Anya smirked. She'd had enough high school and undergrad art classes to know cadmium red when she saw it, not to mention mars black, and if she wasn't mistaken, a hint of phthalo blue. One didn't paint interior walls in oils. The woman had to be the worst liar Anya had ever met. Moreover, Sidra had to know that she had seen right through her feeble attempt to deceive her.

All at once, the darker implications of her fact-finding mission began to sink in. Anya's euphoria and so-called courage faded—forthwith, replaced by the cold chill of newly rising fear. She decided it was time to go.

"Well, then, I'll be off. Sorry to interrupt your breakfast. Have a nice day," Anya said, hastily exiting the gallery. She was so flustered that she almost forgot she'd parked a few doors up in front of Smoky's. Shakily, she gunned the engine and sped toward McClean's.

The sheriff's Blazer and a moving van were parked out in front of the emporium. He and Sam were in the process of loading up what looked to be the antique breakfront from Martine's dining room.

Sheriff Wakefield frowned at her as she skidded into a parking space up ahead of them.

"Where's the fire?" he grumbled, as she leapt from her vehicle.

Anya chose to ignore his comment for the moment. She was desperate to tell him about her recent findings. He would know what to do. She rushed over to him, breathlessly.

"Martine's coming home today," he continued. "I thought you and Desda were going to clean up a little bit in there," he said.

"Where are you going with that?" Anya asked, pointing to the breakfront.

"The Cruz sisters' place. Martine's got another moving van on the way to deliver some furnishings from her sister's house and her antique store. She's getting rid of some things to make room for it all."

"Desda and I will get right over there and straighten up, but first there's something else that I think needs your attention," Anya insisted urgently.

The sheriff gave one last heave-ho to the breakfront, and Sam dragged it on board the truck. He leaned against the tailgate and wiped his brow. "I gotta pick up Martine. Can it wait?" he asked.

"Well, I guess it can, but it is important. Something strange is going on over at the art gallery," Anya said, pressing on as he and Sam pulled the rear cargo door down and hitched it tight.

"At the gallery?" the sheriff replied, frowning and

checking his watch. He seemed in no mood to hear whatever it was she was about to tell him.

Sam shoved his hands in his pockets and listened with interest.

"Are you aware of anyone staying at the gallery other than Sidra? A partner, relative, gentleman friend, anyone?" Anya asked.

Sheriff Wakefield sighed and shook his head. He looked puzzled. It was the same look she'd detected on Tate's face when she'd sought to convince him of the clandestine associate's existence. Though she could practically hear the blood rushing through her veins, Anya worked hard to keep her voice calm and controlled.

"Well, someone is there. For some reason, she's hiding somebody upstairs in her office. Whoever it is, they have not made themselves known to anyone in town. Don't you think that's odd?"

The sheriff considered this for less than half a second before saying, "Well, *Anya*, I'll admit that's *odd*, but I can't go rushing in there, guns blazing, and demand to know who's upstairs."

Anya instantly realized that she had picked the worst possible time to bring this up to him. He was clearly fatigued and in a hurry to pick up Martine.

"No crime has been committed," he went on to say. "She's not a suspect in any kind of wrongdoing. She has a right to her privacy. Now, I've got to get this stuff unloaded over at Kathleen and Donna's place and get to the airport, but I will do what I can to look into it, OK?" The sheriff shifted his hat farther back on his head and got into the truck with Sam. "Meantime," he added, leaning out the window, "go get Desda. Do something about that mess in there."

It took less than an hour for her and Desda to restore some semblance of order to Martine's shop. In the process, they noticed something interesting. Strangely enough, the intruder had focused most of his or her attention on a thorough search of the vault. What had they been looking for?

It was about 10:30 when an even larger moving van, with Louisiana plates, pulled to the curb in front of the emporium. At 10:35, the sheriff's Blazer rolled up and parked right behind it.

Anya and Desda hurried out to greet Martine; however, the woman who emerged gracefully from the passenger's side was virtually unrecognizable as the Martine Decoudreau they knew.

They stared in stunned silence at the woman in the well-tailored, dove gray suit and matching heels. Instead of the musical jingle of bracelets, a designer handbag dangled from the imposter's wrist. Her long braids were sleekly wrapped together and gathered near the back of her collar. When she removed her sunglasses,

Anya could swear she was wearing eyeliner, which was completely uncharacteristic for Martine. The sheriff tried to hide a grin as he registered their surprise.

Martine noticed their dazed expressions too and huffed indignantly. "Don look so shocked, you two. My sista was not da only one to receive her education unda da Paris lights. Deez are my business clothes, as I have been away on business. Dere—dat's all," she said in mock protest, adding a wink and a smile.

Martine hugged them both and was most immediately worried about her cats. Anya assured her that all was well, but she could tell they missed her.

"Ching has been acting a bit strange," Anya said, as Martine led the way upstairs to, what was now—an empty dining room.

Martine laughed. "Stranger den usual?"

Anya recalled with a certain degree of amusement that Ethan had said the same thing.

"Well, for one thing, are you aware that he's obsessed with your desk? He's been nesting in the top drawer," Anya went on to elaborate while purposely omitting her discovery of the drawer's false bottom. "He's also been messing with a photograph on the wall over the sideboard, causing it to hang crooked. Every time I re-center it, he turns it all topsy-turvy again.

Martine smiled. "My sista had da most fabulous dining room set in her shop, and a baby grand piano da magistrate allowed me to have before da estate goes to probate. Wasn't dat nice of heem?"

Anya frowned, immediately perceiving Martine's attempt to sidestep her. She knew Martine's tactics all too well. This cagey ploy to divert attention away from the topic of Ching's behavior meant that she knew exactly what his motives were. She just hadn't decided yet whether or not to reveal them to Anya.

Not to be so quickly dispatched, Anya followed her into her bedroom. "Martine?" Anya pressed, watching as the Cajun Queen unwound her braids and deposited a myriad of tiny hairpins into a silver jar on her dresser.

"Dere is something Ching wan you to know about dat desk and da picture. Sometime he even surprise me, you know?" She chuckled.

"So you've seen him tip that picture and nap in your desk drawer?" Anya asked.

"No, I never see heem do dat," she replied, dissolving into peals of laughter. "But he and I both know da secret of da desk and da picture. He wan you to know too. He must trust you very much!"

Anya leaned against the door frame. "Well, are you going to explain it to me, or should I ask him?"

Anya could see that Martine had no intention of spoiling the mystery. Quite the contrary. Through her evasive responses, she'd managed to create a delicious air of suspense—and she meant to prolong and savor it.

"I will tell you everything and so much more, but not today. I wan to go home to da lake. I need to recover my spirit and spend time wid my furry friends, and maybe da sheriff too," she added coyly. "You come out to da lake tomorrow. We'll have breakfast and talk, OK, Sha?"

In acknowledgement of Martine's present state of exhaustion, Anya gave a silent nod of agreement and left her to settle in.

Wending her way across the catwalk to McClean's, she paused to watch the sheriff and the movers below. Her curiosity intensified when Sheriff Wakefield removed a desktop computer, hard drive, and laptop from the back of the moving van. He placed these items in the trunk of his Blazer. Were they Tame's computers? Had Martine uncovered valuable information about her sister, the circumstances behind her death, or possibly the bombing of the hotel?

The sheriff closed his trunk and looked directly up at her. The lawman's uncanny sixth sense had told him someone was watching. There was an uncomfortable moment as their eyes met; then he climbed into his vehicle and sped away.

Most of the cats were napping when Anya arrived at the lake house to pack up her things. They regarded her with hazy eyes and groggy expressions when she announced to them that Martine had returned. She couldn't help feeling that on some level they understood, especially Ching, who appeared in the window, parting the curtains with his whiskers as she was pulling away. Anya felt a wave of sadness wash over her. She had enjoyed her time with them. She was going to miss all of this beauty and serenity and the loving company of the cats.

It was nearly 2 a.m. when Anya crawled into bed after closing McClean's. By 2:22, she was dreaming.

She and Ching were walking through the forest together, Anya tramping heavily and Ching springing along beside her. It was getting dark. He was leading her along a crooked, overgrown path, deeply shadowed by the towering presence of hundred-year-old aspens and even older pines. He moved deliberately, deeper and deeper into the forest, as though he had a destination in mind.

Martine's words swirled like phantoms in her head. "Ching wan you to know something."

Anya trailed the cat as closely as she could in the receding light, scrambling over piles of deadfall and, turning her ankle twice on the rocks and furrows that lay in wait. If he hadn't paused now and again to let her catch up, she might have lost sight of him altogether.

Soon she began to recognize her surroundings. She could hear the gentle lapping of the waves coming in off of the lake. They were somewhere up near the beaver's dam.

They embarked upon a clearing, and Ching stiffened and crouched. Anya crouched too. Ching lifted his chin, flaring his tiny nostrils as he sniffed the air. The smell of smoke from a campfire enveloped them. Anya heard the distant wail of a locomotive whistle, and the clatter of metal on metal as the cars rattled across the Lake Increase train trestle bridge.

There was a lone encampment in the clearing, where a tent had been raised and a small fire burned. Beside the fire, she observed the figure of a man. He was hunched over what looked like a primitively constructed spit. He had a string of fish hanging from it, but they were black and on fire. The man didn't care. He crouched there, slowly turning the smokejack, watching with indifference as large chunks of burnt fish flesh disintegrated and dropped into the flames.

His form and figure struck a familiar chord in her, though she couldn't see his face. Anya felt afraid of the man. She and Ching didn't belong there. They were already at great risk of being seen.

She looked around for Ching then, panic mounting in her chest. A rustling of leaves above her disclosed his whereabouts. He was perched in a tree, high above her. Anya gasped in horror as the limb to which the cat clung swayed dangerously beneath his weight. It wouldn't sustain him long. A low growl rumbled deep within his chest as the branch cracked, and Ching fought to stay aloft. Anya scrambled into position, praying she could catch him. Rising steadily, the grumble became a howl, and then a bloodcurdling scream that tore Anya from sleep in an instant.

She awoke in a state of panic and confusion, unable to recall many details of the dream.

SIXTEEN

Anya arrived early for breakfast at Martine's. She'd been missing the cats and was looking forward to seeing them. Ching flew down from one of the beams overhead. He catapulted off one of the overstuffed chairs and raced to the door to greet her. Zia came trotting swiftly after him, as quickly as her short little legs would allow. The other cats followed, caroling warm greetings. They encircled her legs, tails waving joyfully. Maybe they'd missed her too? Anya bent to give attention to each one of them, imparting words of endearment for such an enthusiastic reception.

"Anya! Is dat you, dear?" Martine called out to her from the kitchen.

"Yes, but I've been intercepted by the welcoming committee! Need any help in there?" Anya asked.

Martine poked her head out of the kitchen. "Let's have breakfast on da deck, yes? Come fix your plate. I have coffee too," she said.

The old Martine was back, looking radiant in a sea-green batik-dyed gown, braids swinging about her slender shoulders, and armfuls of bracelets jingling at her wrists.

She had filled the house with fresh flowers from her gardens. Vases of deeply fragrant, late-blooming lilacs, perfumy peonies, and antique roses had been placed all around the main room, out of reach of the cats. Anya could see that there was also an enormous bouquet on the table outside.

Martine had prepared a rich breakfast casserole, country fried potatoes, and fresh fruit, all of which was served on china and accompanied by the "good" silver.

At first, Anya thought it odd that, over breakfast, Martine wanted to talk about James Beckwith, Charles Firth, the history of the partnership, the town, and the legendary treasure. She was beginning to suspect another one of Martine's diversionary tactics until the conversation took an unexpected turn that shattered the fabric of Anya's reality forever.

"We were jus a couple of single businesswomen, and she a single mother as well," Martine said, referring to Anya's mother, Kate. "It was like a game, searchin for da hidden treasure. A little excitement in what were otherwise long, dull days of tireless work. Da search added intrigue and a sense of adventure to our colorless lives. One weekend we were here, sippin scotch in front of da fire, when we heard a commotion in da study—a kind of scrapin, bangin sound and loud howlin from

Ching. Thinkin he was injured—we rushed in and saw heem sittin cock-eyed in my desk drawer. The bottom of da drawer was tilted upward, revealin a hidden compartment I had never known existed. Do you wan to guess what we found inside?"

Anya couldn't breathe. She had never told Martine that Ching had led her to discover the secret of the desk that night. There hadn't been anything inside of it, though, when she had made her finding.

"Da map … in James Beckwith's own hand, detailing where he had stashed heez loot! It was accompanied by a bank ledger dat notated each bank note and bond, as well as total deposits of silver ingots and gold bars dat he had squirreled away!" Martine clapped her hands together and squealed with laughter as she recalled the pivotal moment.

Anya dropped her fork, chipping the delicate china plate. She stared at Martine, eyes fixed, mouth agape.

A triumphant smile played at the corners of Martine's lips. She was clearly enjoying Anya's reaction and allowed for a greatly extended pause to relish it before continuing with her story.

"We dashed into town—unable to wait for mornin to investigate. Da fortune was in da exact place named by da map, and a very clever place it was! I doubt dat we would have ever found it if it wasn't for Ching. We were still debating about who to entrust wid our finding when your mother passed away. I've shared all of dis with da sheriff. He recommends leaving it where it is until Tame's murder is solved. Den I will turn it over to da law offices of Sterling, Nithercott, and McSwain—let dem handle da details, taxes, and such," Martine explained.

It was a logical course of action. Beau Nithercott of Sterling, Nithercott, and McSwain was Noni Landale's father. He and his wife, Martha, were dear friends of Martine's.

Anya was stunned! The legend was true! James Beckwith had hidden his money and died without ever revealing its location. It was surreal to learn that her mother and Martine had unearthed it more than a hundred years later.

Anya's head was spinning as she tried to process all of what Martine had told her. Randomly she wondered if Martine could make Bloody Marys.

She suddenly realized that Martine had let another detail slip that had been previously unconfirmed. "Wait … murder? So, Tame was definitely the target in the hotel bombing?" Anya whispered the words.

Martine nodded sadly. "Tame wasn't alone in her quest to get to da Beckwith fortune."

Simply put, Martine went on to explain that she had seen some disturbing evidence on Tame's computer that indicated Tame didn't have a blackmailer so much as she had a partner, a male accomplice. At this point, they had his username, but his true identity was still unknown.

Email exchanges on Tame's computer indicated that the two of them had come to believe that Martine was in possession of the Beckwith fortune after Tame had come across a picture of the desk in a book, *Trappers and Traders—North American Legends*. As an experienced antiques dealer, she knew by its origins that the desk likely had a hidden compartment. It was a common feature employed by the maker. Tame became convinced that the desk might have held a map, or perhaps even a diary, that had revealed the location of the money. She'd come to believe that Martine had probably laid her hands on the treasure many years ago.

She and her partner then devised a scheme in which Tame would get Martine to give her half of the money, or reveal its location if she was shielding it from tax considerations, by claiming that she was being blackmailed.

"I was suspicious from da start, of course," Martine confessed. "She didn't even much try to disguise da real purpose behind her visit. She didn't wan to discuss da blackmail at all. Instead, our talk centered around James Beckwith's desk. Tame insisted to take a look at da desk. When I refused, she immediately accused me of having found Beckwith's treasure and demanded her fair share. Naturally, I denied it. I tol her she was mistaken. Dere was no secret compartment, no papers, no map, which was true enough since Kate and I had moved da map to a new hiding place years ago. It is behind da photo of da original Beckwith cabin, hanging over da sideboard. I tol her dere was no treasure to be found, but dat I would be happy to offer her legal assistance to resolve dis attempt to blackmail her. Tame was incensed. She called me a liar and stormed out."

Martine went on to say that the sheriff had done some checking of his own, starting with a call to the New Orleans P.D. He'd been able to determine rather quickly that the blackmail claims were, in fact, false. They'd informed him that they had not had any contact with anyone named Tame Decoudreau.

The sheriff also surmised that when Tame failed to get any money out of Martine, her partner had chosen to cut his losses and eliminate her by blowing up the hotel where she was staying. He probably hadn't expected any evidence of the pipe bombs to be left behind. This miscalculation ended up drawing a lot of unwanted attention when the explosion was ruled a double homicide instead of accidental death. Getting his hands on Beckwith's money, however, had become an obsession for him. That's when he'd broken into the emporium to search for it himself.

Martine sighed and stared out at the lake. "Da sheriff is goin to stay wid me up here until Tame's accomplice is apprehended."

Anya pushed her eggs around her plate, mulling over all of what Martine had shared. As impossible as it seemed, she was sure that Ching had been trying to tell her the story of the map, the desk, and ultimately the Beckwith fortune by exposing the desk drawer's false bottom and by tipping the picture that concealed the map—but why? When she eventually looked up, she saw that Martine was staring at her. Her amber eyes were glowing.

"You know what dis means, don you, Sha? I don think you're gettin da whole picture! You're a rich woman! Half of dat money was your mother's. She and I agreed to split it if we ever found it! So, now her share will be passed to you."

"Mau-OW!" came a loud retort from Ching who had been listening at the screen door.

Utterly shocked, Anya collapsed backward into her chair and gasped, "I don't believe it."

"Shhh .... ," Martine whispered, as a hummingbird swooped in unexpectedly to sample the flowers on the table.

Anya froze while the tiny creature hovered directly in front of her—inches from her face. For the briefest of moments, they were eye to eye, each studying the other. She was mesmerized by the brilliant iridescent green of his minute body and the vibrating whir of his wings, and then—zip—he was gone.

Martine exhaled softly. She'd been holding her breath during the hummingbird's visit. She reached for her fork and said, "You won't tell any of dis to anyone, of course. When it's safe, we will let da attorneys sort it out."

Seeing the look of shock and disbelief etched on Anya's face, Martine turned to Ching and said, "Uh-oh Ching, I think da shock was too much for her." She chuckled and added, "Anya … dear … , would you like a Bloody Mary?"

SEVENTEEN

After that fateful breakfast on Martine's deck, the rest of the week was pretty much a blur.

On Monday, Anya had been in the position of having to leverage her pub and forego a portion of her salary for the next five years to pursue a new dream—a rescue bar and grill named Cats 'n' Cocktails— the first of its kind.

On Tuesday, she'd learned that she was about to become an heiress to a multimillion, perhaps billion-dollar fortune, so long as she and Martine kept breathing. She'd also realized on that day that Martine had stealthily refrained from divulging the exact hiding place of Beckwith's treasure. It was a fact that had made Anya smile.

On Wednesday, Ethan had called to cancel dinner for the second time in a row. He'd been forced to work overtime all week.

It was on Thursday, however, that Anya awoke filled with dread as she groped her way to the kitchen for coffee. Today was the day she had promised to help

Jimmy Shaw steal dogs from dangerous gangsters in the middle of the night.

Anya combed her fingers through her tangled hair and sighed. She would do almost anything for Jimmy and his dogs. In fact, she'd decided that, once she was in possession of her half of Beckwith's money, she was going to donate a sum large enough to build that new wing Jimmy wanted—to expand his facility. She was looking immensely forward to that, but these rescue missions were a whole different story. They always held the potential for peril to people and animals, and something about this particular raid was setting off alarm bells in her head.

To add to her misery, tonight would be the first time she'd seen Ethan since Sunday, and the conditions would be less than auspicious.

Anya poured coffee and took the catwalk over to Martine's, enticed by the spicy aroma of whatever the Cajun Queen was preparing for breakfast. Martine had been staying at the lake as planned but returned early each day to open the emporium. Upon reaching the kitchen, Anya was surprised to see the sheriff seated at Martine's table—though she didn't know why. All things considered, she should have anticipated his presence.

"Good morning, Sha!" Martine greeted her cheerfully.

"Anya," the sheriff mumbled. His greeting was more of a reproachful acknowledgment of her presence than anything else, but that was characteristic of the lawman's nature.

"Good morning. I'm sorry, I didn't know you had company," Anya replied, suddenly feeling self-conscious in her pajamas and tattered old robe. She pulled a hairband from her wrist and worked to contain her bedraggled locks into something resembling a ponytail.

"I saw da gator man while I was down in Louisiana. Got some fine gator boudin from heem! I'm makin it now wid some eggs hussarde and lost bread for da sheriff here. How 'bout you? You wanna try some? Dere's plenty!" Martine announced.

Anya knew boudin was a special kind of Cajun sausage made with onion, celery, bell pepper, cooked rice, and apparently, in this case, alligator meat. It was a delicacy unique to Acadian and Cajun culture and hard to find outside of southern Louisiana unless you found yourself in Martine's kitchen. Eggs hussarde was a little like eggs benedict. It was served with hollandaise sauce, but there was some kind of red wine sauce involved, as well. It was all a little complex for Anya's admittedly underdeveloped palate. She wondered in amusement what the sheriff thought of Martine's authentic dishes.

Martine laughed and shook her head when Anya politely declined the boudin and eggs and chose instead to stick with coffee and two pieces of lost bread—basically French toast—which she proceeded to eat over the sink.

Anya's attention was drawn to the doorway when Ching entered the room. He must have somehow persuaded Martine to provide him with a change of scenery. Ears forward, whiskers back, he paused to sniff the air before gliding smoothly to the counter beside her.

Anya held the plate of lost bread toward Ching so that he could get a good sniff. She'd learned long ago that cats don't so much want to share what you're eating. They just want to smell it.

Ching sniffed the bread as if it might jump off the plate and bite him. He immediately recoiled in disgust, curling his lips and opening his mouth in revulsion. It was a reaction known as the Flehmen Response. Anya had read that it was a behavior not exclusive to cats. It had been observed in many other animals too. It didn't necessarily indicate an offensive smell; however, it always seemed to in Ching's case.

The breakfast conversation was light, and the sheriff appeared to enjoy the food, savoring each bite and remarking on it favorably more than once. They were a strange pair. Strange, but oddly perfect.

Feeling like a third wheel, Anya inhaled her bread, thanked Martine for breakfast, and bid them both goodbye.

She took a quick shower, skipped the makeup, and dressed in a hurry before heading downstairs to McClean's. The place was empty, save for her faithful friend and manager, Desda March, who was keeping company with her husband, Paul. Paul was enjoying what looked to be a cup of Irish coffee. Since his retirement from an accounting firm in Chenoah Falls, he'd become something of a permanent fixture at McClean's—at least when he wasn't on the golf course. The Marchs were both grinning at her like a couple of Cheshire cats.

"Greetings, you two. What could possibly be so humorous at this hour?"

That's when she noticed that the sheriff's Blazer was parked right out front rather than in back of the emporium. In the absence of any pressing police business to explain it—the visit signaled that it was a social call. "Ahhh, I see," she said, with a nod of understanding.

"Looks like they've decided to take it public—their relationship I mean," remarked Paul.

Desda giggled. "Yeah, we've been debating about what Martine is cooking up there for poor Sheriff Wakefield!"

"Let me assure you, that's one breakfast party you wouldn't want to attend. She's rolled out some pretty hardcore Cajun fare this morning," Anya said, laughing.

Seeing that her comment had served to further pique their interest, she decided to entice them with a couple of details. "Two words … gator boudin."

"Gator?! As in alligator?" Desda rightly guessed.

"I've had alligator before," Paul replied matter of factly.

Desda and Anya stared at him incredulously.

"See there, Desda," Anya teased. "After all of these years together, the mystery's not dead. The man remains an enigma."

Paul polished off his coffee and gave Desda a quick kiss. "Gotta go, honey. Got an early tee time," he said. He gave them both a parting wave on his way out.

"He sure is enjoying his freedom, isn't he?" Anya correctly deduced.

Desda smiled. "He keeps busy."

Ever since Anya had learned about the Beckwith fortune, she'd been struggling to keep from telling Desda everything she'd learned. Desda and her mother had been the best of friends, and now she was one of Anya's nearest and dearest.

Desda and Paul were planning on taking a trip while McClean's was closed for renovations. She'd had the brochures lined up behind the bar for weeks trying to decide on a destination.

Anya wanted so desperately to tell her she would pay for the trip. After so many years of devoted service and friendship, no one deserved it more, but Anya had no way of knowing when the funds would be available. She'd also promised Martine to keep it a secret for now, but she would make it up to Desda down the road.

Anya also had yet to fill Desda in on her misadventure at the gallery, to include Sidra's reveal that Ethan had purchased *The Pero Cat*.

"I knew it!" Desda shouted, pounding the bar with her fist. "I knew she was hiding someone up there. I can't believe the sheriff isn't more intrigued by this. In my experience, if you feel the need to hide something or someone, it's because you're up to no good. Talk about a red flag, more of a solar flare if you ask me."

"I don't know. I guess he has other things on his mind these days," Anya replied, wishing she could tell Desda what those things entailed.

"I suppose so. They still haven't arrested anyone in the hotel bombing, and the break-in at Martine's will probably never be solved."

Anya cringed as Desda, unknowingly, touched on the truth she'd been hiding.

"Don't let on to Ethan that you know about *The Pero Cat*," Desda warned. "I'm the one who suggested it to him. He's planning to give it to you to commemorate the opening of Cats 'n' Cocktails."

Anya assured her she wouldn't.

"So, tonight, you get to help Jimmy with one of his crazy rescues. Oh, boy … ," Desda huffed.

"Ugh, yes. Let's not talk about it. I'm nervous enough as it is," Anya replied. "I've got to get rid of that Land Rover."

It was a busy day at McClean's. The lunch crowd was larger than usual. They also had a little inventory to perform, followed by orders to replenish their stock—and to top it off, Craig had called in sick with the flu.

Anya made it her first priority to call Sarah Katz over at Drexsler's Deli. She hoped she'd be interested in collaborating on the benefit for CF Stray Rescue.

Sarah and Jason Katz were the owners of the premier deli in Four Oaks. They had initially wanted to name the deli Katz's Kosher Kitchen. When it was dutifully pointed out that there was already a famous delicatessen with a similar name, the couple had elected to use Sarah's maiden name instead, and Drexsler's Deli was born.

"I'd love to cater for you! Thanks so much for thinking of us!" Sarah exclaimed when Anya pitched the idea to her. "I'll shoot a menu over to you, and you let me know what you'd like us to provide. I'm so excited!"

As the time drew near to meet Jimmy and the others

at the Notahs' ranch, Anya was running low on energy and decided coffee was the answer. She swigged down a few cups, hoping for a second wind, but to her consternation, it failed to help her generate any real strength. Instead, it left her feeling edgy and jittery, which only increased her exhaustion.

She was on her way out the door when she noticed that one of the business cards customers routinely pinned to the corkboard near the entrance was lying on the floor. When she bent down to retrieve it, she saw that it wasn't a business card at all, but a parting gift from Ching, who had already been carted back to the lake by Martine and the sheriff. It was one of Martine's divination cards belonging to a deck known as The Lenormand. It was a small game deck or "jeu de petite".

Anya had been fascinated by the tiny cards when she was a child, probably because they featured colorful illustrations of squirrels, mice, and bears, to name a few, and some very mysterious looking people. Before their use as oracle cards, they'd been used by children to play games with curious sounding names like Sheep's Head. Martine had told her that the cards had been named after a famous nineteenth-century French fortune-teller named Marie Antoinette Lenormand. Interestingly enough, it was said that she never actually used the deck that became her namesake.

This particular card depicted a dog, a beagle to be exact—gripping a leash in his teeth, besieging his owner to take up a walk. Anya slipped the card in her pocket and trudged to her vehicle.

She was the last to arrive at the ranch. Stepping out of her truck, she noticed that there were two other vehicles parked in front—Tate's blue pickup and a gray Toyota Sequoia. Anya presumed that the Sequoia belonged to Jimmy's volunteer, Kelly, a tough-looking girl dressed in fatigues.

Everyone was gathered up on the porch waiting for her. The sheriff and Old Sam were there too. Jimmy, Nigel, Ethan, Tate, and Kelly came out to greet her. Ethan climbed into her truck to recline the rear seats for her. That's when Anya noticed that he, Nigel, and Jimmy were all wearing Kevlar vests, undoubtedly on loan from Sheriff Wakefield. Anya felt a chill creep under her skin.

"Anya, I'll ride with you," Jimmy said. "We'll be the pilot car. Nigel and Kelly will be behind us, and Ethan and Tate will bring up the rear. Kelly and I timed the trip yesterday. The compound is about twenty minutes from the bridge down a dirt road marked only by a post with a blue flag tied to it. There are two houses and two outbuildings. We'll focus on the first of the two outbuildings. That's where we think they're keeping maybe around eight dogs, give or take. The drivers will stay in their vehicles with the engines running. The three of us will go in and grab the dogs."

Ethan handed out headlamps to Nigel and Jimmy and gave Anya a wink. "Dark out there," he said with a sinister grin. He bent down to give her what was meant to be a reassuring kiss. "I've missed you this week," he whispered.

His attempts to dispel her fears with jokes and affection were in vain. She couldn't wait for it all to be over.

Briefly, Anya thought about the night Tate had asked her if she and Ethan were getting back together. She still couldn't fathom where his interest lay in that, but she guessed he had his answer now.

"We'll cut to running lights only—once we make access to the dirt road," Jimmy continued. "We'll get as close as we can to the first outbuilding, then circle around so that all three vehicles are pointed out toward the road, with rear doors facing the enclosure. We'll load up fast and move out, hopefully undetected, fingers crossed."

Anya registered nothing but confidence in the faces surrounding her. Old Sam didn't look the least bit concerned, rocking away in his chair up on the porch, but he was a stoic. The sheriff was even more aloof, as he chewed off the end of a fresh cigar and set about stoking it.

"OK, let's hit it," Jimmy said, sending everyone to their vehicles.

Sensing her apprehension from afar, the sheriff called out to her, "Don't worry, young lady. We'll see you at the bridge."

Anya turned to look at the sheriff. "Tell me something, Sheriff, was that really gator in that boudin?"

Holding a match to his stogie, the sheriff neither confirmed nor denied it. He would eat burnt shoe leather if Martine served it, she thought.

The three vehicles caravanned toward the Chenoah Falls Bridge and made the Dixon County line about twenty minutes later, just as Jimmy had said.

They turned off down a dirt road with only the dim orange glow of their vehicles' running lights to guide the way. They hadn't gone far when the faint gleam of lights from the two houses on the property first became visible through the trees. About thirty yards from the first of two outbuildings, they circled the vehicles.

Tate and Ethan rolled up silently next to Anya. Kelly and Nigel pulled alongside of them.

Jimmy gave everyone a thumbs-up. He strapped on his headlamp, and grabbed his leads and a bolt cutter to gain entrance to the building.

"Keep the engine running," he whispered to her.

All three men, clothed in black, slipped away into the darkness. It was not unlike watching a SEAL team infiltrate a terrorist camp. Anya clicked the release that unlatched the rear door and kept watch for their return in her rearview mirror.

Once she glanced nervously over at Tate, sitting in his truck beside her. He'd been monitoring the scene in his own mirror. Peripherally glimpsing her movements, he met her gaze and gave her a wink.

The minutes ticked by as Anya searched the darkness for any signs of the men when suddenly she heard a loud humming noise. She jerked her head in Tate's direction. His eyes were wide with recognition. Instantly there came a loud BANG, and night became day. Floodlights lit up the area like the noonday sun. Jimmy and the others must have triggered a silent alarm.

Shouts could be heard coming from the houses on the property. The whole thing was heading south. Anya shot a look of sheer terror at Tate. Tate raised a hand, calling for calm, and jabbed his thumb over his shoulder.

She could see their three friends coming up fast now. Each had two or three dogs leashed in each hand. They were barreling toward the vehicles as loud popping sounds were heard ripping through the air. At first, Anya thought it was a backfire from Tate's truck, but he was still parked, waiting for Ethan. When projectiles started pinging off the vehicles—Anya realized they were under fire.

Tate ducked down and motioned with his hand for

her to do the same. He mouthed the words, "Get ready to go," and pointed toward the road.

Anya ducked down and looked over her shoulder. She could see the silhouettes of several figures in close pursuit of Jimmy, Nigel, and Ethan. There were many more muzzle flashes as Jimmy whipped open the rear door, catapulted four dogs into the back of her truck, and dove in after them.

All hell was breaking loose. Kelly's vehicle dug out first in a spray of dirt and gravel. Ethan hurtled into the bed of Tate's truck, shouting, "Go! Go!" He had four dogs with him too.

Tate lit out then, and Anya jammed her foot down hard on the gas to follow. She nearly clipped Tate's truck as she moved out in last position. Jimmy hadn't had time to secure the rear door. It came down hard on one or both of his legs, she couldn't tell. He struggled to grab hold of it and secure it as Anya careened wildly out onto the main road.

It wasn't long before she could hear Jimmy's voice crooning softly to the anxious dogs, soothing them with his gentle, reassuring tone. She could also hear the clicking sounds from his camera phone as he took pictures of what he called "the freedom ride". He posted photos from all of his rescues on his social media site. He would also use them as legal documentation when this case eventually went to court.

A dense fog obscured the road up ahead, as the bridge came looming into view. The cold water below mixed with the warmer air above, creating a swirling mist and an eerie yet welcoming sight. Anya glanced in the rearview mirror again, and seeing no evidence that they were being tailed, she began to relax.

There were two vehicles off to the side of the road, Sam Notah's truck and the sheriff's Blazer. The sheriff had his dog, Billy, with him. He was still puffing away on his Havana, with his shotgun resting casually against one shoulder. Sam was standing on the opposite side, holding stop sticks. Anya tapped the brakes as they raced by, slowing to the speed limit for the rest of the trip.

"Damn," she heard Jimmy curse and sigh from the rear.

Anya glanced back to see him reclining beneath a pile of snorting, snuffling, and seemingly grateful dogs.

"You OK?" she asked.

"Yeah, but you better drop me off at Chenoah Falls Memorial. I'm gonna need somebody to dig a bullet out of my leg."

Anya stepped on the gas.

EIGHTEEN

The hospital was only a block down from Jimmy's center. Tate looked confused when Anya cut around him and sped past the entrance to CF Stray Rescue.

She'd called ahead to the ER. A team of doctors and nurses were standing by when she skidded to a stop at the entrance. A preliminary assessment revealed that Jimmy had a nine-millimeter bullet in his calf, but he was expected to make a full recovery.

Before they whisked him away to surgery, Jimmy made Anya promise to go home after dropping off the dogs.

"Go home," he said. "I've got plenty of people who will check on me later. They'll probably overrun the waiting room and get themselves kicked out."

Anya told him she would return in the morning with breakfast.

"Thank you, Anya! Tell everyone thank you for me," he called out as he disappeared through the hospital's sliding doors.

Anya drove back to Stray Rescue with her surprisingly calm canine cargo. She passed Tate again on the way. After dropping off Ethan and their dogs, he must have somehow surmised that she was heading to the hospital. He made a bold U-turn and fell in behind her.

Arriving at the center, the scene was exactly as she had expected. Jimmy's business approach was steeped in traditions that allowed him to reward his volunteers and celebrate the work he loved so much. Tonight was no exception.

The backlot was strung with party lights. There were tables and chairs, party sandwiches, chips, and kegs of beer. Blues music, of which Jimmy was a big fan, was playing over the loudspeakers.

A triage unit of sorts had been set up to assess the new intakes. It was attended by about twenty volunteers and two local veterinarians, Ethan and Doc Lafferty.

This was how Jimmy liked to do things. For him, it was a victory celebration. He would be disappointed to be sitting this one out.

Everyone rushed over to inquire about Jimmy. Anya assured them that he would make a full recovery. They all breathed a sigh of relief and escorted the dogs from Anya's truck over to the triage area.

A casual inspection of the rear of the truck revealed that the old Land Rover had taken some fire, evidenced by several bullet holes.

A quick check of the dogs turned up no emergencies. All would require only minor medical attention.

Anya noticed that Nigel needed a little minor medical attention himself. He was trying to disguise it, but his hand was bleeding quite a lot. He was pouring bottled water between his thumb and forefinger.

"Hey, what happened?" she asked, taking Nigel's hand and leading him over to her truck.

"Nothing, just a little cut. One of the leashes sliced through my palm," he said.

Anya dug out her first aid kit. She cleaned and dressed the wound while Nigel winced.

"At least you don't need stitches," she said.

Nigel smiled gratefully and hugged her.

Ethan was busy assisting Doc Lafferty for about twenty minutes or so, after which he rejoined their little group where they were gathered around one of the kegs.

"Better slow down there," Ethan said to Nigel. "You have an engagement party to go to in about fourteen hours. Barely enough time to sleep and get dressed. Barely enough for you anyway," he said, laughing.

Anya had completely forgotten about the engagement party. She needed time to sleep and shop for a new dress. More importantly, she had a breakfast date with Jimmy.

"Not me," Tate said. "Sorry, Nigel, but I already sent

along my regrets. I'm going to sleep right here in my truck, grab my gear at first light, and then me and Rob are hitting the road. We're exploring a new location in Ohio for the website. The donations were off the charts for this one. I've never seen a locale generate so much interest."

Everyone pressed him for more information, but he refused to reveal the target. "You'll have to wait and see," was all Tate would say.

Anya studied Tate's expression. He was grinning with anticipation of a new adventure even as the adrenaline from the last one still surged through his veins. Backlit by the glow of the string lights, the disheveled layers of his hair falling in his eyes, Anya couldn't imagine how such a good looking, talented guy had managed to stay single.

Since Tate was planning to camp at CF Stray Rescue—Anya was tasked with driving Ethan and Nigel home. The sun was coming up by the time she finally burrowed beneath the covers, safe and sound in her own cozy bed. As she drifted off to sleep, she wondered how much she could get for a bullet-riddled, 2010 Land Rover Defender.

It was little more than three hours later when Anya breezed into Jimmy's room with breakfast for two. He was in high spirits, but she got the distinct impression that he was in more pain than he was letting on.

"I hope you haven't eaten yet," she said, unzipping an insulated catering bag. "Bacon, eggs, hash browns, biscuits, and gravy, commonly referred to as breakfast combo number seven on the Landale's Log Cabin menu," she announced.

"You and Noni Landale are lifesavers," Jimmy said with a wink.

Anya gave a thumbs-up. "So, you look great! How are you feeling? How long are they gonna keep you?"

"Not too bad and only a couple of days. Luckily, it wasn't too serious."

Anya poured coffee for them both from a thermos she'd brought from home. They spent the next hour chatting about light-hearted topics, such as Nigel and Cecilia's engagement, Martine cooking gator boudin for the sheriff, Desda's growing hoard of travel brochures, and the fundraiser. Jimmy was excited to hear that Drexsler's would be catering.

"I don't know how well I'll be able to tend bar, though. Doc says I'll probably be on crutches or using a cane for a while."

"You never tend bar well. That's kind of the point!" Anya teased. "Don't worry. We'll have a full staff that day. The patrons will still be able to play stump the bartender. You just do what you can," Anya reassured him.

At about eleven-thirty, a few of Jimmy's volunteers showed up for a visit. They'd clearly made a run into

Four Oaks first. Anya recognized the huge flower arrangement they'd brought him as Rheina Sheridan's work at The Twisted Tulip, and the colorful jar of jellybeans was from Candy's Canes. They had also brought Jimmy pictures and medical reports on all of the dogs taken in the previous night.

Anya took this opportunity to make her exit. She had a little shopping to do before the party that night. She hugged Jimmy, said goodbye to everyone, packed up, and left.

The invitation to the Bennedetto-Notah Engagement Party had read: *black tie optional*, which meant that the male guests could opt out of wearing a tuxedo; however, the dress code still called for formal attire. Anya needed something "designy".

She found exactly what she was looking for at a little boutique called Palmieri's. It was a faux wrap dress, platinum, with a sheer overlay embroidered in metallic silver thread. The sleeves were three-quarter length with bell cuffs. Très chic, Anya thought. It was elegant, though understated, and she had a pair of silver Brazilian leather slides that would match perfectly.

In less than an hour, Anya was on her way home with her purchase. Having had little to no sleep, she was looking forward to a nice long nap ahead of the party.

When she eventually opened her eyes, she felt refreshed, but with an all too familiar feeling of heaviness on her chest. Ching was sound asleep on top of her again, his breath coming in soft, warm puffs against her chin. She stroked him gently to awaken him. Reluctantly, he raised his head to look at her through half-closed lids. He yawned so broadly, she could nearly see his gullet. Stretching one long elegant leg toward her shoulder, it was clear he meant to resettle his head and resume his nap.

"Sorry, your majesty. I've got to get up and get ready," Anya said, sliding out from under him. His lordship's body language indicated that he considered the willful displacement of royalty to be the height of impertinence. He jumped down and strolled to the door with an air of self-importance—shooting her a disapproving glare before slinking off down the hall.

Anya was ravenous, having slept through lunch, and went downstairs to grab something from McClean's. She noticed that Ananda was behind the bar. Desda and Paul were invited to the Bennedettos' tonight as well. Desda must have gone home to change. Anya microwaved a taco in the kitchen and ran back upstairs to get ready herself.

No sooner had she climbed into the shower when she heard the musical refrains of a piano being played. It was coming from the direction of Martine's apartment. She recalled that Martine had mentioned acquiring a piano from her sister's house.

Anya shook off the distraction to focus on her own preparations for the evening. She wanted to look her best, and that meant layers of fragrance, from lotions to perfume, artfully applied makeup, and she was planning to try her hand at a waterfall braid.

As expected, she was all thumbs when it came to executing the intricacies of the braid; however, after several failed attempts, the end result was most satisfactory. Anya surveyed the completed look in the Syroco leaning mirror that graced her living room. The platinum dress had a lustrous sheen visible beneath the embroidered overlay—the delicate silver threads of which glinted when they caught the light.

She grabbed her keys, and a small silver beaded clutch, and made her way over to Martine's. She wanted to show off her new dress and take a peek at the new piano.

There was indeed a beautiful, white, Story & Clark grand piano in the living room, but Martine was not at home. A note had been taped to the door that read:

Anya,
If you happen to see Ching—don't be surprised. He wouldn't come out of hiding when it was time to go, so I had to leave him here for the night. I left him some dinner and water. See you at the Bennedettos'.
Love, Martine

It was not surprising that the piano's lid was closed or that it was covered by a fringed brocade throw to protect the surface from claw marks. Ching was seated on the piano bench using his paw to activate the piano's MIDI touch system. The piano had a player component that Ching had remarkably learned to operate! He effected a smug look in her direction as the keys sprang to life, and music filled the space.

"Ching, you are truly an amazing cat. Does Martine know you've learned to play the piano in her absence? Quite an accomplishment. I stand in awe of your greatness," Anya said, bowing slightly in deference to the feline phenom.

As a means of response, Ching affected a statuesque pose and lifted his chin in a catly kind of nod.

After working long hours at the clinic all week, Ethan ended up having to work late that night too. Anya agreed to meet him at the Bennedettos'. To her surprise, she was met by a valet when she arrived, a young man whom she recognized to be one of their restaurant's waitstaff.

The Bennedettos were another one of the old money families. They ran a successful restaurant, Bennedetto's Surf & Turf, but their real money had been inherited. Alessandro had descended from a long line of winemakers who had once owned more than three thousand acres of vineyards in Umbria,

Italy—some with restaurants and hotels attached. The vineyards and accompanying properties had been sold off many years ago, enriching all future generations of Bennedettos.

The house was more of an estate, a five-thousand square-foot Italianate villa with a swimming pool, tennis courts, lake view, and overlooking it all a gorgeous terrace that ran the full length of the house.

The door was answered by another familiar face, a hostess from Bennedetto's, whose name Anya couldn't readily recall. Stepping inside the grand hall, where an even grander serpentine staircase rose majestically toward the second floor, she marveled at the gleaming marble floors and the spectacular floral arrangements that encircled the space. There were more members of the Bennedettos' waitstaff milling around the interior, some with silver trays of champagne and sugar cubes, others with an array of hors d'oeuvres.

Cossima, Martine, and Jules were gathered near the entrance to the hearth room. Jules was on the arm of a very attractive man. They motioned for her to join them.

"Anya, don't you look lovely!" Cossima exclaimed, slipping a glass of champagne into her hand. *Plop- fizz* went the sugar cube that immediately followed. "Never let the devil see you happy, eh?" She winked as she referenced the old Italian superstition surrounding sugar cubes and champagne.

Anya smiled and raised her glass in tribute. "Everything looks so beautiful, Mrs. Bennedetto, absolutely stunning."

Anya and Cecilia had been friends since childhood, and Anya had been to the mansion many times over the years, but it was still a wonder to behold.

"Oh! Thank you, thank you! You're so sweet to notice." Cossima smiled, giving her an exuberant sidearm hug. "If you ladies will excuse me, I have some other guests to greet. Make your way out to the terrace. There's a lovely breeze coming off the lake!" Cossima exclaimed, hastening away in a rustle of taffeta.

Martine was wearing a dress Anya hadn't seen before. It was a satin gown in a rich amber color that closely matched the Cajun Queen's eyes.

"Martine, are you aware that Ching has taught himself to play the piano?" Anya raised the question playfully.

"Tch! Dat cat! He been playin wid da coffee pot too, started brewin a pot at five o'clock in da mornin!"

Anya snickered, "No, Martine, I reprogrammed it while I was staying there. I forgot to reset it for you!"

Anya noticed that while she, Jules, and Martine were laughing at this, the man at Jules's side seemed slightly confused. Anya also realized that Jules had yet to introduce her gentleman friend.

"Excuse me, I see da Cruz sisters over dere. I have

a chair from da shop in New Orleans dey might like," Martine said, leaving the group.

"Would you be a dear and get Anya and I another glass of champagne, sans sugar cubes?" Jules asked her date, who agreeably decamped in search of a waiter.

"Jules! Aren't you going to introduce him to anyone?" Anya admonished her once he'd gone.

Jules wrinkled her nose and shook her head. "No need. You'll never see him again."

No one had ever made it past the first date with Jules. She wasn't a snob—far from it. She just hadn't found what she was looking for.

"Come with me. I want to show you something," Jules whispered, pulling Anya over to the staircase in the Bennedettos' grand hall. "Look up there," she urged.

Anya was stunned to see the elongated face, crooked nose, and mismatched eyes of the woman in the Modigliani portrait staring down at her.

"Ugh. Déjà vu."

"C'mon," Jules said, carefully lifting a corner of her pale blue gown as they ascended the stairs.

"What's *that* doing here?" Anya asked, giving a shiver.

"Wretched thing, isn't she? Modigliani was a strange character," Jules remarked.

"Has Elizabeth approved its authenticity?"

"No," Jules shook her head. "Elizabeth is still in

Sweden. I was unable to convince Cossima to wait. She wanted it on display for the party tonight. It's on loan from the gallery, but I think Cossima has already put a substantial deposit down on it." Jules unzipped her leather clutch purse and produced a tiny gadget that looked like a microscope equipped with a light.

"What's that thing?" Anya whispered. She looked around to see if Jules's gentleman friend was making the return trip or if anyone else was nearby. They were alone for the moment.

"This is a jeweler's loupe. It's a powerful magnifier. I want to have a look at those thread patterns and the signature."

Jules tossed her long blond hair over one shoulder, held the loupe to one eye, and leaned in close. She inspected several areas of the painting, hovering for an extended period of time over the signature in the lower right-hand corner.

"Here, have a look for yourself," Jules said, passing the mini microscope to Anya. She pulled up an image of the portrait on her cell phone for comparison.

Nervously, Anya took a quick look through the loupe at the signature, which, to her untrained eye, matched the image on Jules's phone precisely.

"Modigliani's signature was admittedly unpredictable. He was known to randomly sign in the upper corners as often as the lower corners of his paintings.

Sometimes he capitalized his name, sometimes not, and he frequently signed in color, not always in black."

Anya couldn't see any difference between the two. Both were signed in yellow, with lower-case lettering at the bottom right-hand corner of the canvas. She squinted uncertainly at Jules.

"You don't see it, do you?" Jules smiled archly.

Anya shook her head.

"Take a look at the letter *d* in the signature. See the loop and the way it curves to the right? He sometimes looped the *d* in his first name, which was Amedeo, not a factor here, but never in Modigliani. See the *d* in the original on my phone. It has a closed stem that curves distinctly to the left. His *d's* always curved left whether looped or closed stem," Jules pointed out.

Anya was amazed. "Then, it's a forgery?"

"To be certain. I'm going to approach Sidra with this first, but if she fails to acquiesce and refund Cossima's money, I'm going to the police. Oh, thank you, darling," Jules said sweetly, switching gears as her date reappeared with the champagne. She slipped the loupe back into her purse, and they all made their way out to the terrace.

"Anya!" Cecilia waved to her, looking very glamorous in an off-shoulder, full-length gown. It was made entirely of champagne-colored Chantilly lace—a champagne gown for a champagne party.

Beside her stood Nigel, who had not been given the "option" this evening. He was looking predictably uncomfortable in his tux.

"Gorgeous dress," Anya commented as they approached.

"Yours too! Palmieri's?" Cecilia guessed correctly.

"As a matter of fact, yes." Anya looked incredulous.

"We shop there all the time. My mother knows the owner," Cecilia explained. "Did you do that waterfall braid yourself?!"

Anya heaved an exasperated sigh. "Yes, it took many, *many* attempts to succeed."

"It's beautiful. What do you think of this?" Cecilia asked, pointing to her own hair. "I've been trying out new styles for the wedding." Her gleaming black hair was loosely curled and arranged in an unstructured ponytail that cascaded over one shoulder. It was lovely, and Anya told her as much.

"Eck," Cecilia said, frowning into Anya's champagne. She snatched a sugar cube from the tray of a passing waiter and dropped it into Anya's glass. "Don't let the devil know you're happy, am I right?" she remarked.

She's becoming her mother, Anya thought, smiling to herself. Admittedly, there were worse things you could aspire to.

A string quartet was setting up at the far end of the

terrace. A parade of floating lanterns drifted serenely across the pool below, and beyond that were the shimmering waters of Lake Increase.

"Such a beautiful setting. You couldn't ask for more," Anya sighed.

"Oh, you know my mom lives to entertain. She hasn't so much as popped her head in at the restaurant all week. She's been working so hard on all of this. She always says the real art of entertaining lies in appearing to pull it off seamlessly," Cecilia replied.

"Mission accomplished," Anya affirmed.

Nigel was tugging at his collar. "Can't I at least remove this bow tie? I'm being strangled here," he huffed.

It was then that Ethan arrived, typifying the bad timing he was famous for. His tie was stuffed into his side pocket. His collar was unbuttoned and askew. "Greetings all!" he said, jingling the cubes in his glass of scotch. He looked more like an interloper than an invited guest.

Cecilia bristled as Nigel started to complain again. Anya gave Ethan a reproving glance, pulled his tie out of his pocket, and held it out to him. Ethan traded his drink to her in exchange for his tie. He promptly set about redressing his neckwear, as the call came that dinner was served.

Anya nodded her approval. "Just in time," she said.

Ethan smiled, kissed her forehead, and offered his arm to escort her to the dining room.

NINETEEN

When the call came that dinner was served, everyone moved inside to the opulent dining room. A spectacular setting awaited the guests replete with bone china, Waterford crystal, and sterling silver. Three twenty-four-inch candelabras, embellished with greenery and red roses, lent a touch of romance to the tablescape.

The guests, in turn, expressed their utmost praise and appreciation for the efforts of their host and hostess. Cossima was highly complimented.

There was a bit of fumbling around as everyone located their place card. Anya had been seated between Martine and Jules and across from Ethan—but at an awkward angle.

Everyone in town had been invited to the after-dinner cocktail party on the terrace; however, dinner had been reserved for a group that represented Cecilia and Cossima's closest friends.

Anya noticed that fourteen places had been set, but there were only thirteen people at the table: Cossima and Alessandro, Nigel and Cecilia, Jules and what's his name, Lila and Mason Stevens, Sharon Bailer, Elijah Whip, Martine, Ethan, and Anya. The empty seat and place setting was to Ethan's left.

Jules immediately noticed the questioning look on Anya's face and whispered, "That seat was originally for my sister, Elizabeth, but she got held up overseas. When word reached Martine's ears that the number of guests expected to attend totalled thirteen, she urged Cossima to set the table for fourteen anyway."

It came as no surprise to Anya that the mysterious fourteenth place setting was tied to some ominous superstition of Martine's.

During the first course, which was Italian wedding soup, a bowl was also set at the empty place. This prompted multiple requests from the guests at their end of the table for Martine to recant the tale of London's Hotel Savoy and the curse of the thirteenth dinner guest.

"Many of da superstitions regarding da number thirteen have dere origins in da Last Supper. It is believed dat thirteen people were at da last supper. Within one week, da first to leave—da one who was da betrayer, was dead. And so began da superstition dat thirteen guests at a dinner party is a bad omen.

"Did you know—many fine restaurants, worldwide, do not have a table thirteen? In London, da Hotel Savoy takes it one step further.

"In 1898, a diamond dealer, named Woolf Joel, held a dinner party at da Hotel Savoy for fourteen guests. One of da guests dropped out at da last minute, reducing da number to thirteen. Another guest shared the superstition at dinner dat night, predicting dat da first to leave would die or be killed. Joel dismissed da warning and became da first to depart. Weeks later, he was shot and killed.

"Da hotel was so distraught over da news, dey had staff members join any tables composed of thirteen diners. Finally, in 1927, dey commissioned da sculpture of a black cat. Da cat would be placed at da table whenever a party of thirteen was seated. He is called by da name of Kasper, and as da fourteenth guest, he is always served all of da dishes brought to da table. True story. What do you think of dat?!" Martine asked. She burst into a fit of laughter then, as did her listeners, drawing curious looks from the other end of the table.

The main course offered a choice of three dishes: baked ziti, caprese chicken, or shrimp penne, all served individually in white ceramic crocks. Anya, Jules, and Martine decided they would each request a different one so that they could share.

Anya noticed that Ethan seemed a little lost and lonely next to the phantom fourteenth guest—who was incidentally served baked ziti. Fortunately, he was close enough to Lila's and Sharon's husbands to overhear topics of interest. To his right was Jules's date, who had yet to be introduced to anyone. As the main was being cleared, she saw Ethan introduce himself to the gentleman, but no conversation followed.

Over the salad course, which is always served last in Europe—a cleansing course before cheese or dessert—Jules elaborated on some of the finer aspects of their well-appointed surroundings.

"Most of the furnishings throughout the home are Neoclassical, Rococo, and Empire, seventeenth and eighteenth century," she began. "There is a credenza, however, in one of the upstairs guest rooms, that is Baroque, circa 1700. This dining table is Rococo, in the Regency style, very unusual. It's comprised of Kingwood with rosewood banding and multiple bronze inlays most strikingly on the outer legs. Their ancestors had it shipped over, in one piece, from Italy sometime in the early 1900s. It's twenty-one feet long and can seat twenty-two people when all of its leaves are in place."

She went on to confirm that the three chandeliers were Venetian crystal, the flatware was Lunt sterling, and the Waterford stemware dated back to 1788. It had been crafted at a time when Waterford was still run by the Penrose brothers, who were the original owners, and created by John Hill, the company's original glassmaker.

Over dessert—fruit-filled crepes dusted with powdered sugar and drizzled with chocolate—Martine asked how Jimmy was doing. The sheriff had told her all about the previous night's rescue mission. It prompted Anya to remember the Lenormand card she'd scooped up on her way out that night.

"He's doing really well, actually. He should be released from the hospital in a day or two. We're having a benefit for him next Friday. Which reminds me, on my way to meet Jimmy, I found one of your Lenormand cards on the floor by the entrance. It was the card of The Dog. I think the sticky paw of Ching, our resident cat burglar, must be responsible. What does the card mean?" Anya asked.

Martine smiled. "Dogs are loyal creatures. He probably sense dat you are a good friend."

More likely the cat was bored and had been rummaging around in the vault again, Anya thought.

Once the servers had cleared the dishes, Nigel rose to make a toast. Anya was stunned to hear him attempt it in Italian.

"Bacio per la sposa. Tanto amore e grazie al mio futuro suoceri," he emoted, kissing Cecilia on the cheek.

Everyone clapped and cheered with Cossima clapping the loudest of all. Alessandro was grinning from ear to ear, shaking Nigel's hand, and patting him on the back while Cossima hugged him repeatedly.

"A kiss for the bride. Much love and thanks to my future in-laws," was the rough translation later supplied by Cecilia.

With the dinner portion of the evening memorably concluded, everyone again adjourned to the terrace.

By eight o'clock, the after-dinner party guests had arrived to celebrate with the happy couple. Among the revelers were Desda and Paul, Kathleen and Donna Cruz, Nick and Lisa Larkin, Sheriff Wakefield, Sam Notah, Noni and Larry Landale, Smoky and Helen Mabrey, Freya and Henry Hale, John and Nancy Goshen, and many others.

"Wow, look at that," Kathleen Cruz whispered, pointing discreetly to something or someone over Anya's shoulder.

"It's about time they went public. It's not like we didn't already know," Donna said with a smirk.

They were referring to a couple dancing alone near the edge of the terrace. That couple was Sheriff Kieffer Wakefield and Martine Decoudreau. They were soon joined by Alessandro and Cossima, and Nigel and Cecilia, thereby designating a small portion of the terrace as the official dance floor.

For a split second, Anya feared she was losing her grip on her wine glass before realizing it had been slipped from her fingers by Ethan. Without a word, he took her hand and led her out among the other dancing couples.

Hating to be the center of attention, and believing herself to be a rather poor dancer, Anya tried to protest. "Ethan, I don't want to dance," she insisted.

"Yes, you do," he alleged, pulling her close. "Look at that sensational dress, your beautiful hair. You're just afraid that everyone's watching. Let them watch," he whispered. "We're the best looking couple here."

Anya noticed he had again forsaken his tie. His long black hair had all but escaped its ties as well. The sleek, dark strands spilled over his shoulders and across the lapels of his tux. He was a study in contrasts, which only served to heighten his allure. Not only was he utterly, devastatingly handsome—he was also a smooth dance partner, so refined and elegant as he spun her about the terrace. Anya started to relax. They hadn't been able to converse during dinner, and she was secretly thrilled to have this time alone with him.

"You smell like scotch and cigars," she teased, wrinkling her nose.

Ethan shook his head. Closing his eyes, he said, "No, come closer." He drew her in against him, nearer to his collar, where she imagined she could detect some hint of cologne.

He'd been unable to clearly overhear Martine's explanation of the fourteenth guest and asked Anya to recount it. He was tremendously entertained by it. He laughed so hard that he had to twirl her away toward a table with two empty seats.

"I'll get us a drink," he said, trying to recompose himself.

Moments later, he returned, wearing a look of concern.

"What is it? What's the matter?" Anya asked.

"Probably nothing to worry about," Ethan replied. "I ran into Larry Landale inside. Apparently, Elijah isn't feeling well. They're driving him home."

"Probably that Sidra York sticking pins in his voodoo doll," Anya blurted out, instantly realizing Ethan would have no idea what she was talking about.

Dumbfounded, he cocked his head to the side and asked, "What's this?"

Anya hesitated, considering whether she should confide in Ethan. Like Tate, Ethan could be very practical. There was going to be a row if he dared to suggest that she'd let her imagination run away with her. She decided to take a chance on him, beginning with Sidra's references to "we" and "us". Ethan's jaw dropped when she described slipping into the gallery to investigate the rumors that Sidra had a secret partner lurking in the background.

"Someone was definitely upstairs. No doubt about it. I was on my way up for the unmasking when Sidra came back. Luckily, I had a ready excuse as to why I was there in the first place. While I was explaining the purpose of my visit, trying not to fumble my words, I was certain that I heard the door to her office close," Anya said, steeling herself for whatever Ethan's response might be.

"Wow, murder she wrote!" Ethan exclaimed. "I'm shocked by these cloak and dagger activities of yours. I've never seen this side of you," he avowed, genuinely surprised.

Anya bounced her foot in agitation, ready to reassert her theories, when Ethan's overall tone suddenly shifted. He frowned and glanced over his shoulder at the table where the sheriff, Martine, and his father were sitting.

"What is it? What are you thinking about?" she asked.

"Something Pops told me this afternoon. Remember the campfire we saw out by the beaver's dam that night?"

Anya nodded.

"Well, I reported it to the sheriff, and he went out there to run them off. When he got there, they were already gone," he said.

"Yes, I know. I heard he found evidence that someone had been injured, some traces of blood?"

"Yes, that's right. Well, Pops told me that the sheriff has gotten several calls since then about smoke from a campfire—same location. Whoever it is, they evidently have no idea that their activities have captured the attention of local law enforcement. The sheriff is planning to run back out there to investigate."

Anya was astounded by the obvious implications.

"You think there's a connection, don't you? Maybe the person holed up in Sidra's office and the person camping out by the dam are one and the same."

Ethan shrugged his shoulders. "Due to your none-too-subtle sleuthing and the small town scuttlebutt, it may have become too risky for this character to stay at the gallery full-time. Camping in the woods, hunting, and fishing, is a good way to stay under the radar—unless you camp in a restricted area that is."

Ethan's exculpatory comments left Anya feeling instantly justified in word and action.

"When Nick Larkin told me about the traces of blood found at the campsite, I immediately thought about the break-in at the emporium. I think the mystery camper is the one who broke into the shop. He must have cut his hand when he smashed the glass door. If he's the same person who's been hiding up in Sidra's office—she's guilty of aiding, abetting, and harboring a criminal," Anya alleged. "Something strange is going on around here, and Sidra York is at the center of it all."

They lapsed into silence while Ethan contemplated this information before abruptly asking, "By the way, what did you have for dinner tonight?"

Anya frowned at this non sequitur.

"Because Elijah had the shrimp," he whispered.

Anya's face fell, realizing that she'd had a small

portion of all three main dishes, including the shrimp penne. She started to feel a little queasy until she noticed that Ethan had covered his mouth to hide a grin. He was such a delinquent.

When he'd finally stopped laughing at his own little joke, he said, "I've got four tickets to Monday night's Wildcats game. Want to go with me, Nigel, and Cecilia?"

The Wildcats were the Chenoah Falls Varsity High School baseball team. Too small to attract professional sports franchises, the city had opted to build a modern stadium anyway to host the local teams. The Wildcats games were widely attended and often sold out.

Anya happily accepted.

"Good, it's a date, and I promise to get off early enough to pick you up," he added.

TWENTY

The engagement party for Cecilia and Nigel had been an enormous success, aside from the incident involving Elijah Whip. He had taken ill shortly after dinner, causing an anxious Cossima Bennedetto to interrogate the kitchen staff regarding the shrimp penne. Fortunately, it was soon reported—via the Four Oaks grapevine, that his episode had been short-lived and unrelated. Elijah had felt completely recovered upon arriving home. None of the other guests had experienced anything unusual.

In other news, Nick Larkin and Larry Landale, both city council members, had announced that, while the owners of the old hotel had no intention of rebuilding, the property had been sold to new owners. They were planning to construct a new modern hotel on the site. Anonymous sources relayed the following details: they were a nice young family from Madison, Wisconsin, by the last name of Williams, who had left corporate jobs to go into the hospitality industry. They had chosen Four Oaks with the thought that their young son would benefit from being raised in a small-town setting. They hoped to be open in time for the Super Solarbration, a special event, still in the drafting stages, meant to commemorate August's Great American Eclipse.

Anya had arisen early on Saturday and was about to go downstairs to open McClean's when she heard soft strains of piano music drifting across the catwalk again. Martine was probably already downstairs in her shop, unaware that Ching was giving a concert in her living room. Anya thought she'd better have a look.

On her way over, she glanced out of the windows in time to see someone directly below her hurriedly crossing the street. She instantly recognized the figure as Sidra York. It looked like she had just exited the emporium. Anya monitored her progress as she continued on up the street to the gallery. What business could she have possibly had with Martine?

Anya found Ching and Don Pedro huddled together on the piano bench—muscles tensed, ears alert, heads wagging as they tracked the flurry of black and white keys. Anya couldn't bear to intrude on this harmless preoccupation and withdrew from the scene on tiptoe.

Spring was quickly giving way to summer. It was time for the changing of the umbrellas again. Anya noticed that the city council had already dispatched a crew to change the lamp post flags from those that read *Spring is Here* to the sailing flags that would fly until fall.

They didn't have enough space at McClean's to store all of their umbrella sets, so making the seasonal changes was a bit of a chore. The Stevenses had been generous enough to store the extra sets for them in the vast subterranean recesses that lay beneath the ark—but Two By Two was at the far end of Main Street. The umbrellas were heavy. If she elected not to use the truck to make the swap, it would take her two round trips to the far end of the street to complete the task. It was such a beautiful day, though, that Anya determined she would go on foot.

Passing by Mystic Treasures, she ventured a peek inside. Holly Landale was there, alone behind the counter—minding the shop for Martine. When she wasn't waitressing at her parents' restaurant, Holly sometimes picked up hours working in the emporium, especially when Martine had readings to do. Had Sidra come for a reading? As Anya struggled past with her arms full of umbrellas, she thought she could make out another small, dark shape inside the shop. Ching had resumed his position of authority on the newel post.

Continuing her trek down Main Street, Anya saw a young boy playing near one of the giraffes outside of Two By Two. Drawing nearer, she saw that he wasn't so much playing as measuring. He was measuring the shadow of the tallest giraffe and recording his calculations in a small handheld notebook.

Nick Larkin was conversing with a young couple, directly across the street, in the now vacant lot that had been the site of the old hotel. These must be the new owners she'd heard about at the Bennedettos' the night before, Anya realized.

She huffed a sigh of resolution when Nick waved her over. She was already beginning to regret her decision to walk the umbrellas down to Two By Two. Anya gave a wave in response and crossed the street, dragging the umbrellas along beside her.

"Anya! I want you to meet Mr. and Mrs. Williams. They're building the new hotel here in town. This is Anya McClean. She's the owner of McClean's Pub at the far end of the strip," Nick said, making the introductions. As an aside, he added, "Those umbrellas look heavy. Why didn't you load them in your truck and drive them down here?" He gave her a bewildered look.

"Seemed like a nice day for a walk," she mumbled—fully conscious of the error of her ways. "Nice to meet you, Mr. and Mrs. Williams. Welcome to Four Oaks," Anya said, hoisting the umbrellas awkwardly against her shoulder to shake hands with the friendly-looking couple.

"Thank you so much, but please, call me Keisha, and this my husband, John," Mrs. Williams replied.

"And this young man is our son, Derek," said the father of the giraffe-measuring boy, who had wandered over to get a closer look at the umbrella-toting woman.

Keisha tapped her son on the shoulder, and the boy and his mother engaged in a brief exchange using sign language. As far as Anya could tell, the conversation centered around something to do with the giraffe from the boy and something about good manners from his mother.

Years ago, Anya and her schoolmates had been taught the basics of sign language from their third grade teacher, Mrs. Forester, and a classmate named Jep Hollister, who was deaf. That year, when winter weather required that most recesses be held indoors, they had all begged Mrs. Forester to teach them to sign.

"As I'm sure you can see, our son, Derek, is deaf. He has some residual hearing, and can speak perfectly well, but he prefers to sign."

Anya laid the umbrellas down on the sidewalk. "Well, as luck would have it, quite a few of your new neighbors have a rudimentary grasp of sign language, provided they still remember it, that is," Anya replied, after which she succinctly recounted the story of Jep Hollister.

"Why were you measuring the giraffe?" Anya signed.

Derek's face lit up. Enthusiastically he signed back, "I wanted to know how tall it was to see if it was true to size. I measured its shadow. When the height of something and the length of its shadow form a three-sided right triangle—the length of its shadow will tell you approximately how tall it is."

Derek's mother repeated aloud what Derek was signing for the benefit of everyone present.

"The giraffe is fourteen feet tall," he concluded to everyone's amazement.

"Wow! That's pretty impressive!" Nick Larkin exclaimed. "I happen to know that giraffe is *exactly* fourteen feet tall. One of the owners, Mr. Stevens, told me so!"

Derek smiled proudly, seeing his mother sign that his calculations were accurate. Correctly sensing a captive audience, Derek proceeded to expand upon the topic by signing, "That one must be the boy giraffe. It's taller than the other one. Boy giraffes are taller."

Everyone burst out laughing at Derek's informative summation.

"Derek is homeschooled by myself and an online school for the deaf. He wants to be a veterinarian or an astronaut someday," Mrs. Williams said, smiling proudly.

"Why not both?" Nick ventured.

Derek read his lips and gave him a thumbs-up and an emphatic nod.

Anya expressed what a pleasure it was to meet them all and invited them to Friday's Stray Rescue Fundraiser. She thought Derek might enjoy seeing the dogs, meeting Jimmy, and of course, Ethan, with whom he might have much in common. Ethan might enjoy taking an eager young protégé like Derek under his wing. He might remember a little sign language himself. Nigel and Jep had been best friends until the family moved away.

Anya struggled onward with her umbrellas over to Two By Two. She was relieved to see Mason was already loading their tiki-style umbrellas into his truck, apparently with plans to deliver them and Anya back to McClean's. Desda, in her wisdom, must have seen her starting out on her ill-conceived errand and called ahead.

When they arrived at McClean's, he also helped her unload and raise the new umbrellas, before loading up those she'd been unable to carry on her initial trip.

"Thank you, Mason! You're my hero!" Anya called out.

"Anytime!" he shouted back, waving as he drove away.

Holly was returning to Landale's Log Cabin. Anya could see through the window that, with the exception of Ching, who was still on guard duty, Martine was alone in the emporium.

Anya breezed through the door and cut right to the chase. "Was that Sidra York I saw leaving your shop earlier?" she asked.

Martine looked uneasy. She'd been unpacking a box of candles and other decorative notions when Anya entered. Wordlessly and without so much as a glance in her direction, she nodded in the affirmative.

"Did she want a reading from you?" Anya pressed, strolling over to stroke Ching's head.

"She did," came the tight-lipped response. As a professional, Martine always kept her clients' confidences, but she seemed reluctant to even confirm Sidra's visit at all for some reason.

Anya could see that it was pointless to persist. It was like trying to pry open a clam, so she decided to let it drop. "The piano upstairs is beautiful. Ching was giving Don Pedro a lesson this morning," she said. Hearing his name, Ching gave a little chirp. "Have you signed up for lessons as well, or do you already play?" Anya asked in an effort to infuse a bit of humor into the situation.

"Thank you, it is an exquisite instrument, isn't it? Yes, I play. From da time we were perhaps five or six, we had a teacher who came to our house to give lessons," Martine replied. Her manner remained stilted and strained. Anya knew the "we" to which she referred included her sister, Tame.

"Well, I would love to hear you play sometime. Everything going OK up at the lake?" Anya asked, moving toward the door.

"Mm-hmmm," Martine murmured, looking up to feign a smile.

Anya meandered into McClean's in time to see an interesting exchange take place between Desda and

Craig. Conspiratorial grins were plastered on both of their faces as a twenty dollar bill was traded between them. The positive flow of this transaction was in the direction of the venerable Mrs. March, identifying her as the winner of some private wager.

"Hmm ... and what is this about, dare I ask?" Anya was forced to inquire.

"Your weak arms and recent comedy of errors just cost me twenty bucks," Craig confessed.

Anya was initially confused until, all at once, she remembered the umbrella farce. Obviously, they'd been watching her from the door, since one of them must have placed the call to Mason for his assistance.

"I knew you'd never make it," Desda confirmed, enjoying the theater of tucking the bill into her bra.

Craig raised a hand in protest. "No, not until you saw Nick throw in that detour. That was the curveball. Just wait. I'll be looking for an opportunity to go double or nothing in the near future."

Desda smirked and waved him off. "Bring it on, laddie."

Anya flushed. "Thanks to whoever blinked first and called Mason. Those umbrellas were heavier than I thought."

Craig gave an exasperated sigh on his way to the kitchen.

"Don't play with the master," Anya wisely advised him.

Desda listened with rapt attention while Anya told her all about meeting John and Keisha Williams and their son, Derek. She laughed when Anya shared his future career aspirations.

"I guess you didn't take your cell with you. Jules called here looking for you. She said to tell you that Elizabeth was back and had confirmed her suspicions. She said you would understand. Care to fill me in?" Desda asked.

The news that the Modigliani was a forgery was certainly no surprise, although she hadn't expected to hear it from Desda. Anya decided there was no harm in sharing the latest news flash surrounding Sidra York. It would be all over town by tonight anyway. There were no secrets in Four Oaks.

Desda was predictably shocked, and her disbelief continued when Anya reported that she'd seen Sidra leaving Martine's shop earlier. "I asked Martine if she'd requested a reading, and she confirmed that she had. I tried to get more details out of her, but she was locked up tighter than a safe. Weird, huh?"

"Well, if you ask me, it's not a tarot card reading she needs so much as a ticket out of town! Her reputation is ruined! She might as well shutter the gallery and move on before the authorities catch up to her," Desda said, shaking her head in disgust.

At that moment, Jules marched into the pub. "I

assume you got my message?" she barked, looking from Anya to Desda then back to Anya again. Anya was about to reply when she was silenced by an outpour of indignation from Jules. "I've just come from the gallery to demand a refund for Cossima, but the place is dark, and the door is locked. I'd say she's taken off for parts unknown, but her car's still there. You two haven't seen her?"

"As a matter of fact, I did. She was coming out of Martine's shop..." Anya had started to reply, when Jules pivoted on a dime and started toward the door.

"Wait! She's not there now. That was more than an hour ago," Anya added.

As if in answer to Jules's growing frustration, the door swung open again, and Martine entered looking uncharacteristically dismal, Anya thought.

Jules practically pounced on her. "Martine, I'm looking for Sidra York. You saw her this morning. Did she mention where she was going? Maybe some errands she had to run, or appointments she had to keep?"

Martine shook her head no.

"Well, if you see her, you tell her I'm looking for her. Should she decide to cut and run—Cossima will be out ten thousand dollars! We're all a little too trusting around here, if you ask me. We opened our arms wide and welcomed her in! What, if anything, did we ever know about her?"

There was a long pause after which Jules gave a withering sigh and made her exit.

"Anya, could you possibly come over to da shop wid me? I cannot make out da small print on one of da invoices. If you could come read it to me," Martine meekly requested.

"Sure, I'd be happy to," Anya replied, following her over to the emporium.

Anya was bewildered to see Martine lock the door behind them and flip the sign to closed.

"What's going on?" Anya asked. "Forgive me for saying so, but you've been acting strangely all day." Anya stared at her questioningly.

For the second time, in less than a month, she was wholly unprepared for what Martine said next.

"Da sheriff's investigation into da circumstances surroundin Tame's death is ongoing, and he has strictly warned me not to tell anyone what we've discovered. If I tell you—you must promise not to tell anyone."

Anya knew then that something big was coming. She slipped into a chair behind the counter and braced herself for the worst.

"We *do* know somethin about Sidra York dat I didn't tell you initially. It involves information dat I found on Tame's computer. Before she came here, Sidra had been employed as a clerk in my sista's shop. Her name appears on many documents, as well as da payroll records. Her employment was terminated without explanation."

Anya was shocked beyond belief! Sidra and Tame had known one another? Her brain went into overdrive trying to connect the dots. What exactly did it mean? Martine had told her that Tame had a *male* accomplice who had encouraged her to pursue the Beckwith fortune. When she had been unable to get any money out of Martine, he had murdered her by blowing up the hotel, but his search for the legendary treasure hadn't ended there. He had broken into Martine's shop to search for the cache himself. Now Martine was telling her that Sidra was somehow involved?

"Sidra's presence here in Four Oaks is no coincidence. It looks like Tame may have been double-crossed. Da sheriff's theory is dat Tame's accomplice was, in actuality, Sidra's partner. He believes dey are a couple of fortune hunters who were usin Tame to get to da Beckwith treasure. Sidra opened da gallery as a front operation from which dey could keep an eye on Tame and on me while dey plotted ways to get dere hands on da money. Dis man, whoever he is, was most likely da presence you detected upstairs in Sidra's office. He and Sidra had probably always planned to do away wid Tame once dey had da money. Poor Tame was nothin more den a pawn in a much larger scheme, a quest to steal a king's ransom. She never even knew dat dey were both right here in town when she came to see me."

Anya was dumbstruck. "I know you never share client information, but why on earth would Sidra seek you out for a reading, and why didn't you turn her away?"

"Dere was no readin. Sidra came into da shop unda da pretense of wantin a readin, but I was already wid a client. Holly told her dat she was welcome to wait, but afta dat—Holly got busy with some other customers, and Sidra soon left da store. Dat's when Holly noticed somethin strange. Da door to the supply closet was standin open. When she told me dis—I went straight to da closet to inspect da shelves and noticed dat a bottle of diethyl ether was missin."

"Ether? Why do you have ether?"

"You may be familiar wid its use as an anesthetic. All of da men in my family were doctors. My great-grandfather was a surgeon and used it as an induction agent. I use it as a solvent to extract essential oils from anise and other botanicals used to make my own blends."

"You think Sidra took it? But, why? For what purpose?"

Martine raised her eyebrows in worriment. "I don know, but I don think her purpose for its use is da same as mine."

"Did you report it to the sheriff?"

"Yes, but no one saw her take it from da closet. He needs somethin more to get a search warrant."

"Well, here's something more," Anya said. "Fraud! They've been using the art gallery as more than a hide-out. They've also been using it to traffic in forgeries. Cossima Bennedetto was sold a fake Modigliani for ten thousand dollars, and it looks like Sidra's planning to abscond with the money. Call him."

After Martine had finished speaking to the sheriff, she returned to where Anya was still seated at the counter. She pulled three tarot cards from the pocket of her gown. The first one she placed on the counter was the Five of Swords.

"Ching left dis card in da kitchen dis mornin," Martine said. "He left two more at da foot of da stairs."

Ching watched from the newel post as his mistress lay the other two cards on the counter beside the first. All three belonged to the swords suit, the five, the seven, and the queen.

Anya studied the images. The soldier on the Five of Swords looked as though he'd won his battle, but at a brutal and ruthless cost to his enemy. The Seven of Swords plainly depicted a thief making off with five swords belonging to whoever was in the tent behind him. The queen, with her upright sword, was less clear in her intentions.

"What do you think it all means?" Anya asked.

Suddenly, Ching went airborne, landing on the countertop with all four legs widely splayed. There was a faraway gleam in his yellow-green eyes like someone in the throes of a trance. He bushed his tail, arched his spine, and let loose a shriek that made Anya's blood run cold. The eerie cries continued as did the pagan circle dance in which Ching marched his paws to some unhearable drum beat.

Anya covered her ears and cringed. She remembered that Ching had performed a similar ritual on the top of Martine's desk the night the hidden compartment had been revealed.

Once his howls had reached an earsplitting crescendo, he began to slowly wind down. The marching ceased, his tail diminished in size, and his eyes regained their focus. He gave himself a stiff shake and glanced around to get his bearings. Whimpering slightly, the cat sought to comfort himself with a few swipes of his tongue to his shoulder before racing away up the stairs.

"Ching's death march," Martine whispered. She held up the Queen of Swords and said, "I think da Queen wan to cut ties. Someone's goin to get da sword."

By Saturday afternoon, the news of Cossima's fake Modigliani was out. Her fellow Main Streeters were incensed and vowed to keep watch on the gallery around the clock for signs of Sidra's presence.

By Sunday night, Sidra York had yet to surface. The gallery remained shuttered in darkness. The little compact Ford was still parked out back, but Sidra herself had disappeared into thin air.

TWENTY-ONE

Ethan had suggested that they have dinner at Sawyer's before meeting Nigel and Cecilia at the Wildcats game. Sawyer's was just over the bridge, near the stadium, overlooking the picturesque Chenoah Falls River. In its day, it had been the largest working lumber mill in the region. Now it was a restaurant and a local hotspot. The owners had wisely retained much of the mill's original features, making it something of an attraction.

Once upon a time, loads of debarked timber had been brought by train to the mill for processing. The windows on the south side overlooked the old train tracks and a decommissioned diesel. Above the tracks were large pipes that connected to giant waterwheels on the river. The wheels no longer turned—frozen in time. Inside, some of the scaffoldings, saw frames, sluices, and smaller wheels had been preserved, skillfully incorporated into the overall design. The walls were decorated with black and white photographs dating back to the days when the mill had been in operation. Longtime residents in the area were proud to point out their ancestors in these photos to their children and grandchildren. Even the name Sawyer's was a reference to its lumbering days. Sawyers were the operators of the mills' band saws. It took years to become a skilled sawyer.

On the way to their table—a private booth situated beneath an ominous looking replica of a whipsaw, Ethan spotted some faces they knew.

"Hey, look, it's the Landales and the Nithercotts."

"Looks like some kind of a celebration," Anya replied.

For Anya, seeing Beau and Martha Nithercott immediately brought to mind her hard-kept secret regarding the monumental change in her financial status. It was Beau's law firm, Sterling, Nithercott, and McSwain, that would ultimately be charged with the details of processing Beckwith's vast wealth.

Larry Landale smiled and waved to them as a group of five servers delivered a birthday cake to his party's table. Ethan and Anya looked on as "Happy Birthday" was sung, a wish was made, and the candles were extinguished. Larry then excused himself and hurried over to their table to say hello.

"Hi, guys! On the way to the game, I'm guessing?" he asked—an easy supposition deduced from the game jerseys she and Ethan were wearing.

"Yeah, the home opener is tonight," Ethan affirmed.

"Sounds like fun! Great weather too!" Larry said.

"Is it Martha's birthday?" Anya asked.

"Yep, my mother-in-law is seventy years old today. Doesn't she look great? Good genes. Nice people, my in-laws. Hey! What about the latest news on the whole Sidra York disappearance?" Larry asked, abruptly steering the conversation toward the day's hottest topic. His brown eyes conveyed the shock value contained in the newly emerging details.

The media had picked up the story of the forgery and Sidra's subsequent vanishing act. Formal charges had now been filed. Pictures of her were all over the news, and law enforcement had put out a nationwide BOLO alert. In addition to these charges, the media was also reporting that Sidra and an unnamed male suspect were being sought for questioning in the break-in at Mystic Treasures and the double murder that had resulted from the bombing of The Four Oaks Hotel. Although Tame had been identified as the bomber's intended victim, the media had yet to uncover Tame's former ties to Sidra and her male accomplice.

The leak hadn't come from Anya or Martine, leaving Sheriff Wakefield as the only possible source of this information. The motive for the crimes had been withheld from the media—a step the sheriff had obviously taken to protect Martine.

"Noni told me Sharon Bailer thought someone was

hiding out up in Sidra's office the day of the grand opening," Larry remarked.

Ethan glanced at Anya. "Anya suspected the same thing. Looks like they were both right. It also looks like the Bennedettos are out ten thousand dollars."

"Terrible business. Just terrible," Larry said anxiously. He smoothed his full head of dark brown hair and stepped aside for the waitress who arrived to take their order of two lumberjack burgers, medium well, with seasoned steak fries—extra seasoning—and a couple of bottles of beer.

"Well, if she's guilty, she'll be going to prison, and an auction will be held to liquidate the art and any other salable contents of the gallery. Maybe Alessandro and Cossima will recoup at least some of their money," Anya submitted.

"Maybe," Larry replied, doubtfully. "Tate Blackledge tells me that she paid him for his services, but I have a feeling she might have stiffed the Colburn sisters. I don't know if there's enough value in the contents to cover everybody's losses."

Anya realized that Tate must be back from Ohio and had probably heard the latest news. She smiled to herself, thinking how surprised he must have been to learn that she had been right about Sidra York.

The conversation paused when the waitress returned with their drinks and a request to substitute seasoned waffle fries—extra seasoning—in place of the seasoned steak fries as they were presently out of steak fries. Anya nodded, and Ethan gave the OK.

"You know my mother-in-law became suspicious of Sidra when she asked her to come out to the house to appraise a couple of paintings she and Beau bought last summer in Naples," Larry continued. "She got the feeling right away that Sidra didn't know her stuff. She didn't seem to be familiar with the documentation Martha showed her—you know, the papers that supposedly prove something's legit and what its approximate value is." Larry paused to glance over his shoulder and check on the progress of the birthday party. The guest of honor was about to open her gifts. "Oops, time to open the presents. Gotta run. Good seeing you guys! Enjoy the game!" he called out as he rushed off to rejoin his family.

Anya stared at her beer glass thoughtfully, twisting it between her thumb and forefinger. She wished she could tell Ethan what Martine had confided about Tame, Sidra, and the unknown male accomplice. She knew she couldn't. She had promised Martine that she wouldn't. Any mention of it would also call for an explanation of the motive, which was, of course, the Beckwith millions. Anya had decided in recent days that she might never tell Ethan or anyone else about her share in the money. There was a certain stigma that came with possessing that kind of wealth. She didn't want to change the way her friends and neighbors saw her. She was happy with her life and had no desire to see it altered.

"Well, whoever this mystery man is, if he was also the one camping near the beaver's dam, the authorities have a sample of his blood. They'll be able to identify him pretty quick, provided he's already in the system, of course," Ethan pointed out. "Here's hopin'," he added, raising his beer.

When the food came, the conversation shifted to plans for the Fourth of July. The top three celebrations were always held in the communities of Chenoah Falls, Four Oaks, and Lake Increase.

"The Bennedettos have invited us to join them at the Lake Increase Silver Pines Hotel this year. They've reserved a few tables for family and friends, and they're also going to dust off their old ski show routine. Cecilia and her folks are all gonna perform in the show. Nigel's driving the boat!" Ethan said, laughing uproariously.

Cecilia had been skiing since she was about seven years old. Back then, the Bennedettos had always skied in the Independence Day water show, but that was years ago, and never with Nigel at the wheel.

"Has Nigel ever piloted a ski boat?" she asked, knowing full well what the answer would be. Nigel Notah at the helm of a ski boat, towing his bride-to-be *and* his in-laws, sounded like a recipe for mayhem!

Ethan was laughing so hard at the obvious implications attached to her question that he could barely respond. "No … , but they've started practicing!"

On their way out of Sawyer's, Jimmy Shaw's fluffy yellow dog, Nate, came trotting through the door. CF Rescue was about half a block away, and Jimmy and his volunteers dined there regularly. Nate had the distinct honor of being the only dog allowed inside, often unaccompanied. He enjoyed the attention and scraps of beef and chicken the staff slipped him whenever he popped in. This time Jimmy was right behind him, slowed up by the use of a cane he hadn't quite mastered.

"Well, well, well, two of my favorite people! How are you guys doing?" Jimmy greeted them enthusiastically.

"Hi, Jimmy! Doing great. On our way to the game. You here for dinner?" Anya asked, bending down to hug Nate and ruffle his neck fur. Nate responded with a few wet swipes of his tongue before heading in the direction of a waitress who was offering him a treat.

"Oh, yeah. Sawyer's is like our second home," Jimmy replied. "Speaking of home, great home opener tonight. Should be a win against the Batteau Bears," Jimmy predicted.

"Yeah, we're gonna beat 'em. Got a hell of a pitcher on the team this year. Hope it isn't a no-hitter, though. Those kind of games are great for the stats, but boring for the fans," Ethan correctly pointed out.

"First pitch is in twenty minutes," Anya noted. "We better get moving, but we'll see you Friday. We'll get you a chair set up behind the bar so you can amuse a few people with your abominable bartending skills. Desda and I will do the rest."

"Right on! Looking forward to it. Enjoy the game!" Jimmy replied.

They made it to their seats with beer and bags of peanuts by the opening pitch. Nigel and Cecilia were already there, and the two couples settled in with high expectations.

Unfortunately, Ethan's no-hitter nightmare scenario was playing out, with the game still scoreless by the seventh-inning stretch. Ethan and Nigel groaned and complained as they rose from their seats to stretch their legs. Stadium seating simply wasn't designed to accommodate individuals of exemplary height, at least not comfortably so.

"You girls want another beer?" Nigel asked.

Cecilia and Anya nodded.

"Bring me back a hotdog too," Cecilia added as the brothers departed.

Once they'd gone, the conversation predictably turned to plans for the upcoming nuptials.

"I'm going a little out of my mind over the wedding cake. Would you mind giving me your input?" Cecilia asked—pulling up images on her phone for Anya to view. "You wouldn't believe how many choices there are these days. They're even injecting cakes now with booze or special flavorings."

She and Anya began perusing pages touting the latest in modern wedding cake design.

The top three entries were as follows:

- Coconut cake with key lime filling and white buttercream fluff
- Hazelnut-almond cake with chocolate ganache and mocha buttercream frosting
- Orange Galliano-infused cake with orange curd filling and Galliano-infused frosting

"Wow, wedding cakes sure have come a long way," Anya said, thinking of the pictures of her parents' wedding cake, white on white with a miniature bride and groom on top.

"I know, right? Nigel wants this one for the groom's cake," Cecilia said, pulling up another picture. "It's called chocolate bourbon craze. It's a three-tier chocolate cake, made with espresso and bourbon and filled with bourbon mascarpone. It's covered in chocolate fondant."

Until this moment, Anya had been unfamiliar with the concept of a groom's cake. She had to admit it looked sinfully delicious. "What a stunning cake! I've never seen anything like it. Sounds scrumptious."

"So, considering that, what do you think of the main

cake being lemon-raspberry ripple with buttercream frosting and fondant ruffles?" Cecilia asked, swiping to a picture of a towering, five-tiered, confectionary marvel, that looked more like a wedding *dress* than a cake.

"Beautiful!" Anya exclaimed. "I love them both. You and your white gown might want to steer clear of the chocolate bourbon craze, but other than that, what's the dilemma?"

"Well, I hope everyone isn't disappointed by the bold flavors. Some people will be expecting a traditional white wedding cake, you know?"

"I think people's tastes have evolved. I imagine they'll appreciate a more adventurous approach. I'd go for it. I'm going to have a piece of each!" Anya affirmed.

The game turned out to be a nail-biter with a tie in the ninth that took the game into extra innings, but the Wildcats brought home the win—three to two in the twelfth.

Nigel and Cecilia invited them out for a nightcap afterward, but Ethan declined, saying he had to be at work early in the morning.

"I have a confession," Ethan announced on the drive home. "I do have to go into work early, but I turned them down because I wanted to spend a little time alone with you. I thought we could go to your place for a nightcap instead of going out with them. Is that OK?"

Anya smiled. "I have a little confession and a secret plan of my own."

"Oh?"

"Martine has been staying at the lake house with the sheriff, so there's no possibility of her dropping by unannounced. She's not the only one with a set of backstairs, you know? Want to stay over?" Anya asked, hopefully.

Ethan parked his truck behind McClean's, and they dashed up the stairs to her apartment. By sunup, your personal life would be bantered about and tossed across every breakfast table in town if you failed to take such measures.

Unfortunately, as luck would have it, the fates conspired against their attempts at discretion. By 6 a.m., the jig was up, and all hell was breaking loose again in the tiny town of Four Oaks.

As the first rays of sun glinted on the horizon, most of the townspeople were asleep in their beds, blissfully unaware that federal agents had descended upon The York Gallery.

Sheriff Wakefield's growing concern that Sidra would come back for her car had led to the decision to impound it. While waiting for the tow truck driver, he'd detected the extremely foul and distinctive odor of decay emanating from the vehicle. He made two calls, one to state law enforcement, which in turn contacted the FBI, and one to wake a judge in Chenoah Falls, who finally issued the search warrant.

Anya awoke surprised to find Ching curled up on her chest, softly stroking her face with his paw. She shot straight up in bed, realizing that Martine must also be somewhere nearby. What was she doing here so early?

Satisfied that he'd done his job, Ching thumped to the floor and sauntered out of the room. That's when Anya heard voices coming from the direction of the catwalk.

"Ethan, wake up," Anya whispered, jostling him awake. "Something's going on. Ching's here, and I heard voices coming from the catwalk."

Anya pulled on her robe and went to investigate. She was astonished to find Martine, Desda, Paul, and all seven cats gathered at the windows, making a study of the street below. Anya cinched her robe up tighter. Moving in for a closer look, she saw that a grim, chaotic scene was unfolding at The York Gallery.

Crime scene tape surrounded the exterior where numerous federal agents in blue windbreakers were combing the site. They were inspecting the windows and doors, dusting for fingerprints, and carting out computers and multiple boxes containing office supplies, paperwork, and files. Others were loading up artwork from the gallery into vans that were standing by. A group of three agents were huddled near the curb, examining what looked like a cell phone.

The central focus seemed to be concentrated on Sidra's car, which was parked just out of sight behind the gallery. Two crime scene units and the medical examiner's van were visible there beyond a wall of agents that were guarding this area. Sheriff Wakefield and Sam Notah were across the street, available, but standing down, as the federal agents took control.

That explained why Martine had arrived with her cats so early, Anya thought. She must have been the sheriff's first call to warn her to get into town before they blockaded the street. He'd probably suggested that she bring the cats with her in case she couldn't get home by noon to feed them. Martine must have, in turn, phoned Desda. She'd probably called her too, but Anya couldn't say exactly where her cell phone was at the moment.

"Here comes a tow truck," Paul whispered, as Ethan walked up beside Anya. Everyone was so engrossed in the scene they barely noticed him.

"I better call Doc Lafferty," Ethan murmured. "Looks like I'm gonna be late."

They watched as the tow truck lumbered toward the back lot.

"They must have found something in the car," Desda whispered.

Minutes later, the wrecker reappeared with Sidra's car in tow, followed closely by the ME's van. The trunk was tightly wrapped and taped.

"The medical examiner is going too. There must have been forensic evidence in the car. You don't think *she's* been in the car all this time, do you?" Paul shook his head in disbelief.

Desda shuddered. "Someone would have seen her … unless she was in the trunk."

Anya and Martine exchanged worried glances as the piano suddenly began to play. Anya was certainly no expert when it came to opera or Broadway show tunes, but she thought she recognized the melody. It was from the opera *Carmen*.

"What the heck is that?" Paul exclaimed, jerking his head in the direction of Martine's apartment.

"Ack—dat is Ching!" Martine huffed and rushed away to quiet the feline prodigy.

"Martine's new piano has a player component. Ching's figured out how to operate it." Anya explained, dispelling the baffled looks.

After Martine returned, they continued to watch the activity going on below until Desda wisely suggested that it might be best if they all tried to go about their normal daily routines. There was really nothing else to be done anyway. Numbly each departed: Martine to her home accompanied by her cats; Anya, Desda, and Paul to McClean's; and Ethan to begin his walk to the outskirts of town where Nigel would pick him up and take him to work.

By nightfall, as they had after the explosion at the hotel, many of the townspeople had gathered at McClean's looking for answers and awaiting the first news reports to air.

Desda rang the tip bell. "Shh—here it is!" she shouted, calling for silence and reaching for the remote to turn up the volume on the TV.

A female newscaster read the details from a teleprompter as video from that morning's scene played in the background:

"At approximately seven a.m., the body of an unidentified, deceased individual was found in the trunk of a car parked behind The York Gallery in Four Oaks. The car is registered to Sidra York, who has not been seen since early Saturday. As previously reported, a warrant for her arrest had been issued recently, in which allegations of fraud and grand larceny were sighted. Miss York is currently charged with selling a portrait, known to be a forgery, to a local woman for ten thousand dollars. She and an unnamed associate were also being sought for questioning in a double murder, resulting from the bombing of The Four Oaks Hotel last month and a burglary at a local business known as Martine's Mystic Treasures. The name of the victim in this homicide is being withheld, pending notification of family."

The media wasn't releasing her name, pending notification of family, but the townspeople were sure it was Sidra York. The citizens of Four Oaks, in fact, knew a little something more, as they always did, about this morning's tragedy. It was a grisly detail, either unknown or merely unreported by the media. The only part of the deceased that had been hidden in the trunk of Sidra's little Ford coupe was a dismembered torso. The arms, legs, and head were missing. It looked like the queen herself had been the one to be cut out—literally, Anya thought.

As the word of this quickly got out, Sheriff Wakefield did his best to reassure everyone that there was nothing to fear. The murder had not been the random act of a serial killer on the loose, but a crime in which the individual alone had been targeted. He even went so far as to address this with the crowd gathered at McClean's that night, assuring everyone that they were not in danger and that the case would be quickly solved.

His efforts to restore calm to the town, however, proved futile. In the coming days, the residents of Four Oaks would reel in horror as body parts started turning up all over the place. They had been distributed across the area in widely ranging locations beginning with the, now defunct, Ice & Fuel Company where both arms were recovered. Some local boys, playing near the railroad tracks, made the gruesome discovery of the victim's legs. This was initially wrongly reported as an unknown casualty, the result of someone being struck by an oncoming train, but Sheriff Wakefield had known better.

In fact, it would ultimately be Sheriff Kieffer Wakefield, and not the FBI, who would go on to solve the case. In an amazing breakthrough, he would first recognize and then decode a mnemonic, a kind of secret code that was being utilized by the deranged killer. It was this brilliant bit of detective work that would help him put the last piece of the puzzle in place.

It would still be weeks before a suspect was apprehended, and an arrest was made, but the sheriff would test and confirm his theory as early as Friday.

TWENTY-TWO

Friday was the day of Jimmy's fundraiser. The official groundbreaking ceremony for the new hotel had also been scheduled to take place a few hours beforehand. After breakfasting at Landale's Log Cabin, Ethan, Anya, Nigel, Cecilia, and Larry Landale walked up Main Street together to attend the ceremony. A small crowd had gathered to cheer on the new owners and their son, who stood by beaming proudly—shovels poised.

"That's the future veterinarian I told you about, Derek," Anya said, pointing out the Williamses' son to Ethan. "I'll introduce you after the ceremony. Do you remember any sign language?"

"Absolutely, but I'll have to practice if we're going to be partners someday," Ethan joked.

"Greetings, folks! Beautiful day! Anya, did I hear you've got Drexsler's Deli lined up for Jimmy's thing today?" Mason Stevens asked, joining their little group.

"You heard right, Mason. I hope you and Lila can get away for a while to stop by," Anya replied.

"Oh, we'll be there. Wouldn't miss it for the world."

"Us too. Noni and I are looking forward to deli, draft, and dogs," Larry chimed in, eliciting groans from his neighbors. "What? Not funny? I thought it was funny. I've been working on that one all morning," he admitted, drawing laughter from the group.

Anya noticed that Cecilia was frowning.

"What's that? Is an alarm going off?" she asked, swiveling her head in every direction. There was a hint of foreboding in Cecilia's voice.

The baleful wail of many sirens could be heard, approaching from the direction of the Chenoah Falls Bridge. A hush fell over the crowd. The shrieks grew louder. The sheriff was immediately on the scene, arriving in advance of several state police cruisers.

"Sorry, folks! I'm afraid the ceremony is canceled. Please go home. I need everybody to leave the area!" Sheriff Wakefield ordered.

The crowd withdrew to a safe distance.

"What now?" Cecilia murmured, as more state patrol cars flooded the area.

Officers hurriedly exited their cars and began securing a perimeter. The Williams family was whisked away to wait inside of Smoky's BBQ.

"I don't know, but I better get back to The Cabin," Larry mumbled.

"Me too. Lila will be frantic," Mason said, pushing his way through the crowd to return to Two By Two.

Several minutes later, federal agents in unmarked cars arrived, followed by a flatbed truck that delivered a heavy construction crawler/excavator to the site. As the crawler rolled slowly off the ramp, the crowd was instructed to vacate the area and stay off the street until further notice.

Once again, Anya found herself on the catwalk with Desda, Paul, Martine, and Ethan, along with Nigel and Cecilia. It wasn't the best vantage point. The hotel was much farther up the street than the gallery, so their view was limited.

"What are they looking for?" Paul sighed, squinting hard at the scene. "What we need is a pair of binoculars."

"They must have gotten a tip or something. It has to be related to Sidra's murder, right?" Nigel surmised.

They were unable to tell exactly what it was the excavator dug up on the old hotel's site, but it wasn't hard to guess. It would soon be confirmed that a macabre grand finale had been planned in connection with the town's most heinous murder case. Whoever was responsible had intended for the unearthing of the victim's head to take place at the very well-attended public groundbreaking ceremony. The psychopath had probably delighted in imagining the crowd's horror when the last of the remains were uncovered.

Out of the blue, like déjà vu, the piano in Martine's

living room sprang to life. It was the same piece as before, something from the opera *Carmen.* Martine hurried away, and Nigel and Cecilia turned to Anya—puzzled looks on both their faces.

"Ching," was Anya's singular response. The mere mention of the cat's name was self-explanatory and instantly allayed their confusion.

By two o'clock, Main Street was open for business. Despite the two hour delay, many were already in attendance when Jimmy and Nate got there, along with four other dogs that were up for adoption that day.

None of the candidates had been among those they'd rescued in Dixon. Those dogs had been tougher breeds that had suffered abuse. In preparation for adoption, they would require months of loving care and rehabilitation to restore their true and gentle natures.

Jimmy always brought family-friendly strays to functions—easygoing dogs that would be unfazed by the noise and the crowd. Today Jimmy had brought a border collie mix, a shepherd mix, a flat-coated retriever, and a dog Doc Lafferty guessed to be a whoodle, a stroodle, or a golden doodle.

Anya noticed that Jimmy was still leaning pretty heavily on his cane as Desda guided him to a chair they'd set up for him behind the bar. He'd been told by his doctors to expect a full recovery if he committed himself wholly to therapy.

"Where's my buddy, Ching?" he asked, noticing that Zia alone was curled up on the bar beside Paul.

Ching loved Jimmy Shaw and always insisted on being present whenever Anya threw these benefits. He would yowl and scratch at Anya's access door, demanding admittance until she finally relented. He paid no attention to the dogs, who, by contrast, displayed a deep interest in him. Ching preferred to expend his energy presiding over the activities, always positioning himself on the bar beside Jimmy.

Presently, Ching was on the stairs—perched on the third step, warily eyeing Jimmy's cane. He had a look of worriment in his eyes, but once Jimmy took his seat—he was moved to action. He army crawled toward him down the length of the bar prompting Zia to swiftly vacate her spot. He settled in next to Jimmy—gathering himself into a compact bundle, reminiscent of a hen nesting on eggs. Jimmy chuckled and stroked the length of his back, as the patrons began lining up.

Desda rang the tip bell to signal the start of the event, and Jimmy passed Anya a Blues Destroyers CD to play over the house system. The Blues Destroyers were his favorite local band, as well as personal friends. They'd been forced to cancel earlier in the day when they'd arrived to set up and found that Main Street had been blocked off. Officers manning the blockade had turned them away.

Hearing the bell, Sarah Katz and her waitstaff came from the kitchen to distribute menus and take food orders. Anya got the music going while Desda, Craig, and Jimmy tended bar.

The crowds at these fundraisers tended to be mostly local. They'd all seen Jimmy on the news after the Dixon rescue—interviewed from his hospital bed. For the most part they were taking it easy on him when it came to their good-natured attempts to stump the bartender; still, there were a few requests that none of them knew how to concoct. Anya and her staff repeatedly scrambled for their cell phones to look up the ingredients.

The Cocorita was one such unusual request. It was nothing more than a margarita made with coconut milk, but it had to be frozen, so they mixed up a couple of pitchers and tossed them into the blast freezer. Mission accomplished!

The Green Ghost and the Pop Rocks Rita were the other two head scratchers. The Pop Rocks Rita called for equal parts Grand Marnier and tequila, sweet and sour mix, cranberry, and lime juice, to which the candy known as Pop Rocks was added. They were at a loss for a moment concerning the Pop Rocks until Craig suggested a run to Candy's Canes—after which the Pop Rocks Ritas were a go.

The Green Ghost was a mix of gin, a liqueur called

green chartreuse, and lime juice. Due to the lack of green chartreuse, the Green Ghost had to be ghosted.

Additionally, a group of girls from Pulaski ordered French 75s, but Desda knew the mix called for gin, sugar, lemon juice, and champagne. It was a twist on the mimosa, and she had a batch made up in seconds.

Over the next two hours, the crowd kept them hopping. Jimmy rang the bell three times to cheers from the crowd. Each clang signified that one of the dogs had been adopted. As they headed into the final hour, Ananda came on duty to relieve Anya. She was happy for the opportunity to break away and join Ethan, Nigel, and Cecilia, who were seated in a corner booth.

"Hey, big turnout today! Jimmy's gotta to be thrilled about that," Ethan said, as Anya flopped down beside Cecilia.

"Yeah, I was a little worried about the time delay, but I don't think it had an impact. He's already secured homes for three of the dogs," Anya was pleased to report. Suddenly she heard an odd crackling sound in her ear. It sounded like something was fizzing. She looked questioningly at Cecilia, who had placed her hand discreetly over her mouth. Anya looked down at her glass. "You're the Pop Rocks Rita?!"

Cecilia grinned through her fingers, trying to contain the mini explosions that were going off in her mouth. "Remember how much we used to love these things as kids?" she asked awkwardly. She held up one of the packages Craig had bought at Candy's Canes. "At this point, I'm really just eating the candy," she confessed, pouring the rest into her mouth.

Anya shook her head. "I should have known. Have there been any new developments regarding our town's most recent headline?

Nigel shook his head. "No. The media covered it, but they still aren't releasing Sidra's name or a motive. Pops says the sheriff thinks he's onto something, but he's keeping it under his hat. It was his hunch, and on his order, that the groundbreaking ceremony be halted. Somehow he knew."

The sheriff and Martine entered then, as if on cue. Anya watched them make their way over to the bar. As soon as Ching spotted his mistress, he was on his feet, deftly navigating around customers and their drinks to reach her.

"The sheriff is a sharp guy. He's going to get whoever's responsible for all of this. You can bet on it," Ethan assured with the same confidence in the sheriff they all shared.

Anya decided to change the subject. "So, how about the wedding? Have you set a date yet?"

"As a matter of fact, we have! On Martine's advice, the date will be May fifth." Squinting and tapping a finger on her lips, she added, "I can't remember whether she said the moon will be waxing or waning, but the sign of Taurus will be transiting the sun."

"And Jupiter will be aligned with Mars," Ethan mumbled.

Anya nudged his knee under the table. "That sounds perfect! A spring wedding!"

"Also, Martine is throwing me a wedding shower! You'll be getting an invitation! I'm so excited," she beamed.

Nigel put an arm around her, hugging her affectionately. They were such the happy couple, a truly good match.

Cecilia was continuing on with more details about the wedding, but Anya was barely listening. She was watching Martine and Sheriff Wakefield conversing at the bar. Did Martine know what it was the sheriff was "on to"?

Minutes later, the bell rang again to signify that all four dogs had been adopted just as the festivities were drawing to a close.

"Gotta wrap this up," Anya said, sliding out of the booth. "I have to get Jimmy a check and see him off. Can you all stick around?" she asked. "I haven't eaten all day, and I think Sarah has plenty of food left over. I thought we could head upstairs with some beer and deli sandwiches when I get done. I need some peace and quiet after this day."

"Thanks for the invite, but Nigel and I are supposed

to have dinner with my folks. We'll see you at Tate's tomorrow, though," Cecilia replied.

Anya had no idea what she was talking about. "Tate's? Tomorrow?"

"Yeah, he's back from Ohio and has some really creepy footage to share. He's invited us all to a barbeque at his place tomorrow. Didn't Ethan tell you?" Cecilia asked.

All eyes converged on Ethan. It was obvious that she wasn't the only one who had noticed how indifferent he'd become when it came to socializing with Tate.

"I just got the text today! I haven't had a chance to tell you," Ethan protested, springing to his own defense. "How about it? Wanna go?"

"We'll see you both there," Anya affirmed, shooting a disapproving glance at Ethan as she made her way through the mob toward Jimmy.

Jimmy was addressing the crowd, expressing his deepest gratitude to Anya, the devoted patrons of Chenoah Falls Stray Rescue, and the four families who had opened their hearts and homes to the dogs he'd brought along that day.

Joe Hop, owner of Hop's Market, approached Anya to bestow a donation check of his own—courtesy of the Patawomek Street Chamber of Commerce. Anya was stunned to read the amount. She hugged him with many thanks before announcing the day's results.

"Thank you all for coming to show your support for Jimmy and the dogs of CF Rescue! Not only did we raise five thousand dollars in donations here today, but I've also received this check from Joe Hop of Hop's Market. I think you all know Joe," Anya said, pausing while the crowd hollered and waved to Joe. "The proprietors on Patawomek Street have authorized him to match that amount, bringing today's grand total to a record-breaking ten thousand dollars!" Anya presented the two checks to Jimmy as the crowd erupted again into whistles, whoops, and applause.

Jimmy waved the two checks in the air triumphantly. Then he hugged Anya and whispered, "Terrible start to the day, but hey, we managed to turn it around, didn't we? Thank you so much." To the crowd, he shouted, "Thank you! Thank you all so much! Thanks to McClean's and their staff, and thanks to Sarah and Drexsler's Deli! You guys are the best!" He made a hero's exit, brandishing the banknotes, with Nate trotting along beside him.

Anya could see Martine and the sheriff outside at the curb loading Ching and the others into their cars for the return trip to the lake. She felt a pang of sadness. Except for Ching, Zia, and occasionally Don Pedro, Anya rarely got to see the cats anymore now that they were all staying at the lake house full-time. She couldn't wait for all of this to be over, for their blissfully predictable, happy lives to resume.

Back upstairs, Ethan said, "Wow, it's so strange seeing the sheriff and Martine together in public. I'm still trying to get used to it."

"Yeah, it's weird ... kind of, but I'm happy for them. They're great together," Anya replied.

No sooner had they settled on the couch to eat when Anya noticed a book lying on the floor near the fireplace. Ching must have been in her living room earlier, she thought as she went to retrieve it. Upon inspection, she saw that—this time—there were no teeth marks, and no pages were torn.

"I knew Ching had recently taken up the piano, but has he become a literary critic as well—suggesting titles in his spare time?" Ethan joked. From where he was sitting, he could just make out the title. "*Once He's Gone,*" Ethan read aloud. It was a very entertaining novel by Brooke Matheson. Anya placed it back in the bookcase.

Ching wasn't the only one of Martine's cats who enjoyed dislodging books from shelves. She imagined they enjoyed hearing the loud thumps they made when they hit the floor. Anya had seen Don Pedro do it too. If it had been Ching, why had he chosen the Matheson book? Ching never did anything without a reason.

"Wow! I hope that's not one of his cryptic messages directed at me!" Ethan howled.

Anya raised an eyebrow. "Better watch your step," she teased.

At that moment, there was a ding from Ethan's cell phone.

Ethan responded with a waggish grin, "Hmmm, my cell phone. Maybe it's Ching. He knows we're talking about him."

Anya made a face at him as he dug his cell out of his pocket.

"Nope. Text from Tate. I'll let him know we're coming tomorrow."

TWENTY-THREE

Many of the communities that surrounded Chenoah Falls derived their names from French and Native American words or terms that stemmed from the fur trade or lumbering industries. The town of Punkin, for instance, took its name from a word lumberjacks used to describe a particularly nice log. Pulaski's namesake was the inventor of a tool—a combination ax and hoe. When timbering operations called for blasting, a hole was dug into which a powder charge was placed. The community of Coyote Hole was named for this practice. Staghead's name was taken from the term given to trees with dead tops. Four Oaks, as well as Five Pines, were references to the number of oak and pine tree varieties that were indigenous to the region.

Tate Blackledge lived in a town known as Batteau—a type of boat once used by French fur traders. It was about twenty minutes southwest of Chenoah Falls, and Tate had built a magnificent house there. The home had been initially slated for teardown until Tate bought it from the county, tore it down himself, and rebuilt it from the ground-up.

He and his brother Rob had done all of the work themselves, including the pouring of two thousand additional square feet of concrete, increasing the original square footage to almost three thousand square feet.

With the help of the Colburn sisters, Tate had incorporated all of the best modern finishes on the interior. There were beautiful hand-scraped hardwood floors throughout the living room, dining room, game room, study, and four bedrooms. The ceilings were all opened up to the rafters exposing rough-hewn beams, augmented by gothic-style black iron light fixtures and fans. The house also contained three masonry wood burning fireplaces, which was not entirely unusual in this northern clime.

The furniture, however, was another story. Jules and Tate had gone round and round when it came to selecting the furnishings and artwork. In the end, Tate had gotten the final say. All the chairs and sofas were black leather, all of the area rugs were cowhide, and all of the picture frames held enlargements of vintage horror movie playbills. No decorative bowls, vases, or sculptures had been approved, and there was not a throw pillow in sight.

Ethan had suggested that Cecilia and Nigel ride with them on the day of Tate's party. When they arrived, there were quite a few cars lined up in front of the house and along the road, so Ethan was forced to park on a side street. They were greeted by a couple of girls who were sunbathing in the back of Tate's old blue pickup. He'd put a liner in the bed and filled it up with water for them. He'd even thrown in a couple of pool floaties. They raised their glasses and waved as they passed by.

"Ahhh … ," Nigel sighed, "This is exactly what I need. Time to put this week in the bag and blow off some steam," he declared.

Their host was just exiting the kitchen when they all eventually trooped through the door.

"Hey, guys!" Tate greeted them enthusiastically. "Wow, I missed a lot while I was gone, huh? Four Oaks is all over the news. I can't say I remember anything like this ever happening around here," he added. He gave Anya a knowing look and shook his head in awe. She knew it was his way of capitulating to her superior instincts when it came to Sidra York.

"Sure, what about the Finley case?" Cecilia replied, referring to a particularly disturbing 2001 murder/suicide. It had happened in the town of Pulaski. A teenage boy had killed his parents and two siblings before shooting himself. It was a gruesome reminder.

Tate stared at her, momentarily dulled by Cecilia's dispassionate response. "Keg's over there," Tate continued, clearing his throat and pointing them toward the bar near the kitchen. "Food's in there too: burgers, brats, dogs, potato salad, someone brought a cake. Make a plate, grab a beer, and come on outside on the deck."

Tate had assembled a small coalition of friends for the day's festivities. They were all local people—local to Batteau. Some Anya recognized, some she didn't, but they were all very friendly and quick to introduce themselves.

After a stop by the kitchen for food and beer, Nigel led the way toward a table near the edge of the deck, where he presumed they could enjoy a pleasant view of the tree-lined property. Instead, they found themselves staring down at a deep muddy hole. It was the general consensus that Tate was in the process of adding a pool.

While they were eating, Anya couldn't help but overhear a lot of talk about the case in Four Oaks, drifting over from nearby tables. Much of it was rife with rumor and innuendo that was utterly false. She was tempted to interject some truths into these discussions but decided to raise the topic of Fourth of July instead.

"What's this I hear about you dusting off the old ski show?" she asked.

Cecilia nodded emphatically. "We've been practicing for a couple of weeks now. Mom and Dad have still got it! I'm really looking forward to skiing with them again."

"Nigel's a competent ski boat runner I gather?" Anya asked with a sidelong glance at Nigel.

"Oh, yes, very. He was a little nervous at first, but I have the utmost faith in his ability," Cecilia said proudly.

Nigel raked his fingers through his long dark hair and heaved a pressure-filled sigh in response.

Ethan started laughing. "Are we going to see any new stunts in this year's performance?" he asked.

"I wanted to add a jump, you know, off a ramp, but Nigel was too apprehensive about it, so we're sticking to the tried and true," Cecilia affirmed.

"By the way, Cossima tried to book three rooms at The Silver Pines, so you and Anya could stay over too," Nigel said to Ethan, "But they're completely full over there." Ethan and Anya were nonplussed by such a thoughtful gesture.

"How generous and kind of your mom, Cecilia! Please thank her for thinking of us," Anya said.

"Yes, please do, but I'm kind of relieved to hear that she was unsuccessful. Doc Lafferty is taking his wife and kids on vacation that week, and I have to be at work by eight. Don't worry though. I'm still planning a late night and one hell of a hangover in the morning!" Ethan announced, drawing a burst of laughter from them all.

Anya noticed that Cecilia had made a plate that consisted primarily of olives. She was popping them into her mouth, three and four at a time.

"We have a group of tables reserved under the pavilion on the back terrace," Cecilia struggled to explain with her mouth full of Gordals. "VIP, all-inclusive, open bar, a fabulous lunch buffet, and full table service for dinner. Mom and Dad will probably have to run into town after dinner to check on the restaurant, but they'll leave us the keys to the boat. We can watch the fireworks from out on the water." She glanced expectantly at Nigel, who promptly remitted his cache of olives. Anya pushed her last two across the table to her, as well.

As soon as the guests had eaten their fill, and the leftovers had been cleared away, Rob was excited to share the news about the soon to be infamous trip to Ohio.

"I'm not gonna bore you guys with the full report. If you want to see everything, you can go to the website and check it out. If you want to see some highlights, come in the game room. Don't feel like you have to or anything! You won't hurt my feelings!" Rob assured with a laugh.

Of course, everyone followed him inside. Whenever Tate and Rob said they had great footage to share, everyone knew they meant it.

Anya took a seat on one of the couches with Ethan, Cecilia, and Nigel taking up positions to her left. She wasn't surprised when Tate took a seat to the right of her. He always left the presentations to his brother. He was uncomfortable when it came to addressing groups.

"After this is over, come into the study with me. I have something important to tell you," Tate whispered in her ear.

He kept his eyes forward, refusing to acknowledge her questioning look. Clearly, he didn't intend to expand on the request, so Anya turned her focus back to Rob.

The laptop was already connected to the big screen TV, so once everyone had gathered, Rob proceeded to share what proved to be an impressive compilation of captioned stills and raw narrated video footage of their latest spine-tingling adventure.

"The subscribers on the website voted to send us on a trip to Kenyon College in Gambier, Ohio." Rob displayed a picture of the college.

Anya was struck by a pulsating sense of foreboding that emanated from the structures and the surrounding landscape.

"The semester had ended and commencement ceremonies had been held the week before, so the campus and all of the residence halls were closed," Rob continued. "We had the place to ourselves, with permission to explore. This is one of the creepiest places I've ever visited. It was built in 1824, and the original buildings were designed in the gothic revival style, brick and stone facades, spires, pointed archways, real medieval-looking stuff."

Rob clicked to the next slide. "These are the south

campus gates. They're two old stone pillars marking what they call *The Middle Path*. Unofficially, the students call it *Hellsmouth* or *The Gates to Hell*. The students observe two superstitions connected with what they say is an evil portal. They never pass between the pillars without touching one of them, and they never pass between them when the Church of the Holy Spirit's bells are chiming midnight, for fear of being transported to hell. Here, of course, is a little video of Tate standing between the pillars, holding up the time on his phone, which reads midnight. You can hear the church bells in the background! As you can see, my brother is still with us!"

Everyone burst out laughing. Someone asked Tate if he was crazy. Tate swirled his scotch and nodded yes.

"This is the Church of the Holy Spirit I just mentioned. It's an amazing old gothic chapel that is also supposed to be cursed. Legend has it that the church sits over the pits of hell. It has these black, sooty scorch marks you can see here by this window, but there has never been a fire there. A priest was said to have gone crazy and hung himself in its bell tower. Many believe his lost soul haunts the church, but we weren't able to uncover any evidence of that."

The next slide was entitled: Old Kenyon Hall. "This is where things got interesting. Old Kenyon Hall was the first structure to be built on campus. It was a residence hall for male students. It burned down in 1949. Tragically, nine students died. They say the blaze began around four a.m., originating from one of the four old fireplaces—ironically the only one that is still in use to this day. Here it is in the middle parlor. After the fire—much of the hall had to be rebuilt, which was done the following year."

Rob clicked ahead to a slide entitled: New Kenyon Hall. It was equally as ominous as its predecessor with its menacing medieval facade. "Since being reconstructed, there have been many reports of ghost sightings, cold spots, shadowy images, and muffled sounds of disembodied voices crying, 'Wake up! Fire! Fire!' We let the cameras roll all night. That's us getting into our sleeping bags there. When I edited this, I fast-forwarded to show two places in the footage we thought showed the presence of shadow figures. Here's the first one."

Anya and Cecilia both sucked in their breath as the amorphous outline of a shadow appeared. It floated into camera range from stage right, hovering above Tate and Rob while they slept. Stunned spectators looked to one another in disbelief, and wary whispers circulated. Anya shifted uncomfortably on the couch beside Tate. The shape-shifting apparition hung around for several minutes and then startled the onlookers by zooming off stage left. A few people jumped and nervous laughter erupted.

"Here is the other one, a little harder to see, but watch the doorway. I circled it in red," Rob said, cueing up the second video. There did indeed seem to be a vaguely defined energy lingering in the doorway of the middle parlor. It remained there, nebulous, unmoving for several seconds before slowly oozing from the room.

Everyone was impressed, and many went so far as to proclaim it as irrefutable evidence that the supernatural exists.

"Wait, you haven't seen the best part!" Rob exclaimed. "This is the last bit I have to show you. This is the video we shot outside of the door to Stuart Pierson's room on the fourth floor. This poor guy was a pledge left by his frat brothers on a train trestle bridge. They knew in advance that there were no trains scheduled to come through that night, except one did. The engineer never so much as tapped the brakes. They never knew they hit him. Watch this," Rob said, clicking play.

The viewers watched in horror as the open door to Stuart's old room slowly swung closed. It quivered for a moment as Tate or Rob whispered, "Look, look at that." Suddenly it began to shake violently, rattling against the door jam and quaking mightily on its hinges! The video reeled wildly amid a hail of curse words as Tate and Rob took off running down the hall!

Yelps and gasps were again accompanied by strained

laughter, and Rob ended the show. Even Tate laughed and shivered his shoulders as if to shake off a residual chill attached to the experience.

"That place has the creep factor for sure!" Rob said. "I'll end it there, but if you want to see the rest—you can go online and check it out. At Lewis Hall, a student supposedly hung himself in the attic. Nothing happened while we were inside, but while we were getting a shot of the exterior, the whole place lit up for a total of five seconds, and then BAM, total darkness again!"

While the party moved back outside, Anya excused herself, telling Ethan, Nigel, and Cecilia that she would be right out.

When she made her way into Tate's study, she saw that he was waiting for her—seated in a chair behind his desk. Rob was standing beside him.

"Looks like I owe you an apology, Anya," Tate submitted. "I spoke to Jules the day Rob and I got back from Ohio. I guess you were right on the money about Sidra York, huh?"

Anya folded her arms across her chest and smiled wryly. She was feeling a certain amount of satisfaction that Tate had been forced to eat his words.

Tate smiled in that boyish, charming way of his and said, "I see you're going to gloat. That's OK. I get it. I should have taken you much more seriously. I won't make that mistake again. I promise. Now, for the new business, and believe me—if you have any inside information—you can trust Rob. Have they been able to identify Sidra's secret partner yet?"

Anya tucked her hair behind her ears and fiddled with one of her earrings. "I would love to tell you what I've been able to learn so far, but I'm under orders by the sheriff to keep quiet."

"Naturally," Tate replied facetiously. "Well, as luck would have it, I have an interesting detail that I *am* at liberty to share with *you.* My brother here recently informed me that he *did* happen to see Sidra in the company of a male associate. It happened on the first day that we were on the job. I'd gone into town for supplies. Rob had stayed behind at the gallery to start ripping out some old partitions left over from when the place was a furniture store. Sidra and some guy in a fishing cap dropped in. She didn't introduce him. They smiled and waved, went up to the office for a minute or two, and then left without a word."

Anya was dumbstruck! She jerked her head at Rob, who had been silent up until now. "Did you get a good look at him?"

Rob shrugged. "Not real good, but he was about five-ten, slim build, dark wavy hair, wearing jeans, a dark blue T-shirt, and a tan fishing cap," he said.

Hearing Rob's description, Anya flashed back to that first tarot card reading Martine had done on the night of Ethan's graduation party. She'd drawn four cards. One of those cards had been the King of Spades, a warning about a self-serving, *dark-haired* man.

"Rob, you have to call Sheriff Wakefield right away. You're quite possibly the only one who's ever seen him!" Anya said.

"We already did," Tate replied with a grin.

Anya noticed Tate's eyes shift to a place near the doorway, directly over her left shoulder. She turned to see that Ethan was standing there. He seemed to have overheard the whole conversation. She got the impression that Tate had intentionally disregarded his presence.

"So, Anya," Tate said, recalling her attention to him.

Anya turned to see that Tate was reclining comfortably in his chair, palms together, fingers interlaced.

"You never called me about the bank. Did you make an appointment?" he asked.

Tate didn't realize, of course, that she was set to inherit millions. No one did. With that in mind, Anya had decided to forego the loan and use her existing funds to get the project underway. She could pay the balance with her share of the Beckwith estate if it was settled in the next month or two. The only reason to seek a bank loan would be if the money didn't come in by the time the project was completed. She couldn't tell Tate any of this, though, and had no idea how she was otherwise going to explain it. He would know that without a loan, she would have to run her accounts to zero, and he would wonder why she would want to do such a thing.

"Actually," Anya said, "after going over my finances, I found that I have enough to cover phase one. By the time you're finished, I may have enough to pay you in full without going to the bank. You can come by anytime and pick up a check for the deposit unless you want me to mail it."

An interminable silence followed. Tate's expression revealed nothing of his reaction to this news, but Anya knew his mind must be full of questions. Tate had a fairly good grasp of her financial situation. He had to know she didn't have that kind of money lying around. Tate stared at her without further comment, and Anya made a swift departure.

On the way home, the two couples had little to say, with each one wrapped up in their own private thoughts. However, once Nigel and Cecilia were dropped off, and she and Ethan were alone in her apartment—Ethan had plenty to say.

"I don't know why I assumed that I was the only one you'd talked to about Sidra York. I guess I shouldn't be surprised that you chose to confide in Tate," Ethan said in an accusatory tone while collapsing on her couch.

"Ethan, all that stuff about Sidra came up during

one of the meetings we had to go over the renovation plans for the pub. We're friends. That's all. You know that. There's nothing to get worked up about."

Ethan stood up and began to pace the room. "I promised myself that I wouldn't ask you if you explored whatever this is between you and him while I was gone. I half expected the two of you to be a couple by the time I got back from Minneapolis. You know Nigel warned me that, if I was sure about you and me, I better lock it down before I left. He told me to put a ring on your finger—get engaged. Know why I didn't take that advice?"

"Because you wanted to be free to do whatever you wanted to do? Because you knew I would have said no? Because we were too young, and everyone knows long-distance relationships don't work? One or all of the above?"

Ethan shook his head. "No, and for your information, I didn't see anyone while I was away. I didn't take Nigel's advice because that's not my style. I always thought we were better than that. I believed that, no matter what happened while I was away—when I came home—you and I would still have the same feelings for each other. I was right to believe that, but I don't trust Tate," he said.

Ethan sank into a chair across the room from her. He drew a hand across his mouth like he meant to prevent whatever he was about to say from coming out.

Ultimately, the force by which he felt compelled to speak, won out, and he continued. “Even now, I get the feeling that he’s waiting in the wings for our relationship to run its course. Listen, Anya, I realize you don’t see it, but I know Tate. I’ve seen how he operates. He’s a good guy, but he’s very smooth. He always knows what he wants, and he knows how to get it. He’s charming, manipulative, and good with the lines. He has feelings for you, Anya. I can see it. It’s more than a friendship to him. I mean, who could blame him? Beautiful girl like you, smart, successful. I could never settle for friendship alone when it comes to you.”

Ethan sighed and rubbed his eyes wearily. He got up again and came to sit beside her on the couch. He pressed his forehead to hers and said, “None of this is your fault. This is my problem, not yours. I’ll try not to bring it up again, but moving forward—your friendship with Tate is going to be a problem for me.”

Anya was about to respond when Ching suddenly strutted into the center of the room.

“What are you doing here?!” Anya exclaimed. “Excuse me,” she said, climbing over Ethan to ascertain the reason for the cat’s unexpected presence.

When she went to Martine’s to see if she was at home, she saw another note had been taped to her door. Once again, Ching had been MIA when it was time to go back to the lake. Martine wrote that she hoped Anya would feed him dinner and breakfast in the morning.

Anya was secretly happy to see the feline fugitive. She'd been missing the cats quite a bit lately. She went into Martine's kitchen to put out some kibble and bits of turkey. Ching sprang into the room behind her, heading straight for the turkey.

She returned to the living room to find Ethan standing near the door, preparing to leave.

"You're not staying? Because of this thing with Tate?" Anya asked.

Ethan smiled and kissed her goodnight. "No, because of work." He pulled her close and sighed. "I love you so much, Anya. I'm sorry about all of this. I don't think I used to be this jealous, was I? I'll work on it."

"I promise you, nothing happened while you were away, and you don't have to be jealous. I love you, Ethan."

After he'd gone, Anya was surreptitiously drawn to thoughts of Tate. Ethan wasn't entirely wrong. She and Tate had always been very close. They had everything in common, and there had been a few times when Anya had sensed that if she were to give him an opening, he would take it. Truth be told, she had fleetingly considered the possibilities of it herself a time or two over the years, but she had never really let go of Ethan while he was away. Anya had always entertained the hope that they would get back together someday. She'd known that she could never move on from Ethan until she was sure there would be no second chance, and now there was.

Anya was exhausted by the time she finally climbed into bed. Ching was quick to join her. He crawled up the length of her body to settle on her chest, their noses practically touching.

"You're lucky you're a cat," she said. "Less complicated."

Ching squeezed his eyes closed and yawned broadly, sticking his tongue out so far it touched her chin.

"You rascal. Did you hide from Martine so you could stay here with me?"

"Tch!" Ching sneezed, rolling off her to the edge of the bed. He dug in his claws as he slid over the side, dragging the sheet and cover with him. Then he left the room without so much as a backward glance.

"*Cats*!" Anya huffed, clicking off the lamp.

TWENTY-FOUR

Summer Festival had brought record numbers of tourists to Four Oaks. It was their busiest season; however, with estimates as high as three times the usual number of visitors, it had been suggested, on more than one occasion, that the recent media attention might be responsible.

There had been no arrests made, no further developments of any kind in the hotel bombing or the Sidra York case. People were already starting to put it behind them and get on with their lives.

It was late Sunday morning, June 25th, and McClean's was preparing to close for renovations in less than a week. Tate had stopped by to get Anya's input on last-minute plans he'd drawn up for a climbing wall he wanted to add to the Cats 'n' Cocktails project. Anya found herself marveling at an interactive system of climbing poles, footpaths, rope bridges, hammocks, perches, and cylindrical hidey-holes for smaller cats, treats, or toys. His designs were phenomenal.

"Well, if you approve, then I guess you know what's

coming next," Tate said. He combed his fingers through the layers of his hair as he accepted the check Anya held out to him. He tapped the edge of it on the counter, his dark blue eyes searching hers for hidden answers. While it wasn't out of the realm of possibility that she possessed sufficient funds to cover the deposit—Anya knew he was still trying to figure out how she planned to pay the balance without taking a loan. Sensing that a question was on the way, Anya swiftly decided to apply a little misdirection.

"When you're finished with the job, we'll celebrate," Anya suggested. "I still have Grandma Luna's leftovers in my freezer."

Tate beamed a smile at her, one that said, "Nice try." He snapped the check, slipped it into his pocket, and left without a word.

"Talented guy," Desda commented as they both watched him go. "So good looking too."

Anya grinned. "Yeah, the new place is gonna be great, isn't it?"

Desda bobbed her head in excitement. "I can't wait. Ever wonder why there's no girl?"

"What? You mean Tate? I wonder about that all the time," Anya said.

Desda raised her eyebrows at her. "I think I know," she said.

Anya wasn't about to take the bait. Today was the day

of Cecilia's wedding shower at Martine's house, and one glance at the clock told her it was time to get moving. She waved Desda off and hurried upstairs to get ready.

Anya had already chosen a dress to wear, a simple, sleeveless, lavender shift, along with a pair of summery, platform wedges that had multicolored vamps. She arranged her hair in the messy half-bun she'd begun to favor, allowing the rest of her glossy black hair to fall in waves past her shoulders.

To her great consternation, Anya discovered that she was out of contact lenses. She used her phone to place an order before grabbing her glasses, purse, and keys.

The gift she'd come up with for Cecilia was a clever one that Anya wished she could take credit for, but in truth—she'd spotted the idea on a social media site. It was a large rectangular beverage basket containing a variety of fine wines, ten to be exact. Each bottle had a fancy tag attached to commemorate ten future firsts Cecilia and Nigel would experience during their first year as a married couple. One tag read: *First Valentine's Day,* another: *First Christmas*; there was also: *First Anniversary,* and so on. Anya knew Cecilia would love it. She'd been storing it downstairs in McClean's wine cellar. The cellar was where all of McClean's beverage stock was kept.

Hugging the heavy and incredibly awkward basket to her chest, Anya eyed the stairs, warily. Judging the climb in three-inch wedges to be more than a little perilous, she kicked off her shoes and wrestled it up to the top in bare feet.

Desda was openly amused by these antics, grinning as she watched her struggle out the door to her truck. Anya pretended not to notice, returning to the basement once more—this time to retrieve her shoes. Breathless from her exertions, Anya took a seat at the bar for a moment. That's when she noticed that Desda was brimming with enthusiasm.

"Paul and I have booked our cruise!" Desda announced. "We're leaving on the first for the Virgin Islands!"

Anya watched Desda gather up all of the brochures she'd had on display behind the bar for over a month. She'd been so consumed with the details, often immersing total strangers in her deliberations, that people had started to avoid sitting directly at the bar.

"I'm going to bring these with me to the shower. Look at this ship!" Desda exclaimed. "*The Mystic Princess*! Isn't it beautiful?!" Anya had to admit that the gleaming white ship, replete with lavish staterooms, grand staircases, elegant dining rooms, and upper deck pool, was very appealing.

"These are the excursions we're taking: On St. Lucia, hot mineral pools and sulfur springs heated by a volcano, followed by an aerial tram ride through a rainforest/

eco-park. On St. Croix, we're going to do a little rum tasting at the Captain Morgan and Cruzan Rum Distilleries. We may even try scuba diving if I can talk Paul into it."

"Rum … not a bad idea," Anya interjected, reaching for a bottle of Malibu and pouring them each a shot.

They were huddled over a brochure that featured pictures of Marigot Bay on St. Kitts when Elizabeth Colburn walked in.

Elizabeth studied the photos of the picturesque little shops and restaurants surrounded by turquoise waters, white sand beaches, and palm trees. In her usual saturnine manner, she grumbled, "You're not going to the Caribbean this time of year, are you? It's hurricane season, for heaven's sake! Everyone knows that!"

Apparently, everyone did not. Desda suddenly looked a little pale. "Hurricane season?"

"Well, it's not peak season. Three out of four hurricanes blow up between August and October. I'm sure you'll be fine," Elizabeth conceded in a rare attempt to soften the blow.

Anya placed a hand on Desda's shoulder to steady her.

"I'm about to order the new tables, chairs, and barstools we agreed on," Elizabeth said, "but I need you to sign off on it first." She shoved the paperwork toward Anya.

"Have you finished taking inventory of the artwork that was removed from The York Gallery?" Anya asked, signing the bottom of the order form.

The Colburn Design Studio had been charged with the task of assessing the value of the gallery's contents for the purpose of an auction, partly to help Cossima Bennedetto recover what she'd paid for the fake Modigliani.

"Yeah, that phony!" Elizabeth snapped, clearly and rightfully exasperated. "What a fraud! Most of the pieces were of modest value. A few had actually been stolen from a gallery in New Jersey, of all places. And get this—it seems Miss Hoity-Toity must have had at least *some* art training in her past since she appears to have painted about *half* of the collection *herself*. Investigators stated that she had a little art studio upstairs, paints, assorted canvases, and a stack of art books with full-color illustrations to use as a guide!

That explained Sidra's Bell Book & Candle purchase, Anya thought to herself, not to mention the paint smears she'd noted on Sidra's person the day she'd visited the gallery to conduct a little detective work of her own.

"Cossima won't recoup a dime!" Elizabeth continued. "Neither will we, for that matter. She took off before we had a chance to invoice her for our part in the gallery project. She ordered those chandeliers and studio couches from us. I'm so furious with that woman that my mind has been playing tricks on me. I know she's dead, but I keep thinking I see her everywhere

I go. Jules says it's because I can't accept that she fooled us all, and my subconscious wants restitution. She's right, of course, but just the other day, I could have sworn I saw her walking into the Palm's Hotel in Chenoah Falls. I was dropping off some chairs at our upholsterer across the street. I even went so far as to call out her name! She didn't turn around because it wasn't her, of course. I must be going crazy," Elizabeth growled. She snatched up the papers and heaved a frustrated sigh. "Well, I'm off. I can't make it to the shower today, but Jules will be there. She's bringing both of our gifts. Have a great day, and if I don't see you—happy cruising," she said, directing the last bit to Desda on her way out the door.

Pink and white crab apple trees were blooming against the shady backdrop of leafy oaks and towering pines that formed a perimeter around Martine's house. The meticulously maintained flowerbeds lining the path that led to the entrance were exploding with a cultivated mix of delphiniums, lupines, petunias, and marigolds. An elegant floral wreath of silk lilies and yards of breezy white tulle adorned the front door.

Anya wrestled her basket of wines inside and deposited it on a table in the entrance hall that had been designated as the official gift table.

Candles in sparkling crystal holders flickered on the fireplace mantel, and there were balloons and streamers everywhere she looked. Several arrangements of fresh roses and lilies of the valley, Cecilia's favorite, had been strategically placed—out of the cats' reach. They filled the space with a sweet, heady aroma. Stations had been set up around the room for fun and games and to encourage the guests to mingle. Next to the gift table was a smaller table with a crystal bowl full of costume jewelry rings. The sign beside it read: *Please take one, but say the word "bride," and someone will steal your bling!* Anya did as instructed, sliding one of the faux diamond rings onto her finger before taking a tour of the other stations.

There was a mimosa and lemonade station, beside which stood a table and a giant mason jar full of candy kisses. The sign here read: *Guess how many to win!* Anya was pretty good at these kinds of challenges. At the state fair, she'd estimated the number of cheeseballs in a thirty-two ounce container and won a thirty-two ounce container of cheeseballs. Another time, at a carnival in Five Pines, she precisely guessed the number of golf tees in a jar and won four free passes to Neon Lights Glow in the Dark Putt-Putt Golf in Pulaski. Anya wrote a number down and tossed it in the basket provided.

The next station had a poster: *How Well Do You Know the Bride?* It was accompanied by a cup full of pencils that had: *Chenoah Falls Bowl-a-rama* embossed in gold on their sides and a stack of question and answer sheets on which questions about Cecilia had been neatly typed. Anya read a few to herself. *Where did the bride and groom meet? What is the bride's shoe size? What is the bride's favorite flower?*

Beyond that, was a table that held a shiny silver receptacle. There were stacks of tongue depressors and magic markers lying beside it. The idea was to record ideas for adventurous or unusual date night ideas on the tongue depressors and place them in the silver holder. They were to be drawn one at a time by the future newlyweds whenever they needed to "keep things interesting". This one would require some thought, so Anya decided to percolate on it and move on down the line.

Why Do We Do That? was the question posed by the chalkboard sign at the next table. Here was another stack of paper copies and another cup of pens, not pencils, imprinted with the words: *For all your legal needs—call Beau Nithercott 779-1800.* Anya smiled and lifted the top sheet from the pile. It was a matching game. The left side was a list of traditional wedding customs, and the right side was a list of how they had originated. *Why does the bride wear a veil? Why does the wedding party dress alike?* Anya noticed, interestingly enough, that many of the answers stemmed from superstitions having to do with disguising the bride from evil spirits.

Martine was nowhere in sight, but Anya heard laughter coming from the direction of the kitchen.

She decided that she better say hello and see if she could be of help. The sign on the kitchen's swinging door read: *Keep your eyes open for more bling! Whoever finds the most rings by gift-opening time wins a prize!*

Anya was greeted by hugs and hellos from the merry group on the other side of the door. Sharon Bailer, Kathleen and Donna Cruz, and Rheina Sheridan were sipping mimosas and swirling white icing on what looked to be about a hundred cupcakes.

"Wow, that's a lot of cupcakes. Need some help?" Anya asked.

"Thanks, but I think we're almost done. We baked fifty-six cupcakes at our shop last night, eighteen chocolate, eighteen red velvet, and twenty vanilla," Donna announced.

"We're going to arrange them on a platter in the shape of a wedding dress," Kathleen added.

Anya wondered briefly why there were twenty vanilla, but only eighteen chocolate and red velvet.

"Rheina, the flowers are spectacular! I can always recognize your work. When Jimmy Shaw was in the hospital, some of his volunteers brought in an arrangement. I knew in an instant it had to be from your shop. You always give it that extra touch," Anya said sincerely.

Rheina beamed, pleased to receive a compliment. "Thank you, Anya! I think they turned out beautifully, kind of a trial run for the flowers Cecilia wants for the wedding."

"Where's Martine? I didn't see her when I came in," Anya asked.

"I thought she was going to get set up in the study for the tarot readings she's going to do later. We're going to draw three names, and those three people will get a free reading from Martine today," Kathleen explained. "You must have passed right by her when you came in."

Just then, a mad scrabbling sound was heard as Ching shorted his ascent to the counter.

"Is that Ching back again?!" Donna exclaimed, shaking her head in disbelief. "We've put him in Martine's room at least three times, but he keeps getting out somehow. We're afraid he might get into the food or try to eat the flowers. They aren't cat safe."

"The door to Martine's room has a lever-style handle. Ching knows how to operate it. I'll put him in the study instead. It has a brass knob. That should present him with more of a challenge," Anya offered, scooping him up in her arms.

"Good idea. The other cats are in the guest room, but it has a lever handle too, I think," Kathleen pointed out.

Ching was straining to sniff the cupcakes and the bowl of icing. He struggled in protest as Anya whisked him from the room. She headed straight for the study, ignoring the loud howling this elicited from her prisoner as he voiced his objection. When she reached the study, Martine was there, clearing an assortment of papers from her desktop.

"Oh! Ching ... ," Martine huffed, shaking her head at the wayward cat. Anya deposited him in the nearest chair and closed the door.

"He keep gettin out of my room," Martine remarked. "Smart cat. Are Cossima and Cecilia here yet?"

"No, not yet," Anya replied. "Just me and, of course, the cupcake brigade."

"Doesn't da place look lovely for da shower today?" Martine asked with a whimsical smile.

"Beautiful, absolutely stunning!" Anya affirmed.

Martine put the last of her correspondence on a shelf behind her, dusted off the desktop, and pulled three tarot decks from her bottom drawer.

"Tell me, how is it goin wid Ethan?"

"Things are going well, I think. We're taking it slow. It's kind of like starting over," Anya said with a shrug.

"Slow? Too slow if you ask me! Dat pot's been simmerin away on da back burner for years! Time to kick up da heat!" Martine exclaimed.

"You mean like you and the sheriff?" Anya said with a wink.

"Da sheriff? Oh, honey, dat's no simmer. He's a rolling boil!" Martine said, after which they both burst into laughter.

"OK, time to get mimosas and greet da guests,"

Martine said, ushering Anya out of the study ahead of her. "I love you, but you stay here, Mistah," she instructed Ching, closing the door behind them.

Cossima and Cecilia had now arrived and were admiring the beautiful table that had been set for the buffet. Martine had broken out her best crystal, china, and flatware for Cecilia's day.

The excitement escalated when the guests learned that Cecilia's wedding plans included a ceremony to be performed at St. Mark's Cathedral and a reception at The Top of the Pines Hotel, to which they would all naturally be invited. The Top of the Pines was by far the glitziest hotel within a hundred miles or more. The reception would include a cocktail party in the grand lobby, followed by dinner, drinks, and dancing in the main ballroom.

Silver trays began arriving from the kitchen then, carried by the attendees that had prepared them. The traditional fruit, cheese, and vegetable platters were in evidence, as well as a tray of heart-shaped tea sandwiches, but the rest of the menu was far more imaginative and inviting. Most notable were the bacon-wrapped asparagus dippers accompanied by a Caesar-style dressing, individual shrimp scampi flatbreads, garlic-parm pretzel knots, and spinach-artichoke spring rolls.

After visiting the buffet, guests gravitated toward either the deck or the living room. Some chose to stroll past the flower arrangements, pausing to admire them or to entertain themselves at the clever bridal shower activities around the room.

When the names were drawn to award the free tarot readings, Anya wasn't surprised to see that nearly everyone was hoping to be a winner. Sharon Bailer, one of Martine's regulars, Jules Colburn, and Donna Cruz were the lucky recipients. Each took turns adjourning to Martine's study for a ten-minute reading, while Anya stood guard outside the door, foiling Ching's multiple attempts to escape his confines. Once, he made it as far as one of the living room sofas, executing a rather well thought out end run past her ankles. To his chagrin, Desda was there to make the interception, and the dejected Ching was returned to his makeshift cell.

"Out of contacts?" Cecilia asked, coming over to keep Anya company.

Anya gave her nosepiece a shove in annoyance and nodded.

"You look great in glasses," Cecilia said truthfully. "You should wear them more. Did you hear the latest about my mother's efforts to recover her losses on that painting?"

"Actually, I happened to see Elizabeth this morning," Anya replied with a sympathetic sigh. "She said she didn't think they would be able to make enough from the gallery auction to recoup your mom's losses. I'm so sorry. How is she taking it?"

"Not too terribly, considering. I think she feels a little foolish about getting taken, but the money is of no consequence to her."

Anya mulled over the idea of ten thousand dollars being of no consequence and began to realize that, considering her upbringing, inheriting half of the Beckwith fortune was going to be a real adjustment for her. Could ten thousand dollars ever really be of little or no consequence to her? Anya didn't think so.

"Here," Cecilia whispered, handing Anya a small sachet purse she had swinging from her arm. "I don't know if you'll win, but I've collected a lot of bling from everyone here today. Take it, but my lipstick's in there too, so don't lose it!"

Anya accepted it with a smile.

Jules emerged from Martine's study, wearing a bemused smirk.

Anya raised her eyebrows questioningly.

"I hate to tell Martine," Jules whispered, coming to stand beside her, "but her spiritual antennae is on the fritz today. She said I'm going to meet a new romantic partner while out of town on business. I am leaving on business next week to catalog a house full of antiques on Martha's Vineyard, but I happen to know the owners are something like a hundred years old."

"No rich, handsome grandsons waiting in the wings?" Anya asked.

Jules shook her head and added, "Also, why didn't somebody warn Desda it was hurricane season before she booked that trip? Love your glasses, by the way. You should wear them more often."

Donna Cruz was obviously delighted by her reading, rushing over afterward to exchange a few words with her sister, Kathleen. Kathleen was equally elated by whatever the news had been.

Sharon Bailer exited Martine's study, red-faced and agitated. She too rushed directly over to Kathleen Cruz and asked to borrow her cell phone.

Anya happened to catch Kathleen's eye. She cocked her head and frowned to convey her curiosity.

Kathleen sidled over to her and whispered, "Bad news, I guess. Sharon was planning to ask Martine about her daughter, Jenny's, new beau. Jenny is quite taken with him. Sharon wanted to know if she's about to gain a new son-in-law. Judging from the look on her face, I'd say the answer was no. She's probably calling Jenny as we speak."

"I hope she isn't upsetting her unnecessarily," Anya said, expressing concern. "I respect Martine's advice, but personally, I still believe a lot of free will goes into the direction our lives take. I think even Martine agrees with that. Donna certainly looked excited about her reading. Anything you can share?"

"Oh, yes! Well, Donna and I have always dreamed

about buying one of those old mansions on the Upper Terrace overlooking Main Street. They seldom come up for sale. Usually, they're passed down to future generations, but last week, one finally came on the market, and we've applied to the bank for a loan. Martine believes we'll be approved!"

Donna and Kathleen had moved in together years ago, after Donna's divorce had been granted.

"That's terrific! I know you'll get it!" Anya replied in earnest.

"Time to open the gifts!" Cossima announced when the tarot readings had concluded. Cecilia's gifts were passed around the room so that everyone could admire them. Anya had never seen so much china, silver, and crystal in her life.

The explosion of wrapping paper, ribbons, and bows were swept up while Rheina announced the winners of the games. Cecilia handed out the prizes. Anya lost the bling contest to Jules by one ring.

"One more quick game and then dessert!" Donna Cruz announced. "This one's called *Name That Cake.*"

The partygoers were supposed to form teams of two or three and work in secret to solve clues resulting in the names of different kinds of cakes. By this time, though, so much champagne had been consumed that everyone fell to shouting out clues and answers.

"What kind of cake do you feed a rabbit?"

"Lettuce!"

"No, silly! Carrot cake!"

"Who said lettuce? Whoever heard of a lettuce cake?"

"What kind of cake do they serve in heaven?"

"Angelfood!"

"What kind of cake do you eat in bed?"

Long pause … "Sheet cake!"

The Name That Cake game had everyone craving cake, and they were not to be disappointed. Everyone oohed and aahed when Kathleen and Donna Cruz brought out the cupcake wedding dress on a silver platter. Next came trays of cookies shaped like hearts, diamond rings, and flowers decorated with royal icing and edible pearls. Finally, Martine brought out a New York-style cheesecake sampler arranged in three tiers, much like a wedding cake would be.

A series of well deserved compliments were still forming on Anya's lips when, out of the corner of her eye, she saw a blur of fur *whoosh* by! She knew in an instant that Ching had again defied containment. She looked around in a panic, eventually locating him sitting atop the mimosa bar beside the untouched pitchers of lemonade. He seemed oddly transfixed by the dessert table.

Before Anya could draw Martine's attention to his

presence, Ching let out an unearthly howl that set the crystal ringing!

Everyone froze … Martine jumped! The three tiers of cheesecake pitched sideways, threatening to topple—wildly righting itself when Martine dropped the tray to the table. Frantically, the Cajun Queen scoured the room for the willful cat.

What happened next could best be described as a kind of feline parkour. The guests watched in stunned silence as Ching went berserk! He began running amok, racing around the room, catapulting off chairs, couches, and tabletops in a frenzied torrent. He made a skidding U-turn near the French doors that led to the deck before doubling back toward the dessert table. Anya tried twice to intercept him as he wove a path around the cupcake wedding dress, zigzagged past the trays of cookies, and zeroed in on Martine's cheesecakes. Ching planted his front paws on the edge of the platter—launching it high into the air. Cheesecake rained down on all of the guests, as the tray went clattering to the floor.

Suddenly the room erupted in laughter! Everyone agreed that the sheer absurdity of Ching's grand finale would make this occasion all the more memorable. The guests' good-natured jokes that at least the cupcakes and cookies had been spared helped to ease Martine's embarrassment, and the shower ended a huge success.

When everyone had left, Anya released the other cats who had spent the day in the guest room. Ching flew down from an overhead beam to greet his royal subjects, strutting in circles around them on his long slender legs.

Martine shook her head. "You naughty boy, who but me would put up wid you, eh?"

Almost immediately, Zia sensed that an act of criminal mischief had occurred. She flattened her body with her belly to the floor and nosed the area, where residual evidence of the cheesecake storm confirmed her misgivings. Ears folded, whiskers twitching, she shot a disapproving glance at Ching and scurried back to the guest room.

Anya had the strangest dream that night—perhaps due to the rich food or too much champagne. In the dream, it was morning, and she alone was seated at Martine's kitchen table. The sheriff was cooking breakfast for her in his shorts, a full-length apron, and his regulation hat and boots.

"I've got some fine gator boudin cookin' here," he announced, one of his Habanos clenched in his teeth.

He divided the contents between their two plates and then held the shiny metal pan up to his face like a mirror. He looked directly into it and asked, "Honey, want some breakfast?"

Anya stared into the skillet too and was astonished to see Martine's face looking back at her.

"How do you make those fantastic eggs I like?" the sheriff asked the skillet.

Martine just smiled and slowly faded away.

TWENTY-FIVE

Traditionally speaking, Independence Day marked the end of the summer tourist season in Four Oaks, with most families returning home to ready themselves for the start of a new school year. This year would prove to be different, due to the fervor surrounding the Great American Eclipse on August twenty-first. It was the first total solar eclipse to span the United States from coast to coast since 1918, ninety-nine years ago. Four Oaks was set to experience something close to ninety percent totality, which wasn't enough to allow anyone to view it without eclipse glasses, but enough to flood the area with spectators.

Eclipse fever would see all of the hotels, motels, and campgrounds completely booked up—including the new hotel, which was on track to meet their opening date the week prior. Rather than celebrating the end of another busy season, the town was somewhat anxiously preparing for unprecedented numbers to descend upon them in a matter of weeks.

McClean's had closed for renovations on June 30th

and would remain closed until sometime near the end of August. Even so, Desda March had ordered three boxes of eclipse glasses from the Chenoah Falls Library before leaving on her trip. "In case Tate finishes early, and we want to be open," she had said.

It was July first, and the focus was on the Fourth of July celebrations to be held all weekend in the towns of Four Oaks, Lake Increase, and, of course, the city of Chenoah Falls.

Martine had been called back to New Orleans. The probate court had finished with Tame's estate, and there were papers to sign. The court date was set for July 6th, but due to the holiday, the airlines were heavily booked. If not for a last-minute cancellation on this afternoon's flight out, Martine would have had to drive.

She planned to stay with three family friends who still lived in the house where Martine had grown up. Two of the current residents had been members of the Decoudreaus' house staff that Martine's mother, Armance, had grown close to over the years. Their names were Ginette and Evrard. The third was a woman named Eulalie Benedictine. She and Armance had met in Paris while Martine and Tame were attending college. In later years, Eulalie had come to live with her in the mansion on Rain Street. It had been Martine's mother's wish that Martine retain the home and allow them to continue living there after her death. She was looking forward to celebrating the Fourth with them.

Reportedly, Ching had gone on a rampage the second he'd seen Martine pull out the suitcases. He'd gone so far as to shred the letter from the judge and even taken her keys—twice.

Anya had happily volunteered to stay with the cats. The sheriff felt he'd been neglecting his dog for some time now, having left Billy with the Notahs, so he could stay with Martine. It would give him a chance to spend some time at home with him, and Anya an opportunity to spend another glorious week at the lake.

She held her breath as she tried on last year's stars and stripes bikini. It was still a winner. Over that, she wore a strapless navy dress and a pair of red thongs with white stars printed on the straps. She stuffed a couple of beach towels, some sunscreen, and a sweater into a navy blue tote, which she loaded into her truck along with the suitcases she'd packed for her retreat at the lake. Ethan was picking her up from Martine's, so she could leave her vehicle there for use during her stay. After that, they would be off to The Silver Pines Hotel for a fabulous holiday! Hooray!

When Anya pulled up in front of Martine's, Ethan was already waiting, and he'd brought along a little surprise for Ching. Anya had told him several times how guilty she felt, leaving Ching alone to brave the fireworks. The cat was already upset about Martine leaving, and he'd always been terribly afraid of fireworks. From up at the lake, the pulsating echoes of all three area pyrotechnic shows could be felt and heard.

"Hey, glasses?" Ethan said as she got out of the truck.

She'd forgotten that she was wearing them. "Yeah, I ran out of contacts the other day. Some things might not be quite the way you remember them. Anyway, I only need them to drive," she explained, feeling a little self-conscious.

"I like them. You look really, really pretty," he said with a kiss.

Anya smiled and rolled her eyes.

"So, this is a thunder jacket," Ethan announced, holding up a little gray felt coat. "The latest in technology. It uses gentle, constant pressure to soothe cats and dogs in anxiety-producing conditions. C'mon, let's try it," he said.

Ethan carried her luggage inside and into the guest room while Anya went in search of Ching. The cat was never around when you needed him. Strangely, all of the cats seemed to be hiding at the moment.

"Ching! Ching, where are you?" Anya called to him.

After an exhaustive search of the main rooms, his royal highness decided to reveal himself, slinking out from under one of the living room chairs. He looked at them groggily and shook himself awake.

The thunder jacket wasn't much different from the harness he sometimes wore that connected to his leash. Martine used it to take him outside when he was bored or running riot. Sire was a bit woozy, so Ethan was able to fasten the jacket around him before the cat had a chance to object. Ching vaguely adjudicated its presence and, with the insouciance of a monarch, gave a hyperbolic yawn.

"Hmmm, well, that was easier than I expected," Ethan admitted.

Anya sighed. "I hope it helps. Poor little guy has no idea that, in just a few hours, it's going to sound like World War III out there."

Drawn in by his own curiosity, Benny poked his head out of the kitchen pass-through. He came over to join them, sniffing the thunder jacket and trilling his concern. In answer, Ching gave Benny's whiskers a swipe or two with his tongue, and the two adjourned to the sofa to resume napping.

The Silver Pines was about ten miles down the road, on the same side of the lake. The ski show wasn't set to begin for more than thirty minutes, but they had missed the fishing tournament that always kicked off the day's packed event schedule.

It wasn't much of a contest really, since Bob "Smoky" Mabrey, of Smoky's BBQ, always took home the first place trophy. Incredibly, it didn't appear to dampen the spirits of the other fishermen, all of whom were Smoky's fishing buddies anyway.

At the first intersection, Ethan had to slam on the brakes when a tow truck, trying to beat the light, nearly smashed into them.

"Damn! What the hell?" Ethan shouted, shaken by the close call.

The tow truck was towing a blue pickup truck. Ethan abruptly fell silent, and Anya noticed that he was squinting as if he were trying to make out the license plates on the pickup. She had missed the plate but had seen that the truck had a crumpled right front fender. Ethan drove on wordlessly, and Anya shrugged it off for the time being.

Arriving at the hotel, he lurched into a parking spot, and in seconds, they were off to find their friends at the marina. Anya practically had to jog to keep up with the pace of Ethan's long strides.

"The ski show will be starting soon, so they're probably already on the boat. I hope we have good seats," Anya said as they passed the grandstand.

The local weatherman, Cole Front, which sounded too close to *cold front* to be a coincidence, was presenting Smoky with the first place trophy. Smoky waved and shook the cup triumphantly over his head as the crowd cheered.

"There they are," Ethan said, spotting the *Bella*

Brezza, or *Beautiful Breeze,* which was the name of the Bennedettos' boat. Everyone was aboard except Cecilia, who was off somewhere changing into her ski-wear. She came jogging down the pier, while they were exchanging warm welcomes all around, and Ethan and Anya were expressing many thanks to the Bennedettos for inviting them.

Cossima and Alessandro were wearing red, white, and blue wet suits. Cecilia had dug out one of her old costumes from her competition days, a red and white one-piece embellished with bright white stars and a blue and silver tinsel skirt. She'd arranged her hair into two little buns accented by hair ornaments that looked like mini fireworks were exploding from them.

Nigel covered his mouth, unable to contain a grin.

"Don't knock it, honey! I was sixteen the last time I wore this little number. Fits like a dream!"

"Well, we'll be rooting for you guys!" Ethan assured them.

"Don't call out my name or anything, though. I'm afraid of getting distracted and wiping us all out," Cecilia mumbled.

Cossima was fiddling with her buns. "It's all in fun, honey, don't worry so much. Besides, it wouldn't be the first time, eh?"

Everyone laughed except Cecilia. She was in competitor mode.

"We'll be lucky to get a third or fourth place trophy this year. We're not doing any jumps or stunts off the ramps. I didn't have time to practice any of that," Cecilia said with a shrug.

"No, but she's been practicing some pretty fancy hand and toe tricks and a few fairly heart-stopping flips and rolls!" Nigel interjected. "Very impressive stuff!"

A few of the other ski boats had begun rumbling away with their skiers to the show's starting point on the lake.

"It's almost time. We better go," Cecilia said, climbing into the boat. "We're the third ski group. Our tables are up there on the hill under the pavilion. You'll see our name on the *reserved for* signs. Oh, and be sure to check out the team skiing last. My old instructor is in that group, and I think the only one ski jumping today. They're going to win!" Cecilia called out as they motored away to rendezvous with their fellow water rats.

Anya cringed as Nigel suddenly punched it—coming dangerously close to tossing their star off the starboard side.

They went to the bar first for Mai Tais before seeking out the tables marked *Bennedetto Party.* It was a beautiful morning, calm, clear, and clement. The Silver Pines had gone to great lengths to create an atmosphere of patriotic aplomb. A multitude of spangled banners and Old Glorys flapped in the breeze, and the rooftops and railings were swathed in stars and stripes buntings.

Bundles of faux fireworks exploded from the floral centerpieces on the tables and from all of the flowerpots that lined the terrace and pavilion. The effect was as elegant as it was festive.

"Hey, grab that waitress!" Ethan shouted over the churning of the other boats that were leaving the slips.

Anya waved her over.

"Miss, please keep these coming," he said, pointing to the Mai Tais and slipping her a generous tip.

As the ski show began, Ethan grabbed the edge of Anya's chair and dragged her over closer to him to give her a kiss.

For some reason, Anya hadn't been able to put Ethan's reaction to the near miss with the tow truck out of her mind.

"I got the feeling earlier that you recognized the pickup that the tow truck was towing. Did you?"

"Hmmm?" Ethan frowned.

Anya's jaw dropped. It was an evasive response, an obvious attempt at guarding the truth, but why? Anya rephrased the question. "I saw you looking at the plates. Did you recognize the truck or something?"

"Oh. No, I mean for a minute it looked like Daniel Freeman's truck, the guy who came up to buy seats for his Mustang. He went fishing with us a couple of times, remember?"

Anya did remember. "Really? What would he be doing back up here?"

Ethan was staring straight ahead. "I don't know," he said, giving a shrug.

"He was from Lafayette. Were they Louisiana plates?"

There was a long pause during which Ethan appeared to gulp his Mai Tai; then to her astonishment, he replied simply, "Yep." He had a sobering look on his face. Clearly, he'd been troubled by this observation.

There was another long pause, more of a stunned silence, as Anya waited for him to offer some explanation.

"Remember Tate's barbecue when Rob called the sheriff to give a description of the man he saw that day with Sidra York?" Ethan asked.

Anya nodded, holding her breath as she anticipated Ethan's response.

"His description sounded a lot like Daniel Freeman, right down to the color of his hat. It's been bothering me ever since. I don't know. It's probably nothing, but I'm pretty sure that was his truck. Seems like Nigel or I would have heard from him if he was going to be in the area, unless, of course, he never left. I've got a funny feeling about it. I didn't want to say anything because I've been really looking forward to today. I don't want anything to ruin it. I'll let the sheriff know tomorrow, but for now, let's drop it—focus on having a good time," Ethan suggested.

The waitress brought another round of drinks, and Anya let it drop. She settled in to watch the ski show that had begun, but in the back of her mind, she knew that he was right. There was something strange going on.

It was an amateur show—hotdogging, but no pyramids. All of the skiers were highly proficient, and the crowd cheered loudly in praise of each skillfully executed trick.

The Bennedettos were incredible! Anya marveled at their grace and precision, watching breathlessly as they skied slalom, wake-jumping back and forth, their paths crisscrossing one another smoothly. Cecilia took the center position, performing side slides like a pro. From there, she moved into backwrap side slides, through which she rotated sharply, making nice smooth cuts. She rounded out the solo performance with a heel slide flip and a back landing flip. For the finale, all three Bennedettos executed synchronized forward rolls and 360-degree spins, after which they released the tow ropes in tandem, and sank slowly into the lake. The crowd roared, jumping to their feet, clapping, cheering, and hollering! They were a big hit!

The last team to ski did take first place, just as Cecilia had predicted, with a tremendous ski jump off a ramp performed by Maria Morento, Cecilia's old instructor.

The Bennedettos took second place, and there were many congratulatory handshakes when they arrived at the tables with their engraved silver cup.

"Best run ever!" Ethan exclaimed, standing to applaud them upon their approach.

Nigel and Cecilia sank into chairs beside them. Cossima and Alessandro waved to them and sat with some friends Anya didn't recognize at another table nearby.

"Good enough to get in the paper!" Cecilia beamed. "And your brother did a great job!" She slid Nigel's sunglasses to the top of his head and kissed him.

When the waitress returned with two more Mai Tais and four plates for the buffet, Nigel slipped her a bill and requested that she start bringing pitchers and glasses of water too.

Over lunch, Cecilia asked her if McClean's had closed for renovations yet.

"We closed yesterday, as a matter of fact. The renovations start Monday." Anya went on to describe the sketches Tate had shown her and Desda for the climbing wall and the built-in tropical fish aquarium, which had been another last-minute addition. There would be a carpeted bench below it where the cats could sit and watch the fish.

"I'm really excited. Your place is gonna be a big hit," Cecilia affirmed with confidence. "Once Nigel and I buy a house, we might have to adopt a couple of your rescues."

"Have you been looking at houses?" Anya asked.

Cecilia nodded. "Houses *and* shops. My folks and Old Sam offered to give us a down payment on a house or to send us on a honeymoon as a wedding present, but Nigel and I came up with something we'd rather have—a bakery." Cecilia delivered this news as if it were somehow an obvious choice.

Ethan and Anya stared at her blankly.

Noting their confusion, Nigel went on to explain their future plans to go into business. "Cecilia and I have already saved up enough for a down payment on a house, probably buy something around Lake Increase. After we're married, Cecilia wants to stop waitressing at Bennedetto's and open her own shop—an Italian Bakery, maybe on Patawomek Street. So, we've been looking at houses *and* shops."

Everyone agreed it was a wonderful idea. There were no other bakeries on Patawomek Street. An Italian bakery would be a goldmine, and with so many years of working in her parents' restaurant, Cecilia had become a master of the culinary arts.

"Oh! I've got it—a name for the cat we're going to adopt from Cats 'n' Cocktails—Mascarpone!" Cecilia exclaimed.

"Isn't that Italian cream cheese?" Ethan chaffed.

Everyone roared laughing.

Subsequent to lunch, the canoe and raft races were held, the latter was for kids, ages ten to fourteen. They competed in rafts of all shapes and sizes—swans, dragons, turtles, and such. It was a hilarious production of flailing arms and legs and kicking feet as each jockeyed into position for the win.

Around two o'clock, Cossima and Alessandro stopped by the table to say goodbye. They were on their way to oversee the dinner service at their restaurant.

"Good job today, Nigel and Cecilia, honey," Cossima said, kissing each one on the top of their head. "We're going into town now. You have the keys to the boat?" she asked.

Nigel produced them from his pocket. "Don't worry, they're safe with me."

"OK, we'll be back to the hotel later tonight, but we probably won't see you until breakfast," Alessandro confirmed.

"Happy Fourth!" Cossima called out to them, giving a cheerful wave.

They spent the rest of the day swimming in the hotel pool and floating around in the lake.

Dinner included full table service with a choice of two entrees: steak and shrimp or steak and lobster; with a choice of steak fries, or baked potatoes, steamed carrots, or broccoli, and dinner rolls.

The sun was sinking low in the sky when the water parade set sail in which water crafts of every shape and size were decorated in the manner of traditional street floats. There was a panel of judges, and the winner for the most inventive design was awarded five hundred dollars and a sterling silver trophy cup.

The vast majority of entries were boaters simply looking for the thrill of being part of the flag-waving flotilla. They tended to decorate with vinyl streamers, flags, and buntings.

A few, however, were in it to win it, and they came up with some very creative themes. Most notable in this year's parade were three entries that were decorated in the spirit of the area's timber history and rich in lumberjack lore.

One was a cruiser that had been transformed into Babe, the giant blue ox. Though they weren't in Paul Bunyan's Minnesota—it was still logging country.

The other two vessels were decorated to represent the legends of two other fabled creatures: the jackalope, a rabbit with antelope horns, and the hugag, a lesser-known entity to anyone outside of the lumber belt. The hugag was a mythical beast said to resemble a moose without knees. Unable to lie down, the hugag was forced to lean against a tree to sleep. When lumberjacks heard a tree fall in the forest, they would joke that a sleeping hugag had felled the tree. In the end, it was the blue ox that took first prize.

They ordered snacks from the bar, another pitcher of mai tais, and talked until dusk when it was time to move into position for the fireworks show.

The barges from which a professional pyrotechnic display would be launched were anchored at the far end of the lake.

Nigel guided the *Bella Brezza* to a central location and cut the engine. They were rocking pretty hard for a while from the wakes of the other boaters as they also motored out around them and dropped anchor for the show. All at once, the rumbling of motors stopped, and the lake grew strangely silent.

Soon after, the first launches could be heard: *thum, thum, thum … BOOM! Crackle-Sizzle-pffffftt!* Nervous laughter from surrounding boats could be heard from a few who'd been startled by the sudden onset of the show.

It was chilly on the water that night, and Anya wrapped her sweater closer around her. Ethan noticed and wrapped both of his arms around her, too. She thought guiltily of poor Ching and said a little prayer that the thunder jacket would help.

Scores of rockets came next, screeching into the black in quick succession. They exploded into brilliant red, white, and blue dahlias, diadems, willows, and comets, accompanied by white-hot flashes that terminated like bombs bursting in air. The crowd clapped, cheered, whistled, and hollered as they were bombarded by a continuous and breathtaking display that set the sky ablaze for over an hour. With every launch came the feeling that nothing could top it—and then came the grand finale. When the screaming of skyrockets, the crackle of chrysanthemums, and resounding booms from artillery shells abruptly concluded, the sky was full of smoke. A deep silence abounded, followed by whooping, shouting, and applause from a crowd that had been holding its collective breath. It was a dazzling display that left the viewers drained.

Back on shore, Anya and Ethan bid farewell to their friends. All agreed it had been an unforgettable day.

"Be sure to thank your parents again for us," Anya waved.

"Will do! I'm so glad you two could join us. Drive safe!" Cecilia called to them.

On the way to the truck, Anya suddenly froze. "Listen … ," she whispered, placing a hand on Ethan's arm.

There was an eerie high-pitched whistling coming from the tops of the pine trees that surrounded them. The winds had picked up considerably, and the moon and stars had vanished. The sky was pitch black except for faint flashes of distant lightning.

"Oh-oh … storm coming in. C'mon let's go," Ethan urged, and they ran for the truck.

Rain began pouring down in sheets. They were

soaked to the bone by the time they dove into the front seat. Loud cracks of lightning and deafening thunder made it prudent to wait out the storm in the parking lot.

"I think this one got by Cole Front. I don't remember hearing anything about storms in the forecast for today or tonight!" Ethan shouted above the hail that was pelting the roof.

Anya's eyes were wide with alarm as some of the wind gusts were strong enough to rock the truck. It was with a heavy heart and a tinge of panic that her thoughts turned again to poor Ching. Having endured the fireworks, he was now being doubly tested by the storm.

"Good thing it held off until everyone was off the lake," Ethan murmured, watching a stream of bunting, ripped from the hotel roof, fly by.

The storm raged on for at least fifteen minutes until it dwindled to a steady drizzle that Ethan was able to navigate. Fallen branches, leaves, and other foresty debris littered the road that led back to Martine's.

The house looked noticeably dark to Anya when they pulled up. Had the storm knocked out the power? If so, why hadn't the generator kicked in? She decided not to mention it. Ethan would worry and insist on coming in. She knew he had to work early in the morning. If the power was out, she would hunt up some candles.

"What a great day, huh?" she said, smiling.

"The best," Ethan agreed. "I wish I didn't have to work tomorrow."

"Come over for dinner when you get off. I'll make spaghetti," Anya suggested hopefully.

Ethan smiled. "I'll be here, and I'll be off for the next two days."

They kissed goodnight, and Anya raced inside to find Ching.

TWENTY-SIX

Just as Anya had feared—the power was out, but that didn't explain why the generator had failed. She dropped her tote in the entry hall and went in search of matches to light the candles in the dining room. She moved cautiously, listening for cats. It was pitch black. Anya could barely see her hand in front of her face as she groped her way to the table. For a moment, she celebrated her good luck—having located a book of matches right beside the candles.

When she struck the match, dimly illuminating the blackness, two things immediately registered in her mind. The first was an awareness that lights were glowing from the houses across the lake. Was it possible that only the south side had lost power? The second was a sound to the left of her—a low, guttural growl.

Anya whirled around to see the dark shape of Ching, crouching on the buffet, still wearing his thunder jacket. A bare nail and empty wall space were visible behind him. The photograph of Beckwith's cabin—the one that concealed the map—was gone!

Anya's blood ran cold, and her heart gave a leap.

Ching's growls grew louder as a beam of light suddenly pooled near her feet. It was the glow from a flashlight. Someone else was there in the dark.

Anya forced herself to turn and face the intruder. Panic began to rise in her chest when she realized that the specter looming in the shadows behind her was that of Sidra York!

Anya had a fleeting urge to try to overpower her, but it vanished quickly when she saw the gun.

"Welcome home, Anya. Get your keys. We're going to take a little ride to the emporium," Sidra said— waving the gun and motioning to Anya to get moving.

Anya's mind was racing. What could she do? Launch an attack with one of the heavy lead glass candle holders? That would be no match for a gun. Maybe she could run the car off the road on the way into town, hope to survive, and escape? None of her options seemed like good ones, as Anya tried to slowly back away.

Then ... from somewhere in the darkness, behind the gun-wielding incarnation of Sidra York, there came a ***chirp***! It was the sudden, jarring, timely chirp from a smoke alarm whose batteries had run out! That little miracle was all it took!

Sidra instinctively turned in the direction of the unexpected sound, and Ching launched from the sideboard. Claws slashing and teeth bared, he tore at Sidra with such ferocity that she fell to the floor in a flailing heap. She was forced to drop the flashlight and the gun to defend herself from Ching's bloody onslaught. It was impossible to tell whether the shrieks were coming from the cat or his now helpless victim.

Anya was quick to recover both the gun and the flashlight. "Ching! Ching!" she shouted, trying to call him off for fear that he'd be injured.

At that moment, the front door was kicked open with so much force, it was knocked off its hinges. It spun away with a crash as Sheriff Kieffer Wakefield, Sam Notah, and Ethan charged into the house. The sheriff and Old Sam had their guns drawn. They quickly subdued the vehement Sidra York and placed her in cuffs.

Anya was completely struck. It had all happened so fast, but the relief that began to seep in was short-lived. She wasn't prepared for what came next.

"How did you know?" Anya gasped, handing over the flashlight and gun to the sheriff.

The sheriff was having trouble collecting himself, so Old Sam stepped in. "We knew Martine had already left for New Orleans, at least we thought she had. We saw the house go dark from across the lake, and then beams of light started sweeping past the windows, like someone was in here with a flashlight. Unfortunately, on our way over here to investigate, we encountered another scene. Martine's car is off the road about a quarter mile away—down in a ditch. We flagged down Ethan when he passed and came straight here. Right now, we have to go back and search for Martine. Ethan will stay with you."

By sunup, Anya, along with the rest of Four Oaks, was in possession of most of the answers to most of the questions that had arisen these past few months—though none would provide any comfort.

It was sometime after three in the morning when Sheriff Wakefield and Old Sam returned to confirm with great sorrow that the worst had happened. Martine Decoudreau was dead. It was devastating news that left everyone's spirits crushed.

Anya admitted to the sheriff that Martine had already imparted some of the facts in the case to her. The sheriff proceeded to fill in the blanks—much of it based on Sidra York's own confession:

"The second we popped the trunk of Sidra's car, we knew the victim to be a man. It was a turning point in the case, and the FBI didn't want that information released," the sheriff said. "The media never actually confirmed that it was Sidra York's body that had been found. Everyone simply assumed that it was her. We couldn't have released the true victim's name anyway, even if we had wanted to, since we had no way to identify him at first.

"We had a body, that of Sidra's male counterpart

who was also Tame's former accomplice. We knew he was likely the man behind the hotel bombing, the break-in at Martine's shop, and the camper spotted near the dam, but we didn't have his name. Once we recovered his arms, at the old Ice and Fuel Company, we had his fingerprints. We decided to run them through the system, hoping he had priors, so we could get a hit on his identity. We were also awaiting results on the blood evidence gathered at the campsite.

"Early in the investigation, I was standing around on the railroad tracks—watching the M.E. bag his legs—when I started focusing in on the locations where his body parts had been showing up. The killer hadn't just tied some cinder blocks to the body and dumped it in the river. They'd gone to a lot of trouble to send a message. That's when I made this list of the first three locations, and his name practically jumped off the page." The sheriff dug out a crumpled piece of yellow legal paper from his shirt pocket and handed it to her. "Sidra confirmed my theory and the use of this mnemonic in her confession." Anya carefully unfolded it and read its contents:

F: ford, the make of the car, location of the torso
I: ice and fuel company, victim's arms
R/T: railroad tracks, victim's legs
H: hotel? the victim's head?

"Firth," Anya whispered the name. "So, that's how you knew you needed to stop the groundbreaking ceremony that day."

"It was only a hunch that the 'H' might be connected to the site of the new hotel—a hunch that proved to be correct," the sheriff confirmed. "His full name was Daniel Firth, and he was the last living relative of Charles Firth—James Beckwith's partner. My guess as to the victim's identity was later proven correct when we got a forensic match to him in the system. He had priors for larceny and felony theft.

"You would remember him as Daniel Freeman, the man who, to avoid suspicion, posed as a customer of the Notahs' from Lafayette. It gave him a plausible reason to be in our midst. He was also the mystery camper and the man you suspected was lurking out of sight upstairs at the gallery.

"Daniel knew all about the legend of the treasure—secretly hidden by Beckwith before his death," the sheriff went on to explain. "It was a story that had been passed down in his family for generations, much as it had been in the Decoudreau family.

"Daniel and Sidra had long deliberated on ways to get access to Beckwith's cabin and the emporium. They knew both were currently occupied by Beckwith's descendent, Martine Decoudreau. Ultimately, though, through continued investigation, they came across another name, another living descendent of Beckwith's—Tame Decoudreau. As luck would have it, her antique shop in New Orleans was less than a block away from where Sidra and Daniel were living at the time. They thought they'd hit the jackpot. Tame would become their unwitting pawn in their quest for the money.

"They made contact soon after, Sidra by taking a job in Tame's shop and Daniel by striking up a false romance with Tame.

"They knew their pursuit would eventually take them to Four Oaks. They needed money to travel and to set up some kind of a home base from which their operation could proceed. Sidra skipped town with more than a month's worth of bank deposits from Tame's store. She traveled directly to Four Oaks, where she opened the art gallery.

"With Sidra's role in the mission fulfilled, Daniel began casually raising the topic of Beckwith's fortune to Tame. He pretended to have taken an interest in it after reading about it in a book called *Trappers and Traders—North American Legends*.

"Naturally, Tame mentioned that she happened to be a direct descendent of the man. Daniel immediately set forth his campaign to convince Tame that her sister had most likely rooted out his secret cache years ago and was keeping it all for herself. He repeatedly asserted that Tame had a right to half of the money and persuaded her to try to get it out of Martine. Together, they cooked up the blackmail story in an attempt to play on Martine's sympathies. When that failed, Daniel and Sidra realized that they couldn't take a chance on Tame discovering their alliance and exposing their scheme, so they eliminated her by blowing up the hotel. Daniel also broke into the emporium to search for the money himself but was unsuccessful.

"That's when Firth suggested they take a more direct approach. Under threat of violence, they would coerce Martine into turning over the money, and then kill her to avoid arrest.

"The prospect of a second murder made Sidra nervous. So did Daniel's willingness to eliminate anyone and everyone in his way. She was afraid that, in his lust for the money, she might be next.

"In a bold move, Sidra decided to cut him out first. She knocked him out using the ether that she stole from Martine's shop—then she suffocated him. He was too heavy to drag out to her car, so she was forced to dismember him. She hid the torso in her trunk, and used his truck to disperse his other body parts. We had a little trouble finding his vehicle until we got a call from a liquor store on the Fourth of July about an abandoned truck on their parking lot."

Anya remembered the tow truck she and Ethan had almost collided with that same day, on the way to the Silver Pines Hotel. Ethan had been sure that it was Daniel's truck being towed behind it. Apparently, Daniel had still been in the area—just not in the way they'd thought.

The sheriff removed his hat, tossed it on the table, and rubbed his eyes wearily. Less than twenty-four hours had passed, but he looked like he hadn't slept in days.

Anya noticed that Ching had entered the room looking similarly distraught. He hobbled in—stiff-legged, ears folded, tail drooped. His forlorn presence prompted her to recall the letter from the probate judge that the cat had reportedly torn to pieces.

"What about the letter from the judge in New Orleans? Was it legitimate, or was that part of Sidra's plan too?" she asked.

"Sidra was the one who drafted the official-looking letter from the probate judge," the sheriff said. "With everyone believing that Martine was out of town, Sidra would have all the time she needed to kidnap Martine, get the money, kill her, and leave the area before Martine was ever missed.

"Sidra intercepted Martine in the driveway as she was leaving for the airport. She forced her back inside at gunpoint. She tried to coerce her into giving up the money or its location, but Martine continued to deny having any knowledge. After a search of the desk and its secret compartment produced no results,

Sidra happened to catch sight of the photograph of Beckwith's cabin. Acting on a hunch, she quickly uncovered the map.

"The map revealed that the treasure lay inside the emporium, stashed away in a most unusual place. Since McClean's was closed for renovation, Sidra determined that they could slip in the back way without being noticed. She took Martine hostage and forced her to drive into town with her. On the way, Martine tried to escape by purposely running her car off the road. Sidra survived. Martine did not. You and Ethan passed right by the wreck traveling to and from Martine's house, but the car was so far off the road, you would have had trouble spotting it. It was the tire tracks that caught our attention and led to the finding."

Anya was stunned. She'd been considering that option herself until the sheriff, Sam, and Ethan had come to her rescue.

"Lacking a getaway vehicle, Sidra snuck back into the house to regroup. She decided to wait until the crowds on Main Street had dispersed and then to go into town alone. In the meantime, you and Ethan showed up. She hid in Martine's closet until you left. Evidently, she'd been under the impression that you were planning an overnight stay at The Silver Pines. She was going to use your truck, Anya, to steal the money and then head for the airport," the sheriff concluded.

"Why was the power out?" Anya asked.

"The storm knocked it out on this side of the lake. For some reason, the generator failed. Lucky for us that it did; otherwise, Sidra wouldn't have been forced to use the flashlight, and we wouldn't have been alerted to her presence over here. I knew that Sidra York was still out there somewhere, but I never imagined that she would go to such lengths. There was so much heat on her, I thought she'd be forced to abandon her quest. It was my every hope that she would be apprehended many miles away from here while trying to flee the charges against her."

Anya closed her eyes. It felt like the whole room was spinning. It was a familiar hollowness that filled her, the same dark void she'd felt when her mom had passed. She leaned heavily on Ethan, who was perched on the arm of the chair she was dissolving into. It felt like the end of everything, like sinking slowly into the depths of the ocean, never to resurface.

TWENTY-SEVEN

In the coming days, Anya felt like she was walking through glue. She didn't shower, didn't dress, and didn't leave the house. It was all she could do to take care of the cats. Caring friends and neighbors kept showing up with casseroles she couldn't eat and flowers she couldn't keep because they weren't cat-safe. She had taken to piling them up in the butler's pantry, transforming it into a kind of macabre floral graveyard.

Tate started the renovations at McClean's in her absentia. He came by every morning to ply her with French toast and waffles and share pictures of the progress. He was the bright spot in her day, and she looked forward to his visits.

Of course, Ethan was there for her too, arriving every night after work.

Anya had heard rumors that the sheriff was taking Martine's death pretty hard—dropping off the radar for days at a time and drinking more than usual.

Ching was also deeply despondent. He seemed to know that Martine would never return and spent most days napping in her study. The other cats occasionally went to the window or wandered around from room to room looking for her, wondering why she'd gone.

Martine's remains were cremated and interred without ceremony at St. Peter's on the Rock Cemetery, as per her wishes known only to Sheriff Wakefield.

Shortly after, Anya also learned the reason Ching had so often sat atop the newel post of the staircase in Martine's shop. He'd been guarding the treasure. The finial on the post opened on tiny imperceptible hinges. Deep inside its hollow recesses, a treasure worth almost a billion dollars in gold, silver, and U.S. banknotes had been hidden away by James Beckwith nearly one hundred and twenty years ago.

The law firm of Sterling, Nithercott, and McSwain promptly took possession of it for its client's future management, one Anya McClean. They also took control when it came to the issuing of an official press release concerning the motive in the case, which had been receiving national attention. It stated that while the so-called legendary fortune of James Beckwith had been the central motive in these recent crimes, and a map pinpointing its supposed location had been found—no money had been recovered from the designated site. Further investigation had led authorities to conclude that it had never actually existed. The legendary tale was nothing more than a hoax created by Beckwith himself.

This repudiation regarding the existence of the treasure was a measure taken not only to protect Anya's privacy as a newly minted billionairess, but also to ensure her future safety by discouraging others who might seek the trove.

In the end, only Anya, her lawyers, and the sheriff knew the truth of the windfall she had inherited.

It was during this time of self-imposed seclusion that Anya began to review what she'd come to believe were clues left by Ching meant to warn them all of the impending tragedies.

The first sign of trouble had been his alarming reaction to the appearance of the Tower card the night before the hotel had been bombed. The scene depicted on the card was not unlike the scene on Main Street that day. And who had left the rune tile of Kenaz, the torch, on the stairs? Had it been Don Pedro, or had he just been the one playing with the tile after Ching had left it there as a warning? There was also the Ace of Diamonds, a card that predicted the possibility of an inheritance or some other large sum of money. Had the cat been pointing to the motive attached to all of the violence that followed?

Ching had exhibited a strong dislike of both Tame and Sidra, stalking, sneering, and hissing at them in Anya's presence. And then there was Daniel. Ching and Daniel had first made contact the morning after

Ethan's graduation party. Ethan, Nigel, and Daniel had stopped by the emporium so that Ethan could thank Martine for the clock. Ethan had mentioned that Ching had remembered him and had been happy to see him. A day or two later, Ching had torn up Martine's kitchen chair—a chair that resembled a bucket seat like the ones Daniel had pretended he'd come to buy from the Notahs. Next, the cat had launched an attack on Martine's fur-lined slipper. Daniel was the thieving, murdering descendent of a fur trader who had lived a hundred years ago. Was there a connection? Had Ching had some kind of premonition? How could a cat be so explicit in his senses and attempts to communicate? It was impossible, and yet, all of the cats had refused to eat the fish that came from Daniel's string the day that he and Ethan had dropped by McClean's with their catch.

Ching had also led her to find the false bottom in the desk drawer. He'd repeatedly tried to draw her attention to the location of the secret map, too, by tilting the photo that concealed it. Ching's death howl had closely preceded Daniel's murder, and there was the book by Matheson that had been pushed off the shelf. The book itself had nothing to do with murder, but the title: *Once He's Gone* was curiously premonitory. Had Ching somehow known that it was Daniel that would turn up in the trunk of Sidra's car? He'd torn the book

Trappers and Trades—North American Legends to pieces too, and what about the New *York*-style cheesecake he'd decimated at Cecilia's shower while sparing the other desserts?

Had Ching known the letter from the probate judge was a forgery when he'd shredded it? Did he know that Martine was in danger when he'd tried to hide her keys to prevent her from leaving?

Was it a string of uncanny coincidences- the overt, yet innocent, actions of an ungovernable feline? Anya didn't think so. There was simply too much evidence to the contrary, no matter how extraordinary it all seemed.

It would be weeks later that Anya would marvel once more at Ching's intuition when she happened to hear a feature story about the opera *Carmen.* A new version had taken the theater world by storm, in which the male character was the victim, murdered by his female lover. Ching had played an aria from Carmen on Martine's player piano when Daniel, or at least part of him, had been located in the trunk of Sidra's car. He'd played it again—the day of the new hotel's groundbreaking ceremony.

By August 21st, the day of the Great American Eclipse, six weeks had passed, and Anya finally felt something inside of her shift. The first glimmers of renewed inner strength had begun to surface.

She was sipping coffee on the couch, staring at the rippling waters rolling gently toward her from across the lake, when she felt something land on her foot. It was a little pink catnip mouse. Ching had dropped it. He stared up at her, his almond-shaped eyes like tranquil, citrine pools of light. Anya stroked his head lightly, twirled the mouse by its tail a few times, and flung it into the dining room. Ching chose not to give chase, but even a transitory interest was an improvement, she thought. Maybe something was slowly beginning to shift in him too. He leaped up on to her lap, and they sat together for more than an hour, Ching sleeping peacefully, Anya watching the ripples meet the shore.

She and Ethan wore their eclipse glasses and raised flutes of champagne while they watched the sun disappear from the sky that day.

Martine had claimed that eclipses were heralds or harbingers of major beginnings and endings. They marked the end of one era and the beginning of the next. She had certainly been right about that.

The Cajun Queen had left everything to Anya when she had departed this world, and a grand new chapter was indeed on the horizon. Anya wondered why the best times in a person's life were so often accompanied by the worst times. Martine would have said it was because you have to take the good with the bad to know the difference, to be mindful, as well as grateful.

On August 23rd, Tate Blackledge finished the renovations, and on September 1st, Cats 'n' Cocktails was finally set to have its grand opening.

"I know it's a little early to be moving back to town. Martine used to wait until the first sign of snow, but I'm going to be working a lot for the next few weeks—so we're all leaving, first thing in the morning," Anya had told the cats the night before. She'd taken to talking to them like people. They were family, after all. At times she could swear they understood her declarations.

As soon as she started digging out the cat carriers for the trip into town, Zia, Hester, and Benny made for the guest room and hid under the bed. Luther and Possum acknowledged their presence with only tepid interest, but Don Pedro and Ching switched on. The inspector general and his obliging sidekick galloped to the scene to conduct a professional inquiry into the matter. They circled around the coaches—creeping, sniffing, and ducking in and out of them until eventually they both squeezed into the smallest one and fell asleep.

Anya rose early the following day, leaving herself plenty of time for one last breakfast on the deck and one last contemplative view of the lake for months to come. In the final moments ahead of their departure, she decided to engage the cats in a spirited game of "string". She thought if she was able to dispel enough of their pent-up energy, they might even spend the rest of the day napping.

Performing a quick head count, Anya realized that about half of the crew was MIA, so she popped in one of Martine's CDs she'd come across, hits from the seventies, to lure them out of hiding. In recent months, they'd come to associate music with playtime after Anya had discovered that the feline collective were music aficionados—of a sort. You had to be in tune with their preferences and cater to their vastly discriminating taste. They responded most positively to uplifting compilations with lively tempos. Incorporating music had taken the experience to a whole new level. The second the melodious refrains reached their ears, the absentees sprinted into the room, and the game was on.

After fifteen minutes of sustained exercise, her feline friends collapsed—tongues lolling, and sides heaving. Lacking the strength and will to resist, they were easy enough to load into their coaches, but a struggle to hoist into the truck. The furballs were much heavier than Anya remembered.

She'd saved Ching for last, as was customary. She found him in the study. He'd opened the desk drawer again and was sitting tall inside of it with the air of a statesman.

"There you are. Time to go, your majesty," Anya said, directing his attention to his waiting transport.

Ching squeezed his intelligent, yellow-green eyes at her. On the desk in front of him was a card, one of Martine's tarot cards. It was face down.

A shiver ran through her until it occurred to her that she was going to have to get used to this kind of thing from Ching. Anya took a few calming breaths before flipping over the card. It was the Sun card—the most positive card in the deck. To her surprise, there were two other cards beneath it, the Two of Swords and the Two of Cups. Decisions in love...

And now for a special sneak peek at the second book in The Cats 'n' Cocktails Mystery Series:

Rise of the King — by Faith Waitstill

Anya McClean was down on her hands and knees, crawling around on her living room floor. She was gathering the soggy remains of what had once been a newspaper ad. In keeping with the latest forecast, Goshen's Market was offering twenty percent off on snowblowers and buy one get one free rock salt.

The WFKS weatherman, Cole Front, a name too close to cold front to be a coincidence, had been predicting the first blizzard of the season for days—pointing to a system still forming out over the Rockies. Satellite imagery now confirmed that his meteorological calculations had been spot on.

"Well, this is it, folks, the one I've been warning you about. The event will begin and end as all snow, and we're looking at accumulations in the one and a half to two-feet range. Expect fifty–sixty mph wind gusts as this thing gets cranking, which means downed trees and power outages. Gas up those generators and make sure you have at least three days of supplies for this one. Look for it to get in here between five and six o'clock this evening, after which local travel will be banned except for emergencies. Stay out of the way of those plows! Stand by for more updates as the first blizzard of the season gets set to take the stage."

Anya stared at the startling radar image and sighed. A massive blue wall was chugging steadily toward the area.

Ching had been staging his own series of winter weather warnings these past few days through a number of clandestine excavations into the hall closet. A pair of beavertail snowshoes had been the first item to appear. The cat had somehow managed to drag them out into the hallway, where he'd left them as an unexpected trip hazard for her to encounter—in the wee hours. On the two consecutive nights that followed, the targets had been an ice scraper, and one of the poles for her cross country skis. The pole had come crashing to the floor at 2 a.m., causing her to spring from her bed in abject terror. The shredded Goshen's Market ad was just the latest in this ongoing stream of communication.

Ching's recent assertions, however, seemed to point to more than a sense that the weather was about to take a turn for the worse. Anya thought she detected an underlying theme, one that involved travel and a change of residence. In addition to the hall closet, Ching had been digging into several boxes containing his former owner's tarot card decks and other tools of her trade. He'd been using their contents to leave rather well-placed hints all over the house.

Ching chose to open this conversation with the tarot card known as The Chariot. He'd left it on the table in the entryway, right beside her keys. Last Wednesday, she'd found an I Ching coin with the trigram for water emblazoned on it in her coat pocket. Most recently, two Lenormand cards: the House and the Ship, had turned up in the bathroom sink— their corners dented by the tiny teeth marks of the perpetrator.

In a mundane sense, the Chariot represented travel—and the house, ship, and water trigram were as specific to the desired destination as one could expect from a cat. He wanted to go home to the lake. The lake house had always been the cats' spring and summer residence, sometimes lasting into the fall or whenever the first threat of snow prompted a move back to town. It was a routine to which Ching should have been well attuned, so why then was he ruminating on a return to the lake now with winter weather on the way, she wondered?

Winters in this northern territory were brutal. Frequent accumulations of snow and ice made driving conditions treacherous, if not impossible. Anyone with living quarters above their business tended to spend the winter in town.

Until her death, Ching's former owner, Martine Decoudreau, affectionately known to locals as the Cajun Queen, had owned and operated an emporium next door to Cats 'n' Cocktails—living in the spacious apartment rooms above it in the winter months.

The two buildings in which they'd each lived and worked were located at the east end of Main Street and were connected by a second-story glass catwalk. Martine's emporium had been called Mystic Treasures, and there she had curated her own crystals and sold handmade candles, oils, teas, and tinctures. More importantly though, Martine had been a seer, a reader of tarot cards, and other tools of divination. She'd given readings and spiritual guidance to her clients in an old vault in the basement of her shop.

The vault was an artifact left over from the days when the emporium had been the site of The First Bank of Four Oaks. Both buildings had been established in the 1800s by a distant relative of Martine's, an illicit banker and fur trader by the name of James Beckwith, and his partner, Charles Firth. There was a long and felonious history attached, to which another chapter had recently been added.

Martine's death had been officially ruled an act of reckless homicide. As her sole heir, Anya's life had been utterly transformed. In the blink of an eye, she'd made the top one hundred list of the richest women in the country, a fact known only to Sheriff Wakefield and Beau Nithercott, who was a personal friend and a partner in the local law firm of Sterling, Nithercott

& McSwain. Beau had been tasked with the management of Anya's newfound wealth. She had inherited all of Martine's worldly possessions, including the two buildings on Main Street, a three thousand square foot lake house, Ching, and his six feline companions, a mansion in New Orleans, and a century-old, ill-gotten fortune that had once belonged to James Beckwith. In total, Anya's holdings now amounted to more than a billion dollars.

All of this meant that she had the power to grant Ching's mysterious request, but with a blizzard bearing down, she was reluctant to indulge him. On the other hand, like Martine, Anya had become a firm believer in Ching's intuition. The cat possessed an uncanny ability when it came to foretelling disaster or recognizing unscrupulous people of ill-intent. He never did anything without a reason. Something was clearly disturbing the cat's mind.

Anya glanced around for Ching, who was conspicuous by his absence. Seeing no sign of him, she decided to head downstairs to discuss this impending weather development with her manager, Desda March.

Cats 'n' Cocktails, formerly known as McClean's Pub, had only been open for about two months. The old pub had undergone a major renovation after Anya had hired Tate Blackledge, a friend and local contractor, to completely transform the venue. It was now a modern bar and grill that doubled as a cat rescue. The concept was similar to that of a cat cafe, but with a newly imagined spin. In the short time that they'd been open, they'd managed to find homes for more than twenty cats that had previously resided at local area shelters.

Desda was behind the bar conversing with her husband, Paul. Since his retirement from a big city accounting firm, Paul had taken to dividing his time equally between a seat at the end of the bar and the golf course. With winter on the way, his options were narrowing. Their attention was predictably focused on the ongoing blizzard report.

"Are you seeing this?" Desda asked, pointing to the screen.

The news crew was reporting live from the more populous neighboring city of Chenoah Falls, where local citizens were on the brink of hysteria. They were emptying the shelves in the grocery stores and hardware centers there, stocking up on staple goods, emergency supplies, and in some cases, wine and spirits.

Anya reached for bottles of orange liqueur, cognac, and lemon juice. Desda took her cue from this and began grating orange zest into a bowl of sugar to rim three glasses for sidecar shots.

"After so many false alarms, I guess it's finally going to hit. Radar doesn't lie," Anya said, glancing up at the clock. It was nearly four. Though it would be dark in less than an hour, and snowing in less than two, she had decided to acquiesce to Ching's repeated requests.

"I'm going to take the cats and move up to the lake for a while. I get the feeling Ching is homesick. Don't ask me how I know," Anya announced.

"The lake?!" Desda veritably shouted.

"Whaaat?" Paul exclaimed, choking on his words as he polished off his drink. "You'll be snowbound!"

"So what? It's the slow season. I don't have anywhere I've got to be for the next few days, and the lake house has a generator just like this place does," Anya pointed out. "It'll power up the whole house if the electricity goes out—when the electricity goes out." She nodded toward the TV, where the coverage continued of the madding crowds fighting over the last loaves of bread and cases of water. "I think we should shut down here for a few days, raid the walk-ins for supplies, and thereby avoid that insanity. We'll reopen once the roads are clear. What do you think?" The question was rhetorical in spirit since she'd already made up her mind.

"I'm in favor!" Paul exclaimed.

"I'll grab some boxes from the storeroom! Meet you downstairs by the freezers," Desda agreed.

"I'm going to run across the street to Goshen's and grab some bags of rock salt, then I'll help you girls load up. We better make it quick too. Looks like this thing is coming in pretty fast," Paul remarked.

The news report had shifted back to Cole Front and an ominous-looking radar screen where the blue wall was in the final stages of its approach.

Before joining Desda to pack up her own supplies, Anya decided to dash over to the Bellemores, who now ran the shop next door. She'd decided to sell Martine's place to them a couple of months ago, the day of Cats 'n' Cocktails' grand opening. The genial couple had driven all the way from Philadelphia in response to a "for sale" ad she'd placed. What had really closed the deal was Nyx Bellemore's line of work. Like Martine—she and her husband, Aedan, ran their own mystic shop. The Bellemores wanted to relocate to Four Oaks and reopen Martine's emporium with the same purpose in mind. They'd even kept the original sign that hung above the shop.

On the first day they met, the Bellemores had surprised her by correctly deducing that there were actually two signs above Martine's store, one beneath the other.

The shop's original sign was a beautiful depiction of tarot's High Priestess with the words: *Your Questions Answered Within.* For reasons unknown to Anya, Martine had covered it up with one that read: *Martine's Mystic Treasures.* Aedan had suggested that it might have had something to do with old laws, still on the books in some states, that made fortune-telling illegal.

When the Bellemores decided to use the original sign for their own shop, they relocated the *Martine's Mystical Treasures* sign to one of the interior walls of their store. It was a heartfelt tribute to the memory of one of Four Oaks' most beloved friends and neighbors, the magnitude of which was not lost on the townspeople.

When Anya arrived, Aedan and Nyx—short for Nyxon, were likewise glued to the weather report.

"Oh, boy, this is gonna be a big one," Nyx murmured, nervously combing her fingers through the pixie-like layers of her dark hair.

"Yes, we generally kick off the season with a bang," Anya confirmed. "It creates several feet of snowpack on top of which steady, albeit lighter, accumulations will fall until spring. That being said, you can never rule out an ice storm or two. Not to worry, though, the generators will keep you up and running. I just popped over to let you know that we're shutting down for the duration. I'm heading up to the lake and taking the cats with me. You're welcome to use anything in our freezers or on our shelves if you run low on supplies. You'll want to avoid the chaos going on in the city at the big chains."

Nyx grinned knowingly. "Ching will be very grateful."

Nyx and Aedan were the only ones with whom Anya

felt comfortable sharing the details of Ching's special gifts. They, like herself and Martine, believed that all cats were prescient and that Ching possessed extraordinary talents. Anya had told them about the cards and coins Ching had been leaving around for her to find. The Bellemores had been helpful when it came to interpreting his clandestine communications.

"Thank you, Anya! We're pretty set here, but we wouldn't turn down a bottle or two from the wine cellar," Aedan said.

"We'd be happy to help you round up that crew of yours, too," Nyx added.

Anya smiled gratefully. "Help yourself to the wine, and I admit—I'd love some assistance. It would really save me some time." Loading seven cats into four carriers was an "all hands on deck" kind of situation. Assistance was always welcome.

Nyx and Aedan followed her across the catwalk to her residence, where Anya began closing doors to possible escape routes before extricating multiple cat coaches from multiple closets.

Wary, but caught off guard, the cats were no match for Anya and the Bellemores. They were able to secure Hester and Possum, Luther and Benny, Zia, and Don Pedro with relatively little effort.

It was well known that Ching preferred to travel alone. He also liked to enter his coach last and at his own behest, but when Anya looked around for him—he was nowhere to be found. Panic rising in her chest, she realized it had been almost twenty-four hours since she'd last seen his royal highness.

The town's annual Halloween festival and parade had taken place on Main Street last night. Along with the traditional seasonal activities—trick-or-treating, games, and costume contests—Cats 'n' Cocktails had hosted a rescue event. Eight cats and kittens, none of which were black, given the holiday, had been adopted. It had been a hectic, fun-filled affair replete with ghoulish cupcakes, bat's wing punch, loads of candy, costumed kids, moms and dads, cats and kittens.

It was after 1 a.m. when Anya had returned upstairs to her apartment and found the remnants of the Goshen Market ad. She'd been too exhausted to attend to it at the time. Instead, she'd opted to navigate around it and go straight to bed. Ching had been absent at breakfast as well, which she'd also noted as odd.

Once again, Anya was on her hands and knees, this time to search under beds, couches, and chairs. She checked all of the closets, bookshelves, and the fireplace mantel, calling his name and his favorite phrase, "Treat! Treat!"

Amid all of the confusion, Desda charged into the room. "What are you doing? What's going on?" she asked, her voice rising relative to the hysteria.

"Ching! I can't find Ching," Anya said, breathlessly.

Desda gasped. "I'll check downstairs," she said, sprinting down the steps.

"Maybe he's napping or something over at our place. I'll go see," Aedan called out, jogging off in the direction of their apartment.

Minutes passed as Anya and Nyx continued to search, hoping Aedan or Desda would locate him in the meantime.

Suddenly Desda's voice rang out from the foot of the stairs, "Anya! Get down here!"

Hearing this, everyone came running—converging in a panic to where Desda had been reviewing the security camera footage from the previous night.

"Look," she choked as she pressed rewind and play.

The tape confirmed Anya's greatest fear. They all watched in silent disbelief as Ching sauntered into the frame. He gave his surroundings a perfunctory glance before ducking into the corner space near the front door. It was clear that he was waiting patiently for some unsuspecting customer to exit. There was a double door at the entrance, a security measure intended to prevent cats from escaping, but it posed little challenge for the resourceful Ching. Within seconds, a group of four or five people made their exit, and he slipped out with them unnoticed. Once he was streetside, he paused, crouched, and jerked his head to look directly into the camera. It was like he sensed that he was being watched. It was a chilling sight his image cast—a ghostly white silhouette shrouded by the pitch black night. His eyes glowed as he stared through the lens at them, and then … he was gone.

Faith Waitstill is the author of The Cats 'n' Cocktails Mystery Series

Did you enjoy this book?

The Cats 'n' Cocktails Mystery Series is a work in which each edition contains a new puzzle to solve, while a galvanizing love triangle is an ongoing saga with many shocking, life-altering twists and turns.

Please consider leaving an Amazon review.

For independent authors like myself – your reviews are the single greatest reason other readers will give this series a try.

Thanks for reading and best wishes,

Faith Waitstill

Made in the USA
Las Vegas, NV
16 March 2022

45789063R00233